Suddenly, from the back of the plane, she heard someone sobbing softly. The smoke was getting thicker and Kate was feeling dizzy again, but she kept moving toward the sound until she saw a young woman, no more than twenty or twenty-five, crouched in the aisle, cradling a sleeping child in her arms.

"What are you doing? You've got to get out!"

"I can't find her sweater," the woman sobbed. "I can't find her sweater and it's cold out there. Can you help me?"

Kate realized that the woman was in shock. The odor of jet fuel was getting noticeably stronger. How much time did they have? A minute? Maybe less?

She grabbed a blanket from the floor and wrapped it around the little girl. Kate reached for the woman's hand. "Come on. We have to hurry."

The woman gave Kate her hand. She took it and began to lead her out, but Kate was feeling weak again. The pain coursing through her legs and her chest was becoming more difficult to ignore.

Kate took the mother's hand and put it on the belt of her uniform pants. "Hold on tight. Don't let go."

HIGHWIRE

KAM MAJD

A DELL BOOK

Published by
Dell Publishing
a division of
Random House, Inc.
1540 Broadway
New York, New York 10036

ISBN: 0-440-23734-3

Printed in the United States of America

Published simultaneously in Canada

February 2002

10 9 8 7 6 5 4 3 2

OPM

To Lori, my best friend, my fiercest critic and quite possibly the only woman on the face of the planet who could put up with me for as long as she has.
Thanks, Babe. We did it.

ACKNOWLEDGMENTS

To my friend James Wade, who always inspired me to write better and shorter, thank you. To my agent, Barbara J. Zitwer, whose enthusiasm for the book was energizing, I also thank you. And many thanks to Mr. Warren Helsley for his time and technical assistance. Finally, to Beth DeGuzman for selecting this book from among the many fine works of writing that crossed her desk, and to my editor, Samantha Bruce-Benjamin for taking it under her wing and making it her own, I owe you both my eternal debt of gratitude.

HIGHWIRE

The sudden jolt and unexpected turbulence caught both pilots momentarily off guard before each reached instinctively for the controls. After a tense moment, when it became clear that the autopilot was still holding, First Officer Edmond Bell cautiously eased his grip and tentatively leaned back in his seat.

"Can't wait to get this damn night over with," he muttered—just loud enough to be heard.

In the dark cockpit, Captain Kate Gallagher's face, illuminated by the faint green glow of the instrument lights, was a portrait of concentration. "Five more minutes and it will be," she whispered back.

Bell shook his head. "With my luck, we'll be up here for another hour, holding, waiting for a clearance to land, then have to go back and try this damn thing all over again tomorrow."

Kate let the comment pass, as she had so many others that day. After fourteen hours, three landings in bad weather, and a night in a cockpit with an irritable first officer who thought he was Superman, all she wanted was a little time with her daughter, Molly, a warm bath, and her favorite Mozart symphonies to unwind to. But first, there was the business of landing the plane.

"I'm showing winds of almost sixty knots up here at four thousand feet. Why don't you find out if there's been any change since the last report?" she asked.

Bell picked up the mike. "Kennedy approach, this is Jet-East 394. We need the latest surface conditions."

"Jet-East 394, this is New York approach control." The controller sounded as weary as they were. "Sir, the latest observation indicates that the weather has deteriorated further. I'm showing a ceiling of two hundred feet overcast. Wind is from the north at two eight, gusting to three five knots with blowing snow. There is a half an inch of packed snow on the runways, but we haven't had a landing there for almost fifteen minutes, so I have no breaking action to report."

Bell replaced the mike in its cradle and picked up a chart. Aiming the overhead light at it, he pointed to a number. "That's as low as we can go. You'd better make this one count. The last thing I want to do is go all the way back to Chicago."

Kate shook her head. She didn't know what the hell this guy's deal was, but the fact that she was a woman certainly hadn't bypassed his attention. Add to the fact that she was barely thirty-four, a full five years younger than he, and in the male-dominated world of aviation you had a problem she could do without.

A woman, especially one as striking as Kate Gallagher, occupying the captain's chair was still a rare sight. She wore little makeup and bothered even less about her burnt-almond hair, which she wore shoulder length.

Her skin was not the fair color of her father's Irish ancestors'; it was a shade darker, olive-hued, favoring her mother's Greek heritage. Her eyes, the bluest green

of the Caribbean Sea, were the only thing she had in-
herited from him. Everything else, from her perfectly
arched eyebrows to her nose, long and narrow and just
the tiniest bit crooked, came from her mother, as did
her independence, stubbornness, and fiery temper. It
was that particular trait she was feeling most of now.
Back on the ground, Kate might have been tempted to
give Bell a taste of it. But up here, her sole priority was
the safety of the two hundred and eleven passengers
and twelve crew members who were anxiously waiting
for that moment of relief when the wheels would finally touch the pavement.

The airport was just to their right and less than fifteen miles away. On a clear night, she would be able to
see not only the lights of the two parallel runways, but
also Brooklyn, Queens, Manhattan, and half of New
Jersey. But tonight, as they fought their way through
one of the worst snowstorms the Northeast had seen in
a decade, she could barely see the nose of the aircraft,
less than five feet in front of her.

"Jet-East 394, this is New York approach control.
Turn right to a heading of three five zero. Descend and
maintain three thousand feet. You are cleared for the
ILS, runway three-one-left at Kennedy International
Airport."

Kate punched the Approach button on the glare
shield in front of her, and the twin-engine jumbo jet
began a shallow, descending turn into the night sky.
With a flick of a switch on the yoke, she kicked off the
autopilot, and with her clammy hands gripping the
controls, Captain Kate Gallagher guided Jet-East flight
394 onto the final segment of its approach into
Kennedy International Airport.

The intensity of the turbulence multiplied almost
immediately. Outside, the beam of the landing lights

illuminated the falling snow, which looked heavier than either pilot had remembered. With one hand still on the controls and her total attention focused on the instrument panel, Kate tightened her seat belt and felt the restraint of the shoulder harness pull against her body.

"Better make sure everybody is down," she ordered.

Bell picked up the interphone. "Are you ready?"

"Yeah, we're buttoned up," the senior flight attendant said.

Dorothy Maples was in her fifties, with dark eyes and brunette hair cut page-boy short. She sat on the jump seat at the front of the cabin facing her passengers, smiling and trying hard to hide her apprehension behind her best business-as-usual face. Like everyone else, she was eager to put an end to this very long night.

The landing gear had already thumped into place and the actuator motors had sounded as they slid the flaps from the trailing edges of the wings and readied the plane for its landing. Preparing themselves for their imminent arrival, the passengers jostled to get a look at the ground below, but all they could see was a wasteland of dense, black clouds intermittently glowing bloodred from the reflection of the flashing beacon light.

Kate could sense the mounting anxiety in the cabin just behind her. She had been a passenger enough times herself to know what it felt like to be trapped in a sea of seats, waiting until that final reassuring voice comes over the P.A. to inform them that they had arrived safely.

She adjusted her five-foot-eight frame in the seat and wiped the tiny drops of perspiration from her brow. *Just like the simulator,* she thought.

"Localizer captured. Glide slope's alive," Bell announced, as the two needles on the instrument panel moved toward each other and formed a crosshair.

"Flaps thirty," Kate instructed. Bell moved the lever to its proper position.

Barely a moment after that, the vertical needle began to move slowly to the right, indicating that the plane was moving to the left, away from its intended course.

"Localizer," Bell called out immediately, but Kate was already making the correction and turning the aircraft slightly to the right. Seconds later, the needle settled back in the center, then started to move again, this time to the left.

They were descending now, less than a thousand feet above the ground, in zero visibility and with no room for error.

"You're off the center line again. Localizer," Bell barked, his eyes darting between the small white needle and the pilot to his left.

"Come on," Gallagher muttered to herself. "You've done this a thousand times before. Trust the instruments. Just trust the damn instruments."

The needle began to move again, but did not stabilize. It oscillated from one side of the instrument to the other, like a broken toy. But this was no toy, and this close to the ground, there was no room for child's play.

"Let's get out of here," Kate said, simultaneously advancing the throttles and pulling back on the yoke. "Initiating go-around. Give me maximum power. Flaps twenty."

The two Ryan engines began to howl, clawing their way into the black, wintry sky.

"Kennedy tower, Jet-East 394 is on the go," Bell announced on the mike.

"Roger Jet-East 394, this is Kennedy tower. Climb and maintain three thousand feet. Contact New York approach on 124.9."

"We'll go to approach."

Flying through the turbulence, snow, and clouds,

the pilots of Jet-East flight 394 retracted the flaps and gear and climbed to the designated heading and altitude. Once there, they prepared for one more shot at landing before lack of fuel would force them to divert to their alternate airport.

"You've got the plane. I'm going to make a P.A.," Gallagher said. Bell took over the controls.

"Ladies and gentlemen, as you can tell, we have aborted the landing. It's strictly a precautionary measure and there's nothing to be alarmed about. We're currently being vectored into position to begin the approach again. We should be on the ground in less than ten minutes."

"I'm back," Kate said. She reached for the controls but felt some resistance. She looked up. . . . Bell was still gripping them.

"I've got the plane," she said, looking over at him. But he didn't even acknowledge her and he didn't let go. He just sat there, his hands wrapped around the controls, staring dead-ahead at the instruments.

What the hell was this, a mutiny? Was he saying that he could do a better job? That she was dangerous? What?

She had never flown with this character before, so she had no way of reading him. Maybe he'd had a bad experience somewhere along the line, something that convinced him women just weren't suited for the job. Or perhaps, and more probable, he was just an ass. What the hell, she thought, she was no mind-reader and besides, she had no time for this testosterone-triggered bullshit.

"I've got the plane," she snapped, and jerked the controls slightly to one side.

Bell silently relinquished control.

Kate looked over at him one last time with a glare that could melt steel. They were going to get on the ground, shut down the engines, and park the plane. Af-

ter that, Bell had better pray that God was on his side
because she was going to rip him limb from limb. She
turned away from him and focused back on the instruments with renewed purpose.

"Landing gear down. Give me flaps thirty after you
get three green," she ordered and Bell did as he was instructed. Kate was back in command.

They were below fifteen hundred feet again, in the
clouds and flying at 170 miles per hour, when the localizer began to twitch again. Kate corrected immediately, but felt a new stiffness in the controls. She
looked at the overhead panel and checked the anti-
icing equipment. Everything was on. If the unrespon-
siveness of the controls was not caused by surface
icing, then what was going on?

The localizer needle came back to the center, but
like a pendulum it began moving in the opposite direction again.

Kate wanted to say something, but hesitated. She
wasn't going to give Bell the satisfaction. Maybe this
was an instrument malfunction, Kate thought. She
glanced over at Bell's localizer, then at the standby instruments. All three indicated the same thing: the aircraft was moving erratically off course and she wasn't
able to correct it.

It was an unwritten rule of piloting that a captain
never hands over the plane to the first officer or sur-
renders his or her command in a time of crisis—especially not to someone like Edmond Bell. But as Jet-East
394 descended below five hundred feet, still unstable
and off course, Gallagher considered doing just that.

Maybe Bell was right, she thought. Maybe they all
were. Maybe she should just let her co-pilot take over
and land the plane. Once they were safely at the gate,
there would be more than enough time to lick her
bruised ego and figure out just what had gone wrong.

She was on the brink of handing the controls over

to him when the aircraft finally stabilized at four hundred feet. Kate sighed and tried to relax.

But passing through three hundred feet, the needle began to swing again, this time faster than it had previously. Again, Kate attempted to correct, but the needle continued to move, and by the time the aircraft had reached two hundred feet, it was fully deflected to one side. They were sinking fast, too fast.

"Go-around. Go-around," Bell shouted, a clear note of panic in his voice.

Kate had already pressed the small go-around button on the throttles. "Going around. Max power, flaps twenty," she commanded a second time. "Push the throttles up, way up." Once again, Jet-East 394 struggled to make its way back into the night sky. Then it happened.

It began with a shallow turn to the right. Kate immediately corrected it by turning the controls in the opposite direction. The plane responded for an instant, then continued to roll slowly back to the right. She applied more pressure, but it wasn't enough. With both hands on the controls, she pushed to turn. Still it wasn't enough. She felt as if something was fighting her—as if Bell had finally decided to take over. But she could see his hands, one still on the throttles, adjusting maximum power, the other reaching for the microphone so he could tell the tower that they had aborted the second approach. He was doing what he was supposed to, they both were. Just as they had done ten minutes ago, just as they had practiced a thousand times before in the simulator. But this was different. Something was wrong, terribly wrong.

"Push with me," she shouted to Bell, who threw down the mike and grabbed the controls with both hands.

"What are you doing?" he yelled, but Kate had no time to explain.

"Terrain, terrain, pull up, pull up," the computer-generated voice warned. A half-dozen red lights began to flash in the pilots' faces.

There had been no training for this kind of scenario. Kate had two choices: continue the go-around and hope that whatever was causing the problem would correct itself in the next second, or—

Instinctively she chose the second option, grasped the throttles and pulled them back to idle. The roar of the engines instantly died and Jet-East 394 began to plunge into the darkness.

"What the hell are you doing? We're gonna crash," Bell shouted, lunging over to force her hands off the throttles. He was too late.

From the corner of her eye, Kate saw an orange and red flash. An instant later, the controls shuddered in her hands as the aircraft was forced violently upright. The tip of the right wing hit the ground, causing the nose to pitch up and veer in the opposite direction, completely out of control. Within an instant all hell broke loose.

There was the sickening sound of scraping metal, and vibrant flashes of red, orange, and yellow erupted all around them. Agonizing screams of terror were followed by a sensation of weightlessness, as the aircraft bounced over and over again. The heat, the smoke, the fire . . . and then, blackness.

chapter 2

She was hanging upside down, held in place by her seat belt and harness. Kate opened her eyes and tried to look up, but she could barely make out anything through the hazy darkness. Her head was pounding, her body was wet, and there was a burning sensation in her throat—smoke.

Panicking, she flailed around with her hands, trying to find something to grab on to, but nothing was within reach. She tried to swing herself, a little bit at a time, in the hope of reaching something she could touch. But other than making her nauseous, the exercise proved pointless—she was suspended in nothingness.

She hung back down and tried to gather her strength, then reached up and hit the button on the seat-belt buckle. As the latch released, Kate fell through the darkness, landing on a pile of fiberglass and wire. She screamed in pain and curled herself up into the fetal position. Dazed, she cautiously raised her head and looked around. Her eyes slowly adapted to the darkness, and she began to discern the ghostly shapes of the victims.

The cockpit had nearly separated from the rest of the aircraft, and through the opening Kate could see the flashing lights of rescue vehicles rushing toward them. Bell lay several feet away, still held firmly in place by his seat belt and shoulder harness, his seat jarred from its tracks. Kate crawled over to him and felt his neck for a pulse. He was alive but unconscious, blood dripping from his nose and mouth.

She looked to the aft section of the plane. The cabin was tilted to the right, probably lying on the collapsed landing gear. She saw a handful of small fires that seemed to be contained by the snow and moisture. But all that could change in an instant. There was still plenty of fuel and plenty of ignition, a deadly combination under the best of circumstances.

The passengers were everywhere. In the semidarkness, Kate could make out their movements. Some moved slowly, others in panic, stumbling over the rubble and into one another, in a desperate attempt to get out and away from the smoke-filled wreckage.

Kate heard Dorothy Maples's voice. She was at the doorway, barely able to stand against the wind and the blasts of snow, her jacket torn, her shirt partially out of her skirt. She was yelling, directing the evacuation.

"Jump, jump! Don't take anything with you!" In the hell that was left of Jet-East flight 394, some passengers had managed to find their carry-ons and were attempting to drag them along, dangerously slowing the evacuation process.

"I said don't take anything with you," Dorothy yelled as she grabbed the bags and purses and threw them into a pile.

Looking around, Kate saw wounded passengers and crew who needed help. How many and how badly, she had no way of knowing, but she had to find out. The emergency vehicles had arrived, their sirens adding to the mayhem. The firemen pulled out long hoses and sprayed white foam on every hot spot they could see. More vehicles arrived and within minutes, a sea of flashing red, white, blue, and orange strobes covered the entire northwestern portion of the airport.

Kate looked down at Bell. He was still unconscious but she had to get him out. The plane could explode at any moment. . . .

She released his seat belt and shoulder harness and, holding on to him as tightly as she could, let his body fall to the ground. Simultaneously grabbing on to the console and the back of Bell's seat for support, she managed to raise herself to a standing position. Almost instantly an acute pain ran up her legs and through her body, causing her knees to buckle. Kate screamed in agony and seized hold of the seat to prevent herself from falling.

As the pain subsided, she glanced weakly in the direction of her co-pilot. With forced effort, she placed her hands around Bell's collar and began to pull, but he wouldn't budge. Kate tried again, this time harder, and managed to move him slightly. Inch by inch she dragged him toward the opening at the rear of the cockpit until she had hauled his body to the jagged gash at the side of the plane. Kate took a deep breath and braced herself for the four-foot jump to the ground.

As her feet made contact with the pavement, streaks of pain shot up though her right thigh and she fell against the side of the plane, clutching her leg. This time, she didn't even wait for the pain to diminish. She put her arms around Bell's body and pulled him out of the cockpit and onto the snow-covered ground.

They had to get away from the airplane, but in the general commotion Kate found no one capable of helping. She pulled again, dragging him foot by excruciating foot until, overcome by nausea. She fell to her hands and knees on the ground next to Bell, her forehead resting against the snow-covered tarmac, as she tried desperately to catch her breath.

Bell's shirt was torn and there were cuts and bruises on his face, but he seemed to be breathing normally. She looked around again. She had to get him into an ambulance. There were others who needed her help.

She got up, ignoring the pain slicing through her body. As she began to walk away, she felt Bell's hands grab her ankle.

Kate squatted down beside him. "How do you feel?"

"Like I've been in a plane crash," Bell gasped. He coughed painfully. "What . . . what happened? Why—why did you do it?"

Kate stiffened, but there was no time for explanations now.

"I've got to get you some help. I'll be right back," she said. She limped toward the nearest rescue vehicle.

"I'm Captain Kate Gallagher," she said to one of the firefighters who was pulling out a hose. "My first officer is lying over there, on the ground. He's injured and needs help. Go," she urged, then turned back to the wreckage.

As Kate got closer, the full extent of the damage started to become clear. The fuselage of the plane, still intact, lay on its side. One wing pointed diagonally into the air and the other, partially broken off and on fire, lay some fifty yards back. Next to the wing was what remained of the black-and-white checkered building that had housed the instrument approach equipment.

As far as she could tell, the fire wasn't extensive, but there was plenty of smoke and flashing lights. People were running in all directions, some screaming, others simply moaning and staggering about in shock, clumps of white foam hanging from their clothing.

With a horrifying shudder, Kate realized that people could still be stuck in the airplane—her airplane. Still limping, Kate picked up her pace and made her way to the tilted fuselage. But the front exit was far too high and the partially inflated slide blowing in the wind was just out of her reach.

She scanned the body of the airplane for the location of the exits. Toward the center of the craft, she found one, half open, almost totally buried beneath the wreckage. She positioned herself beside the door and began to dig her way through the snow and dirt until she had created a small opening. Rolling over onto her back, she squeezed herself through.

Once inside, the distinctive smell of raw fuel hit her instantly. Because of the bad weather, Jet-East 394 had taken on extra fuel for possible diversions and holding. Right now more than three thousand gallons of JP4 sat in bladder tanks, not twenty feet from where she was standing.

The air was so heavy with smoke and fumes that it was almost impossible to breathe or to see. The only light in the cabin came from the flickering red lights that ran along both sides of the tilted aisle indicating the exits. There didn't appear to be any passengers left, or at least none that she could see. The deserted cabin, only minutes earlier reverberating with sounds of panic, was now eerily quiet.

Kate worked her way back, leaning on seats, stumbling over scattered debris and luggage, occasionally entangling in the spiderwebs of oxygen masks that dangled from above. She slowly made her way to the rear of the plane and looked in every direction, but still she saw no one. Dorothy and the rest of the flight attendants had done a masterful job of evacuating the passengers.

Suddenly, from the back of the plane, she heard

someone sobbing softly. The smoke was getting thicker and Kate was feeling dizzy again, but she kept moving toward the sound until she saw a young woman, no more than twenty or twenty-five, crouched in the aisle, cradling a sleeping child in her arms.

"What are you doing? You've got to get out!"

"I can't find her sweater," the woman sobbed. "I can't find her sweater and it's cold out there. Can you help me?"

Kate realized that the woman was in shock. The odor of jet fuel was getting noticeably stronger. How much time did they have? A minute? Maybe less?

She grabbed a blanket from the floor and wrapped it around the little girl. Kate reached for the woman's hand. "Come on. We have to hurry."

The woman gave Kate her hand. She took it and began to lead her out, but Kate was feeling weak again. The pain coursing through her legs and her chest was becoming more difficult to ignore.

Kate took the mother's hand and put it on the belt of her uniform pants. "Hold on tight. Don't let go." With the child in one hand and using the other to feel her way through the mangled remains of Jet-East flight 394, Kate led the way to the rear of the fuselage.

Just as they got to the galley, Kate saw the food carts, coffeemakers, luggage, and pieces of fuselage mangled together, barring their exit. She stopped, wiped her watering eyes, and squinted hard. "We don't have time for this," she muttered, panic welling inside her.

"Where are we going?" the woman asked.

"This way . . ." Kate said, coughing through the smoke. "We have to get out this way. Take a blanket and cover your face," Kate shouted to the woman. She grabbed a blanket for herself, covered her face and the child's, and edged her way forward, struggling to move over the wreckage. Near the front of the plane, she located the main door, through which most of the passengers had exited.

Like everything else in the plane, the exit door was tilted to one side. The threshold was at waist level. On the outer side of the open door, the semi-inflated slide whipped around in the wind. Kate placed the child on the doorway's edge, drew a lungful of cold air, and turned to the woman.

"You've got to go out there and pull the slide down and sit on it," she shouted over the roar of the wind. "I'll give you your baby, you grab her and slide down, okay?"

The woman nodded and followed her instructions. Kate handed her the baby. Then she heard it.

It was a loud whooshing sound, the same sound as when a match is thrown onto a gas grill that has been on for a while. Kate turned to face the noise. To her horror, a wall of orange and red fire had engulfed the cabin and was sweeping forward, igniting the fuel vapors. There was no way she could exit in time.

Kate leaned forward and desperately tried to reach the slide. She pushed with everything she had. The upper half of her body was outside the plane and her lower half was still caught inside when the fire reached her. The force of the blast slammed her legs against the side of the door as the fire shot out through the opening. She screamed, but had already managed to get hold of the back end of the slide. She latched on to it and pulled herself out, falling the short distance on her back, her eyes glued to the exit and the fire and smoke pouring from it.

Looking up into the sky, she wanted to stay there forever. To close her eyes and then open them somewhere else, far away from this nightmare. But two men, one on each side, grabbed her under the arms and pulled her up.

"Are you okay, Captain?" one of them shouted. They were firemen in full gear and hats, and had witnessed the entire scene. Kate's shirt was torn and caked with blood—but the captain's uniform stripes, the epaulets, remained attached to her shoulders.

As Kate nodded, the pain hit her with renewed intensity.

"My co-pilot. Is he . . . ?" Kate stammered.

"He's on his way to the hospital," one of them replied reassuringly.

"I didn't think anyone could have survived that," the taller of the firemen said, pointing to the wreckage. "Okay. The paramedics have arrived and everyone is off the plane. Let's get out of here fast."

The paramedics rushed to carry the woman and her child away from the burning wreckage on stretchers; Kate refused the third stretcher brought in for her.

She shook her head. "I don't need one."

Fifty feet out, Kate turned and took one last, stunned look at the wreckage of her aircraft. Most of the fires were out, but the scene was carved forever into her memory. Every pilot's worst nightmare had unfolded before her eyes.

She felt cold and dizzy. She bent over and put out a hand backward to steady herself, but the effort was futile and she fell to the ground.

Gazing up at the night sky, she watched the snowflakes dance their way to the ground all around her. One of the flakes fell into her mouth. She tasted it as it melted on her tongue.

Turning her head away from the flashing lights, Kate noticed a pair of small dark eyes staring at her, waiting—a rabbit. She had seen hundreds of them.

With the plentiful grass surrounding the runways and no predators to worry about, they seemed to be as much a part of airports as airplanes.

The rabbit froze for a second or two, twitching his nose at the woman in the torn shirt lying there motionless. Then he turned and scurried back to his burrow.

Kate lay in the snow. It seemed so peaceful, so serene. All she could think of was the rabbit, the brown little bunny with its white nose and the dark eyes, living his life in a hole in the ground, seemingly satisfied with so little. How lucky he was, she thought. How lucky, as her eyes flickered shut.

chapter 3

She woke to find an IV drip in her arm.
Monitors were lined up on both sides of
her bed.

Kate wasn't sure how long she had been asleep this
time—maybe an hour, maybe a day—but every time
she woke up, jumbled images of the crash played
through her mind. She could still hear the screams.
Did anyone die? she wondered. If so, how many?

She had a faint recollection of talking to someone,
but she couldn't remember the conversation. She did
recall that he was tall, wore a dark suit, and introduced
himself as someone from "legal."

He hadn't told her much about the accident, but
she did hear him say that the media would pursue her
and she was not to talk to anyone about the incident.
What the hell was his name?

Kate struggled to sit up, but the pain in her chest
and side, and the IV needle in her arm, prevented her
from doing so. She picked up the small controller on
the bed and pressed a button. The back of her bed began

to rise, and she pressed a second button. Moments later, a nurse in her late fifties with short salt-and-pepper hair, glasses, and a dour expression appeared.

"I see you're up again. Any pain?" she asked as she took her pulse.

"How long have I been asleep?"

The nurse picked up her chart and glanced at it. "Four hours, since the last sedatives."

"I—I don't remember being awake."

"That's not unnatural in your condition. You've suffered a major concussion and have been in and out of consciousness for the last two days."

"What's wrong with me?"

She wrapped a blood pressure cuff around Kate's arm and took a reading. "Other than the concussion, the damage is mostly superficial. Except of course for the two hairline cracks in the upper two ribs. But compared to some other people . . . you're lucky," she replied without looking up.

"The others. How bad? Were there any . . . ?"

"I don't really know all that, but there are two gentlemen outside who can answer all your questions." She began to remove the blood pressure cuff.

"Were there any fatalities?" Kate asked, louder this time.

"I don't really know, but the men out in the hall . . ."

Kate grabbed her arm. "Dammit, did anyone die?"

The nurse looked at her over the top of her glasses. "I think they're saying six. There were injuries, some serious, but I don't know anything else. They were taken to several different hospitals."

Kate let go of her arm, fell to the pillow, and closed her eyes.

"Are you okay?" the nurse asked. Kate didn't reply. "I'm going to go and get the doctor. He'll be here in a few minutes. In the meantime, if you need anything, just press the Call button."

Moments after she left, the door opened. When Kate opened her eyes, she saw two somber-faced men in dark suits walking toward her.

The one in the lead was young and tall, with boyishly straight brown hair, which, despite his best effort at keeping it combed back, still managed to fall over his forehead. His brown eyes were framed by oval-shaped tortoise-shell glasses.

He looked tanned—an unusual sight in winter in the Northeast—but in Michael O'Rourke's line of work, he could be in New York today and Singapore tomorrow. In Paris in the morning and Little Rock, Arkansas, before the sun went down. As head of one of the NTSB's Go teams, the only two givens of his career were strange beds and restaurant food.

Immediately after the accident, O'Rourke had been assigned as the investigator in charge, or IIC. O'Rourke and his team had been called up from their Washington, D.C., headquarters, and within hours, nearly two dozen investigators were carefully picking their way through the wreckage, marking the site and photographing everything.

After completing the initial phase of the investigation, the team quickly moved the debris out of the open, where it was in clear view of departing passengers. That work began early the next afternoon, shortly after the black boxes were recovered. The operation took almost two days. By nightfall of the second day, what remained of Jet-East flight 394 sat in a hangar on the east side of the airport, awaiting closer examination.

Altogether, there were some fifty investigators. O'Rourke's team alone consisted of eighteen. Then there were the FAA and the FBI—even the airport police had people on the scene—all scrutinizing the wreckage, and carrying out the meticulously detailed search for the unknown.

They weren't sure what they were looking for. The plane was a confused mass of metal, wire, and fiberglass, any part of which might hold the vital clue as to what had happened. It could be something as simple as a piece of plastic burned in one corner—the melting point would tell them what temperature that particular compartment had reached—and why.

Or the information they gathered could provide more direct answers. Information such as the exact position of the throttles at impact might give the investigators the power setting at the time of the crash. The position that a dial or gauge was frozen at would tell them what that instrument, and thus the airplane, was doing at the moment of contact.

But regardless of how good the clues or the investigators were, the most vital information in any crash always came from two sources. The first was a pair of recorders, each slightly larger than a shoe box and painted bright orange for easy recognition, held securely in the tail of the airplane—the section most likely to suffer the least damage in a crash. Between the FDR—the flight data recorder—and the CVR—the cockpit voice recorder—investigators had access to data that was detailed and precise.

The second and even better source of information was located in Jamaica Hospital, room 629, warily eyeing the men at her bedside.

"Captain Gallagher, my name is Michael O'Rourke, and this is Robert Jenkins. We're with the NTSB. I hope you're feeling better."

With her good hand, Gallagher shook O'Rourke's hand and nodded at Jenkins.

"We just need a few minutes of your time, if that's okay," O'Rourke said.

Kate nodded.

"Can we start off with exactly what happened out there as you remember it."

Kate didn't answer right away. She couldn't shake what the nurse had said.

"Captain Gallagher?" O'Rourke prompted.

"Yeah, sorry. I think we had a control problem. I don't know where or how, but I'm almost sure of it."

"Can you tell us more?"

Kate gathered her thoughts and slowly began to recount the events that led to the second go-around. "I don't know what happened after that. The aircraft began to roll to one side and we couldn't correct it."

"And you noticed this where? On the second go-around?" O'Rourke asked.

"No. It started on the first approach. We couldn't maintain course. We were moving from one side of the localizer to the other. At first I thought it was the gauges, but now I suspect that the aircraft was actually not responding to my commands."

"Why was there was no reference to any of this on the voice recorder?" Jenkins asked, inching closer. Like his partner, he was tall but slightly rounder, with a full head of gray hair, a thick gray mustache, and eyebrows that almost met in the middle.

For a second Kate was tempted to tell them the truth: *I didn't want to say anything to the first officer because he was a jerk and would think that I was making it up.* But this wasn't the time or place to bring up Edmond Bell. "I . . . I don't know. I guess everything just happened so quickly."

"You didn't discuss it?" Jenkins asked incredulously. "Let me get this straight. You are on the final segment of the approach in poor weather, you're off course, the flight controls aren't responding, and neither of you made a peep. Is that what you're saying?"

Jenkins's needling tone caught Kate off guard and for a moment she wondered what was happening. More than anyone else, she wanted to know what had gone wrong. Didn't this idiot understand that?

"No. We didn't discuss it. Maybe we should have, but like I said, everything happened too fast."

"Captain Gallagher. Why didn't you want to turn back to Chicago?" Jenkins asked, slowly removing a small black notebook and gold ballpoint pen from his breast pocket.

"What?"

"On the voice recorder you indicated that you were opposed to going back to your alternate, which was Chicago. With the weather as bad as it was, many flights chose that option. I'd like to know why you didn't."

Kate recalled a comment Bell had made, something like "The last thing I want to do is to go all the way back to Chicago." Her stomach lurched. Had she let him intimidate her into making the wrong decision?

"The weather was still above minimums and the criteria for initiating an approach were within limits. There was no reason to go back to Chicago. If others did, that was their decision. My decision was to make the approach and land at Kennedy," Kate said, her patience running thin.

"Yes, but I want to know—"

"You want to know what?" Kate snapped. "Obviously you've studied the recorders and reached some kind of conclusion. Now, why don't you tell me what the hell that conclusion is, or do you want me to guess?"

"Ms. Gallagher, we're not suggesting that you did anything wrong." O'Rourke glared at Jenkins. "It's just that there are a number of unanswered questions based on the information we got from the tapes."

"Like what?"

Jenkins stopped taking notes and looked at her coldly. "For one thing, the data does not support your claim that there was a control malfunction."

"So what do you think happened?" Kate asked, genuinely curious, but apprehensive about what she might hear.

"We can't answer that at this point," O'Rourke replied. "That's why we need your help."

"Your colleague here seems to think differently," Kate said, pointing to Jenkins.

"Ms. Gallagher, why did you abort the go-around?" O'Rourke asked.

Kate faltered, trying to read their expressions. "The aircraft stopped responding to my commands. I thought it was more sensible to take my chances close to the ground when we were still flying relatively straight, than continue the go-around and have the thing flip over, no doubt killing everyone on board. Have you talked to the first officer?"

The men looked first at each other, then at the floor.

"I see," said Kate. "And what did he have to say?"

O'Rourke paused for a moment before replying. "Well, he's still in Long Island Jewish Hospital. We're waiting for his condition to improve before . . ."

"How is he?"

"He has a concussion, some fractured bones, but he'll be okay."

"What did he have to say?" she repeated, bracing herself.

O'Rourke lowered his voice and looked directly into her eyes. "He says that it was your fault. He insists that you failed to maintain course and that you aborted the second go-around after . . . after you panicked."

Panicked. Kate shuddered. The word echoed through her mind. Had she caused this accident and killed all those people? No, dammit. She hadn't.

She turned to O'Rourke. "How about the passengers? I've been told there were six fatalities. What about the rest?"

"There were thirty-four injuries. Eight of them serious. Three are in critical condition."

"It was very lucky that the snow was really coming

down or things could have been a lot worse," Jenkins added, making no attempt to disguise his hostility.

Without even looking at him, she asked, "What now?"

"Well, the investigation will—"

She cut in, before O'Rourke could finish. "That's not what I'm asking. I want to know if I'm to be charged with something. Will I need a lawyer?"

"If we have given you the impression that you're to blame for the accident, I can only apologize. This investigation is far from over," O'Rourke replied. "As far as retaining the services of an attorney, it's entirely up to you, but it's worth considering."

"I see," Kate said, giving him a frigid stare. "You gentlemen go ahead with your investigation, but understand this. What happened out there was a mechanical malfunction. I didn't imagine it and I didn't panic. I made a split-second decision, and that's why you're standing here talking to me. The next crew this happens to may not be so lucky."

The door opened and a young resident wearing a white lab coat came in. He pulled out his stethoscope and placed it on Kate's chest. Without looking at the men, he asked, "You gentlemen aren't relatives, are you?"

"No, we're just leaving," Jenkins said, turning to go.

"Good idea," the doctor responded.

"Ms. Gallagher, I wish you a speedy recovery. We'll be in touch," O'Rourke said, placing a business card on the table next to the bed.

Once in the hall, Jenkins turned to O'Rourke. "What do you think?"

"About what?"

"About the Knicks. What the hell you think I'm talking about?"

"I don't think we have enough information to make a call."

"Yeah, right. And she's as ugly as my aunt Bertha."

"What's that supposed to mean?"

"She screwed up, buddy. It's written all over the place."

"She's recovering from a concussion and a bunch of other injuries. Maybe you ought to give her a break, huh?"

"Yeah, and maybe you shouldn't let your dick do the investigating."

"What the hell are you talking about?"

"Come on, Mike. I saw the way you were looking at her."

O'Rourke shook his head and started to walk away.

"Not that I blame you. She's about as good-looking a woman as I've seen in a long time. Shame she's wasting her life in the cockpit of an airplane, you know what I mean?"

O'Rourke didn't want to hear any more, but Jenkins wouldn't shut up.

"I mean, I can think of a whole lot of things she could be doing with her talents, other than sitting behind the—"

"Listen, you asshole. Six people died in that accident. Four from one family alone. You'd be wise to remember that. And as far as your personal opinions are concerned, you've made enough of a jerk out of yourself for one day, don't you think? Besides, it's not important what you think. What *is* important is that I don't want to hear it. Got it?"

Jenkins shrugged. "Hey, what's gotten into you? I was just talking."

With a gesture of disgust, O'Rourke turned on his heel and left him standing there.

chapter 4

The nurse's words kept ringing in her ears. "Compared to the others, you were lucky." Throughout the day following her interrogation by O'Rourke and Jenkins, as she was wheeled in and out of her room for various tests, Kate was tormented by that thought.

When the dinner cart was brought in, she thanked the orderly but pushed the cart away. She picked up the remote and began to flip through the channels. When she saw the *Special Report on Flight 394* she sat up in bed and turned up the volume.

The program, a thirty-minute segment prepared by one of the networks, was an alarmingly thorough examination of the crash, including live footage, interviews with the passengers, and computer-generated imagery of what was thought to have occurred. Although no direct reference was made to the captain by name, the words *pilot error* were repeated throughout.

Kate didn't even blink. She simply felt numb. But when the reporter started to talk about the passengers and the screen filled with photographs of the dead, Kate could no longer watch. The image of each of those people would remain with her forever.

The door opened and Doris Fallon, the nurse who had tended to her since the first day, walked in. She saw Kate's glazed expression, took one look at the TV screen, and turned it off.

"A bunch of people were watching that stupid program down in the cafeteria when I came on duty. I was hoping you wouldn't see it."

"Why?" Kate asked.

"Because you need all your energy to heal." She smiled. "Your mother called again. She talked to Dr. Kelsey and he told her that you were okay. You know, after they brought you in here, she sat in this chair right here for nearly two days. She only left after they assured her you were fine. They had to practically beg her to get some rest."

Through the fog, Kate remembered Mama saying that she and Molly missed her, that they wanted her back. She missed them too. "I'm ready to get out of here."

"I think you're checking out tomorrow."

"No, not tomorrow. Tonight."

"I'm sorry. It's hospital policy. All checkouts are in the morning."

Wincing with pain, Kate unhooked the IV from her arm, got out of bed, and slowly walked into the bathroom.

The nurse waited for a few minutes, then asked, "What are you doing in there?"

Kate came out, dressed in a brown turtleneck, black slacks, and a heavy black wool coat that her mother had brought to the hospital. "Leaving." She placed her few personal belongings in a small leather bag.

"You can't do that."

"You don't have to be any part of this and you won't

get in any trouble. Just come back here in twenty minutes and report that I'm gone."

"But . . ."

"I'm walking out of here. If you want to leave the room, this is your chance." Kate looked at her for a minute. When Fallon didn't respond, she began to walk out the door.

"Wait a minute," the nurse said. "You can't go out the front."

"I told you, you don't have to be involved with this. I'll . . ."

"It's not you I'm concerned about," the nurse said, walking to the window and opening the blinds. "It's them."

Kate limped over to the window and glanced down. In the parking lot were three vans with large satellite dishes on top.

"They've been here all day. They're pretty anxious to talk to you."

Kate sat back down on the bed. "Damn."

"Why do you have to leave right now? What's so important?"

"I can't explain it. All I know is that I'm sitting here in this bed while the whole world is crashing down on top of me, and I'm getting the blame for it. I feel like I've got to do something. But I can't do it from here."

Doris Fallon looked at Kate. "Come with me. I've got an idea."

He was standing alone, leaning against a gray Pontiac Grand Trans-Am parked among a hundred other nondescript cars. He wore a long black overcoat and a gray scarf wrapped around his mouth and nose to protect him from the cold, but more importantly, to preserve his anonymity. He glanced up at the fourth floor and then at the television vans a short distance away. He had been waiting there long before any of them had arrived and would remain there long after the last one was gone. . . . Whatever it took to catch a glimpse of her.

He threw down his cigarette and crushed it with the sole of his shoe, then got into his car.

Six floors up, Doris Fallon led Kate down a hallway. Using the service elevator, she accompanied her to the first floor. They walked through the kitchen and out gray metal double doors that led to the loading dock at the back of the hospital.

"One block north"—Nurse Fallon pointed—"and two left turns—you'll see the subway station on your right. But please, be careful. One of our aides got mugged last week just a block away."

"I'll be fine. Thanks for all your help. You'd better get back in, before they find out I'm gone."

Turning up her collar, she plunged her hands deep into the pockets of her thick coat, climbed down the stairs, and began to walk. It was time to go home.

Half a block away, the car slowly turned the corner and pulled up to the curb, just ahead of Kate. Luck was his lady tonight. Blinking rapidly to prevent the rivulets of perspiration from falling into his eyes, he slowly lowered the driver's side window.

He pointed the camera's powerful telephoto lens at Kate and began taking shot after shot. When the infrared film ran out, he carelessly lowered the camera for a second, inadvertently exposing his face to the uncompromising glare of the streetlight. At that very instant Kate turned to look behind her, and for the briefest of moments it was as though she could see straight through him. As if her eyes bored directly into his soul.

He jerked his head back, screwing his eyes shut. He couldn't afford to be seen. Not now. Not ever.

chapter 5

Kate got off the R train on Broadway and limped one block north to the heart of Astoria, Queens.

There it was. Athena's Taverna, the tiny restaurant on the south side of town, its yellow flashing neon sign signaling its presence to the world. Kate smiled, remembering the very first time it had been switched on as she and Mama held hands and watched with pride.

The taverna was her mother's way of ensuring her daughter's independence, so she would never have to endure what she had—never have to be dependent on a man who had picked the bottle over his family and his vows. Her whole life had been dedicated to securing Kate's future.

She had little education when she first arrived in this country and barely spoke English. But what Mama did know was food. From sauces to roasts to melt-in-your-mouth desserts, her talents were unsurpassed by all who sampled them.

Early recognition of her gift led her to spend the

better part of her life in kitchens the length of Queens. Two decades after she arrived in America, using every last penny of her savings, she opened the doors to the taverna and christened it Athena, her daughter's middle name.

Kate took care of the books, and Mama stuck with the cooking. Before long she became as famous as her food and endearingly referred to as Mama by her customers. By the time Kate had finished college, Athena's Taverna and Mama were neighborhood institutions.

The familiar scent of roasted lamb greeted Kate twenty feet from the door. Smiling, she opened the door and found herself in the middle of a crowd waiting to be seated.

The room was small and dimly lit, only sixteen tables squashed side by side with barely enough space for the waitresses to squeeze by. The chairs were wooden and old and looked uncomfortable, but the boisterous crowd savoring Mama's cooking didn't seem to mind.

A small section of the floor was left open for dancing, and next to it stood an open fireplace roaring with crackling fire, hot enough to warm the room on the coldest of New York nights.

Kate was making her way to the kitchen when she heard a squeal and turned to see her little girl running to her, a huge smile lighting up her five-year-old face.

Kate cringed in pain as she picked up Molly, but quickly covered it with a smile. She kissed her on the neck and cheeks, where it tickled. Molly laughed, kicking her feet and screaming, "Stop!" but anyone could tell that she was loving every minute of it.

In the restaurant, the patrons, mostly regulars, watched the reunion of mother and daughter. No one seemed to mind the commotion. One even lifted a glass to toast Kate's safe return, and others quickly followed suit.

Kate acknowledged the gesture with a shy smile, nodding and thanking the regular crowd.

After things settled down, she focused on Molly standing beside her. Seeing her always reminded Kate of him, even though Molly didn't look anything like her father. Everything Molly had belonged to Kate: her eyes, her face, even her smile.

"Okay. Where are they?" Kate asked.

"You wait right here. I'm going to get them, okay? Promise you'll wait right here." Without waiting for a response, Molly ran to the back of the restaurant. A moment later she came back with a stack of drawings and handed them to Kate. Mother and daughter sat on the ledge of the fireplace as Kate looked through the pages.

Molly's sketches, all drawn when Kate was away on flights, could be of a person or an event, anything that she considered special. When she returned from a flight, Molly would tell her the story of each drawing. It was their ritual.

Kate examined each picture as if it were the most precious she had ever seen.

"Hey, what's this?" Kate asked.

It was the sketch of a woman standing, holding a small girl's hand. Behind them was the sun, clouds, and a cross.

"That's a picture of you and me in heaven, Mommy."

Kate almost dropped the paper. She kneeled beside the child and whispered, "Why did you draw this?"

"Grandma said you hadn't come for me because you were sick. When Daddy was sick he went to heaven. I didn't want you to go all by yourself, like he did. I didn't want to be left alone."

Kate felt her eyes misting and quickly hugged Molly so that she wouldn't see.

Molly pulled back and looked at her with curiosity. "What's wrong, Mommy?"

"Nothing, sunshine. Nothing." Kate brushed Molly's bangs away from her eyes. "I'm just so happy to see you."

Kate looked around the busy restaurant and said, "Listen. Why don't you go back to your playroom. I've got to go see Grandma." She playfully slapped Molly on the bottom and the little girl ran to the back office, her braids flapping against her back.

Fighting against the drowsiness caused by the pain medication, and the pain itself, Kate hobbled into the small, bustling kitchen, littered with orders and Mama's magic ingredients.

Leo, the fifty-something Italian chef, was the first to see her. He nodded toward Mama, who had her back to Kate.

She was a stocky woman, no more than five-foot-four. Her hair was gray and tied in a bun, and she wore no makeup. Mama was only fifty-five but looked much older. Looks weren't something, however, that Mama spent a lot of time worrying about. What you see is what you get, she always said. People could accept her or not. It made no difference to her.

It had been a hard life, mostly spent in other people's kitchens. Raising a daughter alone, in a country and a culture she never fully understood, had taken its toll on this once beautiful woman.

For as far back as Kate could remember, Mama was always busy doing something, cutting or chopping or mixing things, and tonight proved no exception. Kate walked up behind her and put her arms around her. Mama stopped cutting and turned around, her face smiling even though her eyes filled with tears. "Katrina," she said, in her unmistakable accent. "You are okay. Yes?"

Kate put her hands on Mama's shoulders, ignoring

Leo and the two waitresses at the serving hatch, who had stopped working to watch the reunion.

Mama smiled, but the tears started again, and she was helpless to stop them. Mama hated anyone to see her like that, especially Kate, but dammit . . .

"Come." She took Kate gingerly by the hand, as if afraid that she might break. "Come, I make your favorite."

Outside, she found the first available table and sat her daughter carefully down. She could see that Kate was in pain and desperately trying to conceal her discomfort. She went back and quickly brought the tzatziki and hot bread. She brought out a glass of retsina, as well as pita, feta, and olives. Within a matter of minutes, the table for four was covered with hot, fresh, Greek food.

"Mama, I can't eat all of this!" Kate objected, but her protestations fell on deaf ears. Plate followed plate until Mama finally came to join her daughter.

"Now, tell me everything."

Kate spent the next twenty minutes giving her mother a detailed account. When she had finished, she waited for her mother to absorb the harrowing details.

"You wait right here," Mama said and made her way to the small office in the back. She came back with a stack of old letters and began thumbing through them. Mama pulled out the one she was looking for, opened it, and put her glasses on. She squinted hard and began to read. Then she stopped and pointed.

"Right here. Read this right here," she said, handing it to Kate.

The letter was written in Greek, a language Mama had insisted Kate learn. It was from her grandfather, whom she had never met, and in it he said that the family still loved Mama, despite the fact that she had gone against their wishes and married the "American soldier." She had disobeyed them and moved to America, and now she was suffering for her mistake. The letter ended by saying that she could return and take her place with her family, but first she would have to ask for forgiveness from her church and her father.

Kate looked up. "Why didn't you go, Mama?"

"Because I was a young woman with a child. A child with no father. Because I had disobeyed and dishonored my family. You would have been an outcast, my Katrina. You would have never been accepted by them. Ever," Mama said, leaning back in her chair. "I couldn't do that. So I stayed here and the rest . . . Well, you know the rest."

Kate bit her lips and squeezed her mother's hand.

"Don't feel sorry for me," Mama said, looking her in the eye. "I didn't do this for you—I did it for me. I was right and they were wrong. You see? If I had gone back and condemned you to that life, I would never be able to look into those beautiful eyes. And I would never be able to look into mine."

She leaned over the table. "Do you remember how scared I was that first time when you took me up in an airplane?"

"Yes."

"Well, you don't know the half of it. I was not just scared, I was, I was . . . how do you say, petori . . ."

"Petrified?"

"I was petrified." She slapped the table. "Those things are dangerous, I still don't like them." She paused. "But I saw in your eyes what it meant to you. I saw how happy you were and how it made your soul free. So I said you go ahead and you fly your airplanes, you don't belong in a kitchen." She reached over to take Kate's hand. "You were born to fly, Katrina. Don't you ever let them take that away from you. If you are right, you are right. You fight for it, and you fight for yourself. Not for Molly and not for me. For Katrina."

The restaurant door opened and two men wearing

thick coats and gloves, one of them carrying a tape recorder and a large Steadicam, walked in. The first man stopped and asked one of the waitresses a question. She pointed to Kate. With little regard for the customers, the men worked their way through the narrow spaces between the tables and homed in on Kate and her mother.

Kate turned her back on them.

"Ms. Gallagher, we would like to ask you a few questions about the Jet-East flight," the first man said as soon as he reached the table, attempting to thrust the microphone into her face. The questions came thick and fast, many of them blatantly suggesting that she was responsible for the crash.

"Look, how many times do I have to tell you guys? I can't talk to you—there is an investigation going on." But they just carried on, questioning and insinuating blame.

It took every ounce of self-control Kate possessed to keep from exploding in frustration. But it was Mama who had finally had enough.

She got up from her chair and turned to face the first reporter. "That's enough. I will now ask you to leave."

The man ignored her and continued with his questions. Mama's face didn't betray a single emotion. She calmly called over to the front desk. "Helena, call 911. Tell them there are some intruders here who might be armed and dangerous." She then turned toward the kitchen and yelled, "Angela, tell Leo to come out here. Tell him to bring his meat cleaver."

The waitress disappeared and the two reporters looked at each other, then at the corridor leading to the kitchen.

"All right, lady. Don't worry, we're leaving. We're leaving," one said as they both backed away.

When they were gone, Mama straightened her hair

and turned to face her customers. She started to apologize for the unpleasant interruption, but they didn't give her a chance. The applause was immediate and resounding. She smiled, the proud smile that only a parent could understand. You don't mess with Mama's kid and get away with it.

chapter 6

It was well after midnight by the time Leo's green Chevy pulled into Greenwich Village, with Kate in the front seat and Molly asleep in the back.

Grove Street was blocked off by a garbage truck with a snowplow attached, so Leo dropped them off on the corner. Kate thanked him and they began to walk the short block home. The night air was frigid and the sidewalks were piled high with grimy snow and ice. At a newspaper dispenser, Kate stopped to look at the headlines, filled with news of the Jet-East flight. She reached in her pocket for change but came up empty. She looked at Molly.

"Do you have any change?"

Molly threw up her arms. "I don't even have any pockets."

"Hmm. Remind me to buy you some pockets tomorrow."

Molly giggled as Kate tried to read what she could through the dirty glass. She could make out only part

of the lead article, which included references to the
"black boxes" and quotes from passenger interviews,
but she saw no mention of Ed Bell. The words *pilot error* took center stage.

Desperate to read the rest of the article, she considered breaking the glass, but try as she might she
couldn't pry a copy out of the machine. Forgetting herself in her frustration, she kicked the dispenser as hard
as she could and instantly felt the pain in her thigh and
her toes.

"Dammit," she cursed at the wind.

Behind her, Molly walked up to the stand, glared at
it with the angriest face a five-year-old could make, and
kicked it too.

"I'm okay, sunshine. Let's go home."

The floor-through apartment had two bedrooms. The
main living area also functioned as a dining room. Two
wing chairs with matching fabric were placed on either
side of the fireplace. The hardwood floors were covered
by Persian carpets in soft, subtle tones, and the small
kitchen included an alcove that housed a desk and a
computer.

Kate threw her coat over the couch and limped over
to the mantel, where pictures of Mama and Molly and
one of Jeffrey were lined up next to each other. She
stood there for a long time, looking at his photograph,
before gently picking it up.

Handsome and strong, black hair parted in the middle, eyes deep brown and gentle. He was leaning
against a tree in Central Park, smiling.

She thought back to his first visit to the taverna. He
came to pick her up carrying a bouquet, dressed to the
max in black wool slacks and a matching V-neck cash-
mere sweater. It was going to be a real date—dinner
and a movie.

He arrived around seven o'clock to find chaos—customers standing around, dirty tables needing to be cleaned, hot food sitting on the counter waiting to be served. He spotted Kate in the kitchen, totally frazzled, her apron covered in sauce. The cook and one of the two waitresses had called in sick, and Kate was up to her eyes in it.

So, on their first proper date, even before he had met the family, Jeffrey Bryan Taylor, a third-year medical student at New York University, took off his jacket and grabbed a tray. He waited on tables and poured wine, laughing and charming the customers as if he had worked there for years.

After they closed the restaurant, Mama grabbed Jeffrey by the arm and sat him down at one of the tables. She brought out her best bottle of retsina, then went back to the kitchen and prepared her specialty: slow-cooked herb-roasted lamb with all the trimmings.

They ate, drank, laughed, and talked, still sporting their dirty aprons. He heard all about their lives and how they had ended up in Queens. They talked about the taverna and what it meant to them. And they talked about Jeffrey. Mama listened carefully and whenever she didn't understand something, Kate leaned over and slowly translated for her. It was one hell of a first date.

Jeffrey was the only man Kate had ever truly loved. She adored him. And when he died of a sudden and massive ventricular failure, a part of her died too.

She needed him now more than ever. Someone who trusted and believed in her. But he was gone, never even knowing that he had a child.

Kate shivered and placed the photograph back on the mantel. She wrapped her arms around herself and went over to the thermostat, turning it up. In the kitchen, she took out a pan and the cocoa, while Molly got the milk. Mother and daughter quietly worked in perfect harmony. One heated the milk and the other mixed the chocolate. One stirred while the other got the cups and the marshmallows. The entire operation was so precise, the Blue Angels would have been impressed.

When the process was finished, they sat across from each other at the wooden kitchen table and drank their hot chocolate, each cradling her cup with both hands, staring into the distance without talking.

"Let's go," Kate finally said.

"I'm not tired."

"I know you're not. But since it's nearly eleven o'clock, let's just give it a shot. What do you say?"

"But I slept in the car the whole time," Molly said, unable to stifle a yawn. Kate reached for her hand and led Molly to the bathroom. Molly brushed her teeth and got into bed. Kate kneeled beside her while she said her prayers.

"Okay, I'm ready," Molly announced.

It was time to go through their ritual evening kiss. Kate leaned over. Eye, eye, forehead, nose, cheek, cheek, lips.

It was another of their little traditions that both mother and daughter had come to savor.

"I'm not tired," Molly objected again, but before the lights were off she was fast asleep.

Closing the bedroom door, Kate walked back into the living room and looked around. She wanted to *do* something but didn't know what.

She should have been exhausted. In fact she was. Not to mention the pain. But as Kate pulled out the first of the four thick aircraft-operations manuals and opened it to the first page, the only feeling she was truly aware of were her anger and frustration and a fervent need to come up with some kind of an answer. So much for the doctor's orders to rest.

She had no idea what she was looking for and less idea of how she would possibly find it, but as she flipped through page after page of notes and schematics, at least she felt she was doing something. The exercise was not totally in vain; thick manuals filled with technical writing can be as calming as the best prescription tranquilizers, and around one A.M. Kate succumbed to their effect and fell asleep on the couch.

It was barely seven A.M. when the phone rang.

"Hello?" she mumbled.

"My name is David Benson and I'm a reporter with—"

"How did you get this number? I'm not listed."

"We want to give you a chance to tell your side of the story. I can be up there in ten seconds, I'm just downstairs."

"You're where?" Kate staggered to the window, almost stumbling over the manuals on the floor next to the couch.

The white WNYK van was parked just in front of the house. She saw a crew unloading equipment and a man in a long overcoat standing by it, looking up at her.

Kate yanked the drapes shut and slammed the receiver back in its cradle. As soon as she hung up the phone rang again so Kate yanked the cord out from the wall. She did the same to the phones in the kitchen and her bedroom, then returned to the window.

She peeked through the gap in the drapes and saw that the equipment was unloaded and the crew positioned. These people were here to stay. Kate picked up a manual from the table beside her, leafed through it, and flung it across the room. This was hopeless. What was she supposed to do? Figure out what went wrong from a bunch of schematics? She was no engineer.

Kate huddled up in a corner of the couch, hugging her knees, gazing in the distance. Then she made her decision.

She took a shower, got dressed, and woke Molly up.

"Come on, sweetheart. We've got to go."

"Where are we going?" Molly asked, sitting up and rubbing her eyes.

"Grandma's."

"Are you going to fly again?"

Kate put Molly's clothes on the bed, then sat down next to her. "No, hon. I've got some things that I need to do, and I have to do them alone. You're going to stay with Grandma for a few days. Then I'll come get you, okay?"

"Can we go see Max?"

Kate hesitated. "I told you not to give him a name. He's just a puppy in a pet store. He may not even be there anymore."

"Don't worry. If he's not there, it's okay."

"All right. All right. We'll go see Max, but hurry up."

Having won the argument, Molly quickly dressed and put her belongings in a little backpack.

Kate led Molly into the kitchen. "How would you like to leave through the window instead of the door?"

"Yeah," Molly said excitedly.

They climbed down the escape ladder, sliding the last three feet. Molly enjoyed the adventure and wanted to do it again. Kate didn't. The medication was helping to ease the pain in her leg but clambering down ladders certainly didn't help matters.

At the end of the alley between her building and the one next to it, Kate peered around the corner. The reporters were still there, waiting. They would be waiting a long time.

Two blocks down, Kate and Molly stopped in front of the pet store. Molly's eyes instantly lit up.

"See, I told you he'd be here," she said, pointing to the little brown-and-white cocker spaniel.

"And I told you that there's no way we can have a dog in the apartment."

"He'll be so quiet, they'll never know."

"Listen, Molly. It's in our lease. No pets. Maybe we could sneak in a bunny or a hamster. But we can't sneak in a dog."

"I don't want a bunny and I don't want a hamster. I don't want anything. You just go away like you always do," Molly said, crying.

"Oh stop that, you're acting like a selfish little kid."

"I am a kid." Molly walked away, still crying.

"Stop your whining. What are you going to do, cry every time something goes wrong?" Kate said. The moment the words were out of her mouth, she shuddered. She could hear the cutting, insulting words her father had used when he got drunk, feel the blows, remember the pain from the first—and last—time he had hit her. She was about the same age as Molly was now. Mama had come storming into the living room and shoved him so hard he fell over the couch. Furious, he almost went after her. But then something stopped him. He just shook his head and walked out of the ramshackle farmhouse. Two days later, Iowa state police found Jack Gallagher and his truck overturned in a snowdrift off the side of Route 104.

As Kate's mother stood next to her in a worn black dress, at the conclusion of a brief and poorly attended service at the local funeral home, she seemed more angry than grief-stricken.

Mama's in-laws seemed relieved when she politely refused their offer to have her and Kate move in with them. "I swore that he could yell," she told them. "He could hit me, yes. But not my child. We have nothing to keep us here. I will write you when we have a place back with my people."

Throughout the service, Kate watched stone-faced, her father's final words ringing in her ears: *Stop your whining. What are you going to do, cry every time something goes wrong?*

She never cried again. Not the day of her father's funeral. Not the day Jeffery died. Not even now.

Molly had either not heard Kate or not cared, because she just kept walking, not looking back.

Kate ran after her. When she caught up with Molly, she put her hands on her daughter's shoulders to stop her. She kneeled on the sidewalk, and, with her eyes just inches from Molly's, said, "I'm sorry, honey. I'm so sorry."

Molly nodded, her eyes brimming with tears. "It's okay."

"I'll tell you what. When I come back, we'll go talk to the landlord. We'll see if he'll let us have a puppy. If he does . . ."

Molly didn't let her finish. She grabbed Kate around the neck and squeezed. "Yeah."

Kate gave her a quick kiss. "Come on, let's catch a cab, okay?"

Wiping her face, Molly nodded.

Kate took Molly back to the restaurant, all the while keeping up the pretense that nothing was wrong. As she left the restaurant she relived the words, making sure that she remembered the shame at the moment she'd uttered them so that she would never, ever repeat them.

Fifteen minutes later, she was at the corner of Thirty-seventh Street and Broadway. It was time to go to work.

She hailed a cab and slid into the backseat. "Kennedy."

chapter 7

The plane pushed back and started a slow taxi. Just before they approached the runway, she saw it. Patches of scorched earth, the partially destroyed checkered radio building, a few remaining pieces of debris in the dirty gray snow—all that was left of her plane. She looked at the spot as long as she could bear to, then turned away.

The Boeing 757 touched down at Miami International Airport just before noon. By the time Kate walked out onto the jet bridge it was already eighty degrees. The Jet-East crew shuttle was two terminals away. She would be there in less than five minutes.

The company headquarters were located in Miami. The core of the Jet-East operation—scheduling, dispatch, or training—was assembled in one facility, on nearly fourteen acres of well-tended lawn, six miles northwest of the airport.

As Kate stepped through the two large glass doors marked FLIGHT ACADEMY, she felt her stomach clench like a fist. The same feeling she had experienced the very first time she'd walked through those doors, a decade earlier, flooded back.

The first female pilot to be hired by the company, her arrival had raised more than a few eyebrows. The fact that she was twenty-five—relatively young for a new hire—had raised more. To compound matters further, there were rumors that female pilots were being taken on only as a last-ditch effort to ward off a federal class-action lawsuit; Jet-East was the only carrier operating without female pilots.

Given all this. Kate wasn't surprised on her first day by the stares and whispers when she walked into a class of almost thirty men. The fact that she wore a skirt said it all.

She nodded, smiled, and attempted small talk, awkwardly taking her place in the room full of jocks and former fighter pilots. For a while she wasn't sure if they were looking at her to size her up or ask her out.

For someone who hated to be the center of attention, Kate Gallagher had an uncanny knack of attracting the uncompromising glare of the spotlight. Her experience at Jet-East would be no different.

She rolled up her sleeves and went to work. She aced all the tests whether they were on paper, in the simulator, or administered by her classmates—like the time somebody stuck a photograph of Kate's face on the naked body of a centerfold and hung the picture on the wall for everyone to see.

Kate walked into the class and, judging from the suppressed snickering from her classmates, knew right away that something was up. She spotted the picture, stared at it for a moment, cocked her head to one side, and then to everyone's surprise took out a pen and rounded the breasts on the centerfold, making them fuller. When she had finished, she stepped back to admire her handiwork. Like an artist satisfied with a masterpiece, she nodded. Then, over the approving laughter of her classmates, she walked to her seat and opened her manual.

It certainly wasn't the last time Kate would be tested by her colleagues. During her seven weeks of initial training, hardly a day went by when she wasn't faced with a special extracurricular challenge. Yet, the more she was tested, the more determined she became to succeed.

Two months later, when she graduated with the rest of her class of flight engineers, not a soul questioned Kate Gallagher's right to wear her wings. She had earned them and proved herself in the process. But could she prove herself now?

At the instructor's desk she asked the receptionist for Spencer Hill.

"He's around here somewhere. Try the cafeteria."

She went to the cafeteria, stood at the two open doors, and looked around. It only took her a few moments to spot him. But that was enough time for several people to recognize her, nudging and elbowing the person sitting next to them.

Kate took a deep breath and walked over. Spencer was sitting with four other instructors. She stopped at the table and tapped him on the shoulder. As he turned, a huge, hearty smile lit up his face.

He was tall, with short, curly red hair. His heavy lidded gray-blue eyes drooped against his pale skin, giving him a kind of hound-dog look. He wore black pants and a soft blue shirt, a red tie, and matching suspenders. It was his best attempt to look professional, but in truth, he looked like the kind of guy who would be more comfortable in a pair of overalls, or in a bar somewhere shooting darts with the guys and drinking beer.

He was the best instructor Kate had ever known. Whether the subject was aircraft systems, crew resource management, or plain old weather charts, Spencer Hill made sure that all his students left his classes with genuine knowledge and skill.

"What are you doing here? I've tried to call you several times, but your phone is out of order."

"I unplugged it."

Hill nodded his understanding. "What's up? How are you doing?"

Kate smiled politely at the four other men at the table. "Is there someplace we can talk?"

"Sure," Hill said, standing up.

Spencer opened the door to his office and Kate saw that nothing had changed. It was still crammed to the rafters with books, manuals, and airplane models.

"Now, give me a hug," he said as he closed the door. She obliged him with a big, comforting embrace.

"How's my godchild?" Hill asked.

"Getting more stubborn every day. I try not to argue with her."

Hill chuckled. "It doesn't get any better when they grow up. Here, let me clean some of this away so you can sit."

He cleared some books from one of the seats, opened a window, placed a small ashtray on the ledge, and lit up a Camel.

"Same old Spencer," Kate said.

He shrugged. "What, this? It's my domain. I'm the king here. I can leave it in a mess if I choose."

"I'm not talking about the mess; Norma's used to that. I'm talking about the cigarettes. Does she know you still smoke?"

"I knew I should never have introduced you two." Hill peered down at her. "What are you gonna do? Spill the beans?"

"If I have to. Remember what your doctor said after the first heart attack."

"Yeah, yeah, I know. I've cut down to like . . . two cigarettes a day. That's all. I promise I'll go down to one. Is that good enough for you?"

"Just remember, your wife doesn't want to lose you. Neither do I."

Spencer smiled. "Thanks. Now what the hell went on out there. You scared me to death."

"They're saying I did it, Spence. That I folded."

"Well, obviously they don't know you like I do. Tell me what happened."

Once again Kate explained the series of events that led to the go-around, including everything about Ed Bell.

"Oh, that idiot," Hill interrupted when she mentioned his name. "I remember him from the flight academy. A know-it-all. Nobody could teach him anything. Now tell me, what do *you* think happened."

"I don't know, Spence. I had all the anti-icing equipment on, there was no warning, no caution lights. Nothing."

"Explain the sensation again. The resistance you felt. Was it solid, like the controls were being locked by something? Or soft, you know, mushy, turning slower than you wanted them to?"

"Started off being slow to respond but then it got harder to turn. When I aborted the go-around, I was convinced we wouldn't have made it."

Hill crushed his cigarette in the ashtray and got up. "You're one of the most competent pilots I've ever known. If you're telling me something was there, then it was." He grabbed a thick manual and placed it in front of him. "Now, let's find out *what* it was."

The moment reminded Kate of her first day. She was sitting alone in the cafeteria, toying with her salad, when a younger version of the man sitting in front of

her today took a seat next to her. Without a word of
introduction he said, "You've been the buzz of the
schoolhouse."

"Yeah? And who, pray, is doing the buzzing?"

"Everybody. They all want to know who the new
girl is."

"Well, I wish they would just ask. I feel like the star
attraction in a freak show."

The stranger laughed. "My name is Spencer Hill,"
he said, shaking her hand. "And my office is directly
down the hall and on the left. Come by whenever you
feel like it."

Kate took him up on it. Soon they were more than
mentor and protégé, they were friends. Kate got to
know and spend time with his wife, Norma, and the
rest of his family, when he invited her over for his famous once-a-month Sunday barbecues.

"Okay, let's see what we've got," Hill said, and
closed the manual. "The way you've explained this to
me, there are three possibilities. The first is icing. As
you know, most icing accidents occur immediately after takeoff, in cases when the aircraft was not properly
de-iced on the ground. But that's not what happened
here. We also can't argue that the amount of ice was
more than the equipment could handle because during
the certification process, these aircraft are tested to the
limits. No." He pushed the manual away. "Icing had
nothing to do with it."

Kate didn't say anything. She was simply listening,
relieved to have someone else do the thinking.

"Now, let's look at the second possibility: pilot error.
That's the most likely cause—at least, that's what the
papers say. That you felt something, perhaps real, perhaps not, and in the split second that it took to make
the decision, you made the wrong one."

"But I didn't make . . ."

"I didn't say you did." Spencer lifted a hand. "I said that's what the papers are saying. The papers don't know you, and they don't know the person they're talking about went through the most rigorous training and evaluation this school had to offer. You didn't know you got special treatment, did you?"

"What!"

"When you were hired, everyone was afraid that it was a mistake; that the company had hired the first female who came along and that maybe you weren't up to the job. Did you know that they made sure you weren't cut any slack? They decided to put you through the works and if you failed, well . . . that was that."

Kate was dumbfounded. She didn't know what to say.

"Do you remember your final check-ride with the FAA representative in the simulator?"

"Yeah."

"And you remember when the simulator broke down just before the ride was completed, forcing you to retake the entire exam the next day?"

Kate nodded.

"That simulator was working perfectly fine."

"Then why . . . ?"

"To test you. To make sure you didn't crack under pressure. Only the company knew about it. They had to be sure, and I don't blame them."

"Is it still like that? Do they still . . . ?"

"No. That's what I'm telling you. You proved to everyone here that a woman could be just as good—or just as bad—as a man. There was no essential difference and no special attention was necessary." Spencer leaned over. "You paved the way for all those other women who were to follow," he said. "You should be proud of yourself.

"A person who did that, a person who passed two

check-rides instead of one and didn't fold under that kind of pressure, wouldn't panic," he said decisively. "That brings us to one last possibility." Hill rose from his seat. "Come. I've got something I want you to see."

In the classroom next door, Spencer prepared the video machine and turned off the lights. "You haven't seen this one. Flight department just put it out for the new hires to familiarize them with our latest systems. I think you might be interested."

He hit Play and the screen filled with a black-and-white picture of an old Mustang fighter sitting on a ramp somewhere, the words *Flight Controls* scrawled across the screen. The narrator began to explain how, during the earliest years, the aircraft control surfaces were mechanically linked. By moving the yoke, the pilot simply pulled a cable that in turn moved the ailerons or rudders, which, like the fins of a fish, maneuvered the aircraft.

The scene changed to an old Boeing assembly line in the mid-1960s, with rows of 707 and 727 jets in various stages of construction. The narrator went on to explain that the next generation of aircraft were considerably larger and required more pressure to move the controls. Cables were out. Enter hydraulics. Large pumps pushed fluid through sophisticated plumbing and applied pressure to the control surfaces, thus moving them. Hydraulics, however, were heavy and required constant maintenance. There was a better choice. One that came with the advances made in technology.

Another image appeared, this time a formation of six F-16s.

The most advanced flight control system in aviation history, the narrator continued, is called fly-by-wire. The system, initially designed and used for combat aircraft, proved so reliable that it was only a matter of time before the concept was applied to civilian aircraft.

Most of the heavy plumbing, pumps, valves, and the actuators were replaced by thin wires and tiny computers. Less weight, less fuel burn, and, ultimately, less maintenance.

The image changed to a schematic and the voice explained that the signals generated from the flight control input are sent to the flight control computer somewhere in the heart of the aircraft, where they are instantaneously translated to binary language. That information, along with millions of other elements that flow from dozens of similar computers, determine how far and how fast a motor should run and how far the flight control should be extended.

No mechanical connections. Even the "feel," the resistance on the yoke that gives the pilots the sense that they are turning the wheel, is artificial; machines that simulate feedback to make the pilot feel as if he is doing something, whereas in fact all he is doing is generating a computer signal that could just as easily be accomplished by a simple tap on a keyboard.

Hill turned off the video and switched on the lights. "I want to stop right there," he said and sat on the corner of a desk. "Obviously this is an oversimplified explanation of the system, but it pretty much tells us what we need to know."

Of course, Kate was familiar with the intricacies of the fly-by-wire system. Jet-East 394 was controlled by it. But what did any of this have to do with what had happened? Hill read the confusion on her face.

"What I'm trying to tell you is that it takes a dozen computers and a million pieces of information for the ailerons to move up one degree. Yes, fly-by-wire is the most sophisticated and dependable system on the planet. Yes, there are backups to the backups to the backups, making the possibility of failure nearly nil. But it is *not* the old cable-and-pulley system where you pulled the yoke and something moved. There are primary-control and secondary-control computers. Then there is the air data computer and at least four backup flight control computers. Navigation computers, engine data programs, all sorts of things. Then there is EMI . . ."

"But I thought the systems were shielded from electromagnetic interference," Kate interrupted.

"They are. At least we think they are. But, heck, every day someone invents a fancy new gadget, and nobody knows how the hell these things react with the computers. That's why we have to make everyone turn off electronic devices for takeoff and landing. Before computers all we used to have to worry about was cross-over electrical charge from one system to another or from lightning. But now . . ."

"Could the problem be with one of these computers?"

"Conceivably? Yes. But remember you're dealing with a system that has more redundancies than the U.S. government. I'm not aware of any history of a problem with it."

"Where does that leave us?"

"I'm not sure. At least not yet. But I can tell you this much: As far as everyone's concerned, *you* did it. You folded and you screwed up, and now you're trying to find somewhere to lay the blame. I wouldn't expect a whole lot of understanding or help from anyone."

"I don't."

"That's my girl. Now, having said that, this is what I want you to do. . . ."

chapter 8

It was just before five P.M. when the 757 touched back down on Runway 13 Right at Kennedy. Kate stopped at the first available phone and dialed the office of the National Transportation Safety Board. She asked for Michael O'Rourke, only to find that he was in New York, conducting the investigation of the Jet-East crash. She knew exactly where to find him.

Using her electronic I.D. card, Kate opened one of the exit doors. At the foot of the stairs Kate stopped to pin her badge to the outside of her jacket, then began to walk around the perimeter of the terminal.

The hangar was located on the opposite side of the runways and getting there on foot was nearly impossible. Trying to ignore the butterflies in her stomach, she flagged an approaching maintenance cart.

"Any chance you can give me a lift to Hangar Three?"

The man looked at her, then leaned forward to look at her I.D., but didn't recognize her.

"Jump on," he said. Taking the airport perimeter road, the ride took less than five minutes. He dropped Kate off in front of a small door to a huge hangar. She slid her electronic I.D. card through and watched the little green light come to life. She held her breath and entered.

The hangar was large enough to house a ten-story building, but for the time being it was occupied only by the carcass of Jet-East flight 394.

The fuselage, still intact but badly bent and broken, with black soot covering most of it, rested on two large, ladderlike stands. The cockpit, hanging by a thread, sat on another stand. Reaching up to the belly of the fuselage, she gently brushed her hand across its cold metal skin, as if it were a sick child she somehow wanted to comfort.

Her thoughts a thousand miles away, she lingered for a moment unaware that Michael O'Rourke had appeared at her side.

"How are you feeling, Ms. Gallagher?" he asked.

Startled, Kate turned around. "I'm fine, thank you. Your office told me I could find you here."

He wore jeans and a white shirt under a black V-neck sweater. He was holding a clipboard and pen. "I'm afraid I don't have a whole lot of new information to give you."

"That's not why I came here."

"Oh?"

"Mr. O'Rourke, I want to go through your research files."

"What files?"

"I want to see the original investigations that the NTSB has conducted for every accident involving this type of aircraft, in . . . say, the last five years."

"Most of that information is a matter of public record. You can get—"

"No. I don't want the public record. I want to see

the raw data, the transcripts, the voice recorders, everything you guys see."

"Why?"

Kate sighed deeply. "I can't explain it. What I felt back there in the airplane, it was as real as you and I standing here. I don't know what it was, but I'm hoping that something in your previous investigations may lead to a clue."

"Captain Gallagher, as much as we like to hear other opinions, you have to understand that NTSB investigations are extremely thorough, and that . . ."

"I'm not looking to challenge the NTSB, Mr. O'Rourke. But I was there. I felt something. Maybe someone else felt exactly the same thing." Kate looked him directly in the eye.

"And what do you want me to do? Open up files, let you listen in on the voice recorders, the final words some of these people spoke before they died? Invade their privacy in the hope that something you hear may be familiar?" His tone seemed uncharacteristically hostile.

"My intention is not to invade anyone's privacy or to dishonor the dead. I think you know that. I want to—"

"The information is public and is available to you, like anyone else. I'm sorry, I can't make an exception beyond that."

"Look at this!" Kate shouted, pointing to the fuselage. "Look at this. They're saying *I* did this. *You're* saying I did this. That I caused this accident and I killed those people. All I'm asking is that you consider the possibility that maybe, just maybe, there is something to what I'm telling you. If I'm wrong, you've lost nothing." She winced as a jolt of pain shot through her side. "But if I'm right, Mr. O'Rourke, if I'm right and this has happened before, what happens the next time? What will you do when the next plane goes down?"

O'Rourke looked at her at length, considering her

plea. Finally he broke the silence. "I'll be at head-quarters in Washington tomorrow. How's ten-fifteen?"

Kate made it back to Greenwich Village just after dark. From the corner, she peeked at her building. At least two of the vans were still there. Dammit. She was losing her privacy, her life. How long could this go on?

She needed clean clothes and a hot bath, but there was no way to reach the escape ladder from the alley. She hung around another minute or two, but when it became clear that they weren't going anywhere in a hurry, she decided it wasn't worth the hassle.

She walked two blocks to a small boutique and bought a pair of black wool slacks and a tan turtleneck sweater, some toiletries and cosmetics, and a pair of brown leather half-boots. Emerging from the store she hailed a cab and headed for the midtown hotel where she was sure she could get a room for the night.

The next morning, Gallagher caught the eight o'clock shuttle from La Guardia and landed at D.C.'s National Airport in less than an hour. Inside the terminal, she turned her cell phone back on. It rang almost immediately.

"I've got something I need you to check out," Spencer Hill told her.

"What?" Kate asked as she made her way though the terminal.

"There are four independent sources of information to the flight control computers. Of these, two are internal and I'm researching those, and one has to do with the engines, which is not relevant. The only source of information that is independent of the flight control system is the navigation system."

"Go on."

"They use a product called STAR. It stands for Satellite Tracking And Receiving system. It's a great system, used in lots of airplanes, but I can't find any information on it."

"Isn't there anyone in maintenance who can tell you more about it?"

"STAR is very complicated. We don't do any repairs on it. If something goes wrong with the hardware, all Jet-East maintenance does is remove it and replace it with a new unit. Then they send the defective unit back to the factory, and they do all the donkey work."

"What's the name of the company?"

"Searchlight. It's in Washington, D.C."

"That's where I am right now."

"Great. Go there and ask to talk to someone who works the system. Find out how their navigational information is translated into data and how it's forwarded to the flight control computers. Find out everything. Then call me back."

Half an hour later, with a map of Washington in her lap, she drove away in a rental car, feeling a sudden, overwhelming sense of hope.

O'Rourke met Kate in the lobby of the National Transportation Safety Board offices.

After her visit to the hangar the day before, she had set up house in the back of his mind—and stubbornly remained. He'd even had a date; a late-night dinner with someone he had met a few weeks earlier. O'Rourke hadn't been very good company, with so much on his mind. When his date finally asked him what was wrong, he excused it as fatigue and overwork. But that wasn't the reason for his odd behavior; Kate Gallagher was.

Maybe it was physical attraction; her eyes, or her radiant skin. Or maybe it was her determination, the way she fought for what she believed in. He wasn't sure why he felt the way he did, but there was something there, something fundamental.

He knew this was insane. This was an accident investigation, not a dating service. There was a conflict of interest, a conflict of personality—a conflict of everything. Not to mention the fact that she seemed to hate him.

"We can work in the conference room in the back," O'Rourke said in a carefully neutral tone. "I'm not sure what you want to look at, but I've got the summary printout, with a brief description of every major airliner incident going back ten years. I think you should go through them first and decide what you want to see. Pull out the ones that interest you and I'll get you the files."

"Thanks."

They walked down a bare hallway, through a white door, and into a small room that contained a large gray metal desk, two chairs, a bookcase, and a stack of computer printouts.

"Our iron kitchen is just outside, first turn on your right. Every type of vending machine available to mankind."

"This is fine. Thank you," Kate said as she draped her black leather jacket over the extra chair.

This was the first time O'Rourke had seen her in anything other than a hospital gown or an overcoat, and despite his best efforts he was unable to take his eyes off her.

"You look nice," he said, immediately realizing his blunder. He stood there, smiling clumsily, trying to ignore the blood rushing to his face.

Kate glanced at him curiously. "Thanks," she muttered.

O'Rourke didn't say any more. He left the room as fast as his mortified legs could carry him. Kate sat down and went to work.

The list was quite simple: headers explaining general information such as the type of aircraft, the location of the incident, the date it occurred, followed by a brief history of the event. There was a reference number for each incident; three hours later, Kate had jotted down sixteen of them.

She got up, stretched, and went to the kitchen. She bought an apple and a bottle of water from the vending machines and went back to the room. She had barely finished the apple when the door opened.

"Did you find anything?" O'Rourke asked quietly.

Kate handed him the list.

He studied it for a moment. "That's a lot of information you've asked for. It'll take you the rest of the day, maybe longer, to go through them."

"I don't have any pressing engagements."

O'Rourke looked up. "All right. I'll have them brought to you."

Ten minutes later, the door opened again and a young man pushed in a cart packed with files and papers.

"Mr. O'Rourke asked that you call him on extension 1143 when you're done," he said, as he unloaded the documents on the table.

Kate picked up the first thick file. She studied the reports one at a time, taking occasional breaks by standing up and stretching or pacing the cramped room. By the time she had finished, she was down to three files. She pushed everything else away.

She studied the first: a Korean Air jumbo jet that ran into a mountainside on its final descent into Guam in bad weather. The accident was blamed on pilot error, as was the second incident, a China Airlines Airbus A300B4 on a trip from Taipei International Airport to Nagoya International Airport in Japan. She studied the reports closely and was dishearteningly convinced by their findings. There wasn't an "i" left undotted or a "t" left uncrossed in any of them. With a pessimistic sigh, she pulled the third and last report.

Flight 86 of Jetway, a small freight carrier based in Miami, disappeared from the radar while flying at cruise altitude from Atlantic City to its destination, Miami. A massive search-and-rescue operation yielded a field of debris in shallow water off the coast but no survivors. Neither of the two pilots had reported any malfunction or radioed a distress call. The report went on to say that subsequent study of the recovered cockpit voice recorder indicated that the captain was not in the cockpit at the time of the accident. Minutes earlier, he had left to use the restroom and the first officer, in accordance with the rules, had donned his oxygen mask and continued to fly the plane.

Study of the flight data recorder indicated that three minutes later, the aircraft began a shallow turn to the right. Shortly after, the autopilot was disconnected but the aircraft continued its roll and completely inverted in the subsequent six seconds.

There were lots of references to the positions of the ailerons and the elevators: a clear indication that they were being manipulated throughout the dive. But with no voice recordings of any kind, and the captain away from the cockpit, the preliminary conclusion pointed to First Officer Kevin Ames and the possibility that the accident was the result of pilot suicide.

Kate recalled reading about the accident. But since it was only a cargo carrier it hadn't attracted nearly the attention that a passenger plane would have. She was tired and tempted to let it go but something about the accident struck a familiar chord.

Kate grabbed the report and placed everything else back on the cart. Just after five P.M., she dialed O'Rourke's extension, and a minute later he stood at the door.

"Find anything to help us out with our investigations?"

"Oh, I don't think you need any help from me, Mr. O'Rourke. But I would like to make copies of this one file, if that's okay with you."

O'Rourke took the file and glanced through it.

"Charlie Waters led the investigation on this one. He's a good man."

"I don't doubt it."

"May I ask what caught your interest in this one report?"

"It's about the only accident with no clear-cut explanation of what happened. Even your own report says that the 'likely' cause is pilot suicide, but there's no definitive answer."

"They did a thorough background check on the crew. I think there were some problems with alcohol. And he had been fired from one of the majors. They think that may have had something to do with it."

"Did he have a family?"

"Yeah—wife, a couple of little kids. But there were problems at home too."

"You think he killed himself?"

"Like I said, it's not my investigation. But the evidence points in that direction."

O'Rourke walked out and five minutes later came back with a stack of copies.

"You know, these files you asked to see, and the rest of the ones you didn't request. They're all filled with pilots making mistakes, controllers making mistakes, even mechanical failures that are on some level to be blamed on human error."

Kate looked at him curiously. "Why are you telling me this?"

"I don't know. I guess I'm just trying to say that we're all human and we make mistakes."

"Is that what you think happened? That I made a mistake because I'm human?"

"I don't know what happened out there. But I promise you I'm going to work very hard to find out."

"Well, you'll forgive me if I don't wait for you to come to my rescue."

"I'm just trying to tell you that—"

"That I destroyed an airplane, that I killed six people because I'm human? That I failed in my responsibilities as captain, but that's okay because others have too? Exactly what *are* you trying to tell me, Mr. O'Rourke?"

He paused for a minute. "I just wanted to let you know that you're not alone."

She shook her head in disgust. "Yes, I am."

chapter 9

She wanted to scream by the time she left the NTSB. Why didn't anyone believe her? Was it because she was a woman or was it the nature of human beings to place blame wherever it seemed most convenient? Either way, the cold hard truth was that she was on her own. It was up to her alone to come up with the answers—providing there were any.

She needed to spend the night in Washington; the company Spencer wanted her to visit was here. She picked the Hilton on Connecticut Avenue. A few minutes after she called and made a reservation, she parked the rental in the lot across from the main entrance and walked in.

Six rows away in the parking lot, he watched her walk away from her car, a duffel bag clutched against her chest. He reached for the folder on the seat beside him and removed the rubber band that contained its contents. The stack of photographs was almost an inch

thick. He gently pulled them from the plastic folder being careful not to smudge them with his fingertips. The
first picture was of Kate as she arrived at Kennedy, on
her way to Washington, earlier that day. Next was a
photo of Kate as she stepped into a cab in the city, then
one of her on her cell phone and one more walking to
her rental car. In the white border below each photograph, notations indicating the time and place the picture was taken were written in felt-tip pen.

There were more pictures. Molly in the back of the
cab with Kate. Her apartment, front and back. The
restaurant. Kate's mother, on her way to church.

His eyes devoured them all, one at a time. At length
he closed the file and pulled the rubber band around it.
Then he opened the door and got out.

Kate walked into the room and threw her bag on the
bed. She sat next to it, picked up the phone, and dialed.

As usual, Molly was at the restaurant, helping the
hostess and the waitresses and seating the customers.

"How you doing, sunshine?"

"I'm good, Mommy. Guess what? I made fifty
cents."

"Fifty cents? How'd you do that?"

"From one of the customers. He said I did good. He
gave me a tip. Can I buy bubble gum with it?"

Kate responded after a moment of pondering the
question. "Did *well* . . . and only if you save half for me."

"Okay, but when are you coming home? I miss you,
Mommy."

Kate felt winded; as if she had just taken a punch.
"I miss you too. I miss you more than the whole
world."

"You sound sad, Mommy."

"I'm okay, honey. You be good and listen to Grandma. I'll see you in a couple of days."

Kate hung up, but continued to sit on the edge of the bed, staring at the phone. She missed her life, she missed her daughter. When would all this be over?

Out in the hallway, he leaned in close to her door. The words were muffled, but he heard just enough. He reached into his pocket and pulled out a small silver gadget, no bigger than a paper clip. He slowly pulled back the clasp with his hand, coiling the spring, readying the device for its intended purpose.

Confirming that there was no one around, he quietly inserted it between the doorjamb and the door, then walked away. Back in the lobby, he picked up the house phone.

Kate answered on the first ring.

"Sorry to bother you, this is the front desk. Are you driving a white Toyota Camry, license plate number AW4612?"

She didn't know the license plate number, but recognized the car. "Yes, it's a white Camry. Why?"

"You left your lights on. You might want to check on that before the battery runs out."

"Thanks."

He waited in the lobby until he saw her come out of the elevator, keys in hand. Now.

He went back to her room and simply pushed the door in. Once inside, he bent over and grabbed the little device, now at the foot of the door, a small needle extending from its tip that prevented the door from closing.

Kate was annoyed to discover that her lights were not on; he must have been talking about another car. She rushed inside to get out of the cold, returned to her room, and locked herself in, using the deadbolt and chain. In the bathroom, she poured herself a glass of water, then walked to the bed and pulled out the NTSB file from her bag.

She spread out the documents and began to read.

Through the tiny crack in the door of the closet he watched every move she made. How she picked up the room service menu, her position on the bed. He watched her phone downstairs for food. Heard her say, "Thirty minutes will be fine."

Inside the closet, he wiped his clammy palms across his pants and reached into his pocket. The cold steel handle of the knife felt reassuring. He wasn't going to use it. But he wouldn't hesitate even for a second if she left him no choice.

She flipped through a few channels, then got up and began to undress. First came the sweater, then the pants, the bra, and finally the panties. He licked his lips as Kate wrapped a towel around her body and walked into the bathroom.

When he heard her getting into the tub, he opened the closet door ever so slowly, making sure the hinges didn't creak.

He looked toward the light in the bathroom. The temptation was so intense he felt it might burn a hole through him. But that wasn't why he was here.

He crept over to the bed, picked up one of the sheets of paper and glanced over it. Then a second one, and a third.

He heard the water stop and turned his head in the direction of the bathroom door and gripped the knife in his pocket. But nothing happened.

He had seen enough. He placed the papers back exactly as he had found them, blew a farewell kiss toward the bathroom, and slipped out of the room.

Kate got out of the tub, dried herself, and put on the hotel robe she found in the closet.

She was brushing her hair when she heard the knock.

She walked to the door and glanced through the peephole. Room service.

Automatically she reached for the chain, but the chain was unhooked. She looked down at the deadbolt. It too was open.

Locking the door wasn't something she would forget, and she distinctly remembered locking this one.

She let the waiter in, then stuck her head out and examined the hallway. The waiter put the food on the table, then Kate asked him to wait until she had checked the room, the closet, even underneath the bed.

Content that no one was hiding in her room, she signed the bill. When the waiter was gone she locked the door, decisively, double-checking that the chain and the bolt were secure.

Trying to relax, she convinced herself that it was just the stress—her mind playing tricks. She dug into the scampi she had ordered. Fifteen minutes later she was back on the bed researching the Jetway flight 86 file page by page.

There were no recordings on the CVR, at least nothing to indicate the first officer was about to commit suicide. As a matter of fact, most of the transcript consisted of idle conversation—references to one of his children's birthdays and an upcoming fishing trip. If this man had planned to kill himself, he offered no indication whatsoever.

Furthermore, there were no signs of mechanical problems. No failures of any kind. Nothing.

But the CVR only saves recordings of the pilots' voices for thirty minutes. All conversation prior to that is taped over and therefore irretrievably lost.

Also, the first officer had his oxygen mask on, which almost certainly would have muffled his voice and maybe even prevented him from saying something that could have been recorded on the CVR. Besides, if someone was going to kill himself, why would he care about wearing an oxygen mask?

The only data on the flight recorder indicated minor fluctuations in the controls for a number of minutes prior to the accident, fluctuations dismissed as clear air turbulence and corrected by the autopilot.

"Fluctuations in the flight controls," Kate whispered to herself. The words had an eerily familiar ring. The more Kate thought about it, the more she was convinced that she had found something.

She spent two more hours on the papers. Sometime after eleven o'clock she turned off the lights.

The Searchlight Tower, an eight-story black marble and glass structure, was located in Crystal City, Arlington. In the lobby, Kate presented herself at the information desk.

"I'm wondering if someone can help me. I need some information about one of your products. It's called STAR."

The middle-aged receptionist looked up and noticed Kate's informal clothes.

"And you are with . . . ?"

"I work for a private firm. I'm doing some research on the system to see if it's right for us."

Clearly dissatisfied with the answer, the woman eyeballed her for a moment, but with the morning rush and the perpetually ringing phones, she was in no mood for a lengthy discussion.

"Have a seat." She waved in the direction of a chair and went back to work.

Several minutes later, a very attractive woman with long blond hair tied back in a ponytail, wearing a tan pantsuit and an I.D. badge, walked up to Kate and thrust her hand forward.

"My name is Dorothy McGuire. I'm the assistant marketing director for Searchlight."

Kate shook her hand. "Are you familiar with the STAR system? That's what I'm interested in."

"I'm familiar with all of our products here at Searchlight. How can I help you?"

"I would like to find out how your system works. How it receives its signal and what method it uses to transmit that signal to the other systems in the aircraft. And if you can give me some literature on it, schematics and data, that would be helpful as well."

"You're familiar with STAR?"

"I've used it before."

"May I ask where?"

"My airline uses your system."

"And which airline is that?"

Kate hesitated for a moment, then whispered, "Jet-East."

An alarm went off in the woman's head instantly but she struggled to keep her face expressionless.

"Why don't you just wait here for a moment," she said, backing away awkwardly as if Kate were contagious.

Dispirited, Kate slumped back down in her chair. She wasn't a crook and she wasn't a fugitive, but being treated this way, seeing the expression of shock as someone recognized her, made her feel like one.

Some fifteen minutes elapsed before Dorothy McGuire reappeared.

"Here, you'll need to wear this," she said, handing Kate a visitor's badge.

Kate clipped the badge onto her jacket lapel and followed the woman past the reception desk.

"Where are we going?"

"You wanted to know more about the STAR system. I'm going to introduce you to the person who helped create it—Mr. Davis Thompson."

"Who is he?"

"The chief operating officer."

They took the elevator to the ninth floor and walked through a long corridor, past a series of glass doors, before arriving at another reception area.

"Go right in." The secretary pointed to the door.

McGuire opened the door, waited for Kate to enter, and closed it behind her.

The corner office was exquisitely decorated, offering a panoramic view of the capital. Two walls displayed an eclectic array of paintings that ranged from Salvador Dalí to Paul Klee, even Picasso. In the corner, two elegant mahogany and glass étagères played host to a variety of awards.

The room seemed empty, so Kate walked up to the window, admiring the view.

"Beautiful, isn't it?" said a voice from behind.

Kate jumped and turned in the direction of the voice.

The man was tall, with jet-black hair slicked straight back. His gentle eyes were cobalt blue and he had a soft smile—a no-nonsense, comforting "welcome to my home" smile that proved irresistible to all women—including Kate. He was in his early forties, and dressed in black pin-striped slacks and a white shirt, with a red tie. There was a jacket hanging on a coat tree.

"My name is Davis Thompson," he said, shaking Kate's hand firmly. "I understand you have some questions about my STAR system."

"Yes, but I didn't expect to be talking to the COO."

Thompson took a seat in the rich burgundy leather chair behind his desk and pointed to chair across from it.

"Why not?"

"The information I need is mostly technical and could be answered by anyone with a basic knowledge of the system."

"Well then, I'll try not to disappoint you."

Kate smiled politely. "Okay."

"But before we get started," Thompson said, "I want you to know that I have a great deal of admiration for you and compassion for your recent ordeal."

"You have an advantage over me. You seem to know who I am."

"Like everyone else, I watched the accident on television. But my interest goes beyond that of a casual spectator. Your aircraft used our system and, well . . . Jet-East is an important client."

"So you've been following the story."

"Yes, quite closely. You know, I saw you on TV the night of the crash. You were quite the hero, saving that woman and her child."

"I did my job."

"And now they're blaming you for it."

Kate didn't say anything.

"Tell me, Ms. Gallagher. Why are you here? Do you think the STAR system had anything to do with what happened?"

"Not at all. As a matter of fact I've always found the system to be amazingly efficient."

"I don't understand. Why then . . . ?"

"Mr. Thompson, something took control of that aircraft and it wasn't me. I have no idea what happened, but I suspect it had to do with the flight control systems, so I'm checking out everything that is in any way connected to them. STAR is one of those systems."

Thompson studied Kate for a moment, then said, "Well, let's get to it then."

"I'm sorry?"

"Ms. Gallagher, STAR is one of the most thoroughly researched and extensively used navigational systems in the world. Its application, from civilian to military use, has been tested for years. And it has saved lives. I can pull out fifty letters right now and show them to you. Letters from lost fishermen and campers who found their way home using the STAR system. We're in the business of saving lives, and that's what I'm most proud of. But if there is any chance that STAR had anything to do with this terrible accident, any chance at all, I have to know about it."

"I'm sure there's nothing wrong with your system—"

"Yet you're here."

"I just want to know how it works."

"Tell you what. I'll get you all of the data on STAR you want. Everything from scratch. I am also going to make our top technicians and our chief software designer available to you. They will cooperate with you in any way you wish. All I ask is that you respect the confidentiality of the information we give you and that I be kept completely informed of any progress you make."

"I—I don't know what to say."

Thompson got up from his chair and walked around to the front of his desk to sit on the edge.

"I think you're getting the raw end of this deal, Ms. Gallagher, but I'm not doing this for you. I'm doing this for my company."

Kate smiled. "Thank you."

Thompson leaned back and pushed a button on his intercom and said, "Please make sure conference room number two is open. Then ask Richard Malkovich to join Ms. Gallagher there." He turned to Kate. "Rich is our chief software designer. He knows more about STAR even than I do. He'll spend as much time with you as you need, and he'll give you the data that you asked for. Here's my card with my direct line and my home number on the back."

"Thank you again," Kate said, getting up and shaking Thompson's hand.

He smiled and waited until she was safely out the door. Then he returned to his chair, grabbed his pen, tapped it on his desk a few times, and put the end of it in his mouth. Chewing the tip, he leaned back in his chair and turned to face the window.

Shortly before noon, and after spending more than two hours with Searchlight's top technical advisers, Kate left the building with a thick pile of documents and marketing handouts on STAR.

From his window, Thompson watched her leave.

"What do you think?" he asked.

Robert Cordelia, a man of fifty-two with thick gray hair parted to one side, lifted his deep brown eyes. "Everything she's got is safe. I don't think she's going to be any trouble. Besides, right now she trusts you. That was a good PR job you did on her."

Thompson was chewing his pen again. "I don't know." He sighed. "There's something about her, something dangerous. I feel it."

"Don't worry. We'll be watching her."

"Do more than that. I want to know everything about her. I want to know which side of the bed she sleeps on and what she eats for breakfast. I want to know who she talks to and when." He turned to Cordelia. "Are we clear?"

Cordelia nodded.

It had been a hectic two days of exploratory research, but Kate felt no closer to an answer than when she'd started.

She stopped at a FedEx office and shipped her package of technical data to Spencer. By early evening she was back in Greenwich Village.

Kate was relieved to see that the television crews

had finally left, having given up on interviewing their star fall guy. She went into her apartment through the front door, which she locked behind her.

At the refrigerator, Kate poured herself a glass of juice, took a sip, and picked up the phone. She hesitated for a moment, then dialed.

"Hello?" a female voice answered on the third ring.

"Hello, Mrs. Brita Ames?"

The line was silent for a moment. "Who is this?"

"My name is Kate Gallagher. I'm an airline pilot. I was in command of the Jet-East flight that went down a few days ago."

Another pause. "I'm Brita Ames. What can I do for you?"

"Mrs. Ames, I need a few minutes of your time."

"I'm just putting the children to bed."

"Would you like me to call back?"

"No, it's okay."

"Mrs. Ames, I know this must be difficult for you, but I need to discuss your husband's accident."

"You said you're the pilot of the plane that crashed a few days ago?"

"Yes."

"Why do you need to know about my husband's accident?"

"Mrs. Ames, I'm not sure how to explain this, but I've studied the information on his crash, and some of what he went through sounds awfully similar to what happened to me."

"In case you don't know this already, he died in his crash. You don't sound dead to me."

"I know this is hard for you, Mrs. Ames. But all I want is a chance to speak with you. It's probably nothing and the investigation is probably accurate, but there is always a chance that—"

"He didn't kill himself."

"Beg your pardon?"

"My husband, they said he killed himself and the other pilot and crashed the plane. He didn't do that. He didn't do any of that."

Kate paused. "Mrs. Ames, is there any way I can come to see you?"

chapter 10

He strode purposefully down the hall, his eyes fixed on the large, solid mahogany door at the end, his fists clinched. He was in his early sixties, lean and tall and in great shape. His ears were large and stuck out somewhat from his massive bald head. A large fleshy nose and dark brown eyes presided over his striking face.

In his former life, before "IPO," "NASDAQ," and "dot com" became household terms, people had considered him a tender soul. He shuddered to think what they said now when the name Marshall Hayes was mentioned.

He was the founder of Hayes Technologies, located in the heart of Silicon Valley, a computer hardware manufacturer that had become highly successful.

Business was brisk and demand high, or at least high enough to persuade him to take the company public. The initial offering was made at four dollars per share and it took a full two years for the shares to reach six dollars. But that was enough, more than enough.

Marshall Hayes had arrived. A lifetime of hard work and persistence had paid off, and, against all odds, the youngest of eleven children born to a citrus farmer and his homemaker wife had made it to the big leagues. It was time to enjoy the fruits of his labor; it was time to enjoy his life. No more eighty-hour weeks, no more sleepless nights.

With his weakness for booze and blondes, it didn't take long for Marshall Hayes to cut back his schedule to fifty, then forty hours per week. Before long, he was barely seen in the office, leaving key decisions in the hands of those far less competent and with motives of their own.

Business slowed to a snail's pace, as giants like the resurgent IBM and Dell gobbled up market shares, growing at warp speeds. But between the scotch and the skirts, Marshall Hayes remained unconcerned. When he finally snapped to, Hayes Technologies had been kicked off the NASDAQ and was trading as a penny stock on the bulletin boards.

As majority shareholder, he had managed to stay on the board and remain CEO, but being the CEO of an ailing company with a dismal future was an unenviable position. Sales slumped, key employees resigned— sometimes without so much as notice—and Hayes Technologies, once a real player in high tech, became almost a footnote, one step away from bankruptcy.

In a desperate but brilliant move to save the company, Marshall Hayes brought in Davis Thompson, the thirty-three-year-old boy wonder. He was a venture capitalist with an MBA from Harvard and his name was synonymous with money and Wall Street. His picture had once appeared on the cover of the *New York Times Magazine*, with the caption *What's Wrong with Greed?* just below it.

The article talked about Thompson and the new breed of tycoons who, through leveraged buyouts, mergers, and streamlining, had managed to revive companies that were casualties of technological change, and in the process made money. Lots of money.

Thompson's name alone quadrupled the value of Hayes Technologies on the day that his appointment was announced. The massive number of shares that Hayes offered him to take the job became worth almost $25 million overnight. But that was just the beginning.

The very first thing Thompson did was to rechristen the company. Hayes Technologies was old and stale and associated with failure. Searchlight. Now there was a name.

In six months Thompson restructured the entire company, changing its core business from hardware manufacturing to software development. But not just any software. Thompson knew better than to compete with the likes of Bill Gates and Larry Ellison. His target was a specific area, a niche, and he found it in global satellite navigation.

He brought in his own people, the best he could find, and moved the company headquarters from Silicon Valley to his home—Washington, D.C. In the process, he put the company firmly back on the map.

Marshall Hayes retained his title as chairman and CEO, but that was all it was—a title. Thompson was president and COO. He ran everything, made every decision. In less than three years the price per share skyrocketed to nearly forty-eight dollars. Then he hit the jackpot.

The project name was STAR—Satellite Tracking And Receiving. It was an innovative and revolutionary technology, equal to or better than its rival, the GPS, or Global Positioning System. Like the GPS, the STAR system allowed any moving vehicle, whether it was a car or a ship or a plane, to be tracked by a satellite signal and allowed the location of the vehicle to be identified immediately, at any place on the globe. STAR had other advantages as well. It enabled the user to find and target a location and follow a path to that destination anywhere on the planet.

For the time being, the satellite usage would be leased, but Thompson had grander ideas: his own chain of satellites circling the planet around the clock, making him more money than any man had a right to have. He implemented his strategy to acquire satellite ownership, and overnight the stock took an 800 percent jump. Each of the men were worth billions, more money than they could burn.

But there was a price to pay for that kind of success. A price that Marshall Hayes was unwilling to pay.

Hayes threw the office door open and, to the surprise of the young secretary seated behind a large teak desk, pointed to Thompson's door.

"Is he in there?" he growled.

"Yes, but he's . . ."

Hayes ignored her and barged into the room. The two men sitting on the couch next to the coffee table bolted upright.

Davis Thompson, behind his desk, put down the black pen he was chewing and looked up.

As usual he was perfectly dressed—a blue Armani suit, its jacket hanging on the back of the chair, a white shirt, a gold tie, and cuff links.

"Well hello, Marshall," Thompson said, flashing his signature smile.

"Leave us," Hayes growled at the men.

They looked at each other, then at Thompson, got up and walked out, their eyes still fixed on the old man. Once they were out of the room, Marshall turned to Thompson.

"Why didn't you tell me?"

"Tell you what?"

"Don't patronize me, dammit. It happened again. There was another e-mail, wasn't there?"

Thompson placed the pen down on his desk and folded his hands in his lap. "Yes."

"When?"

"Last Wednesday. The e-mail was waiting for me when I got in."

"My God, the day before the Jet-East plane went down."

"I'm sure it was a coincidence."

"What did it say?"

"I don't think that's relevant."

"What did the damn e-mail say?" Hayes shouted.

Thompson let out a deep sigh. "More of the same. That another plane would go down within twenty-four hours."

Hayes gave him a piercing look. "And you feel that's not relevant?"

"It was the pilot's fault. Haven't you been reading the papers?"

"So you think it's a coincidence that we get two messages saying two planes are going to go down, and they both do. Do you also think it was a *coincidence* that the pilot of one of these planes showed up in your office yesterday?"

"She just wanted to know about the STAR system. Nothing else. But we're not taking any chances. We're watching everything she does."

"And who's doing the watching? Your goon, what's his name . . . Cordelia?" Hayes didn't hide his contempt.

"You know about him too?"

"I know everything, don't ever forget that. This was my company long before you came along and it will be my company long after your ass is in prison."

"You mean our asses, don't you?" Thompson replied, a hint of a smile playing on his lips.

Hayes's glare seemed to burn holes through Thompson. Then his face relaxed, as did the rest of his body. He slumped down on the couch began to rub his temples.

"My God, man, why didn't you tell me?" he asked.

"Because you would panic. Because you would want to pay."

"And you think paying him would be wrong?"

"And then what? What makes you think he would stop? The e-mail said there were five planes that were infected with this virus. Even if he was right, that only accounts for two. What makes you think he would stop now? And what if we pay him, what have we done then? Have we not admitted that we knew about this? Haven't we left a paper trail that could land both you and me in prison for the rest of our lives? What do you think will happen, Marshall?"

"I don't know," Hayes said in a defeated voice. "I don't know."

Thompson got up to join Hayes on the couch where he put his arm around the old man. "I know how you feel, believe me I do. The last thing we wanted was to hurt anyone, but what could we do? This is the work of some lunatic who has it in for us. Even if we paid the bastard, he still wouldn't leave us alone. He seems to enjoy taunting us."

"We make navigation software, for God's sake. How the hell can somebody use that to crash airplanes?"

Thompson hesitated. "I don't know. But I'm going to find out."

Marshall shook his head. "We should have gone to the authorities when we got the first message."

"And told them what? That someone managed to penetrate our security? That someone claims they've sabotaged five airliners throughout the world? That they are responsible . . . that *we* are responsible and liable for whatever damage occurs? The STAR system is installed on some seven hundred commercial airplanes around the world. To change the entire software would require that each plane be grounded for almost two weeks! You want to tell them that, Marshall? You want to call each of the companies who bought your product and tell them their entire fleet has to be grounded for two weeks so we can act on our hunch?"

"It's not a hunch. They've done just what they threatened to do—twice!"

"Even so, are you ready to take responsibility for what happened to the Jetway flight?"

"Dammit, we should have gone to the authorities when we could."

"And seen a ninety-percent drop in the stock price? We would be worth nothing. And you could kiss the Austin deal goodbye. Do you think their board would approve a merger to an outfit that can't even handle its own affairs?" Thompson moved to sit on the coffee table facing the old man. He leaned over, put his hands on Marshall's shoulders, and looked him directly in the eye. "Marshall, we would lose everything. Everything we have worked for all these years. The company, the deal with Austin, everything."

Marshall Hayes looked up at Davis Thompson with eyes that suddenly seemed old and tired. "That's what it's all about, isn't it? The last buck, the last dime. You're single, barely in your forties, and you have billions. What are you going to do with all that money? Give it away? Have you ever given anything away, Thompson?" Hayes asked with a stony expression. "You can't possibly spend it, and you can't take it with you, so why more?"

"It's not about the money. It's the game."

"A game? There are people dying out there and we might be responsible. Do you think they consider it a game?"

"That's not our fault. Our product is working exactly

as it is supposed to. Save your anger for your enemies. I'm your friend."

Hayes shook his head stubbornly. "I don't want to play anymore; the stakes are too high. People's lives. I don't play with lives."

"Okay, Marshall," Thompson said, his voice as soothing as a mother's lullaby. "You think we made a mistake by not going to the authorities? You want to go to them now?" He pointed to the door. "I won't stop you. This is still your company. You started it. You want to finish it? Go ahead."

Hayes slowly buried his face in his hands. "What have we become, Thompson? What have we done?"

"We've done nothing wrong, my friend. This may all still be a hoax. But if it's not, if someone has decided to go after you and me, I'll find him, Marshall. I promise you I'll find him."

chapter 11

At the small Key West airport, Kate stepped off the Comair commuter plane into the balmy air. The warmth felt good on her skin. If it hadn't been for Mama, she would have moved to a place like this and bought herself a bungalow with palm trees and sand at the foot of the stairs. Molly would love it; she loved the heat, just like her mother.

At the end of the terminal, Kate claimed her rental car *du jour,* a blue Ford Taurus. Armed with a map of the tiny town, she started the drive.

Eliza Street, typical of most streets on the island, was lined with rows of narrow houses. Kate located number 634A and parked the car. The shotgun house, as it was called because you could shoot a shotgun from the front door straight through the back, was long and narrow, all wood, and painted gray with blue trim. The landscaping was overgrown and unkempt, and some of the paint was beginning to peel, but otherwise the house was well kept.

She walked up the creaky wooden stairs and rang the bell. The door opened, and through the screen Kate saw the pretty yet worn face of Brita Ames.

She was very thin, almost anorexic-looking. Her long brown hair was pulled back in a tight bun and she wore no makeup on her fair and freckled face. She could only have been in her late twenties yet she looked much older. And she wasn't trying to impress anyone either—at least not in her denim overalls and gray T-shirt.

"Hi, I'm Kate Gallagher."

The woman studied her, then with a polite, forced smile, nodded. "I'm Brita Ames. Come in."

Kate walked in and found herself in the middle of a sparsely furnished living room. The shades were drawn, making the room relatively dark. Children's toys littered the floor. A ceiling fan was turning, making a continuous clicking sound in a futile effort to cool the room.

"You have a nice home," Kate said, in an attempt to break the ice.

"It's been home for a long time, but I don't know how much longer. I can offer you water or milk. That's all we have."

"I'm fine, thank you," Kate replied, taking a seat beside Brita on the couch.

Brita picked up a Virginia Slim and lit it, taking a deep drag and exhaling slowly. "I'd given the damn things up six years ago," she said, looking at the skinny cigarette.

"Why did you start again?"

"I don't know. I'm weak, I guess." She took another deep drag. "What can I do for you, Ms. Gallagher?"

"Like I said on the phone, the report on your husband's accident sounded similar to what I experienced."

"They're saying that you caused the accident, that there was nothing wrong with the plane," Brita said bluntly.

"They're also saying that your husband committed suicide. Do you believe them?"

She flinched, took another drag, and let it out. "No. No, I don't."

"I spent most of yesterday going over the accident report. They kept talking about possible suicide because—"

"My husband didn't kill himself," Brita interrupted.

"How can you be so sure?"

Brita Ames placed her cigarette in an ashtray and got up. She went to the mantel, grabbed a picture frame, and handed it to Kate. "That's why."

The boy was no more than six, the girl three or four. They were dressed in their Sunday best, smiling into the camera. Two children, both near Molly's age, left without a father. Kate's heart sank as she looked at them, then at their mother.

"What are their names?"

"Matt and Cheyenne. That picture was taken three weeks before the crash."

"Where are they now?"

"Matt's in school. Cheyenne is upstairs asleep. She sleeps a lot since Kevin's been gone. It's only been four months so she still asks for him." She took one last drag and crushed the butt in the ashtray. "You know what the weirdest thing is? She doesn't even cry anymore, just sits there quietly, hugging Mr. Wishes."

"Mr. Wishes?"

"It's a little teddy bear that she takes everywhere— the last thing Kevin gave her, just a few days before he died." She looked up. "They were the light of his life, Ms. Gallagher, the reason he got up in the morning, the air that he breathed. He hated being gone from them so much that he considered quitting. But he was a pilot, and like most of you guys, flying was part of his soul. It wasn't something he could give up."

"The report said something about a drinking problem, that it was partly the reason. . . ."

"He had a DUI when he was eighteen. He was driving home from some party and had too much to drink. The cops stopped him, threw him in jail overnight, and that was that. But still, it was on his record, and he didn't report it on an application when he got his first flying job fifteen years later. When the company found out about it, they fired him. That's how he ended up with Jetway, flying cargo in the middle of the night. When the investigators started looking into his background, they discovered what had happened, and by the time that hit the papers . . . well, everyone's mind was made up."

"Did he have a drinking problem?"

"No more than you or I do. But it was the only explanation they could come up with. How could a perfectly good airplane fall from the sky? It made no sense—but then you add a pilot who has a past, with problems at home, and you have a convenient excuse."

Kate wanted to ask more, but she sensed that they were private issues. Before she could steer the conversation back to safer territory, Brita launched into her story.

"I was only twenty-two, barely out of college, when we got married. I got pregnant immediately and before Matt was even off the bottle Cheyenne came along, and the rest of my life was laid out for me as a housewife and mother. Kevin was thirteen years older than me: he had done what he wanted to do. Besides, he was always gone, traveling all over the place, leaving me here, alone, up to my neck in diapers. I resented him for it. I thought I hated him." Her eyes filled with tears. "But I was wrong."

She lit another cigarette and inhaled deeply.

"I had an affair—no, several actually. It's tough to keep a secret in a small town like this. When he found out, I told him I wanted to leave, and you know what's funny?" she said, wincing at the memory. "He told me that he forgave me. The son of a bitch told me he forgave me and wanted us to try again. But I still wanted to punish him so I left." She took a long drag and shifted in her seat.

"The last time I saw him was the day before he died. He came to see the kids. He played with them, gave them little gifts, Mr. Wishes for Cheyenne and a little sports car for Matt. Then he looked for me, but I stayed in my room."

She leaned over. "Everything that he did, everything that he was, was for those children. Ms. Gallagher, my husband didn't kill himself, he couldn't."

"What happened when you told the investigators all of this?"

"They were sympathetic. They listened. But they had a job to do. Pilot suicide was the easiest probable cause. Either way, it was enough."

"What do you mean?"

"The life insurance company refused to pay the policy because suicide isn't covered. So now I get to live in this house for about six more weeks, then we're all out on the street," she said, her voice trembling. "I don't even know what happened or how we ended up like this." She paused. "But I'm scared. I'm scared for Cheyenne and for Matt, and I'm scared for me, for the guilt I have to live with for the rest of my life." She sobbed, breaking down completely.

Kate noticed something to her left and looked up. Little Cheyenne was standing there, all of three feet tall, her curly brown hair disheveled, wearing her Barney pajamas, and holding a fuzzy brown teddy bear. She looked at her mother's tear-filled eyes and then at

Kate. She slowly walked over to Brita, wiped her mother's eyes, and sat down in her lap.

"Sugar, this is Kate Gallagher. She flies an airplane, just like Daddy used to."

The little girl's face lit up. "Do you know my daddy?"

"No, honey. I don't."

"He's in heaven," she said, squeezing the teddy bear.

"Is that Mr. Wishes?" Kate asked, pointing to the bear.

"Yeah. How did you know?"

Kate leaned over and whispered, "He told me his name."

The little girl gawked in disbelief. Then she slowly left her mother's arms and scooted over to Kate. "He talked to you?"

"Yeah. You want to know what else he said?"

"What?"

"He said that he likes it when you hug him."

The girl squeezed the little bear harder, leaned closer to Kate, and whispered, "My mommy says that my daddy is not coming back from heaven. But he is coming back, you know how I know?"

With her eyes glued to the little child and a huge lump in her throat, Kate shook her head.

"Because he told me. He told me to take care of Mr. Wishes till he got back, and he told me he would be back next week. How much is 'next week'?"

Kate stared at the little girl, her eyes misting over. "You just hold on to Mr. Wishes and you take care of him for your daddy." Her voice cracked. "Everything else will be all right."

She couldn't look at the child anymore. If she did, little Cheyenne might see the pain in her face, the pain she couldn't hide.

The girl had noticed that something was wrong. She took Kate's head in her little hands. Then, her face inches away, and with more intuition than a seasoned psychiatrist, she asked, "Are you crying?"

Kate didn't know what to say. She wanted to tell her that she wasn't crying, that she didn't even know how to. To tell her that she wished she did, so she could cry for herself and for little Cheyenne. She wanted to tell her that her father wasn't coming back and the sooner she got used to the idea, the less pain she would have to endure. Little Cheyenne, little Molly, what was the difference? Daddy wasn't coming home.

"I'm sorry, sunshine," Kate said, hugging her tightly. "Like I said, you just hang on to Mr. Wishes. Everything else will be okay." Kate got up.

She wiped her eyes with the palm of her hand and turned to Brita. "You take care of her. And you take care of yourself and your son. Remember, they need you more than ever. I'll call you as soon as I have something."

Without a backward glance, Kate walked out of the door.

chapter 12

At six-foot-five and 250 pounds, Robert Cordelia was a formidable figure. He was an ex-Navy SEAL, an ex-FBI agent, an ex-alcoholic, and an ex-husband and father. He had no real friends or lovers, at least none who weren't paid for. He was cool, calculating, and deliberate. And for the right price, Robert Cordelia was also deadly.

He headed an operation called SIGNAT, an elite outfit based in D.C., whose unique services were available only to the most discreet and exclusive of clients.

Officially SIGNAT did not exist. They did not advertise or file tax returns, but it was very much a thriving business. The handful of clients who knew of its existence were more than enough to keep it that way for a long time to come.

Davis Thompson was one such client. He had first been introduced to Robert Cordelia and SIGNAT in his earlier years, when Cordelia was kicked out of the FBI after a mob sting went bust. Even though it was never proven, Cordelia was suspected as the snitch who had tipped off the bosses.

There was a brief inquiry, but Cordelia was never suspended, never reprimanded, never officially accused. The fact that he was heavily dependent on alcohol and barbiturates, which had led to the ruin of his private life, prompted the Bureau to offer him early retirement. He accepted. Sixteen months later, with his divorce and addictions behind him, he began to recruit associates from various law-enforcement agencies and other connections from his shady past. Thus, SIGNAT was born.

One of his first clients was the young Davis Thompson, who at the time was in need of specific and intensely personal information regarding the private life of an ailing CEO of a company he wished to acquire. Cordelia delivered the goods, including a video of the chairman giving "oral" dictation to his young secretary. The video made its way to the tabloids and major stockholders, making the acquisition of the company a cakewalk. Cordelia was paid handsomely for his work, and SIGNAT was on its way.

Over the years, Thompson had used Cordelia's services more extensively, for eavesdropping, background checks on potential clients and employees, and most recently for the biggest hunt of all: to find the culprit or culprits behind the extortion of Searchlight.

Just after noon Cordelia entered the offices of his client. Thompson was pacing the length of his office, lost in thought, wearily massaging his temples.

"Headache again?" Cordelia asked as he sat down.

"Yeah."

"You really should try some nonconventional therapies for that."

Thompson's chronic and often debilitating headaches were not the kind of information that he shared with many. But the fact that Cordelia knew about them didn't surprise him in the least.

"Yeah, like what?"

"I can give you the name of a great acupuncturist."

Thompson stopped midrub and looked at the man across his desk. "I don't need a damn acupuncturist. The doctors tell me they're tension headaches, that I need to take it easy. But I can't take it easy. Do you know why?"

There was no good answer, and Cordelia didn't give one.

"Because I'm being blackmailed and you don't seem to be doing a thing about it. Two attempts, both ending up in my very personal mail file and both telling me that an airplane is going to go down and it's all my fault."

"We're doing everything we can."

"It's not enough!" Thompson shouted, and immediately clasped his head to apply pressure on his temples. "It's not enough," he repeated, softly this time, his eyes clamped shut.

Cordelia pulled out a notebook from his jacket. "We traced the first e-mail to a private box at Stanford University in California. They used some second-year math student's e-mail address. We had the guy checked out. I can tell you anything you want to know about him including the color of his underwear, but it wasn't him."

He flipped the page. "We obtained the routing information, including the exact location of the computer from which the e-mail apparently originated. It was one of forty in the chemistry department, inside an office smack in the middle of campus. Access was password protected. Sounds like it may have been some smart-ass computer geek, you know, one of those hackers. They waited until an airplane went down, then wrote you a letter saying they did it and want thirty million dollars."

"And the second e-mail?"

"From the moment you called me I've had everyone in the operation working on it. I've also hired my own hacker, and so far all we uncovered is that it came from someplace in the D.C. area. We're still tracking it."

"They have my private e-mail address, Bob. Not the company one. How did they get it?"

"I don't know. Maybe from somebody right here. Maybe—"

"Screw maybes. That's not what I pay you for," Thompson said, still clutching his head. "Bring me the ice pack in the refrigerator."

Cordelia retrieved the pack and handed it to Thompson, who placed it on the back of his neck. He kept his eyes closed. "I'm going to have to pay him, Bob. If you don't find him soon, I'll have no choice but to pay him."

"This guy is cuckoo. He's just taking you for a ride."

"Yeah, and this cuckoo says there are three other planes that are going to go down just like the first two. He just doesn't tell us when."

"That's because he doesn't know. Because he has nothing to do with it."

"I can't take that chance. There's too much at stake."

"Searchlight is clear of the first incident. There is no way anyone can connect us to the Jetway flight. But this pilot . . . this Gallagher woman, that's the reason I'm here."

Thompson leaned back in his chair but didn't say anything.

"When she was here yesterday, we had her place checked out. Basic stuff: wiretapped her phone, put surveillance around her house. When she got home, she made some calls. One of them was to Brita Ames, the widow of the pilot who flew that Jetway plane. She went to see her this morning."

Thompson's face drained of all color. He squinted

at Cordelia's long and narrow face, trying to digest what he had just heard.

"How did she . . ." He let the words hang in midair.

"I don't know. But in her phone conversations with the widow she kept referring to the accident report."

"What did she say when she went to see her?"

"I'm not sure. We sent two guys down with her, but they didn't have any equipment with them, so we couldn't hear anything. But I'm taking care of that now. We'll be watching the widow too from now on."

"My God. What the hell is going on here?"

"I don't think there's anything to worry about. Not yet, anyhow."

"She was right here, sitting in that chair, dammit. And now she's talking to Ames's widow, and you don't think there's anything to worry about? When do you start worrying, Cordelia, when they put handcuffs on my wrists? I pay you to bloody worry."

"We're on top of it."

Thompson leaned over his desk, ignoring the pain in his head. "Find out what is going on and who is behind it before this thing gets to me. I don't care what it takes, what it costs, or how you do it. You get this son of a bitch, or you can plan on spending the rest of your career as a security guard at an all-night drugstore."

Under normal circumstances Cordelia didn't take kindly to threats. This was different. Thompson had the power to reach out to Cordelia's other clients and he knew it.

"I'll take care of it. And we'll watch Gallagher. If she makes a move, we'll stop her."

"No extreme measures, do you understand? Don't lay a finger on her. She's not a threat yet. Besides, if anything happened to her, we'd get a hell of a lot more attention than we would ever want."

"Whatever you say."

Thompson relaxed a bit, and placed the ice pack on

his forehead. "What about Marshall? He was in here after you left yesterday and wanted to know what was going on."

"That's the other thing I wanted to talk to you about." Cordelia pulled out an envelope from his side pocket and handed it to Thompson. "This one's on the house."

Thompson opened it and glanced through the photographs in stunned silence, his eyes wide with astonishment. The photographs, mostly of Marshall Hayes and a woman in a variety of revealing poses, were taken from a distance using a telephoto lens. Thompson wasn't sure when he was going to use them, but the fact that he would use them was certain.

"Who is she?"

"She used to work here. Her name is Julia Frances. She quit about two years ago. He's put her up in a condo near National. Takes care of her every need."

"The righteous son of a bitch. I assumed he had one, but this is more than I had hope for. I wonder how much more there is about Mr. Hayes that we don't know."

Kate felt as if she were a hundred years old by the time she made her connecting flight in Miami. All she could think of was little Cheyenne and the way her face had looked when she asked, "How much is a week?" It was exactly the way Molly would have asked. Where was heaven, and when she went there, would she get to see her father?

Kate sat back in her seat and closed her eyes. When the flight attendants walked by with the beverage cart, she ordered two bloody Marys. She rarely drank, except for a glass of wine, and then only with a meal. But right now she hungered for oblivion.

Frustration and confusion gave way to loneliness,

and her thoughts turned to Jeffrey. How she needed him; someone to talk to, someone who would understand and believe in her.

She told herself to calm down, to concentrate on the job at hand and to stay focused, but it was hard. She was a doer, and unless she was doing something positive, proactive, she could easily give in to despair and self-pity.

It had been nearly two days since she had talked to Spencer. From the armrest she pulled out the air phone, slid her credit card through, and dialed the number.

"Spence?"

"You know, you and I need to have a better way to communicate," he said.

"What do you mean?"

"Seems like I can never get hold of you."

"I had to turn off the cell phone, Spence—the reporters got hold of my number and kept calling."

"Make sure you carry your pager then. I may need you in a hurry."

"Why? What's up?"

"How are you at stealing?"

chapter 13

You're sure you want to do this?" Thompson asked Marshall Hayes, as he trailed closely behind him.

"Yes, I'm sure. Question is, why aren't you?" Hayes responded without looking back.

Hayes pressed the keypad on the door that led to the heart of Searchlight's research division. The two entered a room with a front wall made entirely of glass.

Hayes stood in front of the window with his arms crossed; Thompson stood beside him.

"Pretty, isn't she?" he asked, nodding.

In front of them, in a large room, more than a dozen people, all wearing surgical gowns and gloves, continued to work, oblivious to their audience. They moved slowly in their sterile white coveralls and caps, stopping only briefly to speak to one another through their surgical masks.

In the center of the room, a large metallic structure resembling a spider was set under bright lights, the words NOVA XIV written in black letters on one side.

Someone pushed a button and an array of solar antennas began to extend from all sides of the machine, expanding like an umbrella, covering the satellite almost completely. Another button was pressed, and half of the panels closed, followed by the other half.

Thompson stood there entranced by it all, a huge smile on his face.

"It's better than sex," he said, unable to control his excitement.

Standing next to him, Marshall Hayes didn't quite share the sentiment, but he understood exactly what Thompson meant. It was moments like this that bonded the two, regardless of their differences, and kept them together—a fascination with the technological revolution that was moving at such great speed that the human mind could barely comprehend it.

Nova XIV, the fourteenth of sixty-three satellites that were to be launched over the next four years, would put Searchlight in a league that would make Rockwell and Hughes green with envy. Nova XIII was already sitting on pad EL2, strapped to the back of an Ariane IV rocket, some forty-five hundred miles to the south in French Guiana. It was undergoing the final stages of preparation for the launch that was scheduled in less than seventy-two hours.

Thompson first got the idea from Iridium LLC, a failed communications venture started by Motorola, which promised customers two-way communication from virtually any two points on the planet. The company wasn't able to deliver because the technology didn't work as they had expected. In one of the biggest blunders in corporate history, Iridium was left with some eighty-eight satellites circling the globe and two options: to send them spiraling down to burn up in the atmosphere, or to continue to operate them, hoping that a buyer would somehow show up. The venture had cost some $5 billion, half of which had been written off by Motorola alone, sending investors scurrying like ants in all directions.

It was a giant fumble and everyone knew it, but the immense potential of the concept was not lost on Thompson. If the new technology proved successful, it would be a first: a number close to Thompson's heart. He allowed himself even more latitude and toyed with various possibilities until he came up with his plan.

What if he were able to link a string of satellites that not only succeeded where Motorola had failed but, in addition to communications, allowed the satellites to identify and track objects anywhere on the globe. With the STAR system already in place and operational, half the job was already done. The system on the ground was capable of receiving data from satellites to let it know where the target object was and where it was headed. All they had to do was give the satellites access to the same information.

The new and enhanced STAR system—STAR II, as it would be called—with its loop tracking capability, would trace the location and path of any object to which it was assigned. The satellites, with their array of radio transceivers, powerful camera lenses, magnetic imaging, and infrared and heat-detection systems, could then zero in on the target, regardless of its location or size. Cars, planes, boats, bicycles, hikers and campers, ordinary people; a world of moving targets, all visible through the eyes of STAR, and at the push of a button available for anyone to see. Nothing would ever be lost again.

All this would be possible with the help of a small and easily installed homing device that would be given free of charge; but the code that was used to feed the STAR system would not.

The fee would be reasonable, and everyone from automobile manufacturers to police departments and private citizens would be happy to pay a monthly charge to safeguard their belongings, and that was just the civilian application. By the time the military potential of the Nova project was realized, Marshall Hayes and Davis Thompson would be rich beyond any man's right to be.

But like most things on the cutting edge of technology, word eventually leaked, and soon there were suitors and eager investors, lots of them. Private individuals and companies alike, large and small, all clamored for information regarding this unique and innovative concept. Searchlight resisted the offers, but the pot only sweetened.

The winner, a European company by the name of Austin Enterprises, was a high-tech, dot-com communications consortium that made its money in the late 1990s selling every service from online banking to caskets. Austin fit the bill because of their high market cap, cash flow, and hunger for acquisitions, and because they were aggressively looking to move away from the dot-com hype and into something with tangible earnings potential. They were also practically submerged under the weight of their coffers. . . .

By midyear, the preliminary talks had been completed under tight security and agreements reached. In their final meeting, Hayes and Thompson prepared a wish list of what they each wanted. Hayes filled a single sheet but it took Thompson two pages of single-spaced lines, neatly typed, to specify his.

The papers were handed across the table, and after studying them briefly, the Austin negotiators smiled. The deal was made and hands were shook. All that was left was to sign on the dotted line. The ceremony was scheduled for two days after the launch of Nova XIII, at a press conference in Washington, D.C.

"Call him," Hayes practically ordered.

Thompson didn't like to be given orders, certainly not by the likes of Marshall Hayes. But Hayes was still the chairman, something that wasn't going to last much longer. He walked over to the intercom.

"Dr. Malkovich, would you please come to the conference room," he said, with perfect grace.

One of the people who was covered from head to toe, with only his horn-rimmed eyeglasses visible, turned around and saw Hayes and Thompson standing at the window. He hesitated for a moment, then separated himself from the pack.

Hayes opened a side door into a room with a large table. Various models of the Nova series were displayed along the perimeter of the room. He and Thompson took a seat and waited.

Two minutes later Dr. Richard Malkovich, age fifty-eight, and still wearing his lab coat and sterile booties, arrived.

He was tall, thin, almost bald, and unshaven. What little hair grew around his scalp was mostly white and unkempt, and he limped. It was more than just a limp; he would step out normally with his left foot, then drag the right foot on its side, and then the left foot again: the ravages of childhood polio.

In mind and in body, Malkovich was the antithesis of the image the company wished to promote. You would never see him greeting a potential client, guiding a tour, or giving an interview on behalf of Searchlight; those things were left to others, the ones with beaming smiles and perfect teeth. His job as the chief program designer was to oversee the nearly two hundred top-flight scientists and technicians who worked in little cubicles throughout the building, and whose collective effort yielded some of the most sophisticated communications software ever produced.

Thompson had found Malkovich putting in sixty hours a week in a cubicle in one of the many companies that he had taken over. He had instantly recognized his personal limitations as well as his compensating brilliance. He knew the man's full potential had not been realized, but that given the right circumstances it could be.

He broke up the company but kept Malkovich. The day would come when he could use this intensely intelligent and private man. That day dawned when Thompson took over Hayes Technologies and renamed it Searchlight.

Richard Malkovich was brought in and placed in charge of research and development. His main objective was to help Thompson transform a failed hardware-manufacturing company into an instantly identifiable name, dominating a niche that few others could fill. After two years of strategic planning, Malkovich and Thompson discovered one in communications and satellite tracking, and the STAR system was born.

Malkovich sat across from the two men, staring through his thick glasses at one, then at the other, his left eye twitching, as it always did when he was nervous.

"Richard," Thompson began. "We need some specific operational information regarding STAR."

Malkovich eyed Thompson suspiciously. He was almost paranoid about preserving the laboratory's innermost secrets, especially the operating code of the new system. "What would you like to know?"

"Does any of the data transmitted by STAR actually translate into some physical activity? In other words, if STAR gave an invalid command to the flight guidance system—let's say it told the system to turn when it shouldn't have—would the flight guidance system accept the command?"

"No, not if it is out of tolerance."

"What do you mean?"

"The aircraft systems are designed to follow a certain criteria. If STAR tells it to go past that—let's say it tells it to make a sixty-degree bank—the computers simply won't accept that command."

"What if the computers are given something out of tolerance? What happens then?"

"There are four flight control primary computers, the FCPCs. These control the primary controls: the ailerons, rudders, elevators, and so on. There are three flight control secondary computers, the FCSCs, which control the secondary flight controls, like the spoilers. And then there are two flight control data concentrators, which provide data from the primary and secondary computers and analyze everything."

"You're losing me with all this," Hayes said.

Malkovich was clearly impatient. To him, this was elementary stuff.

"What I'm trying to tell you is that there isn't one or two or three computers. There are literally dozens, and they all send the data to the main FCCs, the flight control computers, and the FCCs simply decide if the data is valid or not. If it is not, they won't accept the command." He paused for a moment. "Besides, all four FCCs have to agree."

"What do you mean?" Thompson asked.

"The data received by STAR has to be verified by each of four FCCs. If any one computer disagrees with the other three, its data is automatically discarded and the data from the remaining three FCCs are used. If the data on two of the computers disagrees with the other two, STAR lets the pilots know, and then they make the decision by switching computers. So it's a pretty clear-cut chain of events."

"What happens if the system fails?" Thompson asked.

"It's fail-proof because of the redundancies built into it. The architecture, software, hardware, and even the wiring go through special installation and shielding. Now, do you want to tell me what's going on?"

Hayes got up from his chair and went over to the door to make sure it was locked.

"This room is secure, isn't it?" he asked.

Thompson nodded.

Hayes then pulled out the chair next to Malkovich and looked him in the eye. "Are you sure that there's no way STAR could interfere with how an airplane flies?"

"I have already answered that question. No. I can give you a better answer, however, if I know what the real question is."

Hayes leaned in even closer. "Rich, somebody is blaming our system for causing two airplanes to crash."

"Who?"

"We don't know, and it's irrelevant right now. What *is* important is that we find out if there's any truth to this claim. If there is, we have to protect ourselves. That's why I need to know if there is any way that our system could be . . ."

"Oh, my God," Malkovich said, then turned to look at Thompson, who nodded. "Somebody is saying that they have sabotaged STAR?"

"Yes. That's why we need to know if there's any way that STAR could be made to cause a plane to go down."

Malkovich paused, let out a huge sigh, then said, "By itself, STAR could not do anything outside its parameters. But with a little help . . ."

"For God's sake, man. What the hell is that supposed to mean?" Hayes asked.

"You asked me if STAR by itself could cause an airplane to do something erratic. The answer to that is no. You didn't ask me if with some modification, the system could do some harm. The answer to that"—he glanced over at Thompson—"the answer to that is yes."

The men leaned back in their chairs.

"These are the latest-generation aircraft, using

fly-by-wire. That means computers are doing everything that mechanical connections used to do. You've
got computers talking to one another, taking orders
and correcting one another when they make a mistake.
That's how you can take a super jumbo jet and fly it
across the world with only two pilots in the cockpit.
They've taken out the flight engineer and replaced him
with automated systems. If the electrical load is too
much, auto kicks in and reduces it. If they need more
pressurization air, it's auto again. By doing everything
automatically, the need for human touch and interven-
tion, and thus error, is reduced."

He paused for a minute, scratched his fringe of gray
hair. "The problem is that auto is a computer and computers can get sick."

"You mean like a virus?" Thompson asked.

"Precisely. If this is an act of sabotage, it could be
accomplished by a coded virus, something that is
placed in the program to tell it to activate after a number of days or flight hours; there are many ways it
could be done."

"But you said if the information in the computers
does not agree—"

"It could be a transit virus," Thompson interrupted.

"What the hell is that?" Hayes asked.

"He's right." Malkovich nodded. "The virus could
have been designed to move around from one system
to another, from one computer to another. It could
change the programming of the entire computer, or it
could be a subdirectory—you know, a small deviation
from the computer's routine, and very hard to detect."

"So all these interlinked computers could be infected simultaneously?"

"Either all or some, depending on what the virus
was designed to do. You see, in any aircraft, they're all
connected and are all designed to talk to one another
and even monitor one another. That's why—"

"Can they all be infected at the same time?" Hayes repeated impatiently.

Malkovich looked at him, then at Thompson. "Under some very specific circumstances, yes."

The men were stunned into silence. So it may have been true, all of it. The horror, the full implication of it, began to sink in.

"How could something like this get into the system with all of the security we have in place?" Thompson asked angrily.

"The virus could have been introduced at any time—at the time of manufacture, at the time of installation, during the loading of a new software or updates or during any of the intermediate checkup periods. What have the authorities said about all this?"

Thompson and Hayes glanced at each other.

"You haven't told them, have you?" Malkovich asked in a low, frightened voice.

"No."

Malkovich sighed again. "So why are you telling me now?"

"Because we need your help. You have to understand, we don't even believe any of it. I myself don't see how a virus could possibly do all this, but Marshall says we can't take a chance," Thompson said in his best reassuring voice.

Malkovich took off his glasses and wiped them with a white handkerchief. "Gentlemen, as I sit here in front of you today, I cannot think of a single reason why a specifically designed virus could not do everything you have told me and more."

"Let's say it's all true. How do we get rid of it?" Hayes asked.

"If it's a transient virus, you've got to rewrite and then reinstall every program it could have infected."

"But that could take weeks," Thompson shouted.

"That's right," Malkovich replied calmly. "Reinstalling all of the system software would. But there could be a shortcut. We could write a patch that would disinfect the operating system's program, then disable the virus and check out each computer to make sure every system is performing properly. To do that we have to get to each computer individually to do the work."

"That would open this whole thing up. That's not an option," Thompson objected. "There's got to be another way."

There was a period of silence, then Malkovich said, "You could do it during their C checks."

"What?"

"The C checks. Every commercial airline has to go through a C check periodically. That's when they literally take the aircraft apart. All the seats are taken out, the wall panels, everything. The only thing left is the hull. It also happens to take about two weeks, just long enough to rewrite every program that could have been infected—or make the patch and install it. We could say it's a modification, an enhancement to go with the new system, and even throw in some free features to keep the airlines happy. All of it could be done at minimal cost, because the programs are already in place, and no one would have to know anything."

"You think it'll work?" Hayes asked.

"I don't see why not," Thompson responded confidently.

Thompson got up and walked over to Malkovich. He put his arm around him and said, "Rich, you may have saved the day again."

Malkovich gave an uncomfortable smile. He hated being in the spotlight.

"Okay, let me ask you something else. Is there any way we can verify if one of the airplanes that went down was in fact infected by this virus."

Malkovich thought this out for a moment. "The

only way that I can think of is through the FCDC. But even that . . ."

"What the hell is that?" Hayes asked.

"The flight control data concentrator. It's a computer that watches and records the primary and secondary computers' functions. It may or may not hold the clue, depending on when it lost power to its source. But like I said, you have to get your hands on the FCDC, and for that, you need to have access to the airplane itself."

"I happen to know where one of those airplanes is right now," Thompson said quietly.

chapter **14**

Well, can you tell me where he is?" she asked, her voice edgy, her ear still glued to the black receiver.

"I'm sorry, ma'am. He's not . . ."

"I don't understand. This is the third time I've called in two days and each time you tell me he's not there."

"Ma'am, you didn't want to leave a message. If you had, I'm sure he would have . . ."

"How about a pager, a cell phone? Do you have any way to get hold of him?"

"May I ask who's calling?" the female voice asked from the other side, it too now bordering on agitation.

She hesitated for a minute, then said, "Yeah. Tell him it's Barbara. Tell him he has to call his doctor's office and ask for Barbara." She hung up.

Her name was not Barbara. It was Tara, Tara Wilson, and she didn't work in a doctor's office. She was making the phone call from her cramped office on the third

floor of the MIT computer science lab on Massachu-
setts Avenue in Boston.

She was reasonably attractive. Her skin was very
fair, almost transluscent. Her ash-blond hair was long
and wavy and hung freely around her shoulders. Tara
stared at the phone, then leaning back in her chair,
screwed her brown eyes tightly shut.

Her cell phone rang. Startled, it took her a few seconds to fish it out of her tote bag.

"Hello?" she said, then paused.

"Don't tell me I shouldn't have called you there,"
she whispered as she got up and closed her office door.
"I had no choice. You didn't call me." She paused
again.

"Fine. Three minutes," she said, and pressed the
End button.

She rushed out of her office, stopping at the next
door briefly.

"Hey Frank, I need a big favor. Can you cover the
first ten minutes of my computer-graphics group? Just
get them started on chapter nineteen, the basics of educational fusion. I'll be there as soon as I can." Before
the man with the glasses could respond, she said,
"Thanks. I owe you one."

Outside, she rapidly descended the large stone
stairs and ran to the phone booth across the street. By
the time she got there, it was ringing.

"Yeah, I'm here," she said, and paused to listen to
the voice.

"If I had a damn cell phone or pager number, then I
wouldn't have to call you at your office, would I? But
this brilliant idea of me always waiting for you to call
and you not calling doesn't work."

Another pause.

"I need to see you."

Another pause.

"Don't . . . don't you treat me like a damn house-wife. I don't care if you're busy. I need to see you."

She hesitated.

"The Jet-East plane. It was one of ours, wasn't it?"

Pause.

"Don't lie to me," she yelled. "I saw the interviews, I saw the pilot on television. I heard what she said. Now I'm going to ask you again: Did you or did you not in-stall the virus on that plane?"

Another pause.

"Damn you." She banged the receiver against the cold metal booth. "God damn you," she yelled. "You promised me. After the last one you promised me you wouldn't let another plane go down."

Tara listened.

"I don't care about the money anymore. Do you un-derstand?" she said, then realized that she was scream-ing and turned to make sure no one was within earshot. "I don't care about the money," she said, softly this time. "This is not what this was all about. We weren't supposed to kill people."

Another pause.

"How many other airplanes are infected?"

Pause.

"I don't want to hear that. I want to know how many more airplanes you installed the virus on?"

Pause.

"You have to stop this. You have to stop this or they'll trace it to us. Do you understand? They'll find a way. They always do."

She let him answer.

"Don't you tell me to calm down. Don't . . ."

Pause.

"No more deaths," she said, her voice quivering now. "Do you hear me? No one else is going to die."

Pause.

"Fine. I'll see you then."

The phone call was over, but she held the receiver in her hand and stared at it for a long time. Then she gently replaced it and turned her gaze to the snow-covered streets.

chapter 15

Okay. Let's start from the top," O'Rourke said, throwing the dog-eared, coffee-stained transcript on the conference table.

"Come on, Mike. It's after eight," Edward Santayana objected, slouching in his chair.

Santayana was one of six investigators remaining in this ongoing, after-hours marathon session, and it was clear that, like the others, he would prefer to be someplace other than the airless, windowless room deep inside the FAA headquarters.

"One last run and we can all go home," O'Rourke said, and pulled up his chair. He grabbed the headset, as did the five other men around the table, all in their forties and fifties, and all wearing shirts and ties with the knots loosened.

As they put on their headsets and looked at the first page of the transcript, someone hit the Play button on one of the two tape recorders on the center of the table.

"What the hell was that?"

First Officer Edmond Bell's comments were the first words that the inspectors heard on their headsets. Listening intently, the men followed along on their transcripts, which included information such as the person who was talking and the exact time at which the words were spoken.

On one side of the conference table, a large video monitor displayed pertinent information from the flight data recorder on various charts and graphs. Information such as the position of the flight controls, the flaps, gear, aircraft heading, altitude, bank and power settings, sequenced against the actual time that words were spoken in the cockpit, gave investigators an extremely accurate picture of the events that took place exactly as they happened.

21:03:01. CAPTAIN: "Just what they promised. More turbulence."

21:03:06. FIRST OFFICER: "Can't wait to get this damn night over with."

21:03:11. CAPTAIN: "Five more minutes, and it will be."

21:03:17. FIRST OFFICER: "With my luck we'll be up here another hour, holding, waiting for permission to land, and then have to go back and try this damn thing all over again tomorrow."

There was a period of silence. Then the captain spoke. "I'm showing winds of almost sixty knots at four thousand feet. Why don't you find out if there is any change since the last report?"

The inspectors listened and jotted notes, as First Officer Edmond Bell asked for and received the latest weather updates. Then, for almost three minutes, the only sound recorded by the CVR was the radio chatter between the controller and other aircraft, holding in various patterns.

21:09:46. APPROACH CONTROL: "Jet-East 394, this is Kennedy approach. Turn left to a heading of three five zero. Descend and maintain three thousand feet. You are cleared for ILS, runway three one right."

21:10:12. FIRST OFFICER: "Roger." He repeated the instructions.

Sitting around the table, the investigators listened and watched, reliving every second of Jet-East's final minutes, as instructions were given to the flight attendants and the aircraft descended intercepting the final approach course.

21:12:32. CAPTAIN: "Flaps thirty."

The sound of the lever being repositioned was clear. On the computer screen, the flap indication was moved to the thirty-degree mark. By now, the aircraft had begun to deviate from its course, as indicated by a large moving graph on the computer screen.

"Here we go," someone in the room mumbled, and all eyes moved between the transcript and the computer screen.

21:12:58. FIRST OFFICER: "Localizer."

The aircraft heading quickly changed and it intercepted the course again. But not for long. The aircraft began to veer off, this time in the opposite direction.

21:13:46. FIRST OFFICER: "You're off the center line again. Localizer." The voice was loud and clearly alarmed.

The graph indicating the aircraft altitude was now showing it to be at eight hundred feet and descending.

21:14:11. CAPTAIN: "Let's get out of here. Initiating go-around. Give me maximum power. Flaps twenty."

The investigators, all pilots themselves, watched the screen and followed the scripts intently. They had listened to the tapes many times, yet they felt as though they were experiencing it in real time, in the cockpit.

The go-around was completed, and once the aircraft was back at pattern altitude the captain said, "You've got the plane. I'm going to make a P.A."

21:18:19. CAPTAIN: "Ladies and gentlemen, as you can tell, we have aborted the landing." She completed the P.A. in forty-eight seconds.

21:19:22. CAPTAIN: "I'm back."

Silence.

21:19:28. CAPTAIN: "I've got the plane."

More silence.

21:19:46. CAPTAIN: "I've got the plane."

At this point there was a movement on the controls, significant enough that it was recorded by the flight data recorder.

"Stop the tape," O'Rourke ordered, and took off his headset. "What is that?" he asked, pointing to a surge on one of the graphs on the screen.

"There's no question that they didn't like each other," one of the investigators said. "Looks like she yanked the controls away."

O'Rourke was scratching his chin as he looked at the graph. "She had to ask him twice and he still wouldn't give the plane back. That's insubordination and she could have had his butt but she didn't even talk about it, didn't even bring it up in our interviews."

"What do you think that means?" someone asked.

"I don't know," O'Rourke replied, rubbing the back of his neck. "I don't know. But it doesn't fit the mold of someone who would make up a story to protect herself."

He put his headset back on, then nodded to someone who hit the Play button again.

21:24:16. CAPTAIN: "Landing gear down. Give me flaps thirty after you get three green."

Once again, the aircraft settled for landing, but as it descended below one thousand feet, it began to move away from the straight line on the graph, which indicated center-line.

Seven hundred feet. Six hundred. Jet-East 394

struggled to maintain its course, but it was clear that it couldn't.

Five hundred feet. The aircraft turned toward the center, reached it, but instead of intercepting the course and flying in, it went right through. The whole exercise seemed amateurish, as if there were a student at the controls, learning the basics of instrument flying.

Four hundred feet. Three hundred. The aircraft was now fully deflected away from the center course and still descending.

21:27:07. FIRST OFFICER: "Go-around. Go-around."

21:27:09. CAPTAIN: "Going around. Max power, flaps twenty. Push the throttles up, way up."

"This is it," someone whispered, just as the aircraft began its roll to the right. There was pressure on the controls, and the roll was corrected. Then it began again, this time faster. Almost violently.

21:27:26. CAPTAIN: "Push with me."

21:27:27. There was a sound of something dropping. Then the first officer shouting, "What are you doing?"

21:27:42. COMPUTER-GENERATED VOICE: "Terrain, terrain, pull up, pull up."

The aircraft was almost at a sixty-degree bank now and still turning.

21:27:52. On the screen, the power indication on both engines went from 101 percent down to 49, indicating that the throttles had been brought simultaneously to idle.

21:28:01. FIRST OFFICER: "What the hell are you doing?"

With the controls at almost a full deflection, the aircraft was well past the sixty-degree bank, and rapidly descending.

Then they heard the sounds of metal scraping, screams, followed by static, and, finally, nothing.

At the center of the table, the tape came to a stop. O'Rourke took off his headset, and buried his face in his hands for a moment.

"Well?" he asked, looking up.

After a moment of silence, Santayana said, "I hate to say this, but it sounds like a classic case of vertigo."

"It wasn't vertigo," another investigator said from the end of the table. "She flew center-line, dead-on altitude, all the way until the last thousand feet. If she had vertigo, how could you possibly explain that?"

"I don't know. Maybe she got nervous as she came closer to land," Santayana replied.

"I don't think that's it either," O'Rourke said. "I've met her several times. She doesn't strike me as the nervous type."

"So what do you think it is?"

O'Rourke hesitated, still looking at the computer screen, which was frozen on the position of the controls at the moment of impact. "I don't know. But she insists that there was resistance, something interfering with the controls."

"Then why isn't there anything to indicate that on the tapes?"

"There was tension in the cockpit, remember? The guy wouldn't even give her the plane back. Maybe she didn't want to say anything. Maybe she thought he would think she was making excuses for failing to keep the airplane straight."

Santayana shook his head. "I don't know, Mike. I know you want to give her the benefit of the doubt; we all do. But everything points to pilot error. The tapes, the F.O.'s statement, everything."

"You interviewed the F.O., didn't you?" O'Rourke asked.

"Yeah, two days ago," Santayana answered. "He repeated everything that he said before. That she was all over the place during the few minutes prior to landing.

That she panicked and couldn't control the airplane. He said after she pulled the power back with the flaps and gear down, they rapidly lost airspeed. The aircraft stalled, despite their recovery efforts. He repeated his original story."

O'Rourke paused for a moment. "I did some checking on the F.O. He's a real hotshot, you know, the Lone Ranger. Doesn't think he needs anybody, and he's got a real attitude about women."

"That doesn't mean he's lying."

"No. But . . . It just doesn't make sense."

"Well then, you're the only one."

"What do you mean?" O'Rourke asked.

"Dammit, Mike. We've gone over these tapes twenty times, and every time we've come up with the same thing. There's no evidence to verify Gallagher's claim that there was a problem. We've interviewed witnesses, Bell was in the cockpit and at the controls—and what he says match the tapes exactly. Then you've got weather, you've got ice—it's a classic case, and you're saying it doesn't make sense. Well, if it doesn't, you're the only person in this room that it doesn't make sense to, because I think the rest of us here are pretty clear on what happened."

O'Rourke looked at the others, who became suddenly interested in their files. Maybe Santayana was right, he thought. Maybe he had let his feelings about her interfere with his judgment. Maybe he was reading something into all this, something that wasn't there. Would he have felt the same way if instead of Kate Gallagher, Ed Bell or someone else had been behind the controls?

"All right, guys. Let's call it a night. See you all tomorrow." O'Rourke watched them pack up their belongings and file out of the room.

When they were gone, he walked over to the computer screen, still frozen on position of the flight controls. The ailerons indicated almost full deflection to the left and so did the rudders. Yet the aircraft made contact with the ground in a right bank, an indication that it had stalled shortly after engine thrust was reduced to zero.

Letting your aircraft stall that close to the ground was like letting your car run out of gas; it just wasn't supposed to happen, at least not to professionals, and certainly not to the likes of Kate Gallagher. She had over twelve thousand hours of flight time, three thousand of those as a captain.

He had studied her record and tried hard to be objective, but everything he knew about her convinced him of one thing: She wasn't the type to lose control under pressure.

The panic scenario fit, but that was the only thing. The rest made no sense at all.

chapter 16

Kate arrived at Kennedy in a filthy mood. The bloody Marys had not been a good idea, serving only to exacerbate her anger—at the NTSB, at the media, which had all but declared her guilty, but most of all at herself for feeling weak and vulnerable. It wasn't in her nature to sit back and feel sorry for herself. She wanted to fight this thing head-on, as she had everything else in her life, to show them that she was right. But she didn't know where to begin.

She needed to get home, grab her bathing suit, and head out for the pool. Exercise was a powerful tool in getting her mind off her immediate problems, and right now she had a handful.

She got off the subway on West Fourth Street and began to walk quickly home. She didn't even think to look for the news crews. That was a mistake. One block from her building, the first microphone was shoved in front of her mouth, and before she knew it there were four more mikes and a crew following her.

"I've told you guys before, I can't talk to you about

this. There is an active investigation in progress," she said, as she backed away. But her words fell on deaf ears.

She picked up her pace, trying to outrun them, but it was no use. They surrounded her like a mob, asking questions. "Is it true that you crashed the airplane because you panicked?" "Were you given preferential treatment at the airline because you are a woman?"

Finally, she snapped. A cold rage came over her and she turned to the reporters and shouted, "What do you want? You want to know the facts of what happened out there? Or are you here because a woman was at the controls of the plane? This is *not* a gender issue but you turned it into one." She clenched her fists, her nails biting into her palms. "The accident had nothing to do with my sex or my skill as a pilot. There was a problem with the controls, but you don't want to hear about that—you're too caught up in the fact that I'm a woman. Think of that when the next airplane goes down. Think of how you could have helped prevent it, instead of sensationalize it."

She knew that she had said too much, but as she walked away she realized that there was no way she could have stopped herself. She had been bottling everything up for too long.

At home, she grabbed her gym bag and took the fire escape again. She jumped in a cab and arrived at Lexington and Fifty-third Street twenty minutes before closing time.

The building was almost deserted, and that was fine with Kate. She changed into her suit, threw the bag to one side, and walked to the pool. She didn't bother to dunk her toe in to feel the temperature or to put on her goggles. She just dove in, ripped through the water, not coming up for air until she had covered the entire length. She did a rolling turn, and continued her strokes, with the concentration of an Olympic contender. A dozen laps went by before Kate started to feel the pain. The ache in her muscles, the shortness of air in her lungs. But it wasn't enough. She had to push through.

She kept up the pace, length after length, trying to generate enough agony to make the images vanish. Images of Cheyenne and of Brita Ames. Images of the family who had perished that wintry night on board the Jet-East flight. The flashing lights, the smoke, the fire. All of it.

By the time she returned home, she was mentally and physically exhausted. She had only enough strength to call Mama.

Molly was already asleep in her little makeshift bed, back in the office, Mama reported. That was where she usually slept until about eleven o'clock when the restaurant closed. Then one of the employees, usually Leo, carried her upstairs to Mama's little apartment and put her in her own bed.

"How's my Katrina? I worry for you."

"I'm fine, Mama. Don't pay attention to anything you see in the papers or on television. It's all wrong."

"And you think you have to tell me that?" Mama said. "I don't know what they're saying about you but whatever it is, I have prepared you for it."

"What do you mean?"

"You had to be strong. You were growing up without a father, without family and without money. I knew that you would be alone too much, as I was, and I knew that there would come a day when you would have to reach deep inside to the very bottom of your soul and save yourself. That day may be here now."

Kate slept through the night peacefully, dreaming of Molly and Jeffrey and Mama. Just before dawn, her beeper went off. At first she ignored it, then got up and turned it off.

From the dresser she picked up her watch. It was six o'clock.

In the kitchen, she plugged in the telephone and hit the button on the coffeemaker. Then she dialed.

"Flight office, Sharon speaking."

"Hi, Sharon. Kate Gallagher. Somebody . . ."

"Hi, Captain Gallagher. Yeah, I paged you. Captain Dobson would like you to come in this morning."

"Why, what's up?"

"I don't know. He just came in here and asked me to call you. He's *not* in a good mood."

That information alone was enough to make Kate feel queasy. Captain George Dobson was one of those people you rarely saw in a bad mood. The fact that he had called at six in the morning couldn't be good, either.

She was feeling more than a little worried when she arrived at the newly renovated Terminal J, at Kennedy, en route to operations. There she swiped her I.D. through the electronic lock and opened the door.

The operations room was in a flurry of activity, as pilots worked on computers and studied their flight plans. The few who looked up and recognized her nodded their support, but Kate didn't look back, instead walking to the rear, where she was directed to the chief pilot's office. She knocked and entered.

Dobson was sitting behind his desk, his right hand holding the receiver against his ear, his left combing through his silvery white hair. He hung up the phone as Kate entered.

"How are you holding up, Kate?" he asked, as he waved her to a chair.

"Oh, like the world is about to crumble. How are you, George?"

He smiled. "The FAA was here a couple of days ago. They wanted to see your records."

"What kind of records?"

"Everything. Your file, company training, everything."

"Well, I hope you cooperated."

"You have nothing to be concerned about. Your records are exemplary."

"Heck, I'm not concerned about the FAA. They can just take a number, right behind the press and the NTSB."

"I hear you, Kate," Dobson said sympathetically. "I know you're tired, but you've got to hang in there."

"That's all I'm doing," Kate responded grimly.

Dobson paused for a moment, then threw down the pencil he was holding. "Dammit, Kate, why did you do it?"

Kate looked up in astonishment. "Do what?"

"Why did you go out there on television and tell the whole world that there's something wrong with these airplanes and they're going to crash? Why?"

"What are you talking about?"

Dobson picked up the remote and pointed it toward a small television. Kate's face filled the screen, informing the world that there was a problem with the airplane and that it might happen again.

"Is that what this is all about, George? Is that why you called me in? I was tired and those guys had been hounding me for days. I just lost it."

"You were asked not to talk to the media. They even sent someone to your hospital room the first day to make sure you didn't talk," Dobson said sternly. "This was aired all over the country. The bean counters are estimating that eight million people watched you, Kate—eight million. I got a call from the vice president of Ops in the middle of the night. He woke me up and made me watch it. I couldn't believe what you were saying." Dobson's face flushed with anger.

"I thought about taping it, but by the time I got to the VCR the piece had finished. But I didn't have to wait long, because they repeated it over and over again, all night long. You're probably on the front page of USA *Today,* Kate, all because of your little thirty-second speech. Jesus, what were you thinking? Reservations have already seen a six-percent drop in bookings in the last twelve hours, and you know what the people who are canceling are saying? That they're afraid to fly. That they're afraid to fly because of what you told them."

He sat there, fuming, waiting for her response.

"I don't think I've ever seen you this mad," Kate said in a subdued tone.

"I *am* mad, dammit. I'm mad at you for raving all over the television. I'm mad at the bean counters who have already translated this into dollars and cents. I'm mad at the VP of Ops for waking my butt up in the middle of the night and I'm mad at me for what I have to do."

She leaned back in her seat and locked her fingers in her lap. "What do you have to do, George?"

Dobson's shoulders dropped and in a defeated voice he said, "You are hereby suspended from all active duty, pending the outcome of this investigation. The suspension is effective immediately and without pay. I'm sorry, Kate." He didn't even pause before saying, "I'm sorry," just blurted it out, as if it were a part of the same sentence, as if he wanted to make sure he included it. When he finished, he sat there in silence, watching her eyes and reminding himself that he had only fourteen months before he could retire.

"This wasn't your idea, was it?" Kate asked after a long moment.

Dobson shook his head. "No, Kate. You've managed to piss off people far higher up than me."

"Then it hasn't been a wasted effort." She stood up.

"I need your I.D. badge, Kate," Dobson said, his hand stretched out. "I'm sorry."

She opened her wallet and pulled out the I.D. with the magnetic strip. Gently, she placed it on the desk and pushed it toward him.

"When all this is over, you're going to have to show me that trawler you're always bragging about," Kate said, and watched Dobson flash a hint of a smile. Then she left.

Sharon, Dobson's secretary, was waiting for her outside his office. She began to walk alongside Kate.

"What, I get my own escort?"

"It's been killing him all morning. He wanted me to see if there was anything I could do for . . ."

"Thanks," Kate said, and put her hand on Sharon's shoulder. "I'm fine."

At the door Sharon pulled out her I.D. and swiped it through.

Kate suddenly realized that she no longer had access to the facilities. She needed her I.D., it was her lifeline. Everything, all her plans, would be ruined without it.

"Uh, shoot, I forgot to get my stuff from the kit-bag room," she said. "I need to go back and get them."

"Of course," Sharon said, and headed to the small room behind the operations area.

Kate opened the door and stood there, an awkward smile on her face, as if to ask, *Hey, do you want to come in?*

"I'll just wait right here," Sharon said, and Kate nodded.

Inside the room, she went to work quickly. She had to get her hands on an I.D. badge—any I.D. badge.

The shelves against the walls were used for storage

of the crew members' bags and personal belongings. Adjacent to the shelves was a closet that held uniforms encased in protective covers.

Kate began unzipping the covers one at a time, reaching for the jacket lapels in the hope of finding one with an I.D. badge still attached. The uniforms mostly belonged to the commuter crew, who lived in different places and worked out of Kennedy. She went through the row, one at the time. Unzip, feel, zip up. Unzip, feel, zip up, but there was nothing there. Her eyes were darting back and forth between the uniforms and the door; she expected it to open at any second and Sharon to walk in and catch her red-handed.

"Come on, dammit, come on," she muttered as she anxiously continued to feel her way through the uniforms.

The sound was muffled, but it was enough. Kate heard it just in time to shove the open uniform away from sight and turn her back.

The door opened and a commuter with his kit bag and uniform in tow walked in. Neither pilot recognized the other, but it was clear to Kate that her time had run out. She grabbed a stack of papers and walked out.

"Got everything?" Sharon asked.

"Yeah," she responded dryly, nodding to the papers.

At the main door, Sharon again swiped her badge through the electronic lock. As she stood there holding the door open, a pilot in uniform walked in, finished with a flight and now on his way home.

Seeing Kate, he instantly grinned and put down his bag.

"God, Kate, how are you?" he asked, as he gave her a hug and kissed her on the cheek.

His name was Meyer. Karl Meyer. He was a senior pilot nearing retirement but still quite attractive. He and Kate had flown together when she was a first officer. He had always liked and respected her, and like most other pilots, especially those of Jet-East, he had followed her story closely.

"I'm fine, Karl. Thanks."

He pulled away and looked at her for a moment. "What's going on, Kate?"

She smiled. "I guess it's my fifteen minutes."

"Are you okay?" His genuine concern touched her.

"Yeah. I'm not going to let them get the best of me."

"I'm not worried about you. I'm worried about the bastards who are messing with you."

She smiled, but was beginning to feel uncomfortable standing there in full view of the other pilots.

"I've got to go, Karl. I'll talk to you soon."

"Let me know if you need anything."

She nodded her thanks and walked away.

Going down the hallway, she glanced down at her hand. During the brief embrace, she had managed to snatch the clip-on I.D. badge from Karl's lapel. She looked at his picture and suddenly felt cheap and dirty and worthless. Is this what she had come to? Suspended from her job and stealing from a friend, someone who respected and trusted her?

She was fighting for her survival, she reminded herself as she exited the terminal. Karl would understand. After this was all over, she would explain it to him, and he would understand, she had no doubt.

When would he notice that his badge was missing and report it to the authorities? she wondered. The instant he did, they could stop its validation and all this would be for nothing. The sooner she put the badge to its use, the better. It would have to be tonight.

chapter **17**

"**D**o you have to leave?" she asked, sitting up in bed, covering the top half of her naked body with a sheet.

Marshall Hayes had already put his pants on, but he was still shirtless. His upper body was toned and tanned and impressive for a man in his midsixties. He grabbed his shirt and began to put it on. "Why do you always ask me that?"

"Ask you what?"

"The same question. 'Do you have to leave?' You ask me that every time we're together."

"I guess because I don't want you to go."

Hayes shook his head. "That doesn't make sense."

"What do you mean?"

Hayes paused for a moment. "You are twenty-six years old. You're beautiful and intelligent. You meet an old man every week and you make love to him. You let him use you and you always let him come back. Not only that, you ask him to stay. It doesn't make sense."

She sat up on her knees at the edge of the bed,

letting the sheet drop. She moved within inches of Hayes, then began to help him button his shirt. "Maybe it doesn't make sense to you. But love does crazy things to a girl."

Hayes pulled away. "Is that it? You're in love with me?"

She giggled. "Maybe."

"You're an angel." With his right hand he brushed the blond bangs gently off her face, looked her in the eyes as he said, "But you are also a whore. The only thing you're in love with is the condominium, the cars, and the bank accounts. You provide a service and you get paid, money that you well deserve. God knows you earn it. But it will help us both a whole lot if neither of us pretends to be something we're not. Don't you agree?"

She recoiled. "You bastard!" she screamed, and shoved him away. "You bastard!" She began to sob, yanking the sheet up to cover herself again. "Is that what you think this is all about? A house and money? I don't want them. I don't want any of them and I don't want you. Go on, just get out."

Hayes leaned over. "I'm sorry if I've been insensitive. But are you sure you want me to leave?"

"Yeah, I'm sure."

"You don't even want to talk it over with Antonio?"

She looked up. "What?"

"Isn't that his name—Antonio? You know who I'm talking about. Your boyfriend. The guy you'll go to see when we're finished here. The actor you've been screwing for the past four months. The guy you slept with on your second date. By the way, his real name isn't Antonio, it's Dennis. Antonio is just his stage name. Let's see, what else . . ." Hayes looked away from her for a moment. "He's broke, that is if you don't count the money that you give him, and has no permanent place to live. He knows about me, but he doesn't seem to mind, because that's where the money comes from and, by the way, he doesn't have AIDS, or any other communicable disease; I had that checked out too." Then he leaned over even closer. "Now tell me how much you love me and how much you want me to stay."

When it was clear that there would be no response, Hayes walked over to the mirror. He put on his tie and gray jacket and brushed the lint from one shoulder.

"Tuesday. Wear the red dress and high heels," he said, smiling at her in the mirror.

Hayes took the elevator to the lobby of her building. He should have been more discreet, but, he reminded himself, there's no fool like an old fool.

He hated her and he hated himself. He felt dirty. He wanted to go home and take a long, hot shower, wash away all traces of the last hour. He wanted to go home to his wife and tell her that he loved her, and that this was the last time, promise. But what was the point? It was a lie—like all the rest of his lies.

Things could never return to the way they had been, regardless of how much he wanted them to. He loved his wife; he always would. But he also knew that he would be back here in a day or a week, walking through the front door like a junkie desperate for the next fix.

Forty feet from the entrance, Hayes saw a black Mercedes pull up to the front of the recently opened Bartlett Hotel. Two valets quickly opened the front doors and two men, dressed in thick gray overcoats, emerged.

Hayes instinctively followed them. What was Kyle, his son, doing with Thompson?

From a short distance, Hayes watched the pair walk into the Blue Lagoon, the hotel's five-star restaurant, and hand their overcoats to the attendant. They were shown to a table and given thick menus, which they began to study, pausing periodically to talk to each other.

Hayes saw Kyle go up to the bar and order something, presumably a Bombay martini, his favorite. His easy, familiar attitude toward the bartender indicated that he was a regular. He sipped the drink and watched the crowd, waving his glass at Thompson.

One of the waitresses walked up to order a drink from the bartender, and Kyle found his target. Hayes watched him as he began to chat, inching ever so slowly in her direction. The girl, obviously irritated and uncomfortable, backed away until she bumped into the customer on the opposite side. Kyle moved still closer and put his hand on her bare shoulder. She pushed it aside and hurried away, shaking her head in disgust. Like father, like son.

Steven Kyle Hayes, or Kyle as he was called, was Marshall's youngest son, and the only child who had followed in his father's footsteps to Searchlight.

Of the three children, his older son, an attorney living in Seattle, had banished himself from his father's life when it became clear that his father's weaknesses for alcohol and blondes in short skirts were addictions that he could not overcome.

His daughter, the middle child, was married and lived on the West Coast. Like her older brother, she too could not tolerate her father's indiscriminate and hurtful conduct, and eventually had withdrawn from his life.

Both children were close to their mother, and over the years they had urged her to leave. But she had refused to do so, opting to remain true to her marriage vows and her Catholic upbringing.

Steven Kyle Hayes, like the other Hayes children, was born into a life of luxury and abundance, but unlike the first two, he proved to be the family's black sheep. As a child, he was mischievous to a fault, and as an adult, lazy beyond bounds. He had attended only the most exclusive private schools, and by the time he graduated from high school, had been expelled from three. In college, he experimented heavily with drugs and alcohol, and after changing his major four times over a six-year period, in the face of abysmally low grades, it was decided that Kyle should look for his future in an area other than academics.

Like his father, Kyle had a weakness for blondes in short skirts and somewhere along the line married one. The marriage lasted three years, ending in a messy divorce and two children, whom Kyle barely knew. None of it had stopped him from pursuing other blondes in other skirts. His indiscretions weren't limited to women and booze, either. Drugs, dice, and a taste for the forbidden were the three staples of his diet.

Marshall blamed himself for his son's failures and for not being there during the critical years when he was growing up. Consumed by guilt, he decided to commit himself to his younger son and stay the course, whatever that was, to help shape his future.

Kyle was given a job at Searchlight. In fact he was given several jobs, but he managed to fail miserably at each one. He would show up late or not at all. He enjoyed his martinis at lunch, and he rarely let anyone forget that he was the boss's son.

Employees and supervisors put up with Kyle because they had no choice. He couldn't be fired, so he was shoved from one department to another, from one floor to the next, always under the pretense that he needed new challenges. There was even a regular ceremony: a quiet, secretive ritual where all the managers chipped in and sent flowers and a note of condolence to Kyle's new boss every time he was transferred.

It took almost four years, but Kyle eventually found his niche. He was a great talker and storyteller. It was a natural talent, one that he had unwittingly perfected over the course of his life every time he bragged about himself and lied to others. Nevertheless, the talent was real, and with a shove from the top, Kyle found a comfy office on the fourth floor, right in the heart of the marketing department, with a secretary and two assistants.

Advancing Kyle to any serious managerial position was out of the question, so a position was created for him. It was called client relations and Kyle was promoted to vice president. It was a fancy title for a cushy job that required long lunches and a fat expense account to entertain clients—the perfect job for someone with Kyle's slender talents.

Nevertheless, it was a job; the first one that Kyle managed to hold. It came with a paycheck and an office with his name in bold letters on the door—and that was enough for Marshall Hayes.

The only thing that continued to bother him was Kyle's affinity for Davis Thompson, whom he liked little and trusted even less. Given Kyle's abundant weaknesses and Thompson's callous disregard for others, their newfound affection for each other possessed all the hallmarks of the maiden voyage of the *Titanic*.

Hayes waited until late afternoon before going to see Kyle.

"Is he in?" Hayes asked his secretary. Without waiting for an answer he knocked and went in.

Kyle was sitting in his chair, his ear to the phone and his feet on his desk, when Marshall entered.

He was young and would have been considered attractive had it not been for the fact that he barely had a chin. He had a crooked smile, which gave an impish quality to his face, a kind of cut-rate charm that had gotten him out of more than one sticky situation. He had a full head of unruly brown curls, a sharp contrast to his father's bald head, but he was a Hayes through and through.

Kyle was dressed in a black suit with a blue tie set off by a Turnbull & Asser shirt with French cuffs secured by oversized gold cuff links. A long way from the earrings and tattoos he had so favored a few years back.

At the sight of his father, Kyle whispered into the phone, "I'll call you back," and put his feet down. "What brings you here, Marshall?" he said, grinning like a Cheshire cat.

The hair on Marshall's neck prickled. He detested his son calling him by his first name.

"How was lunch?" Hayes asked, taking a seat.

"Lunch?"

"I came to see you earlier. Your secretary said you were at lunch."

"Fine. I just grabbed a bite at the deli."

Hayes grinned and shook his head. "You never change."

"What do you mean?"

"I saw you at the Bartlett with your martini and your . . ."

"Wait a minute. Wait a minute. Are you upset because I had lunch with Thompson?"

"No, Kyle, this is not about lunch and not about Thompson. This is about a son lying to his father."

A rare flash of self-assertiveness made Kyle sit up straight in his high-backed chair. "And did you ever consider that I lied because you made me?"

"What the hell does that mean?" Hayes snapped.

"I like him, Marshall. I want to be around Thompson; I want to learn from him. God, I want to *be* like him."

"You *are* like him," Hayes shouted. "Look at the way you dress, look at the way you talk—and stop chewing on that damn pen. I don't even know if I'm talking to you or him anymore."

Kyle threw the pen onto his desk. "Now hang on here. Wasn't it you who brought Davis Thompson to Searchlight? The one who put him in charge? When I first came here, wasn't it you who kept telling me how much I should be like him?"

"That was before I knew who he really was. Besides, I was desperate to have you look up to someone other than the vermin you were hanging around with."

"You don't think very highly of your son, do you, Marshall?"

Hayes leaned forward. "This is not about you. This is about Thompson. I don't trust him."

"And you think I do?" Kyle asked. "You know what the difference is between you and me? I don't have to like the man to learn from him, Marshall. But I *am* learning. And you know what? I'm gonna be better than him. Someday I'm going to beat him. You'll see."

"Beat him at what? The man is scum."

Kyle jumped to his feet. "Didn't you hear anything I said? And you wonder why I was forced to lie?"

"Dammit." Hayes slammed the flat of his hand on Kyle's desk. "You always have a smart-ass answer for everything, don't you? Tell me this—did I force you to lie when you got kicked out of college because you were caught cheating? Did I force you to lie when you and your buddies were caught breaking into that old lady's house to steal her jewelry? How about the time they caught you with cocaine in the bathroom at school. You were in eleventh grade, dammit. Did I make you lie then?"

"What do you want, Marshall, to relive my childhood indiscretions in all their tarnished glory? Why did you come here?"

"I want to know when it's enough, Kyle. Two years ago, when I picked up all your markers in Vegas and

Atlantic City, you promised me that was it. No more gambling, no more lying, no more breaking your mother's heart."

"You hypocrite." Kyle laughed. "Since when were you ever worried about my mother? Do you know how many nights I sat up and watched her cry, telling her that everything would be okay, that you would *eventually* come home—not that you ever did. Do you have any idea how angry she was, not at you, but at herself, for not being able to satisfy you? She blamed herself for everything you did—your drinking, your women, everything." Kyle slumped back in his chair. "I am all those things that you said, and more. But I am first and foremost my father's son. I am what you made me, Marshall."

The arrow hit the bull's-eye and Hayes conceded defeat, slumping back in his chair. "What did I do wrong, son? Where did I fail?" he said, staring into space.

"Who said you failed? You're Superman. You built a company out of nothing and you put it on the map. You provided jobs for thousands of people and you raised a family. You don't know how to fail."

Hayes grimaced. "When I saw you in that bar in the middle of the day, a martini in your hand, pushing yourself on that girl, I . . . I realized that I could have been a better father. That I should have been a better father."

"Don't worry, Marshall. The guilt won't bother you for long. It never did in the past."

chapter 18

Kate looked at her watch. It was one A.M. The terminal was nearly empty, the last flight having arrived minutes earlier.

At the metal detector, she smiled at the lone guard and asked for a tray. He handed one to her and she dispensed her wallet, keys, and change and walked through. On the other side, the guard gave her back her belongings, surveying her briefly, wondering what a woman dressed all in black was doing there at this hour.

She walked away from the checkpoint, sighing with relief. One down, a whole lot more to go. Now to find out if the badge worked.

She pulled it out and glanced at her picture, which she had hastily glued over the original photograph. She didn't want to wear it yet because there was a chance that someone might recognize her. She held the badge tightly in her hand as she went to the deserted rear section of the terminal. There, at one of the doors, she held her breath and swiped the plastic card through the computerized lock. A green light came on. "Thanks, Karl," she whispered.

At the bottom of the stairs, Kate turned up the collar of her leather jacket against the cold and looked around. With the exception of some activity near the international terminal, the area was eerily quiet. She pinned the badge to the outside of her thick jacket. Moving through the shadows, in her dark clothing, she was almost invisible. But the hangar was on the other side of the airport. It was easily two or three miles, thirty minutes at best if she walked. Thirty minutes in the open, walking through a secure area in the middle of the night with a false I.D. Not a good idea. She needed an alternative mode of transportation, but as the last of the day-shift personnel filed past the security posts, closing doors behind them, that possibility seemed remote.

Instinct drew her to the international terminal some distance away, where the last of the jumbo jets were loading for takeoff. There would be activity in that area as departure time arrived: there was always that last-minute suitcase, paperwork, fuel, catering. All she needed was a break.

She hid behind a wall a hundred feet or so from the nearest light and waited. It was a short wait. Someone with a cart carrying two small dogs in a cage drove up to the main cargo door and stopped.

"Hey, I've got two live animals here. They need to go to the aft cargo," he shouted to a baggage handler standing in the belly of the aircraft.

"Leave them there, I'll be right down," the man answered.

"No, man, I can't leave them, it's too cold. I'll take care of it myself." He drove the cart to the tail of the aircraft, put the cage on the conveyer belt, then started it and jumped on for the ride.

Kate emerged from the darkness and walked nonchalantly to the cart. She looked around.

The engine was still running, a routine procedure in cold weather. The transmission was automatic and the light switch easily marked. She placed her foot on the accelerator.

She parked the cart thirty feet from the hangar, walked to the door, and swiped her card through the electronic lock. When the green light came on, she cautiously slipped through.

The air in the hangar was warmer than outside, but the darkness was almost absolute. The only light came from the small cracks in the corners where the giant hangar doors met the walls. It was dim but sufficient enough to illuminate the jagged, twisted contours of the wrecked Jet-East plane.

Kate pulled out her wallet and removed a small, flat flashlight. It was amazing how much light the tiny battery generated in near-total darkness.

She stepped on the cold concrete slab, trying desperately not to make any noise. She was sure that there was no one in the hangar, yet as she walked she felt as though she was being watched.

She made her way to the first ladder and climbed up. Her heart beat faster as she entered the cabin and pointed her flashlight. Nothing had changed from that awful night of the crash. The interior was completely scorched. Dozens of seats were off their tracks and passengers' charred personal belongings littered the aisles. Just above them, oxygen masks hung like strange sea creatures.

She stood as if in a trance, reliving the nightmare, wondering what went wrong. But there was work to be done.

She moved to the front of the plane and located the E&E compartment. She removed a section of the charred carpet covering the opening and pulled out the panel. Pointing the flashlight deep inside the cavity, she exposed the nerve center and all the electronics of the sophisticated jumbo jet.

The floor of the E&E compartment was twelve feet below but there was a ladder. She put her hands on the sides of the opening and lowered herself in.

On the floor of the compartment, she swung her flashlight again and looked around. The room was less than ten feet square and lined with electronics from floor to ceiling.

From her back pocket, Kate pulled out a piece of paper and unfolded it, shining the light across it. It was a crudely sketched diagram, faxed to her by Spencer earlier that day. There were abbreviations written in boxes and arrows pointing in various directions, all in the hope of directing Kate through the maze of electronics and to her target. As she looked again around the cramped room, it quickly became clear that her task was going to be more difficult than she had thought.

She was searching for a box marked FCDC but all the lettering looked alike—there were FCPCs, FCSCs, and FCCs. There was even one FBIC, but no FCDC—at least none that she could see.

"Come on, Spence," she whispered in frustration. "Where *is* this thing?"

She looked again and again, each time working her way from the top to the bottom of the row, wondering if the box was there at all. On the fourth try, she found it.

It was a little box on the third row, painted black like the others, FCDC clearly stamped across it in white. She looked at the letters, then at the sheet in her hand. Bingo.

From her wallet, Kate pulled out a small screwdriver with a Phillips head on one end and a flat head on the other. Holding the flashlight between her teeth, she began to pry at the box.

Once the screws were out, she pulled out the box. Then, using the other end of her screwdriver, she removed four more screws and finally the top.

Spencer's instructions were clear: Remove the chip only, not the entire box, because the empty space would draw attention. She did exactly as he instructed. Looking at the diagram again, she located the microprocessor, held in place with a male-female lock, and gently pulled it away, separating it from the motherboard.

The job done, she put the chip in her wallet, replaced the first cover, and pushed it back into its slot. Then she heard it.

It was the muffled sound of the door. She recognized it instantly, because she had heard it just minutes earlier when she had entered. Someone was in the hangar.

Kate turned off the flashlight, immersing herself in total darkness and absolute fear.

She reached for the steps of the ladder and climbed to the top, then crawled on her hands and knees to peek out the nearest window. She lifted her head, trying hard to see something. What she saw made her heart stop.

Two men wearing night-vision goggles were headed up the ladder to the fuselage.

Paralyzed by panic, Kate frantically looked around for a place to hide—but where? She could hide behind a seat, but with night-vision goggles she would easily be discovered. Her blood ran cold as she realized that she was trapped.

The two men entered through the far side of the cabin. They began to walk to the front of the plane, a petrifying assuredness to their steps.

To her horror, they stopped above her. At the opening to the E&E compartment the men looked down. The one in the lead signaled the exits, and the other nodded. The first man quickly shimmied down the ladder. He reached for his belt and removed a small device resembling a flashlight. A soft, green glow filled the room.

From behind a rack of radio equipment, Kate caught a closer glimpse of one of the men. He was large, dressed in black, and his head was covered with what looked like a hood. For the time being he seemed concerned only with the electronics on the wall. He looked at the markings, the ceiling, and then knelt down exactly where Kate had been just a minute earlier.

He grabbed something else from his belt and reached for the box labeled FCDC. The holes where the screws were supposed to be were empty; the screws lay nearby on the floor, where Kate had left them.

The man instinctively looked around. When he didn't see anything, he reached for the box and slid it out. He was just ten feet away. She didn't dare breathe.

The man was already undoing the top screws. When the last one was out, he placed his tool on the floor of the compartment and opened the box. There was no chip.

He didn't react, merely examined the open cavity, then placed the box on the floor and stood up. Shining his flashlight in her direction, he slowly walked toward her.

Kate tried to prepare herself for the inevitable. She would put up one hell of a fight.

The man continued his approach, moving his head and the light from side to side . . . looking. Searching.

He came to a stop almost straight across from where she was standing and pointed the light at the ceiling directly above her. Whatever was there seemed to satisfy him. He quickly turned and walked back.

On the floor, he hurriedly reassembled the box and put it back in the wall. Then he climbed the stairs out of the E&E compartment.

Kate listened to the men's departing footsteps. After what seemed an eternity, she heard the hangar door open and close. Even so, she stayed behind the equipment rack for a long time, not daring to move, her eyes closed and her breathing heavy.

She was sure that the men weren't with the government—they were working alone. As to who they were and what they wanted, she had no idea.

chapter 19

She let out a short scream and recoiled in horror from the high-pitched noise. Clutching a pillow, it took her a full second to realize that she was in bed and the noise was her phone ringing.

Kate had made it back at around three A.M., curled up in bed, and watched the shadows dance through her window. She spent the rest of the night haunted by the possibilities, both real and imagined, while she dozed fitfully. Time after time, she arrived at the same two conclusions.

The first was that the resistance she had felt on the flight controls, immediately prior to the accident, was as real as the men she had seen in the hangar. The knowledge that she had been right all along brought her huge relief.

The second, and more troubling, conclusion was simpler to arrive at. If she wasn't responsible for what had happened, someone else was. Someone with a lot more to lose, someone who would go to any length to cover his tracks.

But who that person was and what would have happened had she been seen were questions that had terrorized her throughout the night.

Should she have run after them? she wondered. Should she call the authorities? But what would she tell them? Her mind wavered back and forth through every possibility.

The phone rang again.

"Hello?"

"Kate?"

She relaxed. "Spencer."

"How did it go?"

"I got it, Spence. One computer chip, two inches by one, and very thin. Are you sure this thing can tell us what we need?"

"It holds some information regarding the data from the primary and secondary flight controls. Whether it holds any answers, I don't know. Just get it to me as fast as you can, and I'll go to work on it."

"You'll have it in the next hour. I sent it counter to counter."

"Good. Did the sketch help? Were there any problems?"

"Couldn't have done it without the sketch and the rest of your instructions. Thanks, Spence."

"You're welcome. How did you pull it off?"

Kate didn't respond.

"Kate? Are you there?"

"Yes."

"How did you . . . ?"

"I wasn't alone, Spence. There were two men in there, wearing night-vision goggles."

There was a pause on the other end. "Go on," Spence finally prompted, a catch to his voice.

Kate explained the sequence of events and then added, "They almost caught me. I was hiding behind some electronic equipment, and one of them came within a couple of feet of me. Then he turned away."

"Jesus Christ, Kate. Are you okay?"

"Yeah, I'm fine. Who are they, Spence? What do they want? Why were they looking for that chip?"

"Let me think. Let me think." He was silent for a moment. "You're sure they didn't see you?"

"If they had, I don't think I'd be talking to you right now."

"Holy shit, Kate. What have you gotten into?"

"I don't know. I wish somebody would tell me."

"Listen, I think you're getting close to something, and from what you're telling me, that's not necessarily good. I'm going to send the chip out the second it gets here. I should have something soon. I've also got some vacation coming. I think it might be time to use it."

"Thanks, Spence."

"Kate? One other thing. I don't know what the hell this is all about, but until I figure this out, be very careful."

She hung up and leaned back against the headboard. The phone rang again. She considered not answering, then reluctantly picked up the receiver. "Hello."

"Ms. Gallagher?"

"Who's calling?"

"This is Michael O'Rourke, Ms. Gallagher."

"Yes?"

"I'm sorry to call you so early, but I'm leaving for Washington this morning and I wanted to catch you before I left."

Kate looked at the clock. It was 8:14. "It's okay, I was up. Do you have something new?"

There was a pause, then O'Rourke said, "No, actually, I just wanted to let you know how sorry I am."

"Sorry? For what?"

"I read in the papers that the airline . . . Well, you were suspended, weren't you?"

She hadn't thought about the suspension since the day before. Given everything that had happened during the night, it was the last thing on her mind. "Yes, Mr. O'Rourke, I was suspended. It turns out that you're not the only person who thinks I'm a liar."

"That's not fair."

"Why not? Isn't this what you've been angling for? The reason you've been leaking news to the press?" she snapped, without meaning to.

"What do you mean?" he asked incredulously.

"Oh, come on, Mr. O'Rourke. Your office has been colluding with the press since day one."

"Why would you think that?"

"Just open any newspaper. Practically every line reads 'anonymous sources close to the investigation' said this or that. 'Anonymous sources close to the investigation,' that's press code for *you*, Mr. O'Rourke. You and the rest of your little gang."

"God, why do you do this?" O'Rourke demanded.

"Do what?"

"Turn every conversation into a fight. It seems as if every time you and I talk, you're shouting and I'm defending myself. Is it just me, or does everyone piss you off like this?"

She brushed her hair aside impatiently and responded in a level tone, "You barge into my hospital room and blame me for an accident which I didn't cause. You allowed your office to leak information about me to the press, information that lays the blame at my door, and you continue to disregard everything I have to say. In answer to your question, no, I don't feel this way about everyone, Mr. O'Rourke. I save it for special people."

O'Rourke replied in a heavy tone, "I'm sorry you feel that way, Ms. Gallagher. But for the record,

I've had nothing to do with releasing any information about you."

"Yeah? Then who did?"

"I don't know. But in the short period I've known you, my guess is that it could be a number of people."

"Have a good day, Mr. O'Rourke," Kate said, slamming down the receiver.

She wanted to rip the phone out of the wall and throw it in the garbage and the thing was, she wasn't mad at him, she was mad at herself. What had possessed her to treat him like that? He was the only person, aside from Spence, who really seemed to believe in her, and as recompense, she had treated him to a barrage of abuse. She didn't dislike him. In fact, if she was honest with herself, she found him more attractive than she cared to admit. But with everything that had happened recently, she just had to let loose on somebody, and Michael O'Rourke had just happened to cross her line of fire.

It took her only a moment to gather her senses and realize that she wholeheartedly wanted to right the wrong. She quickly made up her mind to apologize, then to level with O'Rourke and tell him everything: the chip, the men in the plane—everything. She felt she could trust him.

She ran to her desk and rummaged through the mess, trying to find his card. When she finally did, she went back to the phone and dialed.

"I'm sorry, Mr. O'Rourke has left for the day and will not be back till late tomorrow," his secretary said. "Who's calling?"

"Nobody," Kate replied and replaced the receiver.

"You said it was urgent," Thompson said.

"You wanted to be informed of the latest progress," Cordelia replied.

They were walking along the Vietnam Veterans Memorial and seemed oblivious to the light morning snow falling all around them. Cordelia, by far the larger of the two, wore his trademark dark blue trench coat and Thompson had on a tailored charcoal gray overcoat with a matching scarf.

"We couldn't get it," Cordelia continued.

"And why is that?"

"I sent in one of my best teams. Within seventy-five seconds of entering the hangar, they had located the box. But there was no chip. She had already taken it."

Thompson stopped and turned to face Cordelia. "What the hell does that mean, *she* had taken it. Who?"

"Your friend. Kate Gallagher, the captain of the Jet-East plane."

"What? How do you know this?" Thompson snarled.

"We saw her."

"In the middle of the night?"

Cordelia nodded. "When my men didn't find the chip, they looked around. They picked up the heat signature from her body and tracked it. She was in the back of the compartment hiding behind some equipment. The rest of the team was in the support van parked on the perimeter. They saw her on their monitor and the team leader gave the order to abort."

"Did she have the chip?"

"Yes."

"Then why the hell didn't you get it?" Thompson was ready to explode.

"Because they would have to take her out and the use of force wasn't authorized."

Thompson stood there in shock, trying to absorb what he had heard.

"So now what?" He sighed, suddenly seeming much older than his years.

"We have to find out where she sent the chip. Then we'll trace it."

"If there's anything incriminating on that chip, I'll—"

"I know, I know. I've already got people on it."

There was a long pause, then Thompson said, "We can't meet at the office anymore."

"Hayes?" Cordelia asked.

Thompson nodded. "He knows about you, he saw you in my office. A couple of days ago he marched up and demanded to know what you were doing."

"What did you tell him?"

"Doesn't matter. He's an old man with no stomach for this kind of work. And he won't be around forever."

"I've got lots more pictures where that last set came from." Cordelia smirked.

"You just hang on to them for now. I'll let you know when I need them."

"What about the Gallagher woman?" Cordelia asked.

"What about her?"

"You want me to make some preliminary plans?"

"I already told you. No rough stuff."

"It's your call. But we'll keep watching her."

"You do that. I've got plans of my own."

chapter 20

The last phone call came in just before noon. It was from Thompson.

"I'm just following up on your recent visit. I wanted to know whether the information we provided has helped you in any way."

"Well, yes, actually," Kate replied.

"Good. How would you like to take it one step further?"

"What do you mean?"

"Ms. Gallagher, with your cooperation, we'd like to see if we can duplicate what happened to you in one of our simulators."

"Why would you want to do that?"

"Because it's important that we rule out STAR as a possible contributor or culprit in what happened."

"Well, I think we can safely do that now. I don't think STAR had—"

"Ms. Gallagher, let me be completely honest with you. Your recent visit here has stirred up some rumors which don't seem to want to die down. For such a high-profile case as yours . . . well, sometimes that's all that it takes."

"All that it takes for what?"

"Ms. Gallagher, in today's market, the value of a company is not so much what it's worth, but what the investors perceive it to be. A rumor here, an exaggeration there, and you might have a ten-percent drop in the value of your stock, maybe even twenty. We can't afford that."

"I understand. I just don't know how I can help."

"By controlling the damage—that's the only way we can kill the rumors. What we need you to do is to take a ride in one of our simulators that uses the STAR system. We will systematically fail each piece of the system and eventually all of it. Then you can tell us whether your experience mirrors what happened in your aircraft."

"Mr. Thompson, I don't believe your STAR system had anything to do with what happened. Besides, this is not a good time for me."

"Please, Ms. Gallagher. You needed help when you came to us and we gave it to you. Now we need your help. The company jet is already at Kennedy. I can have it fly you down in an hour and you'll be back in the city by dinnertime."

She caught a cab to Kennedy and forty minutes later arrived on the north side of the airport, at Searchlight's private hangar.

The Jetstar IV was white with the Searchlight logo clearly painted on the tail in bright gold letters. The twin-engine jet, with standing room and executive seating for up to twenty, was a symbol of luxury and status and contained every kind of amenity.

A flight attendant was waiting at the foot of the stairs. Kate was shown to the cabin and offered a glass of champagne, which she declined. Sinking deep into a rich leather seat, she focused on the open cockpit door, where the pilots were running through their final checks.

It's been said that a pilot makes as bad a passenger as a doctor makes a patient. This was certainly true in Kate's case, particularly now that she was forbidden to fly. She waited until the plane was airborne before she succumbed to her curiosity and to went to the cockpit. She stood in the doorway, watching the latest aviation technology in action.

The cockpit was almost all glass. No dials, no gauges, few switches. Everything that the pilots needed to know was at their fingertips with a touch of a screen. The condition of the engines, hydraulics and other vital systems, the secondary systems such as cabin pressure and cargo temperature controls, even the condition of the lavs and the reserve water, could be monitored by selecting the proper screen.

Navigation was, of course, via STAR. A clear roadway in the sky depicted by a magenta line, which showed every inch of the course and clearly indicated not only every intersection and navigational aid but every town and airport within a three-hundred-mile radius of the aircraft. All you had to do was take off, punch in a few buttons, and simply monitor the system.

She stood there asking questions and learning about the system. The pilots seemed glad to have someone to talk to, and if either one had an opinion about Kate Gallagher, he kept it to himself.

Twenty minutes after the flight began, the Jetstar began to descend into a bank of white clouds, and Kate returned to her seat.

At Washington's Reagan National Airport, the Jetstar taxied to the north side and stopped just short of the private hangar. Almost immediately the doors opened, and Kate saw two other Jetstars, parked side by side, both identical to the one she had just arrived in.

She thanked the crew and headed to the waiting limousine.

Twenty minutes later, in front of the main entrance to Searchlight, Kate was greeted by Dorothy McGuire.

"Good to see you again, Ms. Gallagher. They're all waiting for you," she said, as she handed Kate a badge and led the way.

"Yeah? Who?"

"Mr. Thompson and the technicians and advisers." She punched in some codes and opened a door leading to a long hallway. "There might even be a couple of the board members; I can't tell. They're all men, they're all anxious, and they're all waiting for you," she said, as she stopped in front of another door.

"I guess I should be honored," Kate replied.

"No. But I know a dozen women who would walk in there in tight sweaters with no bra to get the attention you're getting," the woman said, pushing the door open and holding it for her.

Kate acknowledged the comment with a chuckle and walked in.

She found herself at the top of a landing, looking into a large open bay where four identical full-motion, three-axis simulators stood side by side.

The simulators—square white boxes, each the size of a small room—were supported by an array of hydraulic steel legs that zigzagged beneath them, making them look like alien spaceships. In reality, a simulator was simply a training tool, a machine capable of doing everything that airplanes do and more, at least from a pilot's viewpoint.

The visual references outside—the actual movements of the box itself, the acceleration, deceleration, climbs, and descents, in combination with any kind of

system failure that was possible—were so real that
there was no longer a need to train pilots in aircraft.
Students sat in boxes, learning everything that was required of them without ever leaving the ground. In
fact, in nearly every case, the very first time a pilot
touched the controls of an actual aircraft was the very
first time that he or she left the gate.

The activity around the simulators was impressive.
There were technicians in white lab coats talking,
some running around, others waiting with clipboards
in hand. Kate recognized Davis Thompson, his tan Armani jacket and black slacks distinguishing him from
the herd of men in conservative suits.

He was the first to see Kate and walked over to her,
hand outstretched, a broad smile on his face.

"Thanks for coming. We'll try not to take too much
of your time," he said, before launching into the introductions.

Kyle was also present and introduced as Searchlight's marketing man extraordinaire. "I wanted the two
of you to meet," Thompson said, gesturing to Kyle as if
he were his right-hand man. "If you have any questions
about STAR or Searchlight, he's the person you want
to see."

They nodded and shook hands. The introductions
at an end, Kate was led down a ramp and over a narrow, metallic bridge that connected the simulators to
the ramp. She followed Thompson and nodded uncomfortably at the attentive crowd.

"As you can see, we have four of these machines. In
addition to training our own pilots here, we use the
simulators extensively for experimentation with the different products that we develop. STAR was developed
right here, on the third one." He pointed.

Kate acknowledged the comments and walked over to the box. Someone pressed a button that initiated the rotating beacon and the alarm bell. The bridge lifted away, leaving the simulator supported only by its spiderlike hydraulic legs.

"I realize that there are a lot more people in here than you are used to," Thompson said, when they were inside the box. "But we need them for the process."

"I don't mind, as long as they don't expect to see me ace this thing. I've never flown a Jetstar before," Kate said, as she took the left seat.

"We realize that. You'll have a first officer who will tend to all the systems issues, and all of us back here will help in any way we can. All you're going to do is take off and fly to altitude, then we'll start to fail the system."

"Sounds like a fun way to spend an afternoon. Let's go."

In the cockpit, Kate strapped herself in as a technician acting as her first officer began to give her a quick review of the systems. Kate nodded, trying to calm down. It was the first time she had been behind the controls of an airplane since the crash, even if this "airplane" was bolted to the third floor of a building in Washington.

The others took their places in the back of the simulator. The operator punched another button and suddenly night descended; they were sitting on Runway 22 Right at New York's Kennedy Airport.

"What kind of weather do you want?" the box operator asked.

Kate pondered. "I'm tired of the cold. How about a clear night. Seventy-five—no, make that eighty degrees." She hesitated for a moment, then added, "In Los Angeles."

The operator then punched in the order and *voila*

they were at Los Angeles International Airport, on a smogless night, looking at the control tower and the power plant.

"Your call sign will be Nova 123, and we don't need to do engine starts or taxi. We'll just do the takeoff from here," the operator said.

"I'm ready."

chapter 21

In the simulator, everything happened in real time: real speed, real feel, even real communication with the virtual controllers.

"Nova 123, you're cleared for takeoff."

Kate advanced the throttles and asked for maximum power. In the next seat, the acting first officer adjusted the throttles and called out their speeds.

"V1. Rotate. V2."

Kate eased back the yoke and the aircraft left the ground. The half-dozen witnesses standing in the back of the box reached for anything they could find to steady themselves.

"Positive rate, gear up," Kate ordered. "I don't know the flap speeds. Just raise them as you see fit."

In the right seat, the technician followed Kate's instructions. Somewhere during the climb, Thompson nodded to one of the engineers in the back of the box, his hand poised for action above a keyboard. He pressed a button and the first of three channels connecting STAR to the aircraft systems failed.

In the center display panel, *status* appeared in small, barely noticeable blue letters.

At thirty-one thousand feet, the aircraft leveled off and Thompson nodded a second time. The technician pressed another key, and the second channel disconnected. This time, the words *NAV Channels* lit up in the center console.

"What is that?" Kate asked immediately.

"You've lost two of three channels that connect STAR to the aircraft," Thompson shouted over the sound of the engines. "As you can see, the third channel is capable of flying the aircraft by itself. Now, we're going to lose that one, and see what happens."

He turned and nodded to the technician a third time, and the final channel was disconnected.

Instantly, an amber warning light began to flash in the pilot's windshield. Kate pressed it off, and looked down. The screen read, *Revert to manual navigation*.

"Freeze the simulator," Thompson ordered, and the operator pressed a button. Everything was still running; the visuals, the gauges, the engines. But the simulator and all motion came to an immediate stop. The technicians taking notes paused as well, and Thompson walked to the front of the cockpit, placing himself directly behind Kate.

"We have now disconnected the entire STAR system from the aircraft; it no longer exists. The pilot has now been warned and it is up to him to select an alternate method of navigation. If you're over land, that's not much of a problem. If you're over water, it could be. But that's not what happened to you."

Kate had let go of the controls, because with everything frozen there was no need to hold anything. "You've disconnected STAR altogether. What if that wasn't the case? What if your system was still connected, but it gave the computers faulty signals?"

"Good question," Thompson said, then turned to the operator. "Let's start the motion and reconnect STAR."

The simulator jerked to life again. Everything was working exactly the way it was supposed to.

"Okay. I want you to manually fly it and feel for any changes in tension on the controls. I'm going to ask the technicians to send erroneous signals to the computers," Thompson said.

Kate held the controls, maintaining the heading and the altitude at the correct level. Thompson nodded again and one of the technicians in the back went to work. He took a wire from a laptop computer and hooked it into a special plug in the wall. He selected a program and hit the Enter button.

Almost instantly the amber light began to flash in Kate's eyes. When she looked down, the words *FCCs Isolated* appeared on the screen.

"What does that mean?" Kate asked, her hands on the controls, her eyes fixed on the instrument panel.

"The simulator wasn't programmed for fictitious data from STAR," Thompson replied. "So we wrote our own program and fed it to the machine. What you're seeing are the flight control computers refusing the data they've been fed. If you go through your checklist at this point, it will tell you to go to the computers and decide which data you like best, then make a selection."

"Nothing like that happened to us. There were no lights, no indications, no warnings."

"My point exactly. STAR is simply a navigational aid that informs the aircraft which way to fly. It doesn't fly the aircraft and it is not in any way connected to the controls. Other than what you've seen in here today, STAR isn't capable of doing anything else."

Kate relaxed in her seat. "Thanks for taking the time to show me this. I think I've seen enough."

"Don't you want to go back and land?" Thompson asked.

"Sure. Why not."

A heading was assigned, and the Jetstar began to descend. Somewhere through it all, Thompson jotted something on a piece of paper and handed it to the box operator. He looked at Thompson curiously and Thompson nodded. The man shrugged and turned to the control panel. Seconds later, the amber light in the center pedestal came on.

"Left hydraulic system," the first officer called out, as he saw the level of the fluid diminish to zero. He looked back at the box operator, wondering what was going on.

In the left seat, Kate felt the controls stiffen slightly, but she continued flying. Somebody back there was fooling around.

The aircraft leveled off at three thousand feet, about to begin the approach into LAX. It was still night, pitch black, but the skies had become overcast. And it was snowing. In L.A.

Kate found the little game amusing but chose not to react. Simultaneously, the pressure from the second hydraulic system began to decrease.

"Uh . . . we have a second hydraulic failure . . ." the first officer said, looking at Thompson, who shook his head and waved him off.

"Nova 123, you're cleared for ILS, Runway 25 Left in Los Angeles."

Gripping the controls, her entire attention focused on the approach, Kate reached for the localizer button in front of a captive audience. Suddenly, the red warning light came on, followed by the intermittent wail of a horn.

"What is that?" Kate asked calmly.

"I think we just lost the left engine," the man in the right seat responded weakly, his hands in his lap.

Kate had already compensated for the power loss with the other engine and was pressing hard on the rudder to stay on course.

"I don't know the flap setting in this thing, but you better get them down."

The F.O. reached for the handle, then stopped. "With only one hydraulic system you have partial flaps."

"I'll take whatever I've got," Kate responded, concentrating on the instruments. "After you have your flaps, you'd better give me the gear too. I don't know what else is going to go wrong on this flight."

The flaps were extended, but they came down only to 30 percent of full. The co-pilot then reached for the gear handle, pulling it out and down.

Almost immediately more lights came on and another horn began to blare.

"Right main gear is locked up," the F.O. announced unsteadily, his voice shaking, as if he were fighting for his life.

"Shut down the horn please," Kate said calmly.

The man reached up quickly, pressed a button, then dropped his hands back in his lap, wondering what he was supposed to do.

They were still in the clouds, and under instrument flight rules at two thousand feet. As the aircraft descended below eighteen hundred feet, city lights came into view. The Forum, Hollywood Park—everything looked exactly as it should.

"I see the runway," the first officer almost shouted.

"I see it too," Kate responded. "Call the tower, tell them we have an emergency. I want crash and rescue. Tell them we're going to evacuate on the runway."

The man did as he was told. Instantly, the flashing red lights of ambulances and fire trucks became visible rushing toward Runway 25 Left.

"I'm going to keep the right side up as long as

possible. When she comes down, she'll come hard. When the wing hits the ground, she might veer off to the right. If that happens, I need you on the controls with everything you've got, okay?"

The man was a technician. A lab guy with a white coat and thick glasses. His job was to assist her in some basic systems knowledge, not to come down on the controls; he didn't even know what the hell that meant—but he wasn't going to argue. He didn't want to look ridiculous.

"Okay." He wasn't sure if there was any way he was going to get hurt in this contraption, but if there was, they were about to find out.

The aircraft descended. Two hundred feet. One hundred.

The left main was the first wheel to make contact. Everyone felt the jerk as the wheel touched exactly where it was supposed to. Kate simultaneously reduced the power on the remaining engine and the rudder pressure. The right wing began to come down, but they were still approaching too fast. Kate shoved the controls to the opposite side and the wing lifted again, where she kept it for as long as possible. When the wing would no longer stay up aerodynamically, she gently let it fall.

The contact was hard, and like everything else in the simulator, very real. The box tilted to the side where the gear had failed, then it bounced ferociously as the wing scraped the ground. Even the noise, the sound of the metal as it twisted and scratched, was real.

Nova 123 decelerated and the aircraft came to rest with the nose-gear just off the runway.

"Okay, let's initiate the evacuation checklist," Kate said, glancing at her co-pilot, who looked faint, his mouth wide open.

"I think we've seen enough," Thompson said, and with that slowly he began to clap his hands.

The others joined in, which made Kate blush as she got out of her seat.

"I didn't want your trip here to be wasted," Thompson said when she appeared in front of him. "You're one heck of a pilot and you've got a job here anytime you want."

Kate smiled. "Thanks. I might just take you up on it."

With the session over, the bridge was once again lowered, allowing Kate and the rest of the group to file out.

On the other side, Marshall Hayes stepped forward from the crowd. Thompson acknowledged him and guided Kate over.

"Kate Gallagher, this is Marshall Hayes, CEO of Searchlight."

Kate smiled and shook his hand. "Thanks for inviting me here. It's been most educational."

"We're always glad to show off our facility," Hayes said, then turned to Thompson. "I wish I had known about this. I wanted to be here to see it."

"Well, it was all so spur-of-the-moment and your secretary said you were out. When did you get back?" Thompson asked.

Hayes ignored him and turned to Kate. "I hope you found our little experiment useful."

"Yes, I did," Kate said appreciatively. "But now I've got to get back to New York. Thanks again."

Thompson shook her hand, then pointed to Dorothy McGuire, who was waiting nearby. "Ms. McGuire will see you out. Thank you again for coming."

Both men stood there, watching Kate leave.

"What the hell was that all about?" Hayes said, as soon as Kate was out of earshot.

"Just insurance, Marshall."

"Why wasn't I informed?"

"Do you want me to discuss every decision I make?"

"When it comes to the future of this company, yes," Hayes growled.

Thompson shook his head in frustration. "Look, Marshall. I'm gaining her confidence. We just spent the last hour convincing her that there's nothing wrong with STAR; that it is in no way responsible for what happened. Now you're telling me—"

"I'm telling you two things that you'll be wise to listen to. First, I want to know everything that happens concerning this blackmail business. I don't care how you do everything else, but when it comes to this . . ."

"And the second?"

"I saw you and Kyle at lunch yesterday."

"You want a report on what we ate?"

"I don't like the way you've been manipulating him."

"Manipulating? I don't think you give your son the credit he deserves. Kyle is a sharp kid and he's got a bright future with this company."

"Kyle is weak and impressionable and you know it. And I don't much like the way he worships you."

"Maybe he knows greatness when he sees it. Did that thought ever cross your mind?"

"No, it did not. It's not your *greatness* that concerns me. It's your ethics."

"Ethics?" Thompson said sarcastically. "*You* want to talk about ethics?"

Hayes glared at him. "Stay away from my son, Thompson. Stay away or so help me . . ."

"Okay. Okay." Thompson held his hands up in surrender. "Whatever you say. You're the boss."

Hayes held his glare a moment longer, then walked away. When he was safely out of his hearing range, Thompson whispered to himself, "At least for now."

Thompson had offered to fly Kate back in the company jet but she had politely refused. She needed to spend some time alone, to think things through.

The next shuttle flight to New York wasn't for another thirty minutes, so she decided to check her messages.

"Hello, Ms. Gallagher. This is Brita Ames. I need to speak with you, it's urgent. I think . . . I think someone is . . . Just please call me right away."

She kept listening, skipping the next several messages from media reporters. Then she heard Brita Ames's voice again.

"This is Brita again. Where are you? I need to speak with you. Listen, there's something going on here, and I think it's related to . . . I've got to go. There's someone at the door. I'll try you again in an hour."

Kate quickly dug through her wallet for her number. The call was picked up on the fourth ring.

"It's me, Kate."

"Hi. This is Brita and the kids. You know the routine. Leave a message and we'll get back to you."

A machine. A bloody machine.

"Brita, are you there? Brita? This is Kate."

Kate redialed her own number and replayed the messages, noting the times. Brita's first message was left at two-thirty, the second one just after four. She looked at her watch. Seven-thirty P.M.—three and a half hours ago. Brita said she would call back in an hour.

She anxiously dialed Brita's number again.

"Brita, are you there? Pick up the phone if you're there, this is Kate."

There was no response.

The next flight to Miami wouldn't leave until ten-thirty P.M. It was going to be a long night.

chapter 22

It was nearly ten o'clock by the time Tara Wilson finished teaching her night class in the computer science lab at MIT and nodded to her students as they filed past her. She was packing up her lecture notes when her cell phone rang.

"Hello."

She paused, listening.

"You're here now? When did you get in? I didn't expect you until tomorrow."

Two of her students were waiting at the door to walk her to her car.

"Uh . . . hang on," Tara said. "Thanks, guys. You go ahead. I have to take this call."

The students waved and left.

"I'm . . . I'm sorry. Of course I'm happy to hear from you," she said as she closed the door of her classroom. "But I'll be really happy when you tell me that there are no other planes infected with this virus."

She listened.

"Okay. We don't have to talk about it over the

phone, and yes, I'm alone. Just tell me that you took care of it," she said, rubbing her forehead with one hand.

Something in the caller's voice caused her expression to lighten. She actually smiled.

"Thank you," she said, closing her eyes. "You did the right thing."

Another pause.

"You know, for a while there, I just wasn't sure if you . . ."

Pause.

"Trust has nothing to do with it. Things got out of hand and we had to stop it." She hesitated. "I'm just . . . I'm just glad it's over."

She listened.

"Do you?" she said with concern. "Do you really?"

Pause.

"I'm sorry. I'm sorry. I don't know what I'm doing. These last few days have been so hard. I love you too. You know I do."

Pause.

She smiled again, this time covering her mouth with one hand. "That sounds wonderful. What's the room number?"

Pause.

"I'll see you there in twenty minutes."

There was one final pause, then Tara sighed. "It's good to have you back."

She pressed End, but continued to gaze affectionately at the phone, her smile now dancing on her lips. She put the phone away and pulled out her hairbrush and makeup case.

Five minutes later, her hair combed and lipstick freshened, she grabbed her tote bag and turned off the lights.

At the bottom of the stairs, Tara said good night to

the guard standing at the entry to the building and began to make her way across the campus to the parking lot.

She felt alive in a sea of emotion. She was almost giddy with relief. For the first time in weeks, she allowed herself to relax. Could it really be finally over?

She needed to talk to him again, to hear his voice. She wanted him to reassure her, to tell her he loved her like he used to. To tell her that everything would be okay.

She stopped next to a building and fished out her cell phone. After getting the number from information, she dialed. She asked the Sheraton operator for room 626 and waited anxiously for him to pick up. But he didn't. A moment later, the operator informed her that no one was registered in that room.

"It's room six twenty-six," Tara said slowly. "Please try it again. Six two six." She paused.

"That's impossible. That room cannot be unoccupied. I talked to him barely five minutes ago," Tara objected, then proceeded to give the operator his name. Maybe she had the wrong room number. Maybe . . .

"Of course I want the Sheraton. I told you I was just . . ." Tara didn't finish her sentence. She stood there, stunned, unable to breathe, as the realization hit her with the impact of a shotgun blast.

"Thanks," she whispered weakly, snapping shut the flap of the phone.

With a face as devoid of color as expression, she began to walk slowly, suddenly aware of the all-encompassing darkness.

He wasn't there. He wasn't at the hotel. He had lied to her. Why?

The first airplane had gone down months ago. Two people were killed, but he had refused to stop. Then the second one went down and more people were killed. He still didn't stop. Why would he stop now? What did he have to lose?

Her mind couldn't process the rapidly incoming information, but when the last piece hit, her heart nearly stopped.

He was here. He wanted her alone, in the dark. He was here, watching.

She heard something and spun on her heels, her heart ready to leap out of her chest. She saw nothing.

She picked up her pace, heading for the faint glow of the fluorescent lights surrounding the parking lot.

She heard footsteps twenty yards away. Was this panic or was it real? She wasn't sure, until she stopped. The sound behind her stopped too.

She glanced back toward the security guard, but he was gone, probably making his rounds. She searched the darkness. There was no one there, at least no one she could see.

Flushed, her hands cold and clammy, she reached into her bag and squeezed the smooth wooden handle of the Colt. It was loaded; she had made sure of that.

She didn't know exactly why she carried the damn thing. It was just a hunch, a nagging feeling that told her to be careful. The same feeling she had had since the day she'd handed him the virus in a small, black diskette. The day he'd held her in his arms and told her he loved her. It was a lie. They were all lies. He had used her. And now he was here to finish the job. But she was ready.

Her hand still positioned in her bag, Tara began to walk slowly, acutely aware of the slightest sound. Her hand was shaking. She tightened her grip around the handle of the weapon.

The sound of her footsteps was drowned by the pounding of her heart. She moved faster. She was jogging now, her eyes fixed desperately on the parking lot, but she turned back every few seconds to look behind her. The sound of the footsteps was distinct and getting louder, closer. She was paralyzed with fear. She felt as through she were wading through quicksand, moving through a nightmare.

The car was nearly a hundred yards away. He would surely get to her before she could reach it.

Making the last turn, Tara ducked into a doorway. With her back to the wall, she pulled out the weapon, cocked the hammer, and held it tightly against her chest. Her eyes glued to the corner she had come around, her body drenched in cold sweat, she waited.

Nobody came. The minutes ticked by agonizingly as the cold began to permeate each layer of her clothing with icy precision. How much longer could she stand there?

The phone, she remembered. She could call for help.

She slowly reached into her bag. Fumbling through it, she felt the plastic casing and pulled it out.

A sound at her side got her attention and she swiftly turned toward it, dropping the phone to grip the weapon with both hands.

"Damn," she whispered to herself, as she watched the cell phone, its flap open, the Ready light blinking. It was five feet away; tantalizingly out of reach.

She looked left toward the parking lot. The car was less than fifty yards away. Now she could try to make a dash for it. She could shoot into the air as she ran. The noise would bring somebody out. Where the hell was security?

She heard the sound of a distant conversation. Another class was letting out. This was her chance.

She hesitantly moved out from the doorway, and with her arms outstretched, her hands gripping the weapon, she inched her way to the corner and peeked around. She could see the students now, twenty or more, two hundred feet away and walking toward her.

Her eyes roaming the darkness, she quietly bent to pick up her phone.

When she stood up, he was there. Standing inches away, his eyes red and round like those of a madman.

She raised the gun but he had already placed his thumb between the hammer and the firing pin. He pulled the weapon from her hand. Then he lifted his other hand. She saw the contours of the blade, the reflection of the distant light shimmering against the cold steel.

She tried to scream but no sound came out.

She began to back away until a frigid stone wall halted her progress.

"I . . . I love you," she whispered, her eyes fixed on his.

He smiled as he moved closer, the large blade twisting in his hand like a toy.

"I know," he whispered back.

chapter 23

It was just after five A.M. when the rental car crossed the Stock Island bridge into Key West. It was still dark, save for the glow of dawn. The streets of the city were deserted. Even the early morning joggers hadn't found their way to the beach yet.

She turned left on Jose Martí Street, then south on Eliza Street, feeling her pulse quicken as she neared the house.

A hundred yards out, she slowed down, keeping her focus on the gray and blue house, and on the parked cars that lined both sides of the street. Everything was unnervingly still.

She found a parking space on the opposite side of the street not too far from the house, then switched the car's interior light to the Off position. She opened the door to the darkness.

Kate crossed the narrow street, her eyes on the dim light behind one of the windows. She slowly walked up the steps, hearing the old wood creak beneath her feet. The drapes were drawn. She peeked through the small cracks beside them but couldn't make out anything.

At the door, she looked around, then slowly opened the screen and knocked softly three times.

She waited for the door to open. It remained shut.

"Where are you, Brita?" she whispered to herself as she turned away from the house and surveyed the street. Other than the rustle of the palm trees swaying in the early morning breeze, nothing could be heard. No cars, no people, not even birds. It was as if they all knew to stay away from Eliza Street.

Kate tiptoed around to the rear of the house and tried the back door. It too was locked.

There were three windows on the side of the house. The first was painted shut but when she pushed hard on the second one, it moved. She used a trash can to climb up to the window and pushed until it opened. She cautiously reached in and moved the curtains aside.

As far as she could tell, the bedroom was unoccupied. A faint light came from the hallway, through the open door.

She pulled herself up, perched on the window ledge, then turned and landed on the floor with a muffled thump. She tiptoed to the hallway and discovered a small nightlight plugged into a socket set low in the wall. From what she could see, the living room was also vacant. Where were they?

She stepped on something on the floor and bent to pick it up. It was Mr. Wishes, Cheyenne's little teddy bear. Kate knew instantly that something was wrong. She raced from room to room, opening closets, looking for some clue to what had happened during the hours since Brita's phone call.

Brita's cigarettes, half a pack of Virginia Slims, were on the coffee table next to her battered Ronson lighter and an ashtray. A red plastic child's plate, the food on it nearly untouched, and a coloring book were on the kitchen table. Why would Brita leave for the night and not take her cigarettes?

Kate wasn't scared anymore, she was angry. Angry at herself for feeling like a victim and for subjecting Brita and her children to danger. Angry for lurking in the dark like a thief instead of being at home with Molly.

She walked out to the porch and locked the front door behind her.

The sun was up, and Kate could see all the way down the street. She was just about to head for her car when she saw him.

The silhouette of a tall man thirty yards away was unmistakable. He was standing there wearing a baseball cap, his hands in the pockets of his raincoat, watching her. Why would anyone wear a raincoat on a balmy day?

Keeping him in her peripheral vision, she crossed the street toward her car.

From the corner of her eye she saw him begin to approach her. She quickened her pace, fumbling through her pockets for the key. When she found it, she held it tightly between her knuckles, letting the point stick out to create a makeshift weapon.

At the car, she hit the master switch to lock all the doors and windows, then turned the ignition and shifted into Drive. She stepped on the gas so hard that the car kicked like a mule, then stalled. Desperate, she turned the key in the ignition again, but other than the sound of the starter, she got nothing.

She looked back but couldn't see him. Surely he was there. Maybe a few feet away, maybe a few inches, but he was there. She could feel him.

Again she turned the key and stepped on the gas. On the third try, the engine caught on.

Driving away, she looked in her rearview mirror; the street was empty.

chapter 24

The small Key West police department was overwhelmed by another taxing night of trying to maintain law and order among the invading tourists on spring break. It took Kate nearly an hour to persuade the busy desk sergeant to dispatch a car.

She led the way back to Eliza Street, looking for any sign of Brita or the children, and especially for the man in the raincoat. But there was nothing.

Two officers went through the motions, checked out the house, knocked on neighbors' doors, and asked questions, but nobody seemed to know anything. One neighbor had seen Brita the day before and another had heard Cheyenne crying late in the afternoon, but that was it. No one had noticed that the family's car, a secondhand green Honda that was usually parked on the street, was gone.

Exhausted, disappointed, and still angry, Kate finally gave up. She thanked the two officers who promised to follow up on the case, and got into her car.

She was suddenly worried about Molly. Maybe it

was the man in the raincoat, or maybe it was the fact that she hadn't slept in more than thirty hours, but she felt a uneasiness that she couldn't explain.

At the nearest phone booth, she stopped and called her mother.

"Where's Molly?"

"She's at Mrs. Glady's, like always this time of day. Where are you, Katrina?"

Mrs. Glady was a retired schoolteacher who ran a small nursery out of her apartment one block away from the taverna. She took care of six children. When the weather allowed, you could usually find them all in the small park next door, always under the watchful eye of Mrs. Glady and her elderly Haitian assistant, who made lunch for them.

"When did you last check on her?"

"Fifteen minutes ago. Is anything wrong?"

"I don't know, Mama. But I need you to go and get her. Just keep her with you. Will you do that for me?"

"You're scaring me, Katrina. What's wrong?"

"Nothing. I'll tell you all about it later on tonight. I'm coming to see you."

Mama wanted more of an explanation, but Kate had no time to elaborate.

She hung up, then pulled out a business card from her wallet. She studied it at length before dialing the number.

"Is Michael O'Rourke in?" she asked, half hoping that he wouldn't be.

"Just one moment," the receptionist said. A few seconds later, O'Rourke picked up.

"This is O'Rourke."

"Hello, Mr. O'Rourke. This is Kate Gallagher. I need a favor."

She dropped off the rental car at the Key West airport, paid the hefty one-way charge, and took the commuter flight to Miami.

It took less than thirty minutes, but she slept the entire way. Groggy and exhausted, Kate grabbed her bag and deplaned. Curbside, she flagged a cab.

Ten minutes later, the cab dropped her off next to a maintenance terminal on the north side of the airport. At the security gate, she pressed the star button on the keypad.

"Hello?" a voice answered.

"My name is Kate Gallagher, I'm . . ."

There was a buzz and the voice said, "Push the gate open. Go straight on the tarmac to the gray hangar on the left and tell the guard that Mr. O'Rourke sent you."

Kate was amazed that after the way she had treated him, he was still willing to help her.

At the hangar, Kate pressed another button next to a door and was admitted into a cramped office.

"We don't get many visitors here anymore," the elderly security guard informed her. He had a large black pistol in the holster on his belt and was carrying a walkie-talkie.

"How long has it been since anyone came here?"

"Oh, when this airplane first went down, there were people here every day; lots of them. But that was a while back. I haven't seen anybody here for more than two weeks. I guess the interest slowly dies. I don't even know how much longer they're going to keep her here."

The old man walked forward and gave Kate the once-over. "You from the NTSB?"

"No, I'm just researching the event."

The guard opened the door to the hangar.

"Well, there she is." He pointed to what looked more like a heap of scrap metal; the only thing that was left of Jetway flight 86, the plane in which Kevin Ames had allegedly committed suicide, taking the other pilot with him.

Kate moved closer, examining the wreckage. It was amazing how little of the plane was left. Pieces of aluminum as small as a matchbook or as large as a car were arranged on the floor, in the approximate location where they should have been, each carefully tagged.

"Is this everything?" Kate asked.

"Yeah. It went straight down into the water. The investigators told me that it was like hitting a wall of concrete. If this wasn't a cargo plane, they would have probably spent a lot more money trying to get all the pieces to figure it out, but I think they more or less knew what caused the crash. There's the inventory of the items that were recovered," he said, pointing to a table. "I'll be back at my station. If you need anything else, just let me know."

Kate waited until he left, then picked up the inventory list, which was in alphabetical order. There were names, abbreviations, and numbers, but Kate was interested in only one thing and she found it on the fourth page. "There you are," she whispered.

The FCDC flight control data concentrator, which held the same kind of chip as she had taken off the Jet-East aircraft just two nights earlier at JFK, was among the items that had been retrieved.

If Spencer was right and the commands that were issued to the flight controls somehow left a signature on the chip, her suspicions would be proved true, and Kevin Ames's name would be cleared.

She headed for the area where the cockpit should have been.

The structure was practically vaporized. If it hadn't been for the bent and broken cockpit door, she wouldn't have been able to distinguish one section of the airplane from another. Just to the rear of the door, a tape on the hangar floor indicated the location of the E&E compartment—exactly where she had found it on the Jet-East plane.

The box was waterproof, and even though it was dented, it remained intact. She picked it up and walked over to the table, and with the screwdriver from her wallet she pried open the top.

Kate was completely out of breath by the time she reached the corner of Doral and Eighth. She had asked to use the phone at the hangar, but the guard had told her that it was restricted to certain numbers. "I guess they think I'm gonna call all my girlfriends." He laughed and gave her a wink.

"There's a pay phone over there," he said, pointing east. "But it's not a good area for a single woman."

She ran as fast as she could. There were a thousand thoughts racing through her mind, but she focused on just one: She had to warn Spencer.

She jogged steadily and ten minutes later, under the gleaming hot Miami sun, on a street filled with graffiti, she found the phone booth.

He picked up on the second ring.

"Spencer, is that you?" Kate gasped for air.

"Yeah."

"Listen, Spence. Grab a pen and a piece of paper."

"What?"

"I don't have time to explain. Just grab a pen."

"Got it."

"Write down this number: 305-555-1945."

"Done. Now what?"

"I need you to drive and call me at that number from the nearest phone booth. Do it now, Spence."

"You're in Miami?"

"Yeah, Spence. We don't have much time. Get in your car and call me from a phone booth. I'll wait right here."

He hung up, and Kate waited outside the hot, airless phone booth, pacing back and forth, watching some men across the street, their shirts unbuttoned and baseball caps worn backward. They were sizing her up like prey. She didn't have time for this.

The phone rang. Kate picked up immediately.

"What's going on, Kate?"

"I couldn't talk to you on your phone. There's a chance it's bugged."

"What?" he almost shouted.

"They've seen me, Spence. They know who I am. And they know about the chip. They've got it."

"What are you talking about? I've got the chip."

"No, not that one. I was just at the hangar where the wreckage of the Jetway flight is kept."

"Why did you go there?"

"I wanted to get the flight control data chip, so you would have a second one to test. I think that plane had the same problem as mine. But when I got there, it was gone. They took the chip, Spence. I'm almost certain that the same men who were in the hangar at Kennedy took the chip."

There was no response.

"Spencer?"

"I'm thinking. I'm thinking."

"What's there to think about? If they know about the chip, and they know about me, then they know about you. And they know that you have the other chip. You're in danger, Spence."

"Now wait a minute—"

"Listen to me. I think they're involved with a family that's missing. The wife of the pilot and his two kids. Brita Ames called me yesterday, telling me there was something wrong and promising to call back. When I went to her house, she was gone. No trace. Nothing."

"And you think they're going to come after me because of the chip?"

"Why not? They have a lot to cover up. The crash of one airplane and now another. I saw one of them this morning. They know me. They know all about me."

"What do you want me to do?"

Two of the men ogling her had separated from the gang across the street and were slowly heading in her direction. Kate looked at them but kept talking.

"Where's the chip?"

"It's in Sarasota at a lab. They're reading it for me. They've no idea what it is; it's just a bunch of numbers to them. They said I should have something by tomorrow."

"Then go to Sarasota, or to Orlando, or to Jamaica. I don't care where, Spence, but get out of there and take Norma with you."

"Oh, come on, Kate. The monthly barbecue is this Sunday. I haven't missed one in fourteen years."

"You might be in danger, Spence. Do you understand?"

"If I'm in so much danger, how about you?"

"If they wanted me, they would have taken me out a long time ago. It's the chip they want."

"I don't know."

"Dammit, Spence. People are disappearing around me, others are wandering around in night-vision goggles. . . ."

The men were closer now, maybe fifty feet away, still walking toward her, their friends encouraging them with whistles and shouts.

"All right. I'll take a couple of days off, if that's the only way I can get you off my back. But remember, I'm not doing it because of the bogeyman. I'm doing it because you want me to."

"Thanks. I gotta go."

The men were less than twenty feet away now. She started to run.

Standing in the middle of the road, one of them shouted, "Hey, come on baby, don't be afraid. All I wanted to do was let you use my phone. I give great phone," and the rest of the gang burst out laughing.

chapter 25

Thompson stood at the door to the cluttered office with his arms neatly crossed, observing Malkovich. He was typing at the keyboard, reading something from a printout, and eating lunch, all at the same time. It was a carefully orchestrated effort: two hands performing three tasks, four, if you counted the fact that every time he put down the greasy sandwich, he wiped his hands on the leg of his brown corduroy trousers.

Thompson could stand in the doorway for an hour and go unnoticed. Malkovich wouldn't look up unless his pants were on fire, and even then, he would grab the can of Coke next to his sandwich, pour it on the flames, and go back to work—all without even getting up.

"Make any headway yet?" Thompson finally asked.

Malkovich looked up, squinting through his thick glasses, his left eye twitching wildly.

"Sorry if I startled you," Thompson said. "I just wanted to know how everything's coming along."

Still shaken, he put down his sandwich, wiped his hand on his pants one last time, and said, "Good. But I need more time, maybe a day, maybe two."

"Is there any way this could be rushed? You know how important it is."

"No. *You* wanted me solo on this project. So I alone have to decode more than four thousand commands and translate them to binary language. Do you know how long that takes? Now, if I could have some help . . ."

Thompson closed the door. "You're the only one I can trust. You're the only one who can ever know about this. I don't want to alarm anyone else, and I don't want to create any further complications, not until we know that this chip has been tampered with."

"Well, I can already tell you that. The answer is yes."

"Are you sure?"

"Of course. Come take a look. By the way, where did you get the chip?"

Thompson ignored the question. He walked over to the desk and looked at the computer screen. The display was divided into four vertical columns of letters and numbers, all practically identical to one another.

"What is all this?"

"These"—Malkovich pointed to the first column— "are the commands assigned by the three flight computer primary controls. These here"—he pointed to the second column—"are the commands given by the two flight computer secondary controls. The third column is the information from all of the computers as interpreted by the FCC, which has the final say on what happens to the flight controls."

"What's this last column?"

"This is the data taken from the flight control data concentrators, the chip you brought me. It shows the

actual movement of the controls. Take a look at this."
Malkovich moved his chair forward and nodded toward
the screen.

"All the data from each of these rows have to
match. The primary and secondary flight control computers transmit their information to the FCC, which
interprets it and sends it to the actuators. They in turn
move the flight controls."

Thompson analyzed the columns. "They all look the
same."

"Yes," Malkovich replied. "But keep looking."

He began to scroll down the page, pointing to individual numbers in the two right-hand columns, which
in a few cases were one digit off from those in the
other two columns. "You see this?" he said, indicating
one of the discrepancies.

"Yeah. What is it?"

"The FCC doesn't generate commands. It doesn't
have a brain of its own, it just interprets what it's been
told."

"Then how can they be different?" Thompson
asked.

"Because they have been tampered with," both men
said simultaneously.

"My God. Then it's true," Thompson said, pausing
for a minute to chew on his fingernail. "The anomalies
you showed me—are they enough to cause an airplane
to lose control?"

"No, they're minor, but look at this."

Malkovich scrolled through the pages slowly, leaving his finger on the Down arrow. The numbers on the
two right columns quickly began to change. The farther down the pages went, the more the data differed.

"It's getting worse," Thompson noted.

"That's right. The virus multiplies itself, copying itself over and over until it infects every file. But it takes

a while, maybe ten or fifteen minutes. By the time the plane gets to here"—he jabbed at the screen—"it's almost out of control. And then right here." He pointed again.

"All the numbers are reversed," Thompson noted.

"That's right. By this point, the computer was fully contaminated. The flight controls snapped to one side, and boom. No one could save them."

Thompson was silent for a moment. "Now what?" he mumbled to himself.

"Give him what he wants," Malkovich said quietly.

"What?" Thompson turned.

"You said that somebody has sabotaged STAR and they're asking for money. Give them the money, because if this happens to an airplane in flight . . . there is nothing anyone can do."

"You said this virus could be killed by using a patch. Right?"

"Yes, but now we know the virus and how it attacks. Instead of rewriting the entire program on every computer, we can design a program to eradicate the virus."

"And we can install it the same way. By telling the airlines that this is an update to something from STAR," Thompson said, finishing Malkovich's thought.

"Right. And it could be done in a matter of minutes, instead of days, during the C checks. But . . ."

"What now?" Thompson asked impatiently.

"This—this virus attacks very quickly and without warning. Any plane already contaminated won't stand a chance. What if . . . what if this happens to another plane before we get a chance to neutralize it?"

Thompson gave him a cold stare. "Just tell me if this will work."

"Oh, it will work," Malkovich replied, looking straight at him. "If you get it there in time."

Kate spent the night in Mama's apartment above the taverna.

The place was modest. Three bedrooms, two baths, a kitchen with a dining area, and a living room. It was small but homey, due largely to Mama's decorative touches, which included her grandmother's china displayed in a hutch near the dining table. Besides, it was convenient and safe. Twelve stairs down and you were at the back door of the taverna.

Kate and Molly lounged on the overstuffed couch, watching *Aladdin*. When Molly inevitably asked why they weren't going home, Kate told her, "Let's just call it a vacation at Mama's house."

"Are we on vacation for a long time?"

"I hope not too long, sunshine."

She put Molly to bed and kissed her the same way she had done a thousand times before; eye, eye, forehead, nose, cheek, cheek, lips. Molly was soon asleep, and Kate made a makeshift bed for herself on the floor. It was ironic, but she always felt safer sleeping next to her five-year-old. Listening to Molly's soft breathing, Kate fell into a deep, dreamless sleep.

The beeper went off just before first light. Kate was suddenly wide awake and pressed the button quickly so as not to wake Molly.

She tiptoed into the kitchen and picked up the phone.

"I got it, Kate," were the first words out of Spencer's mouth.

"Got what?"

"The data on the chip. It verifies your claim that something was wrong. It shows a gradual degradation in the aileron and rudder authority until they got to nil. Then it goes the other way."

"What do you mean?"

"The controls went haywire. They started doing their own thing."

"I don't understand. How—?"

"I don't know and that's not important right now. What is important is that you were right. Right all along, Kate."

"I . . . I . . ."

"It's over, honey. It's all over. I'll have the chip and the report in the FAA field office in Miami within the hour."

"I don't think they'll even be open yet."

"Then I'll pound on the door till somebody hears me."

"I don't know what to say."

"Don't say anything until I tell you the rest of it."

"There's more?"

"Oh yeah. The data continued to get recorded until the power to the computers was lost after the crash. I studied the tapes all the way to the end." He paused, then dropped the bombshell: "You were less than fifteen seconds away from complete flight control failure. Complete flight control failure, Kate. If you hadn't aborted the go-around . . . well, you know the rest."

Kate stood there holding the phone, her thoughts centered on that stormy night as she fought the controls. The rules had been clear, the procedures simple, but she hadn't followed any of them. What she had followed was a powerful force deep in her gut that told her to abort the flight and in the process break every rule in aviation safety and everything she had been trained to do. But she had been right. She had been right, dammit, and she had saved lives. The relief made her light-headed and she reached for the countertop to steady herself.

"Kate?"

"Sorry, Spence. I was just thinking."

"What's there to think? Go make yourself a margarita and have one for me."

"It's not even seven o'clock in the morning."

"Then make it a double. You're a hero."

She hesitated for another moment. "Thanks, Spence."

"You're welcome. Just don't forget how to spell my name when you get on *60 Minutes*."

"You know, you still can't go back home," she warned. "Not until this thing is settled."

"It *is* settled, Kate. It's over."

"Where are you?"

"In Sarasota. I flew in on Hill Air."

"You still have that old Cessna?"

"Hey, don't call her old. She's my baby."

"You're right. I'm sorry. But you still can't go home for another day or two. Please."

"Don't worry, I won't. Listen, I've got to hang up. I'll call you in a little bit. I'll also fax you a copy of the report if you tell me where."

"Fax it right here," she said, and gave him the number.

"You will have it within sixty minutes," he said. "And, Kate?"

"What?"

"Congratulations."

The first rays of the sun had begun to paint the eastern sky by the time Spencer Hill hung up the phone and walked to his plane, tied down at Crandall Field, a small airport south of Sarasota. He opened the door and threw in his bag. The air was still, the dawn silent.

Something to his left made a sound and he nearly jumped out of his skin. It was probably a rabbit running around in the bushes.

He smiled and shook his head. He wanted to be at home, in his warm bed with his wife. What the hell was he doing here, frightened by a little bunny.

He made a quick walk-around, kicked the tires, climbed in, and started the engine.

The Cessna was a mid-1950s model painted white with blue stripes. He had bought it years earlier, when he had first thought of retirement, and spent nearly two years restoring it. It was his pride and joy and one of the few luxuries he allowed himself. It was also a great way to travel.

"Crandall Unicom, Cessna Five Four Sierra Kilo is taking the active," he announced on the radio, bringing up the power a notch. He checked the RPM, the manifold pressure, and the temperature. Once he was satisfied with everything, he opened the throttle.

Spencer took off, climbed to fifteen hundred feet, and lowered the nose. Once he left the airport traffic area, he dropped down to less than a hundred feet. There he opened the throttles and watched the Everglades rush beneath him.

He could see every detail of the landscape: the brown-green color of the marshlands and the water flowing through them, the foliage, the occasional dwellings on hummocks out in the middle of nowhere.

It would be a short flight to Miami, forty-five minutes, maybe a little more. He was going to land, taxi right to the FAA ramp, march into the branch manager's office, hand him the chip and the report, and stand there, tapping his foot. He would then ask them to fax a copy to Kate, preferably with their apologies in bold print right along the bottom of the report. Hill smiled at the thought.

Forty miles out of Miami, he pulled back the yoke, and the Cessna began to climb to its intended altitude of three thousand feet. He dialed in the frequency and made the call.

"Miami approach, this is Cessna Five Four Sierra Kilo."

"Go ahead, Cessna Five Four Sierra Kilo, this is Miami approach."

"Roger, Five Four Sierra Kilo is a Cessna 172 Slash Tango, forty miles west of Miami at three thousand, requesting flight following and approach clearance into Miami."

"Roger, Five Four Sierra Kilo, Squawk 7243."

"That's 7243 coming up," Hill said, and reached for the transponder, but he didn't get to dial.

The fall was rapid and Spencer felt his stomach drop, as it would on a colossal roller coaster. He grabbed the controls but she seemed to have steadied herself. Everything but the violent shaking.

"What the hell was that?" he asked out loud. It didn't feel like turbulence or a malfunction. In fact, it didn't feel like anything he had ever encountered before. And what the hell was that shaking?

He trusted his airplane, having rebuilt it from scratch. He knew every nut and bolt. Suddenly, however, there was a nagging feeling in his gut, something that told him to be careful.

Instinctively he reached for the throttles and slowly brought back the power. Less power equaled less stress on the aircraft and that was always good.

He began to look around. He wasn't sure what he was looking for but something was definitely wrong. The instruments indicated nothing to that effect and the engine was running smoothly, so what was it?

Through the side window he looked at the elevators and the stabilizer. Maybe there was something there, something jammed. But there was nothing he could see.

As he resettled in his seat, he glanced at the wing above him and froze.

Below the left wing, he could see the steel cable that connected the yoke to the ailerons. Just aft of the connection, and in plain view, the steel cable was filed almost completely through. Hill looked in horror at the few strands of wire, which were slowly breaking away, their frayed and disintegrated ends twisting in the air.

Another strand snapped. He watched, powerless. How many were left? Three? Four?

He glanced down around him. Could he make it to the airport? he wondered. Could he make to any piece of land, or should he try to bring it down right now, in the Everglades? When he looked up, another strand broke off, then the next.

"No!" he cried as the last strand broke away.

In an instant, the aileron, pushed by the wind, deflected fully to the up position, turning the airplane violently to the left. A moment later, the deep blue of the morning sky disappeared and was replaced by the greens and browns of the Everglades as the Cessna turned upside down and began to free fall.

Hill neither screamed nor panicked. In one final effort, he stepped on the right rudder with all his might, trying to turn the yoke to the right, but with nothing to connect it to the flight controls, it lay limp in his hand.

The Cessna dove almost vertically, spinning down like a drill bit. Spencer couldn't take his eyes off the windshield, watching the marshland as the image grew larger and larger in this never-ending spiral from hell. Wincing in anticipation of pain greater than he had ever imagined, his teeth clenched, he struggled to bring the small plane back under control but couldn't manage it. What would it feel like? What would it feel like?

Somewhere between shock and acceptance, he looked at the picture on the dashboard. There were Norma and Amy, his youngest daughter. His other two daughters were there too, all smiling as they surrounded Spencer at one of his barbecues, standing there in his white apron and silly chef's hat.

He struggled with the controls, pushed and shoved and turned, his vision darting between the photograph and the ever closer image of the Everglades, until the very last turn. Then he turned to the picture.

"I love you."

"Cessna Five Four Sierra Kilo, this is Miami approach."

"Cessna Five Four Sierra Kilo, this is Miami approach. Come in, please."

chapter 26

Kate hung up, dressed quickly, and went downstairs to the back-room office. She stood by the fax machine, watching it, as if at any moment she expected it to flash red lights and announce to the world that she was innocent.

Two hours later, there was still no fax. By ten A.M., worry gave way to panic; something had gone wrong, she was sure of it.

She called his home but no one answered. She called the flight academy in Miami, just in case he had stopped off there, but she was told that he was still on vacation.

She couldn't stand to just hang around anymore; she had to do something. She asked Mama to page her if a fax came through and to keep a vigilant eye on Molly. She hugged her daughter and promised that she would be back in a few hours.

The dreaded low pressure that had been forecast for most of the preceding week had finally arrived and had brought with it cold wind, low temperatures, and a threat of more snow.

At the subway station, she bought a Metrocard, but before she got on the train she decided to make one last phone call. It was to the FAA field office at Miami International Airport. She asked to talk to the facility's manager.

"Hi, my name is Kate Gallagher and I'm looking for Mr. Spencer Hill. I believe he came to see you earlier today?"

"Who?"

"Spencer Hill. He's a tall man with red hair and fair skin."

"I'm sorry, I haven't seen anyone here all day. Are you sure you want this office?"

"Is this the FAA field office in Miami?"

"Yes."

"Is there another office nearby?"

"No, ma'am. This is it. Now if you don't mind I've got a lot of—"

"But he called me just a couple of hours ago. He was coming in to see you. He was bringing some files and documents regarding the Jet-East flight."

"I'm sorry. As I said, I haven't seen anyone here this morning. What time did you say he was coming in?"

"As soon as you opened. He called me early this morning from Sarasota. He was flying in his Cessna and he was going to put into—"

"What did you say his name was?"

"Hill, Spencer Hill."

"And he was flying in?"

"Yes, from Sarasota."

"Did he fly in commercially or—"

"No. He flew his own plane. What difference does that make?"

"What kind of plane? Do you know?"

Kate felt a familiar pang in her chest. "A Cessna. A little blue-and-white Cessna 172."

"Hang on a second, please."

The man was gone for a minute, maybe two, but they seemed the longest two minutes of Kate's life. She stood there at the phone booth, pressing the headset against her ear, covering her face with her other hand. The intense pain at the pit of her stomach, what she had suspected all along but was afraid to admit to, could no longer be ignored.

When the man came back on, the first thing he asked was, "What's your name, ma'am?"

"Kate Gallagher," she whispered weakly.

"You wouldn't by any chance have the tail number on that Cessna, would you?"

Kate didn't know the exact registration number, but she remembered the way Spencer always referred to it as the Sky King and that he had used those letters in the registry.

"It was something with the letters SK, Sierra Kilo."

"Ms. Gallagher, about two hours ago we had a report of an aircraft that went down about forty miles west of Miami International. We're not sure where the flight originated since no flight plan was filed, but the first rescue helicopter dispatched to the scene reported seeing scattered debris belonging to a small, blue-and-white high-wing aircraft. More rescue choppers were dispatched to the site, but as of now we've found no survivors." There was a long pause before the man said, "The tail number was Five Four Sierra Kilo."

Kate felt her heart rip in two; holding the phone clutched against her chest, she stared at the grimy tiled wall of the subway station.

"Ms. Gallagher? Ms. Gallagher?"

She dropped the phone and wrapped her arms around herself, staring mutely at the dangling receiver. He was dead. She knew it. She had felt it.

She began to stagger aimlessly through the station, staring blankly at the morning commuters, who dismissed her as a drunk. She felt weak and numb. She wanted to sit down, but the only bench was occupied.

She leaned against a wall and closed her eyes, knocking her head against the cold, dirty tile. She could see him now, as if he were there standing next to her, asking her what she wanted to do next. *Okay, so I'm dead,* he would say. *Let's deal with it and move on.*

She hit her head harder against the wall. She needed pain, more pain. What had she done? God, what had she done?

He was a father to her, a guide, a mentor. Now he was dead and it was her fault. She had killed him.

She wanted to cry, to pound her fists against the wall till they bled. Why couldn't she cry? Why wouldn't the damn tears come?

She began to walk again. She didn't know where she was going and it didn't matter. She wandered to the open door of a Manhattan-bound train and got on.

Kate stumbled off the subway at Grand Central Station feeling empty, as if all life had been drained from her. She wasn't thinking about herself, she hadn't gotten that far. She was thinking of Norma, Spencer's wife, and his daughters. Sometime this morning they would get a call that would start with, "I'm sorry to have to tell you this. . . ."

She sat on a bench and buried her face in her hands, she couldn't understand how life continued to go on all around her. Spencer was dead. Didn't these people know that?

Ten feet away, at a shoe-shine stand, a radio was playing, but Kate paid little attention. . . . Until she heard her name.

The show was called *The Patriot.* It was an exposé of

"the misguided and wasteful policies of the recent Democratic administrations and how these failed policies had eroded the very fiber of decency and morality in America"—at least that was how the Reverend Bruno Cantwell opened the show. It had never been quite clear what school of divinity had afforded Cantwell's ministerial credentials, but his "congregation" of talk-radio addicts couldn't have cared less. Bruno Cantwell offered fresh, bleeding red meat on every show.

One of his favorite targets, equal opportunity employment, was the subject of today's segment, which was being broadcast live from the hospital room of one Mr. Edmond Bell, the co-pilot of the ill-fated Jet-East flight 394, who was currently undergoing a series of MRIs at New York University Hospital.

"Now, you said in previous statements that it was the captain, Kate Gallagher, who aborted the flight. Is that correct?" the minister asked in his heavy southern accent.

"Yes, that's correct," Bell replied.

"I have here unofficial transcripts from an interview you gave the NTSB, in which you said you thought that she panicked and caused this accident. Is that correct?"

"Well, I can't really discuss the accident with you. The ongoing investigation is still . . ."

"Listen, son, I realize that she has the right to have her day in court and I'm not asking you to jeopardize those rights, but the public has rights too. This pilot panicked and caused six people to die. Many others were injured. How would you feel if your wife and child were on a flight piloted by someone who was hired to fill a quota?"

"Was she hired to fill a quota?" Bell sounded genuinely surprised.

"You didn't know that, did you? Neither did the two

hundred and thirteen other people on the Jet-East flight that night. She was hired not because she was the best person for that job but because she was a woman and because the liberal politicians in Washington had decided that it was the politically correct thing to do. They ignored the public's interest and they ignored the statistics, which indicate that women cause seventy percent of the near-misses and accidents in aviation in this country. And now they're even putting them in combat planes, behind the wheel of two hundred-million-dollar airplanes, not because they're the best for the job but because that's what gets the votes."

"Are you sure she was hired on a quota?"

"I have the facts right here."

"Well, that figures," Bell said.

"Why do you say that?"

"Let's just say, I'm not surprised. Had I known that earlier, I would probably have done some things differently, if you know what I mean."

Kate didn't wait. She ran to the exit as if she were on fire. Outside, she pushed an outraged businessman out of the way and jumped into the cab he was about to get into. One look at her face, and the driver simply asked, "Where to?"

The cab cut over on Forty-second Street and turned down Second Avenue. Kate was at the hospital in a matter of minutes.

She rushed through the main entrance and over to the information desk. "What room is Edmond Bell in?"

An astonished receptionist looked up. "And you are . . . ?"

"I'm his sister."

"Room 325, left down the hall from the elevator and—"

Kate didn't wait for the elevator or the directions.

She ran up three flights of stairs and burst through the door. Two security guards in blue uniforms stood at the entrance to room 325, blocking her way.

"I need to go in there!"

"Who are you with?"

"I'm his sister," she said, her eyes cold and defiant.

The man looked at her, then looked at his clipboard. "I don't see a sister on this list. You have to wait until the show is over."

"I don't care about any damn show. I want to go in there," Kate said, moving forward.

"Well, you can't," the man responded, holding his hand out.

"Listen. I don't want to fight with you. All I want to do is talk to your boss. Now, go in there and tell him that Kate Gallagher is here and wants to see him. And if I don't see him in less than thirty seconds, he'll have a lawsuit on his hands that's as big as his ego."

The guard didn't respond.

"Twenty-five seconds," Kate said, looking at her watch.

Hesitant, he looked at the other guard and said, "Don't let her go in there." He turned and opened the door.

Kate stood there until the guard came back out. He held the door open, letting her in.

Edmond Bell's face was as white as the robe he was wearing. He was sitting up in bed, a microphone clipped to his collar. Two men were sitting at a round-table control panel, handling audio levels and the link to the radio station.

Reverend Bruno Cantwell, dressed in a well-cut pinstripe suit, was sitting in a chair next to the bed, his few long, thin strands of dyed-black hair painfully combed across his nearly bald head.

"Ms. Gallagher, what a pleasant surprise," he said, as he rose to shake her hand, but Kate didn't offer hers. A true pro, he ignored the slight and turned to face the mike. He could feel the ratings rocket. "Ladies and gentlemen, we have an added bonus for you today. We have in our presence Ms. Kate Gallagher, the pilot of the Jet-East flight and the central figure in this controversy."

One of the technicians hurried toward Kate and clipped a microphone to her collar.

"We were joined by Ms. Gallagher just a few moments ago, under the threat of a lawsuit. We have invited her to join the discussions since we always encourage an open forum. Ms. Gallagher, why don't you give us your version of what happened up there?"

Kate didn't say anything. She looked at him and Edmond Bell with a glare that would melt rock. Bell had suddenly become intensely interested in the plastic hospital I.D. around his left wrist.

"Ms. Gallagher, you wanted to be in here, so please go ahead."

She still didn't say anything.

"Ms. Gallagher?"

She shifted her disgusted stare from Bell to Cantwell, then said calmly, "You were right. You were both right. I aborted the flight, which caused the plane to crash."

The minister was caught off guard. "Uh . . . why . . . ?"

"The investigation will explain all that in due course, and when it does, the world will see you for the liar you truly are."

"Now, wait a minute."

"I've waited a long time. Now it's your turn."

"You can't just barge in here and tell me—"

"You can cut the transmission or you can try to throw me out. But you're going to hear me. *Now*."

Cantwell sat back and locked his beefy fingers over his belly.

"You said that I was hired to fill a quota. Why did you say that?"

"Because it's true."

"Then prove it. Show me your facts."

"Well, I have reliable sources."

"Perhaps you could share one of them with us, show me a document, anything that proves your point."

"I can get you the information."

"Go ahead. I'll wait."

"Well, I . . . I didn't say I had it right here."

"I see. You also rattled off some statistics. I think it was seventy percent of the accidents and near-misses were caused by women, isn't that correct?"

"Yes."

"Where are those facts, Mr. Cantwell?"

"Now, what is this? You expect me to carry around verification on everything that I say?"

"There is no proof, is there? They're all lies. You sit there in your fancy suit and you play God and you don't even consider the ramifications of your work. But what if you're wrong—have you thought about that? What if there was a malfunction, and instead of helping to identify it, you and your protégé here have chosen to exploit it. You've turned this tragedy into a circus act. But you're wrong. I know you're wrong. And it's only a matter of time before the rest of the world knows too."

"Are you finished?"

"Not yet." She stared him down with open hatred. "You said the politicians are doing everything to further their agendas; to win elections. What's your agenda, Mr. Cantwell? Why are you here?"

"I don't have an agenda. I'm a public—"

"You're an opportunistic liar and a media whore. You would stand in Times Square and sell your soul to the highest bidder if that meant another point in the ratings. You don't care about public interest, you don't care about anything but Bruno Cantwell. You make me sick. And as for you"—she turned to Bell—"I know why he's doing this, but why are you?"

He kept his head down and avoided looking at her.

When it became clear that he was effectively silenced, she tore the microphone from her collar, threw it on the bed, and stalked out.

chapter **27**

Davis Thompson stood admiring the glistening white plane. He wanted to take his time, to relish the moment.

Three days from now, he would be sitting in this very hangar. With the Jetstar logo in the background, he would participate in a ceremony that would mark the end of Searchlight as it had existed for twenty-five years. The newly formed company, a division of Austin Enterprises, would be a leader in wireless technology and satellite communication.

Soon after the ceremony, some highly compromising photographs of Marshall Hayes would find their way to the tabloids. There would be a scandal, a mind-reelingly embarrassing one; there might even be pressure from the top for Marshall Hayes to resign. Thompson smiled with anticipation.

The arrangement was simple. In a reverse merger, Austin, the larger of two companies, would absorb Searchlight in a stock swap. But the Searchlight name would be retained, while actual control would be in the hands of Austin's board and management—and Davis Thompson. They couldn't afford someone like Hayes at the helm, once the photographs were made public. The old man would be given his golden parachute and put out to pasture, where he belonged.

It would all start here, with the signing ceremony followed by a press conference.

Thompson envisioned it again. Bleachers and chairs filled with people: top executives from both companies, Wall Street, and the media. This was Davis Thompson's forte, what he was born to do. They would shake hands, sign papers and pose for the cameras. The ceremony would conclude with a special treat. The new aircraft, the Jetstar V, was being equipped with STAR II, the latest technology that satellite navigation and communications had to offer. The executives and members of the press would be given a hand for this once-in-a-lifetime chance to test the capabilities of the new system.

The airplane at the end of the hangar was now being worked on by a variety of people. There were maintenance personnel, tech services and others, all there to ensure that all systems were in perfect working order.

As Thompson walked toward the aircraft he saw Richard Malkovich holding a clipboard and talking with someone. Thompson waited until he was finished and beckoned him over.

"What are you doing here? I thought you were supposed to be working on the antivirus," Thompson whispered.

"Well, I can do that, or I can do this. I can't do both. We're having a problem with the PCME. I don't think it's a RAM problem, because that's built in, so we're now having to check all the circuit cards and then we have to—"

"All right, all right," Thompson interrupted impatiently. "Is it serious or can you fix it?"

"I can fix it," Malkovich replied confidently.

"Good. Nothing can be allowed to go wrong during the test. The whole world will be watching."

"Nothing will go wrong."

Thompson nodded. "How about the antivirus?"

"It's almost complete. We give it away as a free upgrade. The antivirus is hidden deep within the subdirectory root, no one will ever see it. Once it runs, any system that has been damaged by the virus will be fixed and nobody will be any the wiser."

"Is there any way they can find out that the antivirus is inside the other program?"

"No. The commands will run at incredible speeds. Once the software is installed, it will backdate itself to the date that the original STAR software was installed and then erase the antivirus program. It's quite simple really."

"How long will it take to install the patch on all the planes involved?"

"The procedure takes minutes. You just have to get the software patch to the customers."

Thompson put his arm around Malkovich's shoulders. "You're a genius, you know that? You're a genius."

"Yeah, I know."

Kate had thought that speaking her mind, putting the "Reverend" Cantwell in his place, would make her feel better, give her some satisfaction. But it hadn't. She felt weak and nauseated as she marched down the hallway. At the elevator, she pressed the Down button. A moment later the doors opened.

"Ms. Gallagher, what are you doing here?" Michael O'Rourke asked as he stepped out.

"I came to see my first officer," she replied sadly and got into the elevator.

Just as the doors began to close, O'Rourke said, "Wait," and stuck his hand between them.

The doors reopened and he walked back in, but neither of them spoke. Kate crossed and went out the exit in the lobby without even looking back. O'Rourke shook his head and ran after her.

"Wait one minute," he shouted.

Kate turned. "What is it, Mr. O'Rourke?"

"What were you doing there?"

"I told you I wanted to talk to Bell."

"Now, why don't I believe that?"

"Why doesn't that surprise me? You haven't believed a thing I've said since day one." Kate walked away.

"I'm not your damn enemy, you know," O'Rourke called after her.

She stopped on the sidewalk, her back to him. He ran up to her and they began to walk along together.

Kate finally broke the silence. "Have you ever heard of the Reverend Bruno Cantwell?"

"Yeah?"

"He was in there interviewing Bell. They were talking about the flight and the captain and how she screwed up."

O'Rourke laughed.

"What's funny?" Kate snapped.

"I'm sorry, it's not funny. It's just that I've seen you angry and I feel sorry for those poor bastards. Are they still in the land of the living?"

Kate smiled. "I'm not that bad. It's just been a difficult time. How about you? Why were you at the hospital?"

"I wanted to have a chat with Edmond Bell."

"What about?"

"His statements. There were some inconsistencies."

"What kind of inconsistencies?"

"Just some minor details." O'Rourke paused. "Hell,

who am I kidding? I just wanted to make him sweat, get some truth out of him."

Kate stopped and turned. "Why?"

"Because I don't think he's telling the whole story, or at least he's letting his opinions cloud his judgment."

"His opinions about what? Me?"

"Perhaps. Perhaps women in general. I don't know."

"Why are you doing this?"

"Why are you doing this, why are you doing that? Why are you always asking questions?"

Kate smiled. "I don't bring out the best in you, do I?"

O'Rourke repaid her with a smile of his own. *If only you knew*, he thought. "Where are you going?"

"I don't know." Kate sighed. "I just need to walk."

"Then will you let me buy you lunch?"

Kate didn't look up. "Why not."

They grabbed two hot dogs and sodas from a street vendor and took a seat on the stone steps of a church. O'Rourke brushed the hair away from his face for the umpteenth time and took a bite. Kate stared at him meditatively, as if she were seeing him for the first time.

He was well built and very fit, not because he spent lengthy hours in a gym but because of his love of the outdoors. His passion was basketball; it was something that had stayed with him since childhood. He could play the game and rattle off statistics and if you ever wanted to know the Knicks schedule, all you had to do was ask.

"Why did you get into this business, Mr. O'Rourke?" Kate asked as she took a bite.

"I was born and raised out in Queens. My parents still live there and most of my friends are the same guys I used to shoot hoops with twenty years ago. It was a pretty close-knit group of people, mostly Irish and Italian. My sister Charlotte used to go out with this one guy, Bobby Malone, who was a friend, well . . . still is." He laid down his hot dog and wiped his mouth with a napkin.

"Anyhow, Charlotte had a friend whose father was a doctor and also a pilot. One day he put his whole family in a little Cherokee and they asked Charlotte to go along on a skiing trip. The weather got bad up in the Catskills and he got lost. He couldn't climb, because he would go into the clouds, so he descended and found himself in a box canyon. The weather was getting really bad, wind, snow, you name it. He panicked and tried to bring the plane down on a farm road. The little Bonanza flipped three times. The rest of what happened wasn't clear, but there was an explosion and two of the family members died."

"And your sister?"

"Charlotte shattered two vertebrae just below the neck. She was instantly paralyzed. I guess she was the lucky one."

"Where is she now?"

"At home. With my parents. They take care of her."

"I'm so sorry."

"That was over twenty years ago. Ancient news," O'Rourke said, removing his glasses. "You know, the funny thing is, I still see Bobby Malone. In fact I'm his son's godfather. I go over to his house and his wife cooks this great meal and is real hospitable and everything, but I can't help thinking that it should have been my sister standing there. Isn't that terrible? I love his wife and I wish her nothing but the best, but I still keep thinking that somehow Charlotte got cheated, that what they have should have been her life."

Kate didn't know what to say. She placed her hand on his arm.

"See what you do to me?" O'Rourke asked, taking a sip of his drink. "How about you? How did you get into the airplane business?"

Kate put her soda on the steps. "On my eighteenth birthday, one of my friends dared me to go up in an airplane with her and jump out. It was one those beginners parachute-jumping deals—you know, the ones where you go in the morning, take a couple of hours of training, and then jump in the afternoon."

O'Rourke nodded.

"I went in the airplane, the first time I had ever been on one, and we took off. When the time came to jump, six people out of the eight backed out."

"You're kidding."

"No."

"Obviously you were one of the two who jumped."

"Yeah. Me and one other guy. He was in his sixties and it was his birthday."

"So your friend, the one who dared you, she didn't even go?"

"No. I still tease her about it."

"Then what happened?"

"Nothing. I went back. I jumped a dozen more times before I realized that it wasn't the ride down, but the ride up, that I was hooked on. I don't know what it was, maybe it was the feeling of freedom I felt, the control, but it changed my life, the way I saw things. Before that, I'd been shy and thought that you lived a life that was planned for you. All of a sudden I realized that I had it all wrong. That it was up to me to choose my life, not the other way around." Kate looked at him, feeling embarrassed. "It's . . . hard to explain."

"If it is, you're doing a damn good job of it."

Kate smiled.

"I spent a couple of years at the old Flushing Airport and got a job at one of the FBOs, doing odds and ends, pumping gas in the planes, what have you. I got my ratings, taught flying for a while, one thing led to another, and here we are."

"I think it was fate," O'Rourke said.

She raised an eyebrow.

"You don't believe in fate? That's what brought us here today, you know."

"It wasn't fate. It was Edmond Bell."

"Him again. He still pisses you off, doesn't he?"

"I can deal with Edmond Bell. I've dealt with Edmond Bells all my life. It's the rest of it—the fact that I can't get anyone to believe me."

"We'll find the truth. I promise you . . ."

"You won't find anything because they won't let you," she said bitterly.

"What are you talking about? Who won't?"

"Thanks for lunch, Mr. O'Rourke," Kate said, collecting her trash.

"Who won't?" O'Rourke repeated but Kate didn't respond. She got up and began to walk away.

"Answer me, dammit. Who won't?" O'Rourke grabbed her hand.

She turned and looked at his hand, holding hers. He let go. "The same people who came into the hangar in night-vision glasses. The same people who did away with Brita Ames and her children," she said loudly. Then she whispered, "The same people who killed Spencer Hill."

O'Rourke sat on the steps, looking up at her in bewilderment.

"Now, will you please let me go and deal with my problem?" Kate said, beginning to turn.

"No." He got up behind her. "No, I won't let you go deal with your *problem*. I'm involved with this situation on two levels. On a professional level, I'm in charge of it. That means that if you have information that's relevant to this investigation, it's your duty to let me know and my duty to find out. On a personal level . . ." He hesitated. "Dammit, why do you have to make this so hard?"

"Because you won't believe me. Because no one will believe me and I don't have the time to stand around and try to convince you," Kate shouted.

"So you're not even going to try?" O'Rourke shouted back.

She stood there angry and frustrated. Then she thought, *Maybe this is worth it. Maybe this is worth a shot.*

They found a coffeeshop and sat down in a corner booth. Both ordered peach pie, the house specialty, and Kate told him the rest of the story. She left out nothing.

When she finished, she watched his face, looking for a reaction. Maybe he would shake his head in disbelief and call her a liar. Maybe he'd simply get up and go, leaving her sitting there. But he didn't do either of those things. He pointed his finger at her, and said, "You owe me a Knicks game."

She wanted to ask what he was talking about, but he didn't give her a chance. Michael O'Rourke reached for his cell phone, and pulled out the antenna. He dialed the number and waited.

"Sherry, this is Mike. I need you to cancel everything for the next two days. I'm not sure where I'll be, but I'll be in touch. One more thing. There are two tickets for the Knicks–Lakers game tonight in my desk drawer. Put them to good use."

chapter 28

What the hell does he mean?" Thompson shouted. His voice attracted the attention of several mourners gathered around a casket a short distance away. Thompson lowered his voice. "What does he mean, 'You will pay. One way or the other, you'll pay?' What's he gonna do? Crash another plane?"

The men were walking on a paved pathway between rows of snow-covered graves. Gray skies loomed in every direction, and though there was no snow now, the cold wind that blew across the cemetery was a clear indication that more was on the way.

Cordelia lifted his head from the single page of white paper he was reading. "When did this come in?"

"Just when I called you. The e-mail was waiting for me like the first two. I printed it, then deleted it."

"Does Hayes know?"

"Hell no," Thompson whispered. "The son of a bitch would write the check before he even read the damn thing. He's so anxious to pay, he doesn't even care about leaving tracks." He stopped, his blue eyes riveted on Cordelia. "If this thing ever comes out, if anyone ever finds out about this . . ." Thompson didn't finish his sentence. He didn't have to.

"It won't come to that," Cordelia responded.

"How the hell can you say that?"

"They would have to prove that you knew about the e-mails. It would be impossible. No knowledge, no liability."

Thompson considered this for a moment. "Other than you and I, three other people know about this. Hayes, Malkovich—"

"And whoever is sending the e-mails," Cordelia finished the thought. "We're watching the first two. And I'll get you the third one."

The men paused. Then Thompson asked, "How about the chip?"

"That's another thing I wanted to talk to you about. The guy's name was Spencer Hill. . . ."

"Was?"

"Yeah. He's dead."

"How?"

"He took the chip to Sarasota to some electronics specialist. I had a team go in to get a copy of the report. It's pretty incriminating."

"And the chip?"

"He was on his way to the authorities with it. He was going back to Miami in a little Cessna, but never got there. His plane went down somewhere over the Everglades."

"Did you . . . ?"

"No, we had nothing to do with it. We were going to stop him in Miami when he landed. I had men waiting there with orders to stop him at whatever cost. But turns out we didn't have to."

"The chip. How about the damn chip?"

"It's gone. Somewhere at the bottom of the Everglades. They'll never find it. And we destroyed all copies of the report so there's no way they can trace anything to you or Searchlight."

"What do you know about the crash?"

"It was sudden, no warnings. He had owned the airplane for a long time, he was an experienced pilot, and—"

"He was murdered?"

"It's a strong possibility."

"By whom?"

"I don't know. Maybe our friend, the one sending the e-mails."

"Stop calling him my friend," Thompson snapped.

"Well, do you think it was him?" Cordelia asked.

"Maybe. But you need money and power to get that kind of information and use it."

"Then who? Hayes?"

Thompson didn't respond. He was gazing into the distance, at the funeral service, which had come to a conclusion. A handful of people gathered around the grave began to slowly walk away. Two men with shovels moved in.

"Life's for the living, Bob. Take what you can and do it now, because sooner or later you'll end up six feet under and after that nothing matters."

Cordelia looked confused.

"It was Austin," Thompson added. "It's the only thing that makes sense. They need this deal more than I thought."

There was a long pause, then Cordelia asked, "What do you want me to do?"

"Find out who's blackmailing me before Austin does," Thompson snapped. "Find out who's behind all this. I need to show Austin that I'm in control. I need to show them that I can take care of my own backyard."

"We're close. We're very close."

"What about the woman in Key West and her kids?" Thompson asked.

"I've got the recording right here."

"I can't listen to it now. Just tell me what it says."

Cordelia cupped his large hands in front of his mouth and blew into them. Looking toward the men who were lowering the casket into the ground, he said, "The day before yesterday, Brita Ames got a call at nine-eighteen in the morning. The caller's voice was disguised. He told her that her husband's death was not a suicide. He told her about Searchlight and about the virus."

"What the hell . . . ?"

"Exactly. Brita Ames called Gallagher. Twice. She wanted to talk. We had to take her out before she did more harm."

"What does that mean? You didn't kill her, did you?"

"No. But she's bought and paid for and, for the time being, living in a condo on Seven Mile Beach in the Caymans."

"But she knows."

"What is she going to do? She has nothing. No money, no savings, no home. All she has is a phone call and she doesn't even have proof of that. Besides, she's got those two little kids to worry about; she's for sale. Anyway, we're watching her."

Thompson let the new information sink in, then asked, "Why would he do that? Why would the black-mailer call her?"

"That's what puzzles me," Cordelia said thoughtfully. "He had nothing to gain by telling the widow about all this."

"Unless . . . ." Thompson paused. "Unless it's his way of warning us. First he calls her. Then this e-mail. That's the only explanation."

"You think he knows we were listening?"

"Of course he knows we were listening. He also knows we would be watching her. He seems to know more than you give him credit for."

"I'll find him."

"I hope so," Thompson said. "How about Gallagher? Don't underestimate her, Bob, she has a fire in her—she's not going to give up."

"She's got to be running scared. But just to make sure . . ." Cordelia paused, ensuring that no one could overhear, "just to make sure, I've got something planned for her that will get the message across."

"What are you going to do?"

"It'll be safe and it'll be effective," Cordelia replied. "Do you have anything else for me?"

"No."

Cordelia nodded and walked away.

They were close, very close, Thompson thought. He could feel it. The stars in his universe were either aligned or about to explode all around him.

Kate and O'Rourke were met by two members of the NTSB at Miami International Airport and driven directly to the helicopter pad. The Bell Ranger was already warming up by the time the green sedan pulled up alongside it.

"We have to get there before dark," O'Rourke shouted over the sound of the rotors. "We only have another hour or so."

Kate took her seat, somber and silent.

With the four passengers strapped in, the pilot increased the power on the collective and gently pushed on the cyclic. The Ranger slowly lifted off the ground, hovering for a moment before flying west.

The flight took approximately fifteen minutes, fifteen minutes that were spent in absolute silence, each person in the cabin staring dead ahead. A few miles out, the pilot gestured to something and everyone turned to look.

There were two crafts in the swamp below, a salvage boat and an airboat with a distinctive big-bladed fan on its stern. They were anchored next to each other. As the chopper began to descend, more of the details came into view. There were men aboard both of the boats. They were looking up at the helicopter, waiting for the team to inspect the wreck before salvage work began.

Kate could see the small pieces of the wreckage now, the tail of the plane, a section of the body, the letters S and K written next to each other, torn away from the rest of the fuselage.

The helicopter hovered over the boats, the backwash from the blades flattening the foliage that surrounded them. It slowly came to rest on a mound of dirt about forty feet from the boats. The salvage boat had begun a slow approach to the hummock as they landed.

"We've been waiting for you," a tall black man told O'Rourke. He, like the other two men, was wearing a blue jacket and baseball cap with NTSB printed on them in bright yellow. "Why the big guns? I thought they saved you guys in Washington for the really important stuff."

O'Rourke pointed to the wreckage. "This is as important as it gets."

The boat carried them over to the crash site, where the remains of Spencer's plane were strewn over a relatively small area. The salvage craft began to circle.

"There isn't much to see," the man told O'Rourke. "We've sent for high-resolution sonar equipment to see if we can find the bigger pieces. The visibility in this water is only a foot or two, so the divers will pretty much have to feel their way around. It's pretty hairy."

Kate struggled to control her emotions. She sat in

the back corner of the boat, her gaze directed down at the murky water, the lump in her throat so large that she could barely swallow. *What have I done?* she kept asking herself. She felt like she was trapped in a bad dream that wouldn't end. Was it just six days ago that she had rolled down the runway in Chicago, on the last leg of her journey home?

The boat moved closer to the center of the crash site. Still, not much was visible. It was impossible to tell where the engine or the cockpit was, and there was no sign of Spencer's body. "He may be down ten feet, buried in the mud at the bottom," Kate heard one of the investigators say, shortly before O'Rourke hushed him up. He came and sat next to her.

"I'm sorry," he whispered.

She didn't answer.

They stayed at the site until dark, even though it was pointless to search for the chip. Other than small pieces of wreckage, all they found was the aircraft registration certificate still encased in a plastic cover.

O'Rourke handed it to Kate. She took it and examined it. "I want to go to the family. I want to be with them," she said.

"They were told this morning," O'Rourke replied. "They've gone to stay with some relatives on the coast."

Kate shook her head and grinned bitterly, her eyes filled with incredible sadness. "I couldn't even do that much for him."

When dusk began to settle, it was time to leave. That was the hardest part. She felt as though she were abandoning Spencer, leaving him there at the bottom of the muck to rot for all eternity. O'Rourke sensed her pain.

"We'll get him out of there, I promise you that much," he said, then he pointed to the chopper, its rotors turning.

As the Bell Ranger slowly lifted off, Kate leaned

her head against the cool glass window in the cabin. The raw pain deep in her gut was overwhelming, yet she welcomed it. With her eyes glued to where her friend lay, the helicopter flew east, away from the setting sun.

chapter **29**

Nine . . . eight . . . seven . . ."
Thompson gripped the arms of his chair.
"Six . . . five . . . four . . ."

He was squeezing now, pressing so hard his knuckles were white.

"Three . . . Main engine ignition. Two . . . one . . ."

The explosion was simultaneous with the count. The plume of smoke expanded, rising in every direction. The engines thundered as they reached maximum thrust. In the center of it all was the exhilarating image of the white Ariane IV rocket shimmering against the night sky as it slowly left the Earth.

The room exploded in cheers as the rocket cleared the gantry. Thompson himself could barely control his excitement. But he maintained his composure and refrained from screaming and whistling like the thirty other people who crowded the room.

The live broadcast was intended for a select audience—the people of Searchlight who at this very moment were huddled around some sixty monitors throughout the building, watching with pride and shaking hands, as the fourteenth in a series of sixty-three satellites began its journey into orbit.

As Davis Thompson watched, he felt a mixture of emotions. His brainchild, his dream and years of work, was one step closer to reality, and that was room enough for significant self-congratulation. But there were new concerns and apprehension; maybe even fear.

His new partners at Austin Enterprises were aggressive and ambitious. They were young and ruthless, and, to a large degree, they reminded him of himself— but they were also dangerous. They knew Searchlight's terrible secret and they had killed Spencer Hill; Thompson was convinced of that. They had killed him to protect the deal and to protect their interests.

If he was right, it was even more disturbing to realize that Austin must have moles at the uppermost levels of Searchlight. What else had they done? What else were they capable of?

On the big-screen TVs in the videoconference room, the feed from French Guiana was still focused on the Ariane rocket as it accelerated into space. The men and women in the room were still glancing at the screen, but they had started to move around now, some stopping to shake Thompson's hand and congratulate him on a job well done. He smiled back and shook hands, trying to ignore his mounting fears about Austin.

The door to the conference room flew open and an out-of-breath Kyle Hayes ran in. He went straight to where Thompson was sitting and took the chair next to his.

"I missed it? I missed the damn launch?"

Thompson pointed to the screen; the rocket was a small dot, the fire from the thrusters barely a glimmer.

"Damn," Kyle said. "They kept me on the phone this whole time and I couldn't get off."

"Who?"

"Austin, who else. Who else would I miss the launch for?"

"What's up?" asked a suddenly alert Thompson.

"They wanted to talk about the STAR system, something about its range and capabilities. When I offered to let them talk to someone from tech support, they said no, they wanted to talk to me."

"Why you?"

"I don't know. I guess they're more comfortable with me. The last time they came here, I spent a lot of personal time with them. All you guys ever did was talk about the deal."

"Well, what did they want?" Thompson impatiently demanded.

"I told you, technical data. I told them what I could and told them to talk to tech support," Kyle replied, his attention still on the screen.

"And then?" Thompson asked.

"Nothing. They said they wanted to talk to you."

"Talk to me about what?"

"I don't know, Davis. Call them. Maybe you can get out of going there."

"Going where?" Thompson asked, grabbing Kyle's arm.

"Oh, I'm sorry," Kyle said as he turned away from the screen. "They want to see you. They wouldn't tell me why, but then again, they never really told me much."

"Well, do they want me to bring anything, or . . ."

"No. They want to see only you. Sounds pretty confidential."

Thompson was chewing the tip of his pen. "When do they want to see me?"

"Tomorrow."

"Where?"

"In their head office. I've already made the arrangements."

"They want me to go to London? We sign in three days, dammit, and they want me to go to London? What the hell is going on?"

"I told you, I don't know. They said for you to come alone. A limo will meet you at Heathrow and take you back a few hours later. They wouldn't tell me anything else, but hell, it was Austin. I couldn't exactly tell them you wouldn't meet with them, you know what I mean?"

Thompson leaned back in his chair and turned away. Why did they want him now? Did this have something to do with the virus? Of course it did, he told himself. Why else would they want him to go all the way across the Atlantic just three days before signing the deal? What other possible reason could they have?

Thompson immediately decided to beat Austin to the punch. He would go to London and level with them. He would tell them all about the blackmailer and the virus—everything. Hell, they knew it all anyhow, so what did he have to lose? He would pitch it to them straight and tell them that he had the antivirus patch. It was simply a matter of time before they neutralized any threat.

Besides, they had asked *him* to come see them, not Hayes or anyone else. That couldn't be all bad, could it? They trusted him more, needed him more. Maybe this wasn't all that bad after all.

All of a sudden he felt good again, confident. He could deal with the Austin boys on their terms.

"I guess I'm going to London," he said.

"What should I tell Marshall?" Kyle asked.

"Tell him just what they told you: that they asked for me to come alone," Thompson replied, turning to

Kyle. "He doesn't want you to hang around me, you know."

"I can handle my father."

"You two aren't that close, are you?"

"We disagree more than we agree." Kyle grinned.

"What would you do if he wasn't here anymore?"

"You mean, if he quit or something?"

"Yeah."

"He'll never resign. My father will die in the chairman's chair."

"Let's just say that he did. How would you feel about it?"

Kyle thought before he answered. "My father has lived a full life, more than his share. The rest of us are just beginning."

Thompson smiled and put his hand on Kyle's shoulder. "You have a bright future here, Mr. Kyle Hayes, you know that? A bright future."

It was just past three A.M. when the van pulled onto Broadway. The driver turned north on Thirty-fifth Street, parked, killed the engine, and turned off the headlights. The side door opened and two men wearing dark clothing got out. The one in the lead was carrying a small black leather bag. Half a block away, they walked through the alley to the back door of Athena's Taverna.

In a matter of seconds they had picked the lock and gently pushed the door open, hesitating only for a moment to confirm what they already knew—the restaurant had a fire alarm and smoke detectors, but no burglar alarm. The man carrying the bag carefully entered and the other followed, quietly closing the door behind him. They crept through a narrow hallway into the main dining room.

The restaurant was dark and cold. The chairs had

been turned upside down and placed on top of the tables so that the cleaners could mop the terra-cotta floor.

The men went into the kitchen, pointing a soft green light into every nook and crevice. When they didn't find what they were looking for, they returned to the hallway and silently began to open every door. They stopped to look into one of the rooms. There were some old cleaning rags in a tin bucket, cardboard boxes filled with provisions, an exposed wood floor. Enough—but not too much.

The man carrying the bag went into the storage room, set down his bag, aimed the flashlight inside, and pulled out what looked like a large piece of brown cardboard. He removed a strip from the edge of the paper, filling the small room with the pungent smell of sulfur. Then he placed an igniter on top of the rags, moved the bucket closer to the electrical outlet, and exited the storage room, closing the door behind him. He gave a signal to his partner and led the way out of the restaurant.

The idea was not to harm the family, just to scare them. Cordelia had been very specific on that point. The men were to go outside, watch the fire, and, if it got out of control, call 911. No one was to get hurt.

They sat in the van and waited. It took nearly ten minutes before the first faint flickers of the flames were noticeable through the taverna's windows. The men looked at each other as the glow went from dull to bright very quickly, but they heard no fire bells.

There were three smoke detectors, one in the main entry and two in the seating area. They had photographed them the same way they had photographed every other detail on their several visits to the restaurant. They even had pictures of the outmoded chemical fire extinguishers installed over the range, that had to be discharged manually. Why the hell weren't any fire alarms going off? Maybe the detectors weren't hooked up to any kind of an alarm. Maybe they were going off inside the restaurant, but above them in the apartment, they could not be heard.

The glow got brighter; now they could see the fire spreading out of the storage room and working its way through the main sitting area; it was moving much faster than they had anticipated. They looked around to see if anyone had noticed, but the streets were deserted.

One of them got out of the van, ran to a pay phone at the corner, and dialed 911. The operator picked up, but before he had a chance to say anything, he heard the explosion. In terror he turned and looked at the taverna. The entire front of the restaurant was now ablaze, the fire rushing out of the shattered windows and the apartment upstairs.

"A building just blew up" the man said, then dropped the receiver so that the location and number could be traced, then he raced back to the van. They stayed there another minute, watching as the first residents of nearby buildings stuck their heads out of their windows. Then they slowly pulled out and drove off.

Upstairs, Mama, shaken by the explosion, hurriedly put on her blue-and-white checkered robe. She opened the door and was greeted by a wall of fire in the hallway. She walked toward it, covering her nose and mouth and trying to breathe through the smoke and heat.

She had been sleeping in the living room, close to the phone in case Kate called, but the living room and Molly's bedroom were separated by the fiery hallway. The explosion had buckled the floor, and flames were shooting through the old building, encompassing everything.

Mama shouted for Molly, with what little oxygen

she had left in her lungs. More than once she attempted to cross the hall but was driven back by the intense heat.

She ran back into the living room, dialed 911, and was told that help was on the way.

"My granddaughter is trapped in a bedroom!" she shouted into the receiver. Not waiting for a response, she dropped the phone and ran back to the hallway. She got there just as the second explosion rocked the building. The force of this one was so intense that it threw Mama back several feet, where she knocked her head against the wall and fell to the floor.

Then she heard another bang. Her head spinning and her stomach heaving, she looked up. Two firefighters wearing respirators had broken down the door and rushed up the stairs.

"There." She pointed through the flames. "There, please. My granddaughter . . ."

"We'll get her," one of the firemen said, his voice muffled by his respirator mask. "You have to go down. That's the best you can do for her."

"No. I'm not leaving."

The firefighter pointed to the next one and a third, who had just come through the door, and the three men struggled with Mama, taking her down the stairs.

"Leave me alone," she rasped, her lungs starved for oxygen. "Save Molly."

But the firefighters concentrated only on getting her out. The fire was too strong and the structure too old and weak. Any moment now, it could give way and entomb them all in the inferno.

Outside, the entire building was swarming with flames. Three engines had already responded and a sea of flashing red, white, and blue lights lit up the street. Neighbors, friends, everyone within earshot of the explosions was on the sidewalk, watching Athena's Taverna burn. Firemen were hosing down the roofs of the buildings adjacent to the restaurant, while others had run hoses inside, attempting to limit the spread of the fire.

On the second floor, fire was rushing out of the two windows facing the street. The third, Molly's window, was shattered, and plumes of smoke escaped from it, reaching skyward.

"That one. She's in there," Mama shouted to the firefighters on a truck. They were positioning a ladder, with a fireman clinging on at the wrong window. "That window. She's in that room," Mama screamed, pointing.

Just as the ladder was shifted, a third explosion shattered whatever windows remained. Firemen and bystanders ducked for cover, but Mama stood still and rigid, as if she were defying the fire.

"*There!*" she screamed again, pointing at the window. "Molly, I see you. Stay at the window, they're coming up. Stay at the window."

Molly, shaken and frightened, struggled to breathe. In her hand she held a picture she had drawn for Kate. A picture of a house in flames. "Fire," she whispered. "Fire."

The ladder was almost there now. As the firefighter on it came closer he shouted to Molly, "Stand back. I'm going to break it in." By the time he was level with the shattered window, he realized that he had only a few seconds left. The room behind Molly was almost fully engulfed in flames.

Molly, despite her terror, obeyed him and stood to the side while he smashed what was left of the window with an ax. As the glass and frame fell into the room, he stuck his torso through the gap, ignoring the remaining shards of glass that cut through his heavy flame-resistant coat and wrapped Molly in his arms.

They had barely made it out when the in-rushing air fed fresh oxygen to the fire and a tongue of flame rushed through the gap over his helmet, searing one side of his face. He cried out in pain and ducked but managed to hold on to Molly. Before he reached the bottom of the ladder, other firemen grabbed him and Molly, taking both of them to a waiting ambulance.

While one paramedic worked on the injured fireman, another checked out Molly. She was coughing from the smoke, her face smudged and wet with tears as it was covered by an oxygen mask. But every ounce of her strength and will was focused on the face of her grandmother, who loomed over her, holding out her arms in a gesture of protection, her nightgown flattened against her body by the cold wind.

Mama looked down at her, muttering a prayer in Greek, one that she had not said since she had been a little girl not much older than Molly.

chapter **30**

The telephone in room 362 of the Marriott at Miami International Airport rang just before four A.M., but Kate wasn't asleep. She hadn't slept all night; she hadn't even tried to. She kept thinking about Spencer and the final moments of his life. What had it been like? she wondered over and over again, as she watched the green numerals of the clock on the nightstand, the hours passing with agonizing slowness.

The phone rang again, and Kate slowly picked up the receiver.

"*Imasti kala Katrina. Imasti kala*. We're all okay. Molly is okay," Mama said in Greek and English.

"What are you talking about, Mama? What's wrong?"

"There was a fire, Katrina. The restaurant, the apartment, everything. But we're okay. Molly is okay."

"Where are you, Mama. What happened? What started it?" Kate asked, trying not alarm her. She knew what had started the fire. She knew why it had happened and what it meant. But there was no point scaring Mama.

"I don't know what started it. But with God's help we both survived. That's the only thing that is important."

"And the taverna?"

"The taverna, the apartment, they're all gone, Katrina. We are at Mercy Hospital."

Kate pressed the phone against her chest and closed her eyes. Her hands trembling, she slowly sat up and moved to the edge of the bed.

"Mama, you stay there. You stay there with Molly. I'll be there in a few hours. I'll take care of everything, Mama. This is over. This is all over."

She hung up and hugged herself in the darkness. She suddenly felt cold; it was the same coldness she had felt when Jeffrey died.

After leaving the crash site the previous evening, Kate had spent hours rehashing every detail of the crash with Michael O'Rourke, searching for a shred of a clue. She explained everything over again, including the disappearance of Brita Ames and her kids. After a brief and very late dinner, they got two rooms at the Marriott on Lejeune Road and arranged to meet in the lobby at six A.M., in time to make a final trip to the site where Spencer's plane had crashed. Why hadn't she just gone back? she wondered, the guilt overwhelming her. Her place was with her daughter and her family, not here, in this place, chasing ghosts.

She picked up the phone and asked for Michael O'Rourke's room. When he answered in a sleepy voice, Kate said, "I'm leaving. I'm going to New York."

"What . . . what happened? What's wrong?"

All she managed to get out was "It's over. I don't want to do this anymore."

"What's going on? Tell me please."

"There was a fire. They almost killed my family."

"I'll see you downstairs in ten minutes." O'Rourke hung up before Kate had a chance to respond.

Minutes later, both of them were standing at the checkout counter, ringing the bell to get the night cashier out of the back office.

"What are you doing?" Kate asked.

"I'm going back with you."

"No, it's not necessary. Besides, the first flight doesn't leave for two and half hours."

"The first flight leaves as soon as we get to the airport," O'Rourke responded. "I've got an FAA jet standing by. We're going direct to La Guardia."

Kate looked at him in amazement. "Thanks."

Two hours and sixteen minutes later, the Lear jet 36 touched down on Runway 4 at La Guardia. By the time the jet had taxied to the west side and shut down its engines, a green sedan was waiting for them.

The car pulled up to the emergency room at Mercy Hospital and Kate jumped out. At the counter, she was directed to the room.

She found Mama sitting on the edge of a bed, wearing a hospital gown. She was stroking Molly, who was wearing a gown of her own, curled up in a little ball, her head in her lap.

Mama seemed relieved as Kate entered the room. She shushed Kate to stay quiet and slowly moved Molly's head from her lap and put it on a pillow before getting up to hug her.

"How is she?" Kate asked, before they were even out of the room.

"She's okay. But she breathed some smoke and they just want to keep her here for a little while."

"What happened? How . . . ?"

"There was an explosion. They think it started from some electrical outlet. But . . . me, I don't know."

Kate hugged her again and held her there for a long moment. That was when Mama broke down. "Molly—I could not get to her. I could not save her. It was all on fire, everything."

"Shhhhh. It's all over, Mama, it's all over."

She pulled away and, wiping her eyes, asked, "What do you mean it's over? How can it be over?"

"I'm not going to fight this anymore. The fire, Mama. I don't think it was an accident."

"Don't you think I know that?" Mama said, coming closer. "Don't you think I could figure that out?" Her eyes filling with fresh tears, she said, "Why do you think I'm so afraid? Why do you think I'm standing here shaking? I'm afraid for you, my Katrina, and I'm afraid for Molly. But you know what I'm afraid of the most?"

Kate shook her head.

"That if you give up now, that if you give up because of us, you will spend the rest of your life afraid, just like I have. You can't do that. I won't let you. We will go to the police. We will go there and let them find the *basterthous* who did this to us. Then we spit in their faces."

"But look at you, Mama. What about you?"

"I'll take care of them," said a voice from behind.

"What?" Kate turned around to face O'Rourke.

"I'll take care of Molly and your mother," he said firmly. "The Bureau already has two men stationed outside and more on the way. I'm going to make sure they're okay. I'm going to take your mother and Molly to the safest place on the planet. Queens. My part of it, not yours. I'm going to take them to my parents' home. I've already talked to them and they'd love to have them. Plus I know everybody on the block. Hell, I can make it so that nobody without the proper I.D. can get within a hundred yards of them."

"Why? Why would you . . . ?"

"Here we go again with the whys. Because I want to, okay? Because I want to get to the bottom of this almost as much as you do, and because I like Greek food. Is that okay with you?"

The way he came across, the way he just showed up and took charge, the way he treated her and Mama as if he had known them for a thousand years, as if he knew exactly what he was doing, reminded Kate of Jeffrey and the first night he had come to the restaurant.

"And by the way, I'm Michael O'Rourke. It's a pleasure to meet you," he concluded, holding out his hand to Mama.

She looked at O'Rourke, then at Kate, then at O'Rourke again. Then she smiled and stretched out her hand, gripping his firmly, with a mother's intuition.

Kate raised the collar of her black jacket as she left the subway station and turned north on Broadway, bracing herself against the cold. As she turned west on Steinway, the knot in her stomach tightened. She could see it now, two blocks away, the blackened remains of the taverna and the apartment above, gutted and charred, wisps of smoke still rising from the rubble.

The area was cordoned off with yellow police tape, DO NOT CROSS clearly printed across it in black. On both sides of the street, people had stopped to gawk at the lone fire truck hosing down the smoldering remains of the building.

She wanted to be left alone to remember. Remember the day Mama had finally put together enough money to open the place. To remember the day they found the building, a pizzeria that had gone out of business, with a little three-bedroom apartment upstairs. And when they had finally opened the taverna, watching a dream become reality. A dream that was now nothing but scorched wood, charcoal and smoke.

Kate jumped as she felt someone tap her on the back.

"I'm sorry if I scared you," the man said.

"That's okay," Kate replied, smiling uneasily. "What . . . what are you doing here?" she asked, her hand on her chest.

"I've been looking for you since yesterday. I tried your house but there was no answer, so I . . ."

"I haven't been home."

"I know. That's why I traced you here," he said, turning his gaze to the smoldering ashes. "I'm so sorry."

"Why were you looking for me?"

"We think we know what happened to your airplane. It was a virus, Ms. Gallagher. Someone purposely set off a virus to extort money from Searchlight."

"What?" Kate nearly yelled.

"It was a—"

"Son of a bitch! A virus? It was a virus?"

He nodded. "We received the message yesterday and contacted the FBI immediately. They've initiated a full-scale investigation. Shortly after that we got a call. Ms. Gallagher, they think they have a lead."

"A lead? FBI?" It was dizzying.

"We need your help. That's why we've been looking for you."

"Well, what do you want me to do?"

"We need to go to Searchlight and verify some of the data. There's a team standing by and the company jet is at Kennedy, waiting. We can be in Washington before noon, and I think we'll have all the answers before the day is over."

"I . . . I need to make a phone call."

"You can make it from the plane. Please, this is extremely urgent."

Two hundred miles away, on the eighth floor of the Searchlight Tower, Marshall Hayes sat at his desk. The flashing icon on his computer indicated that he had sixteen e-mails. He began to click through them.

On the eighth message, he stopped.

Number three is coming up. It's up to you now, to make it right.

Hayes froze. He reread the e-mail, slowly, studying every word as if searching for some secret. He wanted to call somebody. Maybe Thompson, or that creature he used for his dirty work. What was his name? Cordelia?

He felt dizzy. His heart was pumping more blood than his body needed. He reached for his carotid artery and pressed down, hoping that would give him some relief. But it didn't.

He read the e-mail again and again. Finally, in one stunning and agonizing moment of realization, he knew. Marshall Hayes knew. "No, my God, no."

chapter 31

The white sedan arrived in front of a gate at the General Aviation Terminal on the west side of Kennedy, where the driver punched a series of codes into a keypad. The chain-link fence edged with the barbed wire began to open. They drove into the private hangar.

Kate could see the plane, a white Jetstar with the gold Searchlight logo emblazoned across one side. But the plane looked dark; so did the hangar.

"Doesn't look like they're ready to go," Kate said, but he didn't answer.

"Hey . . ." she began, as he silently got out of the car.

Looking around, Kate slowly opened the door and got out. At the fuselage of the Jetstar, she stood on her toes and peeked through the windows. The aircraft was unpowered; everything was shut down. No lights, no pilots, no flight attendants, no one.

Oh my God. It's a trap. I've been set up. Get out. Get out now, she told herself and headed toward the hangar door which stood slightly ajar. Fifty feet out, she heard a sound. The hangar door was beginning to close.

She bolted toward the opening, but by the time she got there all that was left was a crack. She stood frozen as the last rays of daylight disappeared through the opening and the hangar doors closed.

Breathing heavily, with her back to the door, Kate stood in the dark, desperately trying to see. She fought hard to control the fear welling up inside her.

In this new game, there would be no second chances.

She slowly edged forward, her eyes adjusting to the dark, enabling her to see the outline of the car—her only chance. As Kate stumbled toward it, she saw him get into the driver's seat.

Kate froze on the spot as she heard the engine start and the tires spin on the cold concrete. An instant before she and the vehicle were to occupy the same space at the same time, she leaped out of the way.

Falling to the floor, Kate grasped her ankle in pain and focused on the silhouette of the driver. The headlights came on, flooding the hangar with bright light. Kate put up one hand to shield her eyes.

She heard the engine revving some thirty feet away. But he wasn't doing anything else. He wasn't ready.

"Come on, you bastard," she whispered, lowering her hand, daring him. Then both the lights and the engine died.

Plunged again into darkness, Kate squinted to see, but other than residual images caused by the momentary flash of bright light, nothing was visible. When she heard the car door open and shut, she didn't wait. She crawled backward on her hands and butt, until her back hit the front wheel of the Jetstar. She turned, using the tires as support to lift herself off the ground, acutely aware of the distance between her and the car.

Keeping her back toward the plane, Kate extended her arms and placed her clammy palms against the cold, metal skin of the fuselage and began to inch back farther.

She needed a weapon. A wrench, a crowbar, anything. Maybe there was something in the car, or a toolbox somewhere. She got to her feet and limped away from the plane, trying desperately to muffle the sound of her shoes. Where was he?

The contact was violent, the pain numbing. What hit her wasn't a kick or a punch or even flesh, but the blow to the back of her legs was so intense that Kate saw stars. She cried out in agony and fell to her knees on the concrete floor, endless streaks of pain shooting like fire through every nerve.

On her hands and knees, with her head down, she saw his feet as he stepped in front of her. She lifted her head to look up but could only determine the outline of his body as he stood above her, a baseball bat in his right hand. Instinctively, she put up an arm to ward off the imminent blow. Nothing happened. Then he spoke.

"You know I should have killed you that night in the hotel, but I didn't. I thought maybe you would get smart and stop pressing your luck. But no, you had to keep at it, didn't you?" he said, leaning down low enough she could feel his breath on her face. A panting breath that made her skin crawl.

"Well, this is what happens when little girls don't listen," he said, bending closer even. Kate knew that if she was to survive, it was now or never. With her right hand clenched into a fist, she punched him in the groin, hard enough that he howled and fell back, dropping the bat.

Kate jumped up to go after the weapon but the pain in her legs forced her back to the floor. She began to feel around on the floor for the bat. Then she felt him grab her feet and begin to pull. She kicked with both legs, screaming, trying to get up and away, but his grip was too tight. He pulled her closer and closer, his powerful hands wrapped around her legs like the tentacles of a giant octopus. When he momentarily opened one hand to get a better grip, she kicked him in the face hard enough to stun him. "Let go of me, you bastard," she shouted, and kicked him again before rolling away.

Her hand met the bat lying on the floor and she grabbed it. When she felt his hands around her ankles again, she was ready. She brought the bat down on his head, but he moved at the last minute and it caught him in the shoulder. He bellowed and let go, curling himself up into a ball.

She got up and started to stagger away but in the darkness hit a wall. She backed off and turned, dizzy. When she heard him whimpering like a wounded animal, she lifted the bat again. His left hand shot up and grabbed her arm. He placed his right hand on her face and shoved her away, ramming her into the fuselage. Kate stood up, trying to get her bearings, but that was all the opportunity he needed. He rushed at her, cursing and spitting, and rammed her into the side of the plane. He didn't stop there. He kicked her in the stomach and the chest, where her ribs were still healing. She fought back, but when he lifted his fist one last time and brought it down to her face, she saw shooting lights behind her eyes. In the blackness of the hangar, everything seemed to stop.

"You're a whole lot tougher than your friend Spencer, did you know that?" he said between breaths, as he stood over her.

He sat next to her on the floor, lifted her limp body, and leaned it against his. "Come on, honey. Show-time."

He reached into his pocket and pulled out a syringe.

He flipped away the plastic safety cover and lifted Kate's arm.

"Put that down." The voice came from a short distance away.

He looked up, shielding his eyes from the glare of the flashlight.

"Drop the syringe, Kyle."

"Marshall?" Kyle Hayes asked, blinking rapidly, a mixture of sweat and blood from the cut on his head pouring down the side of his face.

"It's over, son. It's all over."

"What? How did . . . ?"

" 'Make it right'—that's what you said in your e-mail." Hayes moved closer. "I don't know how many times I've used those very words on you, and you know the funny thing? I never thought you heard me."

"You don't understand."

"Don't I? What was it this time? Drugs? Booze? What in God's name was it that made you go and destroy your life and mine?"

"Destroy *your* life?" Kyle squinted into the light. "Destroy *your* life?" He shook his head. "You really have no clue, do you?"

"No. So tell me. Tell me what would possess a man—my son—to go out and cold-bloodedly take innocent lives."

"They weren't supposed to die," Kyle shouted. "Nobody was. The virus was designed to activate at three thousand hours of flight time. It was installed on all five airplanes at the same time, which meant that the planes were supposed to reach three thousand hours within a few days of one another. I was watching the flight time on all five, and just before the first one hit I was going to make my demand and let you verify it. You wouldn't have had time to fix the others, so you would give me my money and I would give you the serial numbers of the other four; that was the way it was supposed to work out. But the damn cargo plane reached the three-thousand-hour mark months before the others. How the hell was I supposed to know they flew those things that much?"

"Why didn't you stop after that, Kyle? Why didn't you tell us about the other planes after the first one went down?"

"What the hell difference would it have made? I had already destroyed one airplane, killed two people. Why not make that two planes, or three. Whatever it took to make you pay."

"Is that what this was all about? The money?"

"No, Marshall, that was just a bonus." Kyle squeezed the syringe in his sweaty fist. "I wanted to see you squirm. I wanted to see you in pain, up against the wall with the firing squad aiming their rifles at your heart— if you had one. I wanted you to suffer."

"For heaven's sake, son, why?"

"Don't you dare," Kyle said, his eyes filled with contempt. "Don't you *dare* call me 'son.' You are not my father. No father would walk out of the house day after day and leave his wife begging him to come back. How many of them were there, Marshall? How many mistresses did you have? Twenty? Fifty? No. Marshall, it's not about the money. It's about you. It's about every tear that I wiped from her cheek. It's about a nine-year-old boy standing outside his mother's locked door, listening to her bury her sobs into a pillow so that she couldn't be heard. It's about a promise that I made to pay you back."

"My God, Kyle. What have I done?"

"What you always did. You took care of Marshall."

"Let me make it up to you. Put the syringe down and let me try. I'll get you the best help, I swear. I'll get you . . ."

"And what? Reduce my sentence from lethal injection to life behind bars? No, Marshall, I can't do that. It's too late."

"It's not too late," Hayes called out. "It's not too late. Put the syringe down and we'll deal with this madness calmly."

"No!" Kyle shouted.

Leaning on his shoulder, Kate slowly opened her eyes. The sudden motion caught Kyle's attention and he refocused on her, squeezing her tight. He lifted the syringe.

Marshall ran forward, stopping within a safe distance of Kyle and Kate. "I won't let you do it, Kyle. Let her go, or so help me I will end this misery for both of us, right here and right now."

Kyle couldn't see his father's face, just the outline of a body, holding a flashlight.

"You . . . you don't have a gun," Kyle said with a nervous laugh.

"Are you willing to bet your life on that?"

"Dammit, Marshall, with Thompson gone, she's the only one who can get in our way. No one has to know."

"What have you done, Kyle? What have you done to Thompson?" Hayes shouted.

"He was the one who didn't want to pay. He was the one who didn't care about all those people. Don't you see? It's his fault they're dead."

In a nanosecond, the pieces of the puzzle fell into place. "Oh, my God," Hayes said. "It's the plane. You put him on the airplane that's going down."

Kyle smiled. "A fitting end, don't you think? I finally beat him at his own game."

"No, Kyle. No."

"It's over. In just over two hours it'll all be over. No way to trace him to you or me, or to anything. Just another accidental crash that will never be solved."

"We have to stop it, do you understand? You have to help me stop it."

"It's too late. I can't stop it, you can't stop it, no one can. It's over, Marshall. The plane, Thompson, they're all gone. She's the last one left," Kyle said, squeezing Kate harder.

"No. I won't let you. . . ."

"You owe me."

Kate grabbed Kyle's hand with the syringe, and before he had a chance to defend himself, she butted the back of her head into his face with as much force as she could muster and began to move away.

Kyle screamed and dropped the syringe. "You bitch. You bloody bitch!" He pulled out a knife.

A shot rang out. Kyle fell to the floor, grabbing his stomach. He cursed and shouted and tried to stand up, babbling incomprehensively like a drunk. His legs wouldn't move. He stared down at them mutely then at his father, and crumpled in a heap on the floor.

Hayes was already at his side, shouting, "Call an ambulance. The phone is in that corner, and the light switch too."

Kate limped toward the corner Hayes had pointed to. She turned on the light switch and glimpsed the reflection of her cut and bruised face in the mirror beside it.

Hayes placed Kyle's head in his lap. "I'm sorry, son. I'm so sorry."

Kyle's weak eyes blinked as the blood seeded through his shirt.

"I . . . I can't breathe," he moaned.

"The ambulance is on its way. Just hang in there, son."

"I . . . can't . . ."

"Tell me about the virus, Kyle. Tell me how I can stop it. Help me to make it right."

A thin, trembling smile appeared on Kyle's lips.

"What time is it?" he asked, trying to lift his head.

Hayes looked at his watch. "Eleven-forty."

"Exactly?"

Hayes looked down again. "Eleven thirty-eight."

Kyle put his head back down, a look of satisfaction on his face.

"Eight . . . eighteen minutes."

Kate had made the 911 call and was back now. She was standing over Kyle and Hayes, listening.

"What do you mean, Kyle? What's going to happen in eighteen minutes?"

"Go to hell, Marshall," Kyle said, a smile on his face.

chapter 32

What airline?" Kate shouted.
"What?"
"What airline is he on?"

"Atlantic Air, going to London. I don't know the flight number," Hayes replied, as he pressed on the bullet wound in Kyle's chest. Kyle's head was still in Hayes's lap but his eyes were closed.

Kate ran back to the phone in the hangar, ignoring the pain in her legs and chest, and dialed information. "Do you have a phone number for Kennedy Airport's control tower? It's urgent. Hurry, please."

The control tower number was restricted, but she was given a number for the city's department of aviation. Kate quickly dialed the number and got a busy signal. After calling twice more without success, she slammed down the phone.

She reached into her pocket for O'Rourke's number. But the pocket had been torn in the struggle. His card wasn't there.

She looked around in panic but couldn't see it

anywhere. Keenly aware of every passing second, she searched until she saw the control panel for the main hangar doors. Stuffing her blouse back into her pants, she limped to them and began randomly pushing buttons until the doors started to open. Then she ran back to the Jetstar and took a seat in the cockpit. Drawing from her memories of the simulator, she found the battery switch and flipped it; thirty colored lights illuminated the cockpit. She grabbed the radio, tuned in the tower frequency from memory, and pressed the Talk button.

"Kennedy tower, an Atlantic Air flight departed for London about two and half hours ago. What was the flight number?"

"Who is this?" a man asked suspiciously.

"My name is Kate Gallagher. I'm a pilot for Jet-East. I have important information regarding that flight that left about two-and-half-hours ago. It must be recalled. It must be recalled right away."

In the control tower, the shift supervisor took over the call. "Confirm who you are and what your location is."

"I'm sitting in an airplane on the west side of the airport, in the Searchlight hangar. I have information regarding the Atlantic Air flight. It's in danger. It must return right away."

The supervisor had already written "call security" on a piece of paper and handed it to one of his men. "I need to know why you think flight 671 has a problem."

"It will take too long to explain. Just please make radio contact with them. Tell them that they must return to Kennedy. We only have a few minutes left."

"Listen, Ms. Gallagher. I can't just order an aircraft to divert because someone wants me to. If you have something you want to tell me, please . . ."

"It's a virus in the computer system. Their flight controls will cease to operate unless they get back."

"I understand. I understand. I've already called the appropriate people. They'll be there very shortly. I need you to explain to them everything that you've told me. They'll take care of—"

"Didn't you hear me? We don't have the time," she shouted and threw down the mike. This wasn't going to work. Kyle had told them that they had eighteen minutes. And that was three minutes ago, maybe four. By the time someone arrived and she convinced them that she was telling the truth, it would be too late.

She had an idea.

"Get him out of there. I'm starting the engines," she shouted to Hayes, who was still tending to his son. She closed the cockpit door.

Back in her seat, Kate started the auxiliary power unit and looked up at the overhead panel. "Come on, engine start—we need fuel and ignition. How did we do this in the simulator?"

The first engine started and the second one quickly followed. Kate didn't wait. She pushed up the throttles, and as the power on the two jet engines increased, the walls of the hangar began to shake and the airplane slowly began to move.

Two police cars arrived at the hangar as Kate rolled out onto the tarmac. The men jumped out of their cars and began to wave but she ignored them, instead making a sharp left turn to avoid the cars.

At the main taxiway she stopped for a moment to get her bearings, then made a quick turn onto taxiway Quebec, making her way toward the runways. Runway 13 Right was a short distance away; she could see its threshold. She could be there and in the air in less than thirty seconds. But as she looked to her left, Kate saw a sea of flashing red lights racing toward her.

As if anticipating her next move, a half-dozen vehicles began to take positions on different taxiways, blocking her exit. Four more vehicles approached to form another barrier. They were closing in from all directions.

Kate stepped on the brakes, moved to the right side of the taxiway, then turned the steering column all the way around. The Jetstar shook, its tires shrieking against the concrete as they turned a tight radius. She was headed back to the main part of the airport, away from the flashing lights.

With Kennedy Airport all but shut down, the congested traffic had come to a grinding halt. All takeoff and landing clearances had been canceled, and jumbo jets of every color and nationality were lined up one behind the other like boxcars on a train. In the midst of them, the little white plane maneuvered between taxiways; like a mouse in a room full of people, scuttling its way around their feet. Pilots in the jumbos stomped their brakes and came to a halt, watching the Jetstar in astonishment. A babble of voices asking what in the name of God was going on filled her headset.

She was taxiing back onto Bravo, heading for Runway 4 Left. It appeared to be deserted. She picked up the radio.

"Kennedy tower, this is, uh . . . this is . . ." She needed a call sign. On a private plane, that was always the aircraft's registration number, but that number was marked on the outside of the aircraft or buried in paperwork somewhere.

"Kennedy tower, this is Molly Five," Kate said, smiling at her creation.

"Go ahead, Molly Five."

"I guess by now you can see me," she said. "I'm headed for Runway 4 Left. With or without your clearance I'm going to take off. I need you to clear that runway from all traffic. Then I need you to get in touch with departure control and New York Center. I'm going to do a high-performance takeoff and I want all traffic above me cleared."

"Uh . . . Roger," the controller responded.

"I'm going to squawk 5555. Tell them to look for me and to keep all traffic away."

Her plan was quite simple. She would take off, climb as fast as she could, then try to establish radio contact with the Atlantic Air flight 671.

Long-haul aircraft have a diverse range of means of communicating with ground control. But Kate didn't know what equipment Atlantic Air carried and had no way of finding out. What she did know was that all over-water aircraft had the capability to communicate using high frequency, or HF, channels.

HF was used as a primary source of communication because its signals bounced off the atmosphere and allowed for communication over a vast physical distance. But the HF frequencies were often scratchy and staticky. For those reasons, the radios were normally turned off and used only when needed. VHF, or very high frequency, channels, on the other hand, were clear and never turned off. Their range, however, was limited to the line of sight. If the receiving or the transmitting station traveled beyond the curvature of the earth, the system was rendered useless.

Another problem with using either the HF or the VHF channels was that she would have to know what frequency the aircraft's radios were tuned to. Airlines monitored the VHF emergency frequency of 121.5 on all over-water flights. This was a common frequency used by aircraft in distress; simply by monitoring it, planes watched for other planes in need of assistance.

Flight 671 had departed some two hours earlier. Depending on the wind and their speed, that would place them between eight hundred and a thousand miles away. If the Jetstar was light enough, and if she could climb high enough, maybe, just maybe, she could get above the earth's curvature, creating a straight line between her and the Atlantic plane. Then she could use her VHF radio and transmit on the emergency frequency.

"Jetstar Molly Five is on the roll on Runway 4 Left," Kate announced, bringing up the power. No one acknowledged her transmission.

The two engines roared to maximum thrust. The rapid acceleration pushed Kate back in her seat. She didn't know the systems and she had no idea at what speed the airplane would lift off. She had selected a midrange flap setting; something that she remembered from her day in the simulator, and, well . . . it was time to fly.

Halfway down the runway, she glanced at her speed. The nose column had become light; instinct told her that it was time. She pulled back on the yoke and the Jetstar was airborne. At fifty feet, Kate lowered the nose and began to fly parallel to the ground. She brought up the gear, retracted the flaps, and watched the airspeed climb rapidly from 140 to nearly 300 miles per hour in less than thirty seconds. She leaned back and pulled.

With the yoke pulled some four inches, and the aircraft with its light load and its engines at maximum thrust, the Jetstar nearly stood on its tail. On the ground and in the tower, the people watched as the little white jet climbed vertically like a rocket, flying up to five thousand, ten thousand, fifteen thousand feet, before disappearing into the clouds.

Kate got on the microphone again. "This is Molly Five, climbing out of eighteen thousand feet to maximum flight level. I need you to contact Michael O'Rourke at the NTSB. Call the Washington office, they know how to get hold of him. Tell him—" She stopped for a second. "I need to be able to talk to him over the radio. Atlantic Air 671 is the next target. Tell him that the virus will attack in less than two hours. Tell him now."

chapter 33

O'Rourke was in his car, heading east, watching the traffic crawl along the Van Wyck Expressway, when his cell phone rang. He listened as the shift supervisor at Kennedy hurriedly explained the events that had just taken place.

"When did she take off?" O'Rourke shouted into the receiver.

"I don't know. Six, maybe eight minutes ago."

"And it took you this long to find me?"

"Listen, as far as we were concerned, this lady was a nutcase, somebody who stole an airplane. We had no way of verifying her story."

"Damn!"

"Are you telling me there's something to what she said?"

"What I'm telling you is that you better do whatever you can to get that airplane to turn back right now, or it's going to be too late."

Fourteen miles away, in the control tower at

Kennedy, the shift supervisor's face went white. "She said we only had a few minutes."

The Jetstar punched through the cloud deck at twenty-four thousand feet, instantaneously trading the gray overcast sky for the bright blue and brilliant sunshine above the clouds.

Her deck angle was nearly twenty degrees, practically unheard of for a civilian plane flying at such altitude. She continuously watched the engines and adjusted the throttles in order to gain maximum thrust. She turned off one of the air-supply machines, or packs. The remaining pack was more than enough to pressurize and heat the cabin, and less air going into the cabin meant that more air could be used for thrust.

Unsure how high the aircraft would climb, she was more than prepared to take it to its limit, whatever that might be. Somewhere beyond thirty-three thousand feet, she picked up the radio again.

"Atlantic Air 671, this is Molly Five, come in please."

As expected, there was no response.

"Atlantic Air 671, this is Molly Five. Come in please. This is urgent."

Still there was no response. She had to get higher.

Kate pushed the throttles forward, stopping only after the amber warning light indicated that she was about to exceed maximum engine temperatures.

Two precious minutes ticked by.

"Atlantic Air 671, this is Molly Five. This is an urgent message. I'm transmitting on VHF 121.5. Come in please."

"Uh, Molly Five, this is British Airways 28," a man with a crisp English accent responded. "We heard Atlantic Air 671 make a position report about twenty minutes ago. Do you want us to try and raise him for you?"

"Yes. Yes. Please."

"Atlantic Air 671, this is British Airways 28. Come in, please."

Kate could hear the pilot of the British Airways plane make the call. What a stroke of luck; she hadn't even thought about the possibility. Getting another aircraft to make the call for her was like having a relay station in the middle of the sky. If she needed to, she could contact a dozen planes and have each forward the information to the next, until they got hold of the plane.

"Atlantic Air 671, this is British Airways 28. Come in please. I have an urgent message for you."

Kate didn't hear the Atlantic's response, but she did hear British Airways'. "Roger, Atlantic Air. Stand by."

"Molly Five, this is British Airways 28."

"Go ahead, British. Go ahead."

"Molly Five. We've raised Atlantic Air 671. What's your message?"

"I have to talk to them. Ask them to come in on HF frequency 4465."

"Atlantic Air 671, this is British Airways 28. Switch to HF frequency 4465. Switch now please."

"Thanks a million," Kate said, and changed radios.

"Atlantic Air 671, this is Molly Five, come in please."

A voice came through the static. "Yes, Molly Five. This is Atlantic Air 671."

"I have to speak to the captain right now."

In the cockpit of the Atlantic Air plane, Captain Joseph Gallo picked up the microphone.

"This is the captain. Who is this?"

"My name is Kate Gallagher. I'm currently flying a small private jet off the coast of New York. I have definitive information that your craft, Atlantic Air 671, is in imminent danger."

"What kind of danger?"

"Your computer systems have been contaminated by a virus which will go to work in less than two hours. It is designed to infect the flight control computers. Captain, once this thing hits, there is nothing anyone can do."

"Stand by, Molly Five." Gallo looked to his first officer. "Get hold of dispatch on SATCOM. See what this is all about."

He then picked up the interphone and dialed the flight attendants' station in the back. "Billy, wake up the I.O. Get him up here now." He put down the interphone and picked up the mike again.

"Molly Five, we're running some checks up here. It's going to take a couple of minutes."

"Captain, a couple of minutes is all you have."

Gallo once again put down the mike, held the controls with both hands, and announced, "Autopilot is off."

He pressed a button on the yoke and began to feel the controls. A slight turn to the right, one to left, up, down; everything felt normal.

"Autopilot is back on," he said, and looked over.

In the right seat, First Officer Clayton Dawson had the receiver glued to his ear. "Thanks. Hold on a second." He turned to Gallo. "Dispatch doesn't know anything about it. They're asking what's going on."

Gallo leaned his large frame back in his seat and ran his hands through his silver-white hair. He picked up the mike again. "Molly Five, this is Atlantic Air 671."

"Go ahead, 671, this is Molly Five," Kate replied.

"We don't know anything about a virus. The flight controls are responding normally. No one seems to know what you're talking about."

There was no time for this. "Captain, do you have a stopwatch on board?"

"What?"

"Do you have a stopwatch?"

"Yes."

"I want you to zero it out."

"What is this?"

"Go ahead. Zero it out. Then set it at one hour and forty minutes."

It took a few seconds for Gallo to set the timer on his wristwatch. "Okay."

"Now hit the Run button."

"I think I know where you're headed, but—"

"No, I don't think you do. You see, Captain, when the numbers on your timer hit zero, your aircraft will turn to the right or to the left. Maybe it will do it slowly like mine did, or maybe it will snap, like the Jetway flight, but either way, there won't be a damn thing you can do about it. You will sit there in your seat, and you will struggle with the controls until you plummet down into the middle of the ocean like a meteor, and the biggest part of your plane they will ever recover will be a piece of someone's carry-on luggage. Now, I've done my job. It's your call."

There was a long moment of silence as Gallo held the mike in his hand, a stern expression on his long and heavily tanned face. The two other crew members in the cockpit, First Officer Clayton Dawson and International Officer Gregory Wyles, watched as Gallo finally made his decision.

"Let's descend five hundred feet. Make a left one eighty and set up a parallel course, thirty miles off center," he ordered; then, returning to Kate: "Lady, I hope you know what you're talking about."

At Kennedy, the commotion surrounding the Jetstar's departure and Kate's desperate call to turn back the Atlantic Air flight had received more attention than was intended. Witnesses both on the ground and in airplanes had watched the little jet zigzag its way around the airport, and, in more than one case, captains had made P.A.s explaining to their passengers what was going on. There was also the matter of Kate's first radio call, the one in which she told the controllers that the Atlantic Air plane would be in trouble.

Given all the activity, it didn't take long for word to reach the media. Several stations were already monitoring the ATC frequencies and several others were called by observers and others who had witnessed the Jetstar's bizarre activities. A small jet running loose at Kennedy was definitely newsworthy. The likelihood that there was another plane in distress, a jumbo jet carrying nearly three hundred people, was more than news; it was a ratings slam-dunk.

The first phone call in the tower came from the news director of WKNY, a local station on Long Island, who had gotten the Kennedy tower phone number from a friend who worked for the FAA. The call was directed to the shift supervisor, Robert Quinn.

"What can you tell us about Atlantic Air 671? Is the aircraft in distress?"

"Oh, damn." He realized that not only the personnel in the tower but plenty of others who monitored the same frequencies had heard everything that had happened. Before he had a chance to respond, another phone line lit up. It was another radio station, followed by two TV stations. Atlantic Air flight 671 was headline news.

chapter 34

By the time the first blue-and-white NYPD vehicle entered Van Wyck Expressway in Forest Hills, the beige Hughes 500 helicopter was hovering overhead.

The patrol car was followed by a second and then a third, and all three began to sweep across the lanes. Behind them, traffic came to stop. The Hughes 500, in position, slowly descended to the open freeway and landed just ahead of the police cars.

Two hundred feet away, Michael O'Rourke pulled onto the shoulder, parked, and ran to the chopper. He buckled in and the Hughey lifted off.

"What's going on?" he shouted over the rotor noise.

"The plane's on its way back," the man in the next seat replied.

"Thank God. Did you get to him in time?"

"We didn't get to him at all. He called us and said he was coming back. Apparently she somehow made contact with them."

"Was it in time?" O'Rourke repeated.

"Yeah, I think so. I think she did it."

O'Rourke smiled and shook his head. He wasn't surprised.

"Where is she?"

"Radar's painting her about a hundred and forty miles northeast of the airport. It doesn't look like she's coming down yet."

"Have you established radio contact with her?"

The man shook his head.

O'Rourke leaned over the seat and tapped the pilot on the shoulder. "Take us to the tower. I want to talk to her."

At the base of the control tower, someone was holding the door open, waiting for O'Rourke. He got out of the helicopter and ran to the open door, where both men hustled up the stairs. Four floors up, the man directed O'Rourke into the operations center, where at least half a dozen others were grouped around a large table covered with Jeppeson navigation charts and maps.

"Here he is," the man with O'Rourke said breathlessly.

O'Rourke acknowledged the crowd with a wave. One of them, a slim, tall man with blond curly hair, stretched out his hand. "Hi, I'm Bob Quinn. I'm the shift supervisor. We spoke on the phone."

O'Rourke shook his hand and walked over to the table. "Where are they?"

Quinn pointed to a spot deep over the Atlantic on the map.

"Why are they so far south?" O'Rourke asked.

"It's a random route. They're flying farther south than normal to avoid the bad weather."

"How about Gander, or Halifax? Can't they land there?"

"No good. Both airports will take longer."

"How far were they from the ETP?"

"They were thirty minutes from the equal time point, maybe slightly more."

"So they have to come back to New York."

"We're the closest."

"How many people on board?"

"Including the crew, two hundred and sixty-two."

O'Rourke paused to gather his thoughts. "We need to coordinate direct communication with the plane and I must speak to Molly Five," O'Rourke said, smiling briefly at Kate's choice of a name. "You'd better inform the local authorities. Tell them the airplane's going to be here in about two hours. They might as well prepare for the worst."

"**Molly Five, this** is Atlantic Air 671, come in please."

"Yeah, Atlantic Air. This is Molly Five."

"Looks like I owe you a drink. We just got word from New York Ops confirming everything you said."

"I'll take you up on that offer. But you're critical on time now. Speed it up."

"Roger." Captain Gallo reached over the speed setting and rotated the dial, until the indicator touched the red limit line. "You said this was a computer virus?"

"Yes. It's directed at your flight controls."

"How long before it attacks?"

"All I know is that it's supposed to activate at three thousand hours of flight time. Once it attacks, it works pretty quick."

"Roger. Stand by, Molly Five." Gallo turned to Dawson, his first officer. "Get dispatch back on SAT-COM. Tell them that I want them to stay on the phone until this aircraft is back on the ground at Kennedy. But first ask them exactly how many hours are on this airplane."

"We're checking on the hours. It'll be a minute," he said to Kate. "What kind of a call sign is Molly Five anyhow?"

"I'll tell you all about it over that drink," Kate replied.

Gallo smiled. "You said your name is Kate Gallagher. Where do I know that name from?"

"Do you watch the news?"

Gallo made the connection. "My God, it's you. Is that what happened to you? Was it this virus?"

"Yes," Kate said quietly.

Dawson pointed to the receiver. "Dispatch wants to talk to you."

"I've got to go, Molly Five. I'll call you in a little bit."

"Roger."

Gallo picked up the receiver. "Dispatch, this is Captain Gallo."

"Captain, your aircraft had two thousand nine hundred and ninety-five hours and thirty-nine minutes when it landed six hours ago. The aircraft remained on the ground long enough to clear customs and be reserviced before your departure."

Gallo grabbed a pen and scribbled 2,995.39. The chronometer indicated that they had been airborne for 2.46 hours. He added up the figures. The total flight time as of that minute came to 2,997.85.

Gallo looked down at the computer that indicated the distance and time from Kennedy. This wasn't right; it couldn't be.

"What the hell does that mean, it's going to take two hours, forty-six minutes to get back? Is that at best speed?" O'Rourke shouted at Quinn, who was at the radio section across the room.

The FAA Ops center, two floors below the control tower, was a secondary location for use in emergencies.

It was large and equipped with the best in communications equipment.

"The aircraft can do mach 86. The numbers are calculated at eight-seven. Two forty-five is the best-case scenario," Quinn replied, holding the mike in his hand. "It could take longer."

"How about different altitudes? Can they climb, descend, divert, anything?"

"Two minutes this way or that isn't going to make a whole lot of difference. The low-pressure system goes halfway over the Atlantic."

"Dammit, then what are we supposed to do?" O'Rourke shouted in frustration.

Quinn was still holding the mike. "They want to know if we have any suggestions."

"Just . . . tell them we'll get back to them." O'Rourke said, then walked to the table in the center of the room and pulled out a map from a pile on the table. "We need a plan, we need a plan. Come on, dammit. *Think,*" he kept mumbling to himself.

Others in the room began to join him. Quinn came over and said, "Center is aware of the situation. They've taken control and are going to coordinate the operation from there." He looked at O'Rourke. "Mr. O'Rourke, they're saying that you know more about this virus than anyone else. They want you to make the calls."

With that, all eyes turned to O'Rourke and stayed there. He looked at them one by one. A half-dozen men, ages thirty to sixty, dressed in wrinkled shirts and loosened ties, all about to face the challenge of their lives.

O'Rourke put down the map, took a deep breath, and made his announcement. "Gentlemen, in just over an hour and half, a jumbo jet carrying two hundred and sixty-some people will crash into the Atlantic, some four hundred miles east of us. I know this because I've seen it in two other cases, and in both cases they didn't have a chance.

"I have a fair amount of knowledge of what we can expect, but I don't know how or even *if* we can avoid this accident. Hell, I don't even know your procedures or capabilities."

"You just tell us what you need. We'll get it done," Quinn said.

O'Rourke smiled his appreciation. "Gentlemen, we have work to do." He turned to Quinn. "Mr. Quinn, I don't know how many people you have here, but we need more. This room will do for a command center, since you have radios and communications. I need four teams to go to work on the following.

"Team one is to establish and maintain telephone contact with Atlantic Air headquarters in New Jersey. We need to have a phone link. I want their dispatch, maintenance, load—anyone at Atlantic Air who knows anything about this airplane. In addition, they'll also need to do the same with the EOR.

"Team two is responsible for air communications. Principally, they're going to have keep in touch with both the Atlantic Air plane and Molly Five. They'll also need to be in contact with New York radio, New York Center, the weather people, and every other FAA facility available to us. Try to use discreet frequencies as much as possible; they might not be monitored as much.

"Team three is to work with me directly. We're going to look into the virus and see what we can do about it."

"And team four?" someone asked.

"Team four is to work on the possibility of ditching the aircraft."

"Ditch?" someone to the left of him asked incredulously. "You've got low pressure circling above, whipping out fifty-knot winds plus thirty-to-forty–foot waves. They'll break up on impact. We'll be lucky if we can save six of them."

"What's your name?" O'Rourke asked.

"Newman."

"Mr. Newman, if our last available hope is ditching, then I'll take six over nothing."

The men stared each other out, then Newman concurred. "I'll take care of it."

"Thank you. Gentlemen, before this day is over, each and every one of you are going to be witness to one of the largest rescue operations this country has ever seen. Everything you do, everything you say, will be scrutinized to the umpteenth degree for years to come.

"We're dealing with an area that is new to all of us. There is no protocol or manual we can follow, and none of us have been trained on how to deal with a situation like this. I want your ideas, however crazy they may sound. Now, let's go to work."

"Molly Five, Molly Five. This is Michael O'Rourke. Come in please."

Kate immediately recognized his voice. "Go ahead, Mr. O'Rourke. I'm here."

"I'm glad I got you," O'Rourke said. "Kate, they're on the way back."

"I know. How much time do they have?"

"There's a problem." O'Rourke cleared his throat. "Their course is more southerly than usual, due to the weather associated with the low. The system's also pushed the jet stream down, so what was a hundred-and-forty–knot tailwind is now a head wind."

"How close are we, Mr. O'Rourke?"

"Michael. Try Michael. The flight time is just under

three hours. We've only got an hour and half before the virus attacks."

"What are you going to do?" Kate asked softly.

"I don't know."

"How about ditching? Can they ditch the aircraft?"

"We've just got the latest weather from NOAA," O'Rourke replied, looking at a page in his hand. "The swells are thirty feet or more and there's too much wind. The experts say that the plane will break up on impact. It's hopeless."

There was a gloomy silence. "Dammit, I thought I got to them in time, I was counting the minutes."

"It's amazing that you managed what you did. It's the low pressure and the wind; there was nothing you could do."

There was another pause.

"Do you know anything else about the virus?" he asked.

"It's Searchlight, the company in D.C. that makes the STAR navigation system. Someone there planted it."

"I know. I heard from the FAA that two of their people were taken from the hangar at Kennedy. I guess one of them is in pretty bad shape and can't talk."

"His name is Kyle. He's the one who planted it. The other one is his father, Marshall Hayes. Talk to them and some of the top technical people at Searchlight. Maybe they can help."

"I'll get on the radio now. But, Kate, I don't think we have enough time."

chapter 35

In the cockpit of the Atlantic Air 671, Gallo, Dawson, and Wyles were huddled over their manuals. The timer on Gallo's watch was now set to the exact time. One hour and thirty-one minutes left.

Nearly eight hundred miles away at the Atlantic Air headquarters, in Teterboro, New Jersey, more than thirty people were gathered in the "war room," talking on phones to everyone from the maintenance division and aircraft manufacturer to ATC.

Facts about the virus were slowly emerging. Marshall Hayes had made several calls from the hospital to which Kyle had been rushed in critical condition. The first was to Richard Malkovich. "They've got just over two hours," he had explained desperately. "You *have* to do something."

The second call was to the head of the FBI's New York field office, to whom Hayes disclosed everything he knew about the virus, refusing to shirk even a modicum of responsibility.

The FBI in Washington was immediately informed. By the time Kate had taken off in the Jetstar, a team of fifteen agents were already on their way to Searchlight headquarters to talk to Richard Malkovich and other company members. The bottom line, Malkovich told the Bureau's assistant director, was that the antivirus patch was ready. But it could only be installed manually in the aircraft while grounded. In the air, there was nothing anyone could do.

"**What the hell** does that mean, there's nothing they can do!" Gallo shouted into the radio. "They have the antivirus—can't they just upload it or download it or do some damn thing?"

"The software has to be installed by hand. That means a diskette or a data port has to be plugged into the receiver," the voice came back. "There's no other way we can do this."

"How about the timer? Why can't we just pull a breaker or the whole damned clock? Why can't we stop this clock?"

"We examined that possibility too," the voice responded. "We can stop the clocks on the APU, the engines, even the airframe, but that's not the problem. We're being told that the virus has already read the time off the aircraft's computers. The only way that we can shut off the power to the virus is to shut off the power to the computers. Without the FCCs, you won't have flight controls."

Gallo threw down the mike and leaned back in his chair. The stress was beginning to tell on his face. "If anyone has an idea, now would be a good time," he said quietly.

"Why can't we get a copy of it right here?" First Officer Dawson asked from the right-hand seat.

He was too old for the position he was flying. In his

midfifties, with a rapidly receding hairline and a melancholy disposition, Clayton Dawson was divorced and lived alone in the city.

"Now, how in the world are we supposed to do that?" International Officer Wyles asked wryly from the rear seat.

Wyles was the exact opposite of Dawson. Six-foot-two, with a full head of brown hair and a square jaw, he was rugged and athletic and made of steel—or so he liked to think. Wyles was just thirty-five, a navy veteran with over two hundred carrier landings and an ego that made him bulletproof. He couldn't tolerate weakness and failed to understand why Dawson would select the F.O. seat, when he could occupy a captain's chair.

"We can have the program sent as an attachment to someone's e-mail. Then we'll get that person to retrieve his e-mail through the Internet using the satellite phones. He can back it up onto a diskette, and with instructions from the ground, we could install it."

No one spoke as the magnitude of Dawson's idea took hold. Gallo radioed it in. "Can anyone on the ground tell me why this won't work?"

There was moment of silence. "It's worth a shot, Captain."

"Let's get Billy up here," Gallo told Wyles, who reached for the interphone.

Moments later, an attractive woman in her early thirties opened the cockpit door and walked in. A tall brunette, Billy Wayman represented the best of the latest generation of flight attendants; she was perceptive and sharp, and whether she was dealing with a drunk, a frightened first-time flyer, or an amorous pilot, she seemed always to know exactly what to do.

"Billy, do you or any of the others have a laptop with e-mail capability?"

"I'm not sure. Why?"

"We've got a problem and we're headed back to

Kennedy. About ten minutes ago, we were informed that we're going to develop control problems. We haven't witnessed anything to indicate that yet, but we can't take any chances."

"Is it serious?"

"It could be. We just don't know."

"Do you want to make a P.A.?"

"Yeah, I'll do that shortly. First, I want to make sure we have all our ducks in a row. I don't even know what to tell them right now."

"What do you want me to do?"

"Find me a laptop and and an e-mail address. Get it as quietly as you can. I'll explain later."

The passengers of Atlantic Air 671 had no idea that that they were now headed west. They had finished their meals, settled in their seats, and prepared themselves for the remaining hours of the flight, some trying to sleep, others watching the movie.

In seat 4A in first class, Davis Thompson scrolled back up to the beginning of a file on his laptop. Since he had made his decision to level with the Austin boys the previous night, Thompson had worked into the early hours of the morning checking financial projections and other data. In a separate document, he had a speech that he was prepared to deliver if it became necessary. In it, he would reveal carefully selected information about the virus and the extortion. It wasn't Searchlight's fault. They were victims, pure and simple.

He looked at the speech and closed his eyes, cramming like a student before a test. It was important that the presentation appear flawless and impromptu.

After determining that none of the flight attendants had a computer, Billy began to look through the cabin. Most people were either sleeping or had stowed their computers. Davis Thompson was the exception.

She looked around, uncertain how to approach him. "Can I please speak to you in the galley for a moment?" she asked, kneeling beside his arm rest.

"Why?" Thompson asked.

"Please."

Thompson got up, irritated by the disruption. "Yeah, what do you need?" he asked, and Billy drew the blue curtain over the galley entrance.

"We've got a situation in the cockpit. . . ."

"What kind of situation?"

"Well, there's nothing to be concerned about, but the captain has asked that I find someone with a computer and e-mail access."

"There's nothing to be concerned about, but your captain wants a computer and an e-mail address? What does he want to do, check on his portfolio?"

She wasn't sure how to explain it, and Thompson wasn't making things easy. "Please, why don't you come with me."

They entered the cockpit. "Mr. Thompson has a computer. I'm trying to explain to him, but . . ."

"Thanks, Billy," Gallo said. "I'll take it from here."

She nodded and left.

"Greg, pull down the jump seat for Mr. Thompson," Gallo said. "I'm Joe Gallo, this is my first officer, Clay Dawson, and Greg Wyles, our international officer."

Gallo cut to the chase. "Mr. Thompson, you're the first passenger to know that we're headed back to New York."

"What!"

"It's okay, it's merely a precautionary measure, but they're telling us that we might have a problem. They want us to try and retrieve some software from the ground and install it into our computers. The problem is that we need someone with a computer and e-mail capability access."

"What if no one on board had a computer? What would have happened then?"

"I don't have time to explain everything. All I can tell you is that this is a unique situation."

"Why doesn't this ease my concerns?"

"Mr. Thompson, may we please use your computer?"

Thompson looked at the officers, who were staring at him. "Sure, but first tell me what the problem is."

"Like I said, it would take too long—"

"Captain Gallo, I'd like to know what the problem is. As a passenger I have the right to know. Since you want my help, well, that gives me twice the right."

Gallo looked at the other pilots, then back at Thompson. "We've been informed by ground control that our flight control systems will be contaminated by a virus in about an hour and half from now. They know about this virus and even have the antivirus. We need to install that software here, and the only way we can do that is to first download it through an e-mail attachment."

Thompson's face went a whiter shade of pale.

"Now, can we have your computer?" Gallo asked.

Thompson didn't respond.

"Mr. Thompson?"

chapter 36

The file was attached to a message sent by Malkovich, under the watchful eyes of the FBI agents, to Thompson's e-mail address. "They'll have it in less than ten minutes," he said, looking up.

In the first-class cabin, Davis Thompson plugged his computer into the SatPhone jack. His hands were shaking, his migraine freshly renewed—the kind of blinding pain that throbbed with every heartbeat. He had already taken two painkillers and they hadn't even taken the edge off. He would need more.

He was thinking about the time he had seen the computer readout on the virus in Malkovich's office. He remembered the column that indicated the movement of the flight controls and how it altered as Malkovich scrolled down the page. He recalled Malkovich's words as he pointed to the screen where it signaled a full reversal of the controls: "No one can save them now," he had said.

He hadn't even thought about the people that day.

All that had mattered was the money; all that had ever mattered was the money. Things were different now. They knew about the virus and they knew about the antivirus. That meant that they knew about Searchlight, and they knew about him.

It was over: his plans, his career, the Austin deal, everything—and his life, if the transfer of the patch was unsuccessful.

He slid a credit card through the slide on the satellite phone and, with Billy sitting beside him, checked his mail. There were eleven messages waiting for him. The very last one was from Malkovich.

Thompson clicked on the file, slid a disk into the A drive, and pressed Enter. When it was finished, he pulled out the diskette and handed it to Billy. She hurried back to the cockpit.

Installing the software required that a crewmember climb into the E&E compartment. It would have to be done in plain view of the passengers. Gallo decided that it was time to make his P.A.

"Ladies and gentlemen, I need your attention please." He waited a moment until he was sure everyone in the cabin was listening. "About thirty minutes ago, we were informed that we may develop a mechanical problem in the coming hours. We have evaluated the source and our options and have decided that the safest action is to go back to Kennedy. We've turned the aircraft around and are currently returning to Kennedy. We expect to be there in about two and half hours. In the meantime, we're going to take some precautionary measures."

Gallo was just finishing his announcement when Wyles left the cockpit. He went to the front section of the first-class cabin and kneeled on the floor. He peeled off a section of the carpet and removed the hatch. He then placed his hands on the sides of the opening and lowered himself in.

"This is strictly a precautionary measure," Gallo continued calmly. "The aircraft is functioning perfectly well, but we don't want to take any chances. I'll keep you updated on our progress. Thank you." He switched off the P.A. and looked at his F.O. "Okay, is he down there?"

Dawson nodded, the receiver of the interphone glued to his ear. It connected him down to a phone in the equipment bay. Glued to his other ear was the SATCOM receiver. "Okay, Wyles, do you see it?"

"Yeah. We've got the four FCCs, in two separate cases. To the left of them I see the ports. Damn, it's hot down here."

"It's the heat emanating from the electronics. Read what it says on the ports," Dawson said.

"There's two of them. It says Download Port One and Download Port Two."

"Okay, he's got two of them," Dawson said crisply over the SATCOM link to operations.

He listened for a moment, said, "Okay," and got back on the interphone. "Listen up, Wyles. This is what they want you to do. There's a release button on the lower right side of the panel that says Download Port Two. Press it."

Wyles did as he was told. "Okay."

"All right. You can pull out the panel now."

"Okay, I see it," Wyles said, looking at the keyboard and screen.

"What does it say on the screen?" Dawson asked from the cockpit.

" 'Enter authorization code.' "

"Hang on." Dawson got back on the radio. "What's the authorization code?" he asked, then scribbled something on a piece of paper and picked up the phone to Wyles again. "Okay, make sure you're set in capital letters and punch in the following: MJO96-1E3."

Wyles carefully pressed the keys. He lifted the receiver. "I've got MJO96-1E3."

"Did you use the letter O or the number zero?" Dawson asked.

"O, O. You said the letter O."

"Okay. Just checking. Now push the diskette in the slot in the upper-left corner. Make sure it's face up."

Wyles wiped the sweat from his brow and did as he was told. "Done."

Dawson looked over at Gallo. "We're ready. All we have to do is pull the ground-sensing breaker and begin."

Maintenance work, including the programming of all computers, was something that was done only on the ground, never when the aircraft was airborne. The computers could read the fact that the plane was airborne. They had to be made to believe that they were back on the ground.

With his hands tightly around the controls, Gallo nodded. "Go ahead."

Dawson had already located the ground-sensing circuit breaker on the overhead panel. He sat up in his seat, reached for the button and pulled it out.

"Okay. We're ready up here," he said into the interphone. "Select item number three from the menu. It should read 'Program FCCs.' Do you see it?" Dawson asked.

"I got it."

"It's yours."

Gregory Wyles stared at the keyboard for a full ten seconds, then carefully pressed 3. Almost immediately the screen filled with green letters and numbers and command signs that began scrolling down from the top.

"What's happening?" Dawson asked.

"I think it's working," Wyles replied. "The data is being sent and accepted by the computer."

In the cockpit, the pilots smiled—but the relief didn't last long.

Gallo noticed it first. A light vibration followed by a shallow oscillation up, then down. It didn't feel right, but before he got a chance to give the order to abort, the aircraft shot upward with such force that he and Dawson were slammed back in their seats. Instinctively, Gallo struggled to push the controls forward, at about the same time that the aircraft began to reverse the abrupt maneuver. As the G forces went from positive to negative, everyone and everything that was not tied down became airborne, slamming into the walls and ceiling, filling the cabin with screams of terror.

The jet continued to plunge, pinning unbelted passengers against the ceiling. At the bottom of the dive, where the aircraft began to climb for a second time, the G forces once again reversed, and whatever was airborne came crashing down.

"Breaker. The breaker," Gallo was shouting, as he watched the attitude indicator and pushed and pulled the controls, trying to fight the computers.

In the right seat, Dawson knew what he was supposed to do, but reaching the circuit breaker on top required that he release his seat belt and stand.

"I . . . I can't . . ." he groaned, as he finally hit the Release button on his belt.

They were at the peak of another climb, about to plunge again. Weightless, with nothing to restrain his body, Dawson was propelled upward to the ceiling of the cockpit, his eyes glued to the small black button. The last thing he remembered was reaching it—just before his head plowed into the overhead panel. Then nothing.

With the breaker back in, data transfer with the FCCs came to a stop, and Gallo regained control of the aircraft. They were in level flight again. The extent of the damage was horrifying.

The cockpit was strewn with kit bags, charts, bottles of water, everything that hadn't been tied down. Dawson lay on the back of his chair, hands dangling at his sides, mouth open, eyes closed. There was a large gash on the top of his head where it had hit the ceiling panel. Blood dripped steadily onto his shirt.

Gallo wanted to switch to autopilot and tend to him, but he didn't dare. Another of those maneuvers with him not behind the controls, and they were finished.

Bordering on panic, he grabbed the interphone. He needed Billy or one of the other flight attendants. There was no answer. He tried several more times. All was silent.

"**Molly Five, you're** cleared to land," came the command from Kennedy control tower.

"Roger, cleared to land," Kate responded.

She was at six thousand feet, eighteen miles out. The sky was overcast above her, but below, it was all clear. She could see the end of the assigned runway, 31 Right. It was over. It was finally over. Kate smiled and lowered the gear.

Watching from the control tower, O'Rourke saw the Jetstar as the landing lights came on. Someone handed him a note. He read it. "When did this come in?"

"Just now. There's also a call from Searchlight." The man pointed to a phone. "They say it's urgent."

O'Rourke picked up the phone.

In the control tower, no one paid attention to Michael O'Rourke as all expression was drained from his face. After nearly a minute of listening, he quietly responded, "I see," and hung up the phone.

"Molly Five. Molly Five. Come in please."

"Go ahead, Michael. I didn't think they would let you use the radios in the tower," Kate replied. She was at three thousand feet now, eight miles out.

It was the first time she had called him by his first name and he liked the sound of it, even though he wished it was under a different circumstance. "It didn't work, Kate. The antivirus didn't work."

There was a pause, then Kate asked, "Now what?"

"They want you to go after them."

"Me? What am I supposed to do?"

"I don't know exactly, but they're running out of options. They want to try some crazy link-up, but they need your help."

"Are there any other options?"

He hesitated. "I don't know, but I'll find out. For now, I want you to land and taxi to the base of the tower. I'll wait for you down there," he said, and released the mike. There was no reply.

"Kate, did you hear me? Kate? . . . Kate? . . . Molly Five, come in please."

His eyes—in fact, all eyes in the control tower—were now fixed on the small white jet. It was a couple of miles away, still descending, gear down and lights on, ready for landing. O'Rourke wanted to call her again, but he knew she had heard him.

About three hundred feet above the ground, Molly Five broke off its descent. The small jet paralleled the ground as its landing gear retracted. With its throttles advanced all the way, it flashed past the control tower at nearly three hundred miles per hour.

"Molly Five, Molly Five, what are you doing?" O'Rourke shouted over the radio.

"Going to take a little trip," Kate replied.

"Dammit, Kate. I told you it's some harebrained idea that's not going to work. It's just a theory. Besides, you don't know that airplane. We can get a Jetstar pilot here in fifteen minutes."

"Fifteen minutes could make the difference between touching down on the runway or not making it at all. We don't have fifteen minutes. I don't think we even have five."

chapter 37

Tell her to begin an initial climb on a zero
eight zero heading, straight to altitude,"
O'Rourke shouted as he opened the door and rushed
out. "Clear the traffic in her way. Get everybody out."

With several people racing down the stairs just behind him, O'Rourke shouted another order: "Get
Searchlight on the phone and keep them there. I want
to talk to this guy Malkovich personally. I want to know
what his idea is and how the hell it's supposed to work."

The door to the Ops center, two stories down, burst
open, and O'Rourke walked over to the table and rummaged through the charts till he came across the one
he needed. "I need to know the exact position of Atlantic Air," he shouted to no one in particular.

Someone handed him a note with the latitude and
longitude figures. O'Rourke plotted the location on the
chart and marked it with a circle. He picked a point between the circle and Kennedy Airport and got on the
ATC channel.

"Molly Five. Molly Five, come in please."

"Yes, Michael."

"I'm going to give you a position in latitude and longitude. I want you to plug it in the computer and fly there direct. This will be a preliminary rendezvous point. We'll update this as it becomes necessary."

"Roger. Except someone is going to have to tell me how the hell to do it. I still don't really know this plane."

O'Rourke lowered the mike. "I want a Jetstar expert now. I want him glued to a telephone until this thing is over." He picked up the mike again. "Kate, you were right. It's going to be tight. Real tight."

The cabin of Atlantic Air flight 671 was in chaos. More than a dozen injured people lay in the aisles and were being attended to by the crew and other passengers. There was a doctor on board, busily tending to the most seriously injured. All four of the first-aid kits and the medical kit had been opened, their contents strewn everywhere.

Billy was the first person to open the cockpit door. Her hair was disheveled and there was a deep cut over her right eyebrow.

"How bad?" Gallo asked, as soon as she closed the door behind her.

"Bad," Billy said, resting her hand on Dawson's shoulder. He had come to and was holding his hand over the cut on his head. "Let me get something for this." She walked out of the cockpit and a moment later was back with a towel, which she handed to him. "How are you guys doing?"

Dawson put the towel on his head and pressed down. "I'm okay."

"I'm okay too," Gallo said. "How's Wyles?"

"He's unconscious, lying in the first-class aisle. He has cuts and bruises like everyone else."

"How many are injured?"

"Fifteen or more. It's hard to tell. It's a mess back there, Joe. We have a doctor on board. He's doing all he can. He wants to know how long before we land."

"At least two and half hours. We're still six hundred and fifty miles out."

"What do you want me to do?"

"I'll make a P.A. Just make the passengers as comfortable as you can. I'll call you when I have something more."

As Billy left the cockpit, Gallo looked over at Dawson. "Can you take the plane?"

"Yeah, I'm okay," he replied. But his voice trembled.

"Are you sure you're okay? I don't want to use the autopilot; I don't trust it."

"I'm okay. Go ahead, make your P.A."

Gallo hesitantly handed over the control, then began.

"Ladies and gentlemen. This is the captain. Can I have your attention, please. Let me start off by assuring you that the aircraft is functioning properly at this time. What you experienced was an in-flight test being conducted on our primary flight controls. We've been told that there may be a malfunction with those controls, and that was our attempt to test the systems. Please be assured that this will not be repeated." He switched off the P.A. for a moment to consider his next words. "This is a difficult time, and I'm going to ask everyone for their cooperation. There are injured passengers and crew who need your help. The flight attendants are doing the best they can but they need your assistance. Please help them—and above all, you must remain calm. We're going to be very busy up here, so I'm not sure how quickly I can get back to you. I promise you that as soon as I have anything, I'll let you know."

Programming on at least three TV stations in New York had already been interrupted with breaking news about the situation in the air. The reports were not specific, limited to sporadic eyewitness accounts of the Jetstar as it maneuvered through the traffic at Kennedy, and the radio calls made by both Molly Five and the ATC. Phone calls to the tower had elicited no information, so the stations had taken it upon themselves to do the investigating. They had radios tuned to the Kennedy tower and New York Center frequencies. Shortly after noon, the first recording was played for the public, minutes after the transmissions were intercepted.

The recording was of Molly Five and Kennedy control tower, as O'Rourke told her that the experiment with Atlantic Air had not worked. The viewers turned off their soap operas and talk shows, clinging to every word as the intercepted transmission was replayed over and over. Other stations picked up the news and quickly dispatched their vans. Somewhere along the line, CNN got hold of the story; within minutes, Molly Five was national news.

In the press room of the international terminal a harried FAA spokesman faced a media mob.

"I'll take one last question. That's it," he said, and pointed to a reporter.

"What are you guys doing to help the aircraft in distress?"

"As I already explained, an airplane has been dispatched to aid the Atlantic Air plane," he admitted, under his breath cursing the open frequencies and unencrypted transmissions.

"Who is the woman flying it, and what's she going to do?"

The official ignored the question.

"If you guys want to stay here, that's fine. The FAA will issue another statement as soon as one becomes available," he said, returning to the restricted area of the terminal on his way to the tower, shaking his head.

In the Ops center, he approached Robert Quinn. "They're going nuts down there. There are more news vans in the parking lot than at the World Series, and they all want answers."

Quinn looked up from the weather map he was studying and glanced at the clock on the wall. "When that thing hits one forty-three," he said, "they'll have all the news they can swallow."

"Molly Five, Molly Five, this is New York Center, come in please."

"You're a resourceful man, Mike. How did you end up in New York Center?"

"I'm still right here in the tower building, but you're going to be out of the tower range pretty soon. I'm on a phone patch. Listen, there's some stuff that I have to go over with you."

"Go ahead."

"You're still in radar contact. But in less than fifteen minutes we're going to lose you."

"Okay."

"What's your ETA for the fix?"

"I'm estimating sixty-two minutes until I get to north 3715.6, west 6345.2. I'm right at max speed and I've got one hundred forty-eight knots on the tail."

"That's good. Okay—I need to know your fuel status. There are three gauges overhead, just to the left of the hydraulic panel."

Kate looked at the gauges. "They read about twenty-two hundred pounds each. The center gauge reads zero."

O'Rourke snapped his finger, and the man next to him, who had just finished writing down the numbers, ran to a phone.

"Okay. Now, this is what they want you to do," O'Rourke said into the mike. "Since the aircraft you're in is a Searchlight airplane, it's equipped with special equipment that was used in the development of STAR. I think you've learned a bit about the system."

"Yeah. More than I want to know."

"Their satellites can read your position, your instruments, your gauges, your flight controls."

"Okay."

"The engineers at Searchlight believe that they can take this information and feed it to the flight control computers of the Atlantic Air plane."

"How would they . . . ?"

"They're going to get someone in the airliner to dial up the satellite on one of their other phones. They're telling me that with special codes and accesses, the phone call from the airliner can be guided to download the flight control information from the satellite—your flight control information, Kate."

She didn't answer. The aircraft was on autopilot at thirty thousand feet; she was looking around at the various instrument and switch panels in the cockpit, trying to figure out the function of each switch and button.

O'Rourke continued his explanation. "The telephone in the Atlantic Air plane would then be placed in the modem interphase connection and the satellite would tell the flight control computers what to do. Do you understand?"

"I guess. But can they do that?"

"They claim they can. They use the same modem interphase connection whenever a plane is away from its base and there's a need to update its the flight control computers or check their function parameters. They think they can relay commands to you that will allow the Jetstar to send commands to Atlantic's computers—it means they want you to fly the other airplane."

"No physical connection? Just . . ."

"That's right. You're going to intercept the plane, then fly no more than a few hundred feet above them, and they're going to turn the controls over to you. You will then fly their airplane—right down to the runway, Kate."

There was a long moment of silence, then she asked, "Will this work?"

"I don't know. But it's the only chance they have."

The man who had walked away with the piece of paper returned with another and handed it to O'Rourke. "Stand by," O'Rourke said.

He studied the paper, then looked at the man. "Is he on the phone?" O'Rourke asked.

"Yeah, you can pick it up right here." The man pointed to a white phone on the desk. He hit a button, and O'Rourke picked up the receiver.

"Who am I speaking to?" were the first words out of O'Rourke's mouth.

"I'm Jim Banning, Searchlight's chief pilot. I'm the expert on the Jetstar."

"Are these fuel calculations yours?"

"That's correct. I and my team . . ."

"What team?"

"Mr. O'Rourke. I have three of my pilots here, four people from maintenance, and Jetstar tech support on the phone. We have gone over the numbers. They are correct."

"What if they come down to fifteen thousand feet? What if they come lower?"

"It would burn more fuel in the Jetstar—and the Atlantic Air flight too, but not to the same degree. The Atlantic flight has enough fuel; the Jetstar doesn't. We've studied this thing backward and forward. The best they both can do is come back at the same altitude; that gives them both the longest burn."

"But that doesn't—"

"I understand, I assure you."

"You don't understand a damn thing," O'Rourke replied, slamming down the receiver.

He looked at the paper for several more seconds and threw it on the table. He removed his glasses and rubbed his eyes.

In the Ops center, everyone knew that something had gone terribly wrong. In all corners of the room, activity came to a standstill. The men watched O'Rourke closely as he picked up the mike.

"Molly Five. This is New York Center."

"Go ahead, this is Molly Five."

"Kate." O'Rourke took a long breath. "Kate, there is a problem."

"What now?"

"You don't have enough fuel to get there and bring them back. You're short by about eight hundred pounds."

"There's got to be a mistake. There's got to be another way."

"There isn't, Kate. They analyzed it from every angle. Turn around and come back."

"What happens to Atlantic Air?"

"I don't know, Kate. We're working on it."

"How far would eight hundred pounds get me?" Kate asked, after several seconds.

"I don't know. A hundred, a hundred and ten miles. Fifteen or twenty minutes, I guess."

"That's it? We're going to go through all this and they'll crash a hundred miles from the airport?"

"A hundred miles or a thousand. It makes no difference, Kate. Turn back now. Please."

A minute went by.

"Molly Five. Molly Five. Come in." O'Rourke was back on the radio.

"Molly Five, Molly—"

"What if I catch up with them? Have them

disconnect their flight control computers and stop their clock. Bring them in till they're a hundred miles out, then have them reconnect their computers, so they can land themselves. How much time will that give us?"

O'Rourke wasn't sure if he understood the question, but at least four others in the room did. They began to jot information and pick up calculators. When they were finished, they compared notes, and one of them handed his estimate to O'Rourke.

He studied it. Betraying no emotion at all, he picked up the mike. "They're telling me that if you use the last of your fuel to bring them back, it might work. But either they're going to run out of time a hundred and ten miles out, or you're going to run out of fuel."

chapter 38

Did you hear me, Kate? You're not going to make it," O'Rourke shouted over the radio again.

"Molly Five. Molly Five. Talk to me, Kate," O'Rourke begged.

"This is Molly Five. Michael, could I ask you for a favor?" she asked softly.

"What?"

"I need to speak to Molly."

"Dammit, Kate. It's just a hunch, it probably won't even work. We could lose them and we could lose you."

"Are you willing to live with that?" Kate replied. "Could I?"

For some thirty agonizing seconds, no one spoke. It was as if time, itself, stood still.

"I'll make the arrangements," O'Rourke finally said and put down the mike.

At Searchlight headquarters, Richard Malkovich and his staff had begun to make their final preparations for the three-way relay.

Only fourteen of the sixty-three satellites that formed the STAR II system had so far been launched, but the Nova II and Nova XI were in position and quietly circling the globe, several hundred miles over the Atlantic.

"I'm not getting a reading on the RGI," Malkovich shouted, as he limped over to a monitor.

"You should be. The system's powered," someone yelled back from across the control room.

The room, much like NASA's Mission Control, was lined with individual workstations. Each station was manned by a technician who punched keys in his computer and watched the monitors. Others were so absorbed in their work that they ran into one another from time to time.

"I don't care if the unit is powered. I'm still not getting a reading on the damn monitor."

The technician pushed back his seat and hurried over to Malkovich. He looked at the gauge, then at the power port, he even hit the side of the monitor; smashed it with his hand, as if it were an old TV set he was trying to fix. "I told you, you can't power up these satellites this quick. It takes six hours. Six hours, and you're having us do them in thirty minutes. When we rush things, this is what you get."

Malkovich shoved him away. "Listen up, everyone," he shouted to the room. "I'm hearing complaints because we're firing up the satellites in thirty minutes instead of the normal six hours. If anyone has a problem with this, I need to know now."

His men were dead silent.

"Because if some of you are not clear on why we're doing it this way, then I haven't done my job correctly." He then looked at Marvin, another technician. "In six hours from now the passengers on this airplane will be dead. All two hundred and sixty-something of them. They'll be dead and cold and half-eaten by sharks. Am I clear?"

Marvin nodded.

"Right now, every man, woman, and child on that airplane is depending on you to do the impossible. I personally think it's a goal that can be achieved. If anyone here doesn't agree, then get the hell out of this room now. Because if I hear one more complaint about why we're doing it this way, I'm going to walk up to whoever says it and use my gimpy leg to kick them in the ass. Is that understood?"

There was no question that the message had been received loud and clear.

"Now, somebody give me some damn power to the RGI."

In the cockpit, Captain Gallo picked up his P.A. microphone again. He had just briefed Billy on the interphone and asked her to talk to the rest of the flight attendants. It was time to let the passengers know.

"Ladies and gentlemen, this is the captain again. I promised you that I would give you an update on our situation. I have that information now.

"We have reason to believe that the computers that control our flight control surfaces have been damaged. As I said before, we have no way of verifying this, but the evidence supporting it is strong. About thirty minutes ago we attempted to correct the computer. We now have a second plan."

Gallo proceeded to tell them about Molly Five and how they were going to connect the two airplanes. Halfway into his explanation, some actually began to stand up, shouting their questions and demanding explanations. In the cockpit, Gallo didn't hear any of this, but when the door opened and Billy walked into the cockpit, he stopped the P.A.

"They're not listening," she told him, a note of desperation in her voice. "They're shouting, they want to know why you're doing any of this. Some are saying that if there's nothing wrong with the plane, why don't you just fly it. They're scared, Joe. They're scared, and frankly so am I."

Gallo nodded. "Okay. Let me talk to them again."

He started over, in a more somber tone. "It has just come to my attention that some of you have questions; that you want to know why we're interfering with the controls, when we can't verify that there is anything wrong with them in the first place. That's a good question and deserves a good answer: Because we don't know. And because by the time we find out and confirm our suspicions, we may not have time to react." He paused to make sure that he was clearly understood.

"You see, we've been told that our flight control computers have been sabotaged by a virus. Once this virus begins to spread, we won't have much time; that's why we have to take precautionary measures, and that's why we attempted to reprogram the computer in-flight.

"Now, we do have some advantages. For one thing, we know when the virus is supposed to attack; that's a big plus. We also think that we can make this relay work; that is also a plus. But panic is not helpful and could jeopardize our efforts."

His voice on the P.A. was almost harsh, but the information had to sink in for two reasons. First and foremost, unruly passengers would not only cause panic but could endanger his efforts. Second and more important, deep inside, Gallo wasn't sure if this would work. The theory had never been tested before. If it didn't work—and there were lots of reasons why it wouldn't—Gallo felt they had a right to know.

In the cabin, the message struck home. Passengers quieted down and took their seats, some leaning back and closing their eyes, while others simply held hands. The seat next to Thompson was empty, but as he turned and looked at the people all around him, he realized one simple fact. He was alone.

chapter 39

So you're gonna die. Everyone dies eventually. At least you will have died for a reason, a
damned good one. That would count for something,
wouldn't it?

A tingly sensation ran through her body and exited
through her fingertips. She found herself wiping her
hands on her pants to relieve the sensation, but it
wouldn't go away. Her heart was pounding and her
throat was dry, but somehow she wasn't afraid.

She wondered what it would be like when she lost
power on one engine as it ran out of fuel, then the
next, as she glided into a sea of clouds and reemerged
on the other side, staring at the savage ocean below.
The Jetstar wasn't even equipped for over-water operation. No raft—nothing. Even if she miraculously survived the thirty-foot waves and ditched, how long could
she survive in the frigid water? Five minutes? Less?

She had long since forgotten the pain in her ribs
and her cuts. She had forgotten Kyle Hayes and
Searchlight and everything that had brought her here.

Nothing mattered; nothing but the passengers and crew on board the Atlantic flight. And Molly.

When the call came, Kate was still thirty minutes from the rendezvous point, still lost in her thoughts.

"Molly Five, Molly Five. This is New York Center. Come in please."

"I'm here, Michael."

"I've got someone here who wants to talk to you. We used a police-dispatched radio as a remote signal and patched it through New York Center. Molly is on the line, Kate."

She smiled and pressed the button. "Molly? Honey, are you there?"

"Mommy, Mommy—they said my name on television. They said Molly Five. How do they know I'm five?"

"I always told you that you were special. I guess everybody knows it now. How do you know how to work the radio?"

"There's a policeman here. He's helping me push the button."

The actual count was not one but eight officers, and four squad cars. Minutes earlier, they had been dispatched with the intention of establishing communication and protecting the family. News of the rescue attempt had spread fast. It wouldn't be long before the street was crawling with news crews.

The police-dispatch frequency was open and easy to monitor. The media, now following every development, had intercepted the conversation and, unknown to Kate and Molly, was at this very moment broadcasting it live throughout the Northeast.

A restaurant in Times Square, a deli in downtown Philadelphia, a bar in Boston: wherever there was a radio or a television, people were transfixed by the voices of Kate and Molly.

"Is Mama there with you?" Kate asked.

"Yes, Mommy. She's here. But she's crying. Everybody is crying. Why is everybody crying?"

"Listen to me, Molly," Kate said firmly. "There's a problem here. But we've had problems before, right? And we always got through them."

"Like the time when the heater made all that smoke, and the black stuff came out?"

Kate grinned. "Yeah, honey. Like that."

"Is your heater making smoke?"

"No, this is a little different. There's an airplane up in the sky with lots of people in it. There are mommies and daddies and little kids too, lots of little kids. They're in trouble and I have to go help them."

"Are they going to crash?"

"No, honey, not if I can help it."

"Are you going to crash?"

How was she supposed to answer that? Was she supposed to say that yes, she would certainly crash and probably die before the day was over? That sometimes you have to do what you have to do, no matter the cost? Was she supposed to sit there, in the cockpit of this godforsaken plane, and over a scratchy radio transmission explain to her five-year-old daughter what an orphan was?

"Mommy. Are you going to crash?" Molly asked again.

"No, honey."

There was a long pause, then Molly asked, "Are you going to die?"

A waitress at TGI Friday's on Seventh Avenue dropped an entire tray of glasses on the floor but she didn't even flinch. Nor did anyone else. All eyes in the restaurant were focused on the TV screens.

"Listen to me, Molly," Kate said, her voice quivering. "There is an airplane full of people, and they will die unless I try to help them. I'm not sure what will happen, but regardless of what does, I want you to know one thing. I'll always love you, baby girl."

Tears were beginning to roll down Molly's cheeks, but she didn't want Kate to hear her cry. She wiped her nose with her sleeve, then said, "I don't want you to die, Mommy. Please don't die."

"Listen to me honey. I'm not going to die. . . ."

"You're lying. You're going to die and you don't want me to know."

"I told you I'm not going to die. Now I need you to be strong, Molly."

"I'm five years old. I don't want to be strong. I want my mommy."

"And I want you. . . ."

"Take me with you. If you're going to die, then take me with you, please, Mommy. I don't want to be left alone," Molly begged between sobs.

If ever there was a moment that Kate considered turning back, it was now.

"Do you want me to come back, Molly? Do you want me to leave that airplane and come back? Because if you do, I will, I swear to God I will."

Molly wiped the tears from her face, but it was no use, more came down. Even the police officer holding the microphone bowed his head.

In the Ops center, O'Rourke and others listened in as well. Each man sat back in a chair, hiding his tears as he thought of his own child or grandchild.

"No, Mommy. I want you to go," Molly came back after a pause. "I want you to go and save them."

Something was burning her eyes and making her vision blurry. Kate reached up to wipe them. When she did, she realized that it was tears pouring down her cheeks in an unending stream that she couldn't stop. She wiped her face with the palm of her hands, but there was no way to quell a lifetime's worth of tears.

"I have a surprise for you," Kate finally managed to say.

"What is it?"

"Max. He's yours. When I get back, we're going to go and get him together."

"I'll take the best care of him, Mommy. I promise."

"Close your eyes, Molly."

"My eyes are closed, Mommy."

"A kiss for your eye, and one for the other eye. A kiss for your nose. A kiss on your forehead, and one on your cheek. A kiss on your other cheek. And one for your lips. Remember, Molly. Always remember."

chapter 40

"**C**ome on, give me a hand with this one," the young doctor called to a flight attendant in the aft galley. When she didn't move, he got up from the aisle where he was attending to an injured crew member and walked over.

"Did you hear me? Just cover him up and close the area so he's out of view," he told her, watching for a reaction.

The flight attendant was listening to the doctor's words, but she seemed not to hear him. She just stood there, covering her mouth with one hand, as she stared at the body.

"Listen to me," the doctor said, squeezing her arm. "He's dead. There's nothing you can do for him but there are twenty people, maybe more, who need help, and unless they get it quickly they might join him. Do you understand?"

The flight attendant forced herself to turn away from the man's body.

"I need any medical supplies that you have available,

I need comfortable seats, the ones in first class, and I need blankets and pillows. I also need splints, something that I can use to immobilize broken bones. Get umbrellas, walking sticks, anything."

She took a blanket and covered the body in the galley, then slowly moved to the front of the plane.

The aft section of the jumbo jet looked more like the emergency room of a busy hospital than the cabin of an aircraft. The injured lay in the aisles being treated by passengers and crew.

After attending to their immediate needs, the first order of business for the doctor and the crew had been to relocate the injured to a more comfortable and secure place for the remainder of the flight. The first-class section was the obvious choice. Volunteers were selected and, under the doctor's watchful eye, they carefully started moving the injured to the front.

"We need some of these seats. Let's go!" the young doctor shouted as he backed into first class, carrying a seriously wounded passenger.

The cabin was almost full. One woman began to protest; Davis Thompson got up from his seat.

"Get up and go back there, dammit," he shouted at her. "I've given up my seat—so can you!"

The embarrassed woman grabbed her bag and got up to leave; others began to follow. Some offered their help, and the injured were moved to the large leather seats.

Bowing to the inevitable, Thompson had thrown his coat and computer on the floor, making room in his seat. He went into one of the toilets and locked the door. He took the bottle of medication he used to deal with his massive headaches and held it to his lips, a sense of desolation filling his soul.

A brief conversation with an angry Richard Malkovich over the airphone a few minutes earlier had left him reeling. Malkovich had crisply told him about Kyle's role in planting the virus. Searchlight was attempting a rescue using STAR, but it was a sheer "Hail Mary" pass. Nothing but a theory.

Malkovich had also informed him that a warrant had been issued for his arrest. Thompson clutched the bottle of medicine with one hand and held on to the edge of the sink with the other. His doctor had warned him never to exceed the prescribed dosage under any circumstances; it could result in a life-threatening drop in blood pressure. As he stared at the bottle of small white pills, Thompson tried to summon the strength to twist off the cap and swallow all of them. One way or the other, his life was over.

In the cockpit, the crew had watched the stopwatch on the center pedestal wind its way down. Just under twenty-five minutes left.

"This is going to be close. Dammit, this is going to be too close," Gallo said under his breath, his eyes darting between the stopwatch and his instruments.

The last call, seconds earlier, had indicated that Molly Five was a hundred eight miles away, but she would have to see them first, then turn and lock the controls. Only after that could they disconnect the flight control computers and stop their clocks—and that was just the first part of their problem.

Molly Five would have to fly them back over three hundred miles before she was forced to break away. At that point, she would turn the controls back to them and they would have to start the clocks over again, hoping to land before the stopwatch reached zero. They were going to make it or lose it by a matter of minutes. Everything depended on Molly Five.

Billy opened the cockpit door. Gallo was the only person in there.

"We've had one fatality, Captain. The doctor says it was a heart attack, but there are lots of injuries, and eight of them don't look good."

Gallo closed his eyes and hung his head in defeat. He wanted to let go of the controls and rub away the stabbing pain at his temple and the base of his neck— but he didn't dare.

"Thanks for letting me know," he said quietly. "How's Dawson coming along? Is he ready?"

"I think so. I'll check."

Billy closed the door and Gallo looked at the stopwatch. Twenty-four minutes and thirty-one seconds.

"New York Center. New York Center, this is Atlantic Air 671. Come in, please," Gallo said into his mike.

"Atlantic Air, this is New York Center," O'Rourke replied.

"We've had a fatality and we've got other injuries, some pretty bad."

"Copy that, Atlantic Air. Molly Five is about a hundred and twenty miles ahead of you. You're closing in at about twelve hundred miles an hour. You should see her on TCAS in the next few minutes."

"I'm showing less than twenty-three minutes left."

"We copy. We've got the same thing."

"You're sure about this thing, right?" Gallo asked.

"What do you mean?"

"I mean, I've got a perfectly good airplane flying here, and I'm screwing around, endangering people's lives. You're absolutely certain our computers have this virus, right?"

"Atlantic Air, you've got an airplane on its way to you with a pilot who doesn't have enough fuel to return. She's there for one reason and one reason only. Yeah, I'd say it's a safe bet that you've got a problem."

———

"**New York Center,** this is Molly Five. Are you there, Michael?"

"I'm here."

"How close is this going to be?"

"We're showing them down to about twenty-three minutes. You're going to lock in with them in less than eight. That'll give them fifteen minutes they can use, maybe fourteen. The question is whether you can get them to within fourteen minutes of land."

"How about the people doing the link-up? Are they ready?"

The hotline to Searchlight and the flight computer manufacturers was live. This arrangement had been quickly established because it was imperative that Malkovich and the rest of those working on the problem be able to hear the transmissions immediately and instigate whatever corrections were necessary.

Two hundred miles away, Malkovich was studying the monitors. "We're ready, Captain Gallagher," he said. "I don't know if you remember me. You and I spoke the first day you came to Searchlight."

"Of course, Mr. Malkovich," Kate replied. "I guess you're the one putting this whole thing together."

"Me and about thirty of Searchlight's best, who at this very moment are reading your exact location, the condition of your systems, including your engine, even your instrument panel."

"What about the flight controls?"

"Glad you asked," Malkovich said, looking at a computer screen with six separate graphs, each depicting a separate control element—ailerons, elevators, rudders, spoilers, flaps, and slats. "I've got them all right here."

"What do you want me to do?" Kate asked.

"Nothing. You just fly the airplane. Make sure that you're sitting no more than three hundred feet on top of him. You must be able to see him and how the aircraft responds to your flight controls so that you don't overcontrol. Remember: You must remain visible to the other aircraft at all times."

"What if they get too close to me and I want to move away?"

"Once you establish your position relative to the aircraft below you, you must remain there."

"Yeah, but what if they drift up to me, because of winds or something?"

"Ms. Gallagher, the plane below you is going to copy everything you do, exactly as you do it. You step on the rudder, they step on the rudder. You turn, they turn. Do you understand?"

"Are you telling me that if they start to drift toward me, there is nothing I can do?"

"I'm telling you that we came up with this theory less than two hours ago. It's not perfect, not by a long shot."

"Then let's just hope your theories don't need to be tested twice."

In the Ops center at Kennedy tower, the controllers prepared for contact.

"Atlantic Air 671. We suggest that you turn on your landing lights. You're also cleared to switch to VHF frequency, 132.45. Your host is waiting."

"Roger, New York Center. Here we go," Gallo responded as he strained his eyes to see Molly Five on the horizon. Tapping his foot nervously, he glanced at the clock. Seventeen minutes and forty-three seconds. Then he saw her.

"Molly Five, Molly Five. You're a sight for sore eyes. We have you at eleven o'clock high. Thanks for coming to the party."

"Roger, Atlantic Air. I've got you in sight and I'm slowing. Are you guys ready?"

"I hope so. My clock says just over seventeen minutes."

In the cabin, one of the satellite phones had been retrieved and was ready. The telephone receiver, like so many other receivers on board aircraft, was a unit with no attachments or wires.

To make sure their theory would work in practice, Dawson had taken the receiver down to the E&E compartment and tried it in the modem interphase. The interphase assembly, designed for a specific type of receiver that hooked into it, would not hold the satellite phone. But Dawson discovered that if he held the unit in place against the cuplike device, the two units would fit together, at least enough to do the job. Or so he hoped.

But that meant someone had to be there as long as Molly Five was overhead, making sure that one unit was held against the other. Any disruption of the signal, however temporary, would cause the relays to close and the communication would be cut off. There would be nothing anyone could do after that.

Kate waited until she was about five miles away from the jumbo jet before she made a steep left turn. By the time she completed it, Atlantic Air 671 was a thousand feet below her. "Okay, guys, I have you at my twelve. Slow down to mach 80. I'm coming on top."

She clicked off the autopilot and grabbed the controls.

The maneuver had to be accomplished manually. Pushing the yoke forward, Kate watched the jumbo jet as it got closer and closer, until it was just below and in front of her. Then she lowered the nose and, in a matter of seconds, the small white jet was positioned above the big silver plane, close enough that Kate could read the small letters on top of the plane's wings.

"Okay, guys. You've got to keep it steady at thirty-five. Real steady," Kate said.

In the Ops center, Michael O'Rourke and the rest of the controllers held their breath as they listened.

With the aircraft flying at nearly the speed of sound and no more than two hundred feet away, Kate said, "Okay, I'm ready."

Six hundred miles away, at Searchlight, Richard Malkovich said, "STAR's ready."

In the cockpit of Atlantic Air 671, Gallo looked at his stopwatch. Fifteen minutes, eleven seconds. He pressed the mike switch. "Atlantic Air is ready."

In Ops center at Kennedy, Michael O'Rourke looked at the faces all around him. "Ops center is ready. Let's do it, folks."

With First Officer Clayton Dawson waist deep in the E&E compartment, Billy slid a credit card through the phone slot and dialed the number. She then handed the receiver to Dawson, who placed it against his ear. There was a loud hissing sound, a squealing pitch that lasted for almost ten seconds followed by a short beep, then silence.

"It just beeped," Dawson said, his back to the cockpit door.

"Okay. Press the following numbers on the keypad," Billy said, looking down the access hatch. She lifted the piece of paper in her hand and began to read very slowly: "It's 5672097652."

"Done," Dawson said.

There were at least a dozen people surrounding the two crew members, all anxiously waiting, afraid to move.

"Captain, the code is entered," Billy said, facing the open cockpit door.

"Okay. Cut them," said Gallo, keeping his hands wrapped tightly around the controls.

That was his cue. Dawson jumped the final four stairs down to the floor of the E&E compartment, where he moved to the four identical boxes that read

FLIGHT CONTROL COMPUTERS. In preparation for this moment he had already pulled them out of their housings, exposing their connection ports. He unscrewed the first port.

In the cockpit, an amber light immediately came on and Gallo pressed the switch, shutting off the light.

Seconds later, Dawson cut ports one and three.

Gallo felt the plane jerk and saw the red flashing light that read STANDBY, FLIGHT CONTROL COMPUTER ONLY.

"Okay, Captain, he's down to the last one," Billy said, as she stood over the hole in the floor, just a few feet from the cockpit door.

Gallo still held the controls tight, his attention directed at the instrument panel. "Proceed."

Downstairs, Dawson was looking up.

"Go ahead," Billy said.

Dawson pressed #421 on the receiver, then placed it into the cuplike socket. The screw to the last port was already loose. With his other hand Dawson reached over, closed his eyes, and pulled the plug away.

A sudden jerking motion propelled him back, causing him almost to drop the receiver. He managed to maintain his grip and grabbed the interphase with both hands.

"Are you okay?" Billy shouted from above.

"I'm okay. I'm okay," Dawson replied.

In the cockpit, Gallo relaxed as he heard the words. He maintained his tight hold on the controls, but it was of no use; they were no good to him now. Hesitantly and slowly, he let go, eventually dropping his hands to his lap. To his amazement, the yoke was moving from side to side and even back and forth.

"It's working," he said, then picked up the mike. "It's working, it's working!" he shouted into it.

At the Ops center and Searchlight, the controllers jumped to their feet and hugged one another. Kate, holding her position above the other plane, couldn't let go of the controls but allowed herself a broad smile.

"Atlantic Air, this is Searchlight. Confirm you have a positive lock on the relay," Malkovich asked.

"We have a positive lock here," Gallo said, watching the controls in fascination. "Next to my daughter dating the guy with the purple hair, this is the damnedest thing I've ever seen."

"No stranger than flying two airplanes at the same time," Kate quipped from above. "Captain, with your permission I'd like to take command of your aircraft."

"Molly Five. The aircraft is yours."

chapter 41

How long before they're on radar?" O'Rourke asked no one in particular.

"Anytime now," one of the FAA controllers responded.

"I want them right here," O'Rourke said, pointing to a large, blank monitor. "I also want to see their track and the exact location where she's going to ditch."

"I'll get you an estimate in one minute," Quinn called from the opposite side of the Ops center.

"An estimate isn't good enough. There are only two rescue choppers, and unless they know exactly where she is, she's history."

"How can I give you an exact location?" Quinn asked.

"You know how much fuel she has left?"

"Yeah."

"You've got her fuel burn, true air speed, winds aloft, ambient temperature. Hell, the people at Search-light claim they can read her entire instrument panel, including her ground speed. Talk to them. Get the information. I want to know exactly where Molly Five will run out of fuel," O'Rourke said, leaning against a wall. "Remember, she has to have four hundred pounds of fuel when she starts to ditch. That's the minimum amount she'll need to keep her engines running so that she can control her rate of descent."

Quinn nodded.

"Okay, where's my ditching team?" demanded O'Rourke.

In the corner, someone sifting through a stack of maps raised his hand. At the same round wooden table two other men sat listening intently to their headsets.

"How does it look?" O'Rourke asked as he approached them.

"Not good," replied the man studying the maps. "The low extends all the way south past Halifax. Surface winds are forty-plus knots and the whitecaps are breaking at thirty, thirty-five feet. We've been in touch with the Jetstar experts and with the manufacturer. They both say the aircraft will almost certainly break apart on impact. Neither recommends ditching."

"Then we'll just beam her out of the damn cockpit," O'Rourke yelled, slamming his hand against the table, then quickly regretting his burst of temper. "I'm sorry. Just . . . keep up with the weather, the direction of the swell; you know the drill," he said, flexing his sore hand.

The man nodded. "No problem."

"What about the water temperature?"

"Forty-one degrees," answered another man at the table.

"Medical tells us that if she's in good physical condition, she's good for four minutes. Perhaps five."

"Then we'll have to get to her in three," O'Rourke replied. "What's the status of the rescue equipment?" he called to Quinn.

"The Coast Guard has dispatched a cutter, but it won't get there for at least three hours. They're also getting ready to launch two high-speed choppers."

"That's all?"

"We're pressing, but it's going to take time."

"We don't have that kind of time. Don't they understand that?" O'Rourke ran his fingers through his hair and massaged his scalp. "Okay . . . make sure they have the exact location where we expect her to ditch. Give them the coordinates and tell them to fly there direct. They can do that much."

"I've got the location," someone shouted.

At the table, a man pointed to a chart marked with a red cross.

"How far?" O'Rourke asked.

"A hundred and thirty-three miles from the coast. Hundred and thirty-five from the threshold of Runway 31 Right."

"How long?"

"They still have a hellacious headwind. Then Atlantic Air has to slow down. Extend its flaps, gear, get ready for landing and—"

"How long?"

"Twenty-four minutes. Maybe twenty-five. That's under ideal circumstances."

"They don't have twenty-five minutes. They have less than fifteen," O'Rourke shouted, as if he alone were responsible for the predicament.

The two men stood there, both trying to find an answer to a question that didn't have one.

"I've got them on center's radar," someone shouted from the other side.

O'Rourke rushed over to the monitor. Two moving targets lay over one other, making the information hard to read. He picked up the mike.

"Molly Five, Atlantic Air 671. Confirm you're both on the radio."

"Atlantic Air is here."

"Hello, Michael."

"Kate, we're showing that you're going to be down to ditching fuel a hundred and thirty-five miles from the airport. They're telling me that will take twenty-five minutes of flying time, maybe more. Atlantic Air is down to less than fifteen minutes of computer time," he warned.

"What's my ditching fuel?" Kate asked.

"Don't even think about it, Kate."

"How much ditching fuel do I have, Michael?"

"Four hundred pounds. And you're going to need every ounce of that to keep your engines running and make a controlled ditch."

"How long would that buy?"

"I don't know. Four, maybe five minutes. But it's not going to work, Kate. Forget it. Without fuel, you'll be a glider, with little to no control over your airspeed and rate of descent. It's not going to work."

"Captain Gallo, I can buy you five extra minutes. The rest is up to you," Kate said.

"Dammit, don't you ever listen?" O'Rourke yelled.

"This is my decision, Michael. What do you say, Captain Gallo?"

"You give me five more minutes and I'll get the extra five, even if I have to go out and push this damn thing myself," Gallo replied.

In the Ops center, O'Rourke threw the mike down. Nothing about what she had said or done surprised him. In fact, he would have been amazed if she had done anything else. One life for two hundred and sixty-two. It didn't take a rocket scientist to figure that out. But dammit, why her?

He felt selfish for feeling the way he did, for wanting to save her. But it had taken him a lifetime to find her, and to lose her now, like this . . .

"Calculate her new ditching location and get the information to the rescuers," he said weakly, suddenly feeling like a very old man.

"**Captain, bring up** your throttles to maintain mach 82. I'm going to follow you from up here."

Gallo reached over and brought up the power. High above the cloud layer, the two planes, almost touching each other, began their final journey home.

The stopwatch on the center pedestal had been frozen at fourteen minutes and fifty-seven seconds. Although the numbers on the clock had stopped changing, Gallo seemed unable to stop himself from looking at it. How long could she stay with them?

Three hundred feet above him, Kate wondered the same thing. The airliner was thirty times her size, maybe fifty, making the Jetstar look like a flea on the back of some giant dog.

Rescue craft were already on the way; she knew that much. She would have to find them or they would have to find her. Providing they did, then what?

"Atlantic Air, this is Molly Five."

"Go ahead Molly Five."

"Captain, bring up your power to maintain exactly mach 82. They're telling me that's the best speed and power setting to get max range for this aircraft," Kate said. "I'll try to give you as much notice as I can before I disconnect. It won't be much; you'll have to be ready to hook up the first computer just before I peel off. Remember, your clock starts as soon as the first computer is connected."

"Precisely how familiar are you with ditching, Kate?" Gallo asked.

"As familiar as you are, but they don't even have a raft in this damn thing."

"We have rafts," Billy said from the side. She had been in the cockpit for the past thirty minutes. With one crew member injured and Dawson still in the E&E compartment, she had stationed herself in the cockpit, in case there was something she could help with.

"I've just been duly reminded that that we've got rafts," Gallo said with a smile.

"What exactly did you have in mind?" Kate asked.

"We start down just a bit earlier. We level off at three thousand feet. There, we depressurize and open the doors and throw out our portable raft. It's bright yellow and easy to spot. All you have to do is find it."

"You have to slow down to a hundred forty knots to open the doors, that'll take two minutes. Then you'll have to speed back up again for the rest of the flight, that'll take another two minutes. I'm working too damn hard to get you the five minutes you need to blow it on this."

"Then we'll just throw it out at three hundred knots, or four hundred or five hundred, whatever the hell it takes. But we're not leaving you alone. Do you understand?"

Kate smiled. "When you say it with that much charm, how can I say no?"

A pregnant pause followed before Gallo said, "I have to ask you one question."

"Go ahead."

"Why are you doing this?"

It was a simple question requiring a simple answer. But she didn't have one. She had merely followed her instinct, as she had done all her life.

"I don't know," she answered quietly. "But there's a little girl back there who calls me Mommy, and who has the most beautiful green eyes you've ever seen. I don't think I'd ever be able to look into them again unless I tried."

"You know something?" Gallo asked. "When this thing is over, I'm going to find that little girl. I'm going to look into those green eyes and let her know that her mommy is the bravest human being I have ever known."

Kate felt a lump forming in her throat. "Thank you, Captain."

"Atlantic Air, this is Ops center. Come in please."

"This is Atlantic Air, go ahead."

"I have a message for you from Searchlight. It's ready to be patched in."

"Go ahead."

A second voice came on the line. "Uh, Captain. This is Richard Malkovich at Searchlight. We might have a way of verifying the presence of the virus on your aircraft."

Gallo sat up, his attention focused on the voice. "I'm listening."

"I need you to press two switches at the same time. They are the flight control data connector and the ground-sensing switches. Both are located at the observer's panel."

"Yeah, I know. They're used for maintenance on the ground only."

"Well, sir, that's correct under normal circumstances, but tech support tells us that these switches are used to troubleshoot the system, whenever there are programming errors. Since the virus is foreign to the system, it's possible that the computers may recognize it as a programming error, and perhaps display it for us."

"Stand by," Gallo said, and looked over at Billy. "It's the last button on the top left; the other one is two rows down. Second to the right."

Billy found the switches.

"We've got them," Gallo said.

"Okay. Lift the safety covers and press them both at the same time."

Gallo told Billy to go ahead. She flipped up the

black metal guards, then pressed both buttons at the same time. Instantly the center screen filled up with data and algorithms.

"I . . . I don't know what this is. We've got a page full of numbers and letters," Gallo said over the radio.

"Read some of them for me please," Malkovich said calmly.

"It starts with the letters BBB, then there are some numbers 5620, then BBB again, and what looks like a bunch of music notes. Then BBB again and more numbers. What is this?"

"Center, did you copy?" Gallo asked when he received no reply.

"Stand by, Captain," a voice came back. Thirty seconds later, Malkovich was back on the line. "Sir, we have positive confirmation. Your aircraft is contaminated."

Gallo sat there in shock; the confirmation removed all vestige of doubt. Kate was their only hope. He almost couldn't bring himself to speak. "We've got to get down," he said finally. He picked up the mike. "Molly Five, I guess you heard that."

"Roger, Captain."

"How much fuel do you have?"

"Down to eight hundred pounds. Ten minutes, maybe twelve," Kate replied.

"We're starting down now. At ten thousand, we'll depressurize and throw out the rafts. Then I'll maintain three hundred knots. So help me, we'll keep up the speed all the way to the ground."

"I don't see how you're going to open your doors at three hundred knots," Kate responded.

"You let me worry about that," Gallo said, pulling back on the throttles. The two planes, one hovering over the other, began a shallow descent two hundred miles off the coast of New York.

Down at the bottom of the E&E compartment, Clayton Dawson raised his head. "Hey, I need help," he moaned weakly. No one came.

He looked down at the receiver in his hand, which had become numb from his death grip on it. He could no longer feel how much pressure he had applied, so he continued to press harder and harder, to ensure he didn't lose the connection. Now, with his circulation all but gone, his hands falling asleep and the dull ache in his shoulder increasing in intensity, he needed to get relief quickly. But there was no one there.

In all the mayhem, everyone had forgotten about Clayton Dawson. He looked at the interphone several feet away. If he could reach it he could get someone to come down and help him. To reach it, however, he might interrupt the connection. He couldn't risk that.

He had screwed up once before, a long time ago, when he flew a plane filled with people into a thunderstorm and came out on the other side with two dead engines. They had blamed him for that and they had been right. That wasn't going to happen. Never again.

He tried again. "Can anyone hear me?" he said, and waited. Still, nothing.

The movement was sudden and violent. Dawson felt the aircraft yaw to one side; for one terrifying moment he thought he had lost the connection. Instinctively he squeezed the receiver as hard as he could. Then his head slammed against a rack of electronics. Dizzy and bleeding from the back of his head, he somehow managed to maintain his grip.

Above him, in the cockpit, Gallo could hear the passengers screaming in fright, as the aircraft veered sharply.

"Molly Five, Molly Five. What's going on?"

"Fuel starvation. I've lost the right engine. I'm stepping on the left rudder, but that means you're stepping on the left rudder. We're getting too close, Captain. You have to kill your right engine, like mine; that's the only way we can maintain our distance."

"You want me to *what*?"

"Kill the right engine *now*, Captain. I can't hold it much longer," Kate shouted over the radio, her left foot all the way down on the rudder control.

With his right hand Gallo reached over to the fuel switch and turned it off. The cockpit was suddenly lit up with yellow and red warning lights, but with the reduction of thrust from the right side, the aircraft slowly began to level off.

To his horror, Gallo saw the Jetstar no more than twenty feet away. "Molly Five. Molly Five. You're too close."

There was no time for talk. With total concentration, she was applying just enough control to maintain her distance. Both pilots held their breath as the belly of the Jetstar almost touched the top of the jumbo jet. Then, as slowly as it had closed in, it backed away.

When she had safely reestablished her position, Kate said, "We need to keep up the speed. I'm going to increase the rate of descent to three thousand feet per minute. That should give us a few more knots."

"Billy." Gallo looked up. "Pull out the spare raft from the ceiling. Have it ready by door 4 Left."

"What about you?"

"I'm fine. Get going."

Billy walked out of the cockpit and looked down into the E&E compartment. "Are you okay, Clay? . . . Clay? . . . Clay?"

Billy kneeled over him. His face was expressionless. One hand was still holding the connections together, but he was barely conscious. His eyes registered nothing.

chapter 42

I need help," Billy shouted in alarm, quickly climbing down the stairs into the E&E compartment. She put her hands on each side of the receiver and interphase connector and held them securely in place. "Let go, Clay, I've got it," she said.

The back of Dawson's collar was soaked with blood. Billy knew that he was injured but didn't know how badly.

"It's okay, Clay. It's okay. I've got it," she said again, looking at his masklike face. "I need help," she shouted up at the open hatch.

Two of the flight attendants, along with a male passenger, descended the stairs and helped pry Clay's white-knuckled grip off the connection.

"Hold on to this." Billy pointed to the male passenger. "Hold it just like I am, and don't let go. Not for one second, or we're all dead. Do you understand?"

The man grabbed hold of the receiver and the interphase, but Billy still had her hands on it. "You got it?" she asked.

"I got it."

"You sure?"

"I got it. I got it," the man said, staring at the receiver as if it were a vial of nitroglycerine.

"All right," Billy said, then slowly let go.

She turned to Dawson, collapsed against the wall, and held him by the arms. "Listen, honey, I need you. The captain needs you, the passengers need you. We've already got one injured pilot. We can't have two."

Dawson slowly began to rouse.

"You okay, Clay? Can you hear me? You know where you are?"

He blinked his eyes.

"Listen, Clay, we're on the descent. Molly Five is going to disconnect and leave us in the next few minutes. You have to hook the computers back up. Can you do it?" she asked, watching his eyes.

He blinked again.

"Are you sure? We won't have a second chance."

"Yeah, I'm okay," he said groggily.

"Clay, Wyles is unconscious. The doctor says that he's in bad shape. That means Joe is all alone in there. You've got to get up there and help him. Are you sure you can manage?"

Dawson began to sit up. Billy turned to the two flight attendants. "You two stay here until the computers are hooked back up. Then return to your stations and prepare the cabin for an emergency landing. I'm going to send the doctor down here to take a look at his head."

Billy climbed back up the stairs, summoned the doctor, and ran to the rear of the plane.

The raft was bulky and required assistance from three passengers. They undid the clips and lowered the casing and in less than two minutes the long, rectangular, bright yellow plastic container sat next to the last door, in the aft section of the aircraft. All they had to do was to pull the cord and let it fly.

"**The fuel gauge** is showing two hundred pounds but it's flickering down to zero. It could be anytime," Kate said over the radio. "Get ready."

"You've done all you can, Molly Five. Peel off, we'll take it from here."

"Not yet. I can take you another minute, maybe two."

"Listen to me, Kate," Gallo said. "I'm dropping the raft in the next thirty seconds. I want you to peel off, make a chandelle, and get down and find it. Do you hear me?"

"You don't know this virus like I do. Ten seconds could make a difference. Five could."

"You may not have five seconds. Get going right now."

"Just one more second," Kate said stubbornly. "Just one more second."

Gallo's voice was calm and authoritative. "It's over. You've beaten it, Kate. You've beaten the virus, you've saved your airplane, and now you've saved us. Now go! Go for God's sake and save yourself."

Kate let out a sigh. It was going to be okay now. It was time to let fate work itself out.

"Molly Five, getting ready for the disconnect. I guess it's time for a swim."

"Don't mind a little company down there, do you?" a man's voice came out of nowhere.

"What . . . ?" Both pilots looked all around them to identify the source of the voice.

"Captain James Fisher, squadron leader, at your service. Molly Five, say hello to the 463rd out of McGuire Air Force Base. Ma'am, I've got six F-16s flying wing for you. You folks created quite a ruckus back there."

Kate looked through her side window and saw the F-16s, all painted gray and sporting the USAF emblem on their sides. They were flying in formation: three on each side of the aircraft. One of the pilots looked over and gave her a thumbs-up.

"What are you guys gonna do?" Gallo asked.

"Sir, our squadron was dispatched less than twenty-five minutes ago with instructions to fly chase and report. Molly Five, two of my birds are going to go down to the surface with you. We're going to mark your position and stay with you until help arrives. Other than that, I'm afraid there's not a whole lot more we can do."

"It's more than I expected," Kate said. "Captain Gallo, connect your computers please."

"It's about time," Gallo said to himself. "Hook up number four first, then the other three," he shouted over his shoulder to Billy. "I'm depressurizing the aircraft now. Open 4 Left in fifteen seconds and throw out the raft. Don't forget to pull the cord."

He reached up to the overhead panel and with the flick of a switch placed the outflow valve controller to the full Open position. In an instant a hole the size of a plate opened on the side of the aircraft, and as the air from the outside began to rush in, the pressure on the inside and outside of the cabin equaled.

Passengers and crew felt the pressure change; they yawned and swallowed to relieve the discomfort in their ears. Had he had the time, Gallo would have warned his passengers of pressure change. But he was alone, with one dead engine, surrounded by seven jets and little time to lose.

In the back of the cabin, two husky passengers who had volunteered their services pushed the door handle open. Even though the door barely moved, the abrupt inrush of air created an instant wind tunnel. Papers, cups, and trash went flying through the cabin, creating enough noise to drown out the passengers' screams.

Because of the pressure of the wind against the door, they were unable to create a large enough opening to push the raft out, but they kept trying. When it became clear that they could not push the door open with their hands, they both sat down, using their feet to push against the raft, forcing the raft in turn to push against the door. It still wasn't enough.

A third person had been assigned to pull the cord—something that would have to be done the moment the raft was ejected from the plane. If the cord was pulled inside, the results could be catastrophic.

"Push. Push," the men shouted at the man with the cord, and he joined in, sitting next to them and pushing with his feet.

The raft inched its way forward through the opening, and in one instant, the door opened just enough to push it out.

"The cord! The cord! We didn't pull the cord!"

"**Flight computer number** four is hooked up. I'm connecting the next three," Dawson reported, and hung up the interphone. He was still down in the E&E compartment, with two flight attendants watching his every move.

In the cockpit, Gallo started the stopwatch again. "Molly Five, Molly Five, we have our computers. Peel off now."

"Roger, Captain. Good luck to you."

"And to you, my friend. May God be with you."

Kate eased back the yoke, and the two planes began to separate. Then she gently turned her plane to one side; the Jetstar leaned over and cut toward the earth.

"Red One and Red Four. You're cleared to disconnect from the flight. Get down to the deck and stay with her. Use marker twenties and marker fifties. You know what to do," the squadron commander announced, and watched the two F-16s leave the formation, roll over, and dive vertically into the clouds.

"Reds Two, Three, and Five. Reposition yourselves on the front and rear section of the jet. I'll take the rear left side."

Gallo heard the transmission and watched the jets maneuver away. But his eyes remained on the white Jetstar until it disappeared behind them.

"Good luck, Kate," he said tenderly, almost like a prayer.

From below, Kate watched the Atlantic Air plane move farther and farther away until it was gone. Ahead of her she could see the clouds, fluffy and soft, deceptively peaceful.

There was a compressor stall, then a second one, as the engine hesitated. Then, with no further warning, it shut down, leaving Kate alone with only the sound of her heartbeat.

Red and amber lights lit up the cockpit, but Kate paid no attention to them. She was thinking about Molly now, and Max, her new puppy.

She pictured them chasing each other around the apartment, maybe in the park, with Mama watching every move.

She would be okay. Mama would make sure she was.

She was gliding now, soaring through the clouds, free and somehow at peace. When she popped below the cloud deck at about three thousand feet, she was greeted by the bluest of oceans, peppered with a million dots of white. The waves were running north and south, and even from up there she could see the enormity of the swells. She banked the little jet so that it headed south and continued to glide.

"**Okay, all four** FCCs are hooked back up. The clock shows just over ten minutes, and we still have seventy-five miles to go," Dawson said, as took his seat in the cockpit.

"Are you okay?" Gallo asked.

"Yeah, fine. Let's just get this thing on the ground."

"Okay, start the right engine. As soon as it's established, bring up the power. Bring up the speed, right up to the red line," Gallo said.

The cockpit door opened and Billy rushed in. The expression on her face told him that something was wrong.

"What is it?" Gallo asked, afraid of what he might hear.

"They didn't pull the cord." She gasped, struggling to breathe.

"What?"

"They pushed out the raft, but didn't get to the cord."

"Oh God, no."

Michael O'Rourke was no longer in the Ops center. He had climbed two long flights of stairs up to the control tower, where he took a seat beside a window to watch the final phase of the operation.

His job was done; there was nothing else he could do. From here on in, the best people to deal with this emergency were the men and women surrounding him in the glass-encased tower, who had spent the previous two hours preparing for this event, trying to anticipate every contingency.

The entire length of Runway 31 Left—the longest runway at Kennedy—was covered with two inches of white foam. Fire trucks from both the airport and the nearby stations lined the threshold, their red and blue lights flashing. Six medevac helicopters and three dozen ambulances stood at the ready, and hospitals in Brooklyn, Queens, and Manhattan had paged their off-duty staff and were ready for a major medical emergency. And just for good measure, Kennedy Airport had also closed down. This was going to be the big one and nobody was going to screw it up.

"I want all the traffic cleared out of their path," Quinn said, as he burst through the door. "I mean everything. Get center to reroute the traffic to La Guardia and Newark, Teterboro, everybody. I don't want anyone within thirty miles of these guys.

"Anything yet?" he asked O'Rourke.

He shook his head.

Somebody motioned frantically to him from the other side of the room.

"Uh . . . should we slow down, Captain?" Dawson asked, with a concerned glance at Gallo. When he didn't respond, Dawson asked again, "Captain, we're still at three hundred and fifty knots, descending out of four thousand feet. At this rate you're not going to slow down for flaps or gear."

Again, he said nothing. Gallo's eyes were focused forward, his brow furrowed in intense concentration.

"Captain Gallo? Joe?"

"Yeah, I'm here, Clay. I can't stop thinking about her."

"Joe, we're doing three hundred and fifty knots, descending out of thirty-eight hundred feet."

"I wonder if she's okay."

"I don't know, Joe. But unless we get through the next four minutes not a whole lot will matter."

"You're right," he said, pulling himself out of his trance.

"Good to have you back, Captain."

"Listen," Gallo said. "We may not have the time to slow down. First priority is to make the runway. After that we can worry about the gear and flaps and the rest of it."

"You're gonna fly at three hundred and fifty knots all the way to the deck?"

"If I have to," Gallo replied grimly.

"Okay." Dawson nodded uncomfortably. "The runway is 31 Left. It's foamed, and they have the equipment standing by."

"Talk to Billy. Tell her to get ready. It's going to be a bumpy ride."

Dawson picked up the interphone, just as Gallo felt the first resistance on the yoke.

"Damn, I think it's here," Gallo said, locking his hands around the controls.

Dawson put down the interphone and looked at the stopwatch. "It's not time yet."

"I don't think it likes our clock," Gallo said. "Get them down now. We don't have much time."

Dawson gave the final signal to Billy, who relayed it to her crew and passengers. The cabin was already prepared, and the flight attendants took their seats and tightened their belts.

"Three thousand feet and twenty-eight miles to go," Dawson called out.

"We can't slow down. We can't slow down or we won't make the runway," Gallo said. "This thing is getting worse. I can feel it. Bring up the power. Give me three hundred and fifty knots."

Tightly strapped into the right seat, Dawson shoved

the power close to red line. Looking down below him, he realized that in all his many landings at Kennedy he had never seen the ocean and the land speed beneath him as fast as they did today.

"Talk to the tower. Tell them it's started. Tell them she was right."

"Kennedy tower, this is Atlantic Air 671. We're twenty-three miles out at three hundred and fifty knots. Less than a minute ago, we felt the first resistance. We think it's started."

"Roger, Atlantic Air. Emergency equipment is standing by," the controller responded, just as someone in the tower yelled, "I've got them."

Every eye in the tower turned to the east, just below the clouds, where three bright landing lights were pointed in their direction.

Quinn looked at the plane, then at his screen. "I thought I told you to get all the traffic out of the area," he yelled.

"We did. We've been trying to talk to them for the last thirty minutes, but there are just too many," the man answered from another monitor.

"What the hell are you talking about?"

"The traffic. I've got fifty targets right now, maybe more. There are helicopters, private planes, charter stuff. The whole damn sky is full of them. I don't know where in hell they all came from."

Quinn walked over to the next monitor, pressed a button to extend the range of the radar display, then pulled back. "Jesus Christ. What is this?" he asked, as the screen filled with little lines etched on the glowing green background of the scope, each indicating an airplane and all headed in the same direction.

"That's what I'm trying to tell you. They heard the conversations. The news and the media carried this whole thing live. People heard her talk to her daughter and to the other plane. Everybody is taking off. Everybody is headed for her. It's the damnedest thing I've ever seen, it's like . . . like everybody is trying to save her. We even got a call from the White House. They wanted to know what they could do to help. She doesn't need a raft. All she has to do is step over these things and walk to land."

"Joe, you're fifteen miles out and still doing three hundred and fifty knots," Dawson said quietly from the right seat.

"I know. I know," Gallo muttered. He was having a harder time with the controls now, forcing them rather than turning them. He couldn't stop thinking about what she had said: "Ten seconds may make a difference. Five might."

"Go down, you bastard! Go down!" Gallo cursed as he pushed on the yoke.

"Twelve hundred feet above the ground. You're high and you're hot," Dawson said.

"You're not gonna beat me. Not today," Gallo said through clenched teeth.

"One thousand feet."

"Bring the throttles to idle and give me full-up spoilers," Gallo commanded, still fighting the controls.

Simultaneously, Dawson brought the power back and pulled the spoiler handle. Almost immediately a warning bell went off.

"Shut it," Gallo yelled, and Dawson pressed a switch.

"Lower the gear."

"We're too fast."

"Lower the gear!" Gallo yelled again.

Dawson reached for the handle and lowered the landing gear. The aircraft shuddered as the gear doors opened, allowing the gear to fall. The red light stayed on, indicating that the gear doors would not close.

Another bell rang, louder than the first.

"Shut off the damn bells," Gallo shouted, just as Dawson called out four hundred feet.

"They're too damn hard to move," Gallo said desperately, as he fought the resistance on the controls. "I . . . don't know how much . . . longer . . ."

"I'm coming on the controls with you," Dawson said, reaching over.

"Push it down," Gallo shouted. "Push the nose down with me."

"Glide slope. Glide slope," the computer-generated voice warned them, as if they didn't know.

"Keep it coming down. Keep it coming down," Gallo yelled furiously.

"It's gonna hit hard. Real hard," Dawson warned.

"Fifty. Forty. Thirty." The computer-generated voice counted down the final segment of the flight in ten-foot increments.

"Keep it coming down. Keep it coming down. Don't raise the nose or we'll go back up."

"Twenty. Ten."

With the spoilers still out, the gear hanging and no flaps, the jumbo jet hit the ground hard, splashing the foam in all directions.

"Lower the nose. Lower the nose and give me full reverse," Gallo shouted, and with both feet on the brakes, he pressed harder than he ever had in his life.

The tires were the first to go, exploding in quick succession, as every limit they were designed for was exceeded. The aircraft shuddered and shook as it slid from one side of the runway to the other on the foam.

"Keep it on the runway. Keep it on the runway," Dawson yelled, but it was too late.

A third of the way down the runway the jet veered left and skidded off the foam and the pavement, sliding onto the dirt. Struggling to maintain lateral control, Gallo stepped on the right rudder, just as the main wheel collapsed. The left side of the plane came crashing down, but the momentum was far too great for the craft to stop. It continued to move to the side, the fuselage carving an immense gash in the earth, throwing a cloud of dust and debris a hundred feet high.

With the wing's tip dragging because of the collapsed gear, the stress proved too much for the structure. There was a loud shudder and a deafening sound, followed by a violent upward movement as the left wing broke away.

In the cabin, passengers continued to scream in terror. In the first-class section, Thompson shut his eyes, pressing his eyelids hard against each other, and grabbing the armrest so tight his fingers left an impression.

The momentum was tremendous and when the nose of the aircraft went up one last time, it felt as if they were going to be airborne. The nose came back down with a thunderous roar, slamming into the ground. When Thompson looked down, he saw the crack in the fuselage below his feet. There was nowhere to go.

The aircraft bounced again and again, until the forward section broke away. And then, finally, the sound, the shudder, the movement, everything came to a stop, in a cloud of dust and debris.

In the control tower, everyone watched as the escorting F-16s tore away from formation, flying by, two on each side of the tower. Below them, as the dust began to settle, they could see the jetliner resting on its side like a lame bird.

Almost instantly the aircraft was surrounded by flashing red and blue lights as nearly forty pieces of emergency equipment closed in. White foam was spewed over the red-hot engines and smoking wheels, the fuselage, and the remaining wing.

The controllers held their breath as they watched the aircraft's doors. When the first one opened, and the first yellow evacuation chute appeared, there were smiles, but no one dared cheer out loud. But then came the second door and the second slide, and then the third. People began to jump out onto the chutes from all directions, where they were greeted by their rescuers. Only then did a chorus of hoarse cheers break out from the weary crowd in the tower at Kennedy Airport.

In the back of the control tower, Michael O'Rourke slumped against the wall and closed his eyes.

chapter **43**

Molly Five. Molly Five. This is Red One. How do you hear."

No response.

"Molly Five. Molly Five. This is Red One. If you can hear me, tip your wings."

Still, no reply.

"Red Four, this is Red One. She's down to battery power and may have lost her radios. Stay with her and transmit blind. I'm breaking off to mark the location for the Coast Guard chopper."

With those words, the lead fighter broke off from the formation and dove almost straight down. Above him, the second F-16 followed the gliding Jetstar below the dark, gray clouds.

Kate couldn't hear the conversation. With the primary systems gone, she didn't even know how to work the radios. What the hell was the difference now anyway.

Her thoughts were shifting between what awaited her on the surface and her little girl back in Queens.

How could a five-year-old understand why her mother wasn't there to hold her when she was scared or kiss her when she was sick? Who would be there for the first day of school, or to help with her homework? And how about her birthdays?

Her thoughts were jumbled, but then Kate thought about Molly's last words: "Take me with you. If you're going to die, then take me with you, please, Mommy. I don't want to be left alone." She could no longer stand it. Molly deserved more. They both did.

Kate made a decision. If she was going to die, it wouldn't be because she hadn't tried. As she squeezed the controls in her hand, a powerful surge of determination rolled over her and a will to survive emerged stronger than anything she had felt before.

She looked down at the communications panel and punched in a button. "Air Force jets. This is Molly Five. Do you copy?" she shouted into the mike, her eyes roving the ocean below. The raft. Where was the raft?

She spent a minute longer than she should have, not paying attention to her speed.

"Stall warning. Stall warning." The blare of the computer-generated voice followed by violent shaking gave Kate new priorities. She pushed the yoke forward, lowering the nose but with no power, she wasn't descending anymore, she was falling. The Jetstar was nothing but a gliding coffin.

"Molly Five, Molly Five. This is Red Four. You're sinking too fast. Pull up, pull up now."

The sound came through the overhead speaker loud and clear. She had found the radio. It must have been the last button she pushed before entering the stall. She turned up the volume.

"Red Four, this is Molly Five. Where are you?" Kate asked, looking around.

"Molly Five, look at three o'clock high."

Kate turned right to see the gray F-16, no more than fifty feet away, slowly descending to her level. The pilot in the helmet and dark hood was looking at her.

"Where's the raft? I can't find the raft."

"Molly Five, there is no raft. They were unable to pull the cord in time. I say again, negative on the raft."

Kate hesitated, keeping her gaze at him a moment longer than she needed to. As if she wanted to say something, but didn't know what.

"Molly Five. You have to slow your descent. At this rate, you'll go right through."

She looked down at the raging sea. "I'd like to do that, but gravity has other ideas."

"I copy that. Molly Five, there is an F-16 on the surface, marking the location of the ditch. Do you see it?"

She shook her head.

"Orange and yellow flares. Eleven o'clock, two miles. Do you see it, Molly Five?" the man shouted.

Kate leaned over, sweeping the horizon with her gaze. "In sight."

"Ma'am, that's your target. I need you to ditch as close to those markers as possible. Can you do that?"

"I'll try." She turned the plane to line up for the final approach.

Five hundred feet. Four.

She could clearly see the waves now. Giant mounds of water, running parallel, one after the other, like soldiers marching in a parade.

I don't need a plane. I need a surfboard, she thought, letting go of the controls with one hand and tightening her belt.

Three hundred feet. Two.

She gripped the controls even tighter, blinking away the drop of sweat falling into her eye.

One hundred feet.

She had planned to land on top of a wave and parallel to it. That was how she had been trained. That was what she was supposed to do. But she had no power and was sinking far faster than the airplane was designed to do.

Fifty feet. Forty.

If she was lucky. If she could somehow survive the impact, then run back and open the door, she would have a chance. But as the large wave she had planned to land on rolled below her, it was clear that this was not the day to count on luck.

Twenty feet. Ten.

The wave caught the tip of the right wing of the Jetstar and, like the hands of a giant, grabbed it and pulled it in. Instantly devoured by the sea, the Jetstar twisted and turned, being ripped apart by G forces greater than anything it was designed to bear. With her arms shielding her face, Kate screamed and yelled as the small plane tossed and turned, disintegrating with each passing second. What would it feel like? she wondered. What would it feel like, the moment it all ended?

The wings had torn away at the instant of impact, but the fuselage had remained mostly intact, catapulting through the water like an out-of-control torpedo. But it was also decelerating.

When it finally stopped, Kate was in the cabin, upside down and still belted in. She struggled to free herself, but it was useless. The water moving through the cabin was rising rapidly. She could feel the wetness, the cold, the hunger of the sea to have her. She was sinking, too; she could feel that. It was a only matter of time before the Jetstar would fill with water and take her down to the bottom of the ocean, where she would be inurned for all time.

Then, she saw it. A wave the size of a roller coaster, about to crash on top of her. There was nothing else she could do.

"I'm sorry, Molly."

chapter 44

Six Months Later

He stood at the entrance, wearing brown pants, a beige V-neck sweater, and his customary tortoiseshell glasses. He was also holding a bouquet of flowers in one hand—two dozen red roses.

He expected to be greeted, even fussed over. Certainly he expected at least to be recognized. But as Michael O'Rourke stood at the entrance of Athena's Taverna, all he could see was a room crowded with people, gorging on Mama's food. Beside him at the entrance, some twenty or more additional patrons waited for their names to be called.

O'Rourke strained to look through the crowd, even standing on his toes to get a better look. The waitresses were walking around pouring wine. Then he saw Mama going from table to table, chatting with her customers. But no one seemed to know or care that Michael O'Rourke was there, waiting.

Molly was the first one to notice him. She was bringing bread to the tables and picking up the menus. When she spotted him she dropped the menus and ran over to him with a huge smile. He worked his way to the front of the crowd, where she jumped up and hugged him around his neck.

"Mikie," she yelled.

"Easy, easy. I'm trying to look good for your mommy," he said, then gave her a big kiss. "Is she in?"

"Oh, she's here," she replied, looking at the flowers. "But what's with the roses? Next time get her lilacs. That's her favorite."

"Now you tell me? Six months I've been trying to figure her out, and now you tell me what her favorite flower is?"

Molly giggled.

He put her down, then he pointed at himself. "How about the outfit. How do I look?"

She checked him out from top to bottom, and then with all the authority of a fashion critic said, "You look okay. You look good."

Just then, O'Rourke noticed Kate on the other side of the restaurant, looking around, probably for Molly. He wanted to wave at her and say something—but he was suddenly happy just to be looking at her. She wasn't wearing an elegant dress, her hair hadn't been styled in some new and striking way, and her makeup was understated as usual. In fact, all that he could see under the long white apron was a sleeveless red shirt. Her hands were white with flour, and more flour was sprinkled on her face, but it didn't matter. Standing there like a fool, all smiles and feeling tingly like a teenager, breathless and nervous, Michael O'Rourke couldn't take his eyes off her. When she finally caught his eyes and smiled, he knew why. She had to be the most beautiful woman on the planet.

They had saved her that day. Against all odds and despite the heavy seas, they had saved her.

She remembered very little. The freezing water, the sound of the engines, men shouting. She didn't even know how they had done it. That, along with other fragmented memories of the event, somehow had vanished with the sinking plane.

She had read the reports and seen the videotape of her rescue. Her last clear memory was of the wave, tall and mighty, the size of a building about to crash on top of her.

Well it had, and in the process obliterated what was left of the Jetstar. With the cabin broken into a hundred pieces, she had simply fallen out into the water.

The Coast Guard crew had not waited. Two men in scuba gear jumped in and another was lowered in a gondola attached to the Sea Stallion helicopter with a single cable. They had found her, placed her in the gondola, and snatched her to safety.

It had turned out to be a lucky day after all.

Thirty minutes after they pulled her out of the water, with an entourage of some forty aircraft following the Coast Guard helicopter, Kate Gallagher was taken to Jamaica Hospital, where she remained for nearly a week.

It was in the hospital that she first heard about the fate of Atlantic Air flight 671.

They had made it. They had landed the crippled plane and saved the passengers and crew. Including the heart-attack victim, the total fatality count remained at five. Two of the five had been in the cockpit.

Captain Joseph Gallo and his first officer, Clayton Dawson, along with two passengers in the first-class cabin, were killed when the cockpit was sheared from the rest of the aircraft. As for the other passengers and the rest of the crew, although there were many injuries, some serious, no one questioned the fact that they were lucky. Damned lucky.

She hadn't even met Captain Gallo. She didn't even know what he looked like. But as Kate sat in stunned silence in her fourth-floor bed at the hospital, listening to Michael O'Rourke's unsparing account of the crash landing two days later—she knew she had lost a friend. A dear, dear friend.

It took the authorities less than a week to put the pieces together. Davis Thompson survived the crash and was charged with criminal negligence and manslaughter, and his fate was consigned to the grinding mills of the justice system.

Marshall Hayes faced similar charges, and civil suits would soon follow. Kyle Hayes, the one ultimately responsible for all of the lives lost through his creation of the virus, had died in the hospital's ICU.

For Mama and Kate, life was almost back to normal. Kate was a hero now, a role model. Her face was featured on the covers of major magazines. There were offers from television and print media for her exclusive version of the story, and even one from *Playboy*. She refused them all. She wanted her life back—and her privacy.

O'Rourke held Molly's hand as they made their way toward Kate. He had suddenly become aware of how heavy the bouquet of roses in his hand felt. Why hadn't he tried to find out what her favorite flower was? He didn't even want to give them to her. But the first thing she did when Michael approached her was reach for the flowers.

"They're beautiful. Thank you," she said, smiling warmly.

Molly grinned, and O'Rourke glared at her to be quiet. "I . . . I didn't realize you would be so busy," O'Rourke stammered.

"I'm helping out. Leo, our cook, has the flu," Kate replied. She gazed at him for a moment, then put the roses down on the kitchen pass-through. She turned, held his face in her hands, leaned forward and kissed him.

Twenty feet away, Mama offered a silent prayer.

"You know, we can do this another time. It doesn't have to be tonight," O'Rourke said.

"No, this is fine. Just get a table and sit down, I'm going to help out a little bit more while they're busy. Then we can go."

"I've got a better idea," he said, as he rolled up his sleeves. "I'm not much of a cook. But I'm a damn good waiter. Did it all through college."

"Good move," said Molly, hanging on to O'Rourke's arm. But Kate heard her. She looked at the smiling faces of Molly and Mama, who had witnessed the entire scene from the kitchen door.

"I've got a better idea," she said, taking off her apron and handing it to Molly. "How about Chinese?"

ABOUT THE AUTHOR

KAM MAJD is a pilot. He lives with his wife and two young children in Southern California. Delacorte will publish his next novel, HIGH IMPACT, in spring 2003.

If you enjoyed Kam Majd's

HIGHWIRE

you won't want to miss

HIGH IMPACT

an explosive new Kate Gallagher thriller

coming from Delacorte books

in spring 2003!

THE LAST FAMILY

JOHN RAMSEY MILLER

A harrowing novel of suspense that pits
a former DEA agent against his worst nightmare:
a trained killer whose fury knows no bounds,
whose final target is the agent's own
flesh and blood . . . .

*"Fast paced, original, and utterly terrifying—true,
teeth-grinding tension...Hannibal Lecter eat your heart
out!"* —Michael Palmer

_____57496-5 $6.99/$8.99

Bantam Dell Publishing Group, Inc.	Total Amt	$_____
Attn: Customer Service	Shipping & Handling	$_____
400 Hahn Road	Sales Tax (NY, TN)	$_____
Westminster, MD 21157		
	Total Enclosed	$_____

Name _____

Address _____

City/State/Zip _____

Daytime Phone (_____) _____

FB 23 2/02 JRMiller